This man was her enemy! How could she permit him to handle her, caress her as a husband did his wife? Engulfed by awakening female instincts, Tamlyn's hands smoothed up those bonnie arms and snaked around his neck. She gripped the wet locks and hung on for her very soul.

His arm caught her body and pressed her to his wet chest. Water splashed over the tub's edge and onto the stone floor. The kiss consumed them with hungry flames as they were lost to all.

Julian felt drunk. This woman captivated him as she had in the tent, drowning him in kisses of mead and sweet witch's brew. He wanted to kiss her endlessly. The strength of his craving for her frightened him. It roared through his body until the pounding was agony. He neither knew nor cared who claimed whom.

A RESTLESS KNIGHT

Deborah MacGillivray

ZEBRA BOOKS
Kensington Publishing Corp.
www.kensingtonbooks.com

ZEBRA BOOKS are published by

Kensington Publishing Corp.
850 Third Avenue
New York, NY 10022

All Kensington titles, imprints, and distributed lines are available
at special quantity discounts for bulk purchases for sales promo-
tion, premiums, fund-raising, educational, or institutional use.

Special book excerpts or customized printings can also be created to fit specific needs. For details, write or phone the office
of the Kensington Special Sales Manager: Attn. Special Sales
Department. Kensington Publishing Corp., 850 Third Avenue,
New York, NY 10022. Phone: 1-800-221-2647.

Zebra and the Z logo Reg. U.S. Pat. & TM Off.

ISBN 0-8217-8036-0

First Printing: July 2006
10 9 8 7 6 5 4 3

Printed in the United States of America

To some very special people for being there and being you . . .
Lynsay Sands, Leanne Burroughs, Maggie Davis
Monika Wolermans, Carol Ann Applegate
Roberta Brown, Sue-Ellen Welfonder
Lori and Tony Karayanni
The Ladies in Waiting and the authors of Highland Press
Diane D. White
Detra Fitch
and most especially that hussy Hilary, Queen of the Virgins

"... that something in thyne dominion, heed, it is a dragon ..."

—the Mabinogion

Chapter 1

Highlands of Scotland, April 1296

"My lady!"

The shrill cry rent the stillness of the isolated Highland glen. Startled, scores of ravens took to the sky. Their cacophony echoed the call . . . *my lady, my lady*. For a peculiar instant the world held its breath as the heavens were turned black.

Tamlyn MacShane paused from picking the first violets of spring. Straightening, she arched her shoulders to relieve the crick in her back. Loch winds lifted, swirling about her, playfully tugging wisps of her honey-colored hair from the simple braid hanging down her back. She brushed the stray strands from her face, her eyes following the spiraling path of the noisy black birds.

An ill omen, whispered the kenning to her mind.

Her fey gift to sense things and the peculiar behavior of the birds summoned fragments of the lingering nightmare that had awoken her this morn. Vague, just at the edge of her thoughts . . . something about screaming ravens and a coming storm. She shivered.

When the lad topped the crest of the tor he cried once more, "My lady! *He* comes!"

Shaking the somber fit of mind, Tamlyn smiled at the boy tumbling to a stop at her feet. "Och, Connor Og, catch a breath before you turn the shade of these violets."

"My pony tossed me. You must come, my lady," he gasped, "so they can bar the gates."

"Pray, who comes that we must close Glenrogha's gates?"

"*Him* . . . the one heard tell about." His words were whispered in fear. "Riders from Lochshane brought word—Kinmarch had been put to siege by the English king—the dread Edward Longshanks. Raised the Dragon Standard they did. Your da is feared dead." Tears streaked down his dusty face.

Hadrian of Kinmach dead? Nonsense. With the power of the kenning, she'd have felt that. "The laird is not dead, lad. I'd feel it here." Her fisted hand clenched to the center of her chest.

The frown on the boy's face softened. "Mayhap it is so. You were touched by the blood of the Sidhe. Still, they sighted his standard on the road from Lochshane near the sacred passes—the green dragon on the field of black!"

"The Dragon of Challon—*he* comes?" For an instant laughter bubbled up in her throat. Surely this was a jest. A dragon coming on St. George's Day? Her smile faded, then her heart jumped as if she'd taken a pinch too much foxglove.

"Hurry to Glenrogha, Connor Og, and do not look back. I shall fetch my palfrey."

Dropping the basket of violets, Tamlyn hastened to the far side of the hill where she'd left the mare munching grass. Bansidhe ignored her as she knelt to unfasten the leather straps hobbling its fetlocks. Pushing her mantle over her shoulders, she attempted to mount, but the horse jerked the reins from her hands, stubbornly wishing to remain and eat its fill of the spring faerygrass.

"Few animals dare to eat the blades within a faery ring, so you believe the Wee Ones think you special. Do not fash me or I shall speak to the tanner about lining my new mantle with dapple hide, you silly beastie."

The mare's head snapped up with the recoil of a whip. Its whole body stiffened. Taking advantage, Tamlyn scrambled upon its back. The palfrey ignored her heels kicking against its ribs as it issued a shrill whinny.

A rumble came from the distance, deep as thunder from a summer storm, only steady, persistent. The sound sent a shiver up her spine, the eerie noise preternatural—almost with the portent of the Bansidhe's wail. Once more, dark impressions rose of the nightmare that had broke her slumber at dawn. Trembling, Tamlyn pushed the thoughts aside. A storm must be building on the other side of the passes. She turned to search the purple hills ringing Glen Shane. The morning sky near Dun Kinmarch was strangely gray.

Coldness streaked with icy fingers through her soul . . . as if someone of great power just crossed through the sacred passes.

Finally, the horse obeyed her tugging on the reins. Tamlyn felt a rising urgency to reach Glenrogha. Her mantle flying behind, she leaned forward, encouraging her mount to break into a gallop. Once they reached the flatland, she glanced over her shoulder. The skyline above Kinmarch was blacker. No storm filled the heavens with this spreading shadow.

Topping the rise, Tamlyn spotted warriors mounted upon heavy horses of war pouring into the glen. English! The mists that had shielded the sacred passes of Glen

Shane for centuries had failed to hide their valley. How could this be?

A vanguard emerged from the stand of ancient evergreens. Breaking away, several riders traveled at a swift pace. Their monstrous horses chewed up the turf with broad strides. At first she thought they hadn't spotted her. Shouts told otherwise. Slapping the reins against the horse's neck, Tamlyn chose a path into the grove. It curved around the hill, then along the steep cliffs of Lochshane Mòhr. She used the narrow trail to weave through the dense oaks, limes and elms.

The horsemen were compelled to pick their way amidst the undergrowth of rose briars and woodbine. Her smaller mount wove like a needle, threading passage into the forest. She breathed easier as the pursuers lagged behind.

Her best hope was to flank the riders, then double back to the sea caves that ran under Glenrogha's cliffs. A secret passage connected beneath the ancient Pict broch, which would allowed her to come up within the safety of the fortress. Breaking free of the woods, she urged Bansidhe onward.

Five horsemen cleared the trees bordering Glenrogha's dead angle. The fearsome warhorses churned soft dirt clods high in the air.

Tamlyn's mantle flew into her face and tangled about her arms and the bridle, costing precious time. Fleeing to the tidal caves would only reveal their existence to the men following. That path was now blocked. All she could do was make for her sister's fief of Kinloch.

Her lips pressed thin, feeling the palfrey's exertion. If she could just reach the forest of Kinloch, escape would be possible. Suddenly, the mares's hoof hit a depression in the rain-soaked earth, and Tamlyn and the horse went flying heels over head into the ground. Head spinning, she staggered to her feet, then nearly fell as searing pain shot up her right leg.

Three warriors were upon her before the dizziness cleared. Shaking, she warily faced the enemy as they dismounted. In cornered animal panic, she tried to shove past them. With the twisted ankle she couldn't run. Laughing, taunting, they shoved her from one to the other—pack dogs tormenting helpless prey. They wore the green and black of the Dragon of Challon, the dragon rampant emblazoned upon their chests.

"Comely wench," one said, shoving a hood of mail off his head.

Tamlyn knew she was tall for a Scots lass, yet she had to look up at these Norman warriors. With helms off, their dark hair gleamed, a match to their piercing eyes.

"Seems the move northward offers some sport," one smirked. "Come, give us a kiss, wench."

"I'd rather kiss a bloody leper!" Tamlyn spat the words. Never would she allow them to see she tasted fear.

"No lepers here, but you may lavish kisses upon my pet snake." The others laughed when the knight lowered his head trying to kiss her.

Tamlyn flinched as the meaning of the Norman words sank in. Widening, her eyes stared in revulsion. She shoved against his covered breastplate, sending him backward against his horse.

A handsome warrior stepped to box her in. He spoke in a soothing tone. "No need to fear us, sweetling. We're a damn sight cleaner than your filthy, skirt-clad countrymen."

Tamlyn swallowed the lump in her throat, the kenning seeing into their minds. These vile dogs intended to rape her! Forcing back mind-numbing dread, she focused on reaching the dagger in her boot.

Beginning a spell of warding, her lips barely mouthed the ancient words of empowerment, "*Adhnadhe oothras beytharde dethiale*—" She paused, horror spreading through her as she realized the ancient spell of protection summoned the breath of the dragon. Wrapped up in casting the charm, Tamlyn was caught off guard as the youngest knight seized her about the waist, then spun her around, pushing her back against the chest of another man.

Two more mounted warriors cantered up, wearing the Plantagenet colors of scarlet and gold. Three faded golden leopards were on their surcoats. One called, "Might've knowed Sir Dirk would flush out a bit of quim."

Tamlyn pushed this knight as she had the other. Solid, immovable, he towered over her. Hard, jet-black eyes roamed over her peasant's sark.

Placing a hand on either shoulder, Sir Dirk slid them up her throat, a bizarre gesture of threat and sensuality that paralyzed her. "You prove a surprise. They warned us Scots females were sisters to swine and had blue scales upon their bellies and breasts."

Her blood vibrated. "Take your filthy hands off me, you cur."

"These prideful Scots are raised with tongues too free. Let them learn," the second man growled, "starting with this bitch."

She tried to push away from the knight. Repulsed, Tamlyn watched as his hands splayed over her flesh. A smile curved his face as he clutched the bodice in his fists and ripped it down the middle. The thin material offered little resistance. Cheeks burning bright, her hands flew up to cover her full breasts.

Sword-callused hands took hold of her wrists. Bending them back, the knight compelled Tamlyn to release the grip on the torn sark. He leaned toward her and lowered his mouth to the slope of her pale breast. Her twisting against his hold only elicited an evil grin. Foul darkness possessed this man's soul.

"Truly, Dirk of Pendegast deserves his name. He is the finest swordsman of the Black Dragon," one laughed.

The knight nudged the material of the ripped sark with his nose until her pale breast was exposed. Leering, he announced, "No scale of any shade."

Seething with humiliation and rage, her body arched as his hot lips latched around her areola and sucked painfully hard. A whimper, a wounded animal sound, shuddered through her. Tears scalded her eyes. Again, she silently chanted the charm of making, this time to draw within herself, bespell her mind far away where it could not be touched by their brutality.

"Want us to hold her down for you?" a warrior offered.

The tall knight bore her down to the ground with the weight of his body. His muscular thigh pushed through the split in the long mail hauberk, shoving roughly between her legs. Swallowing bile, Tamlyn nearly strangled on the bitter, hot taste. She was terrified she might vomit, fearful she'd drown in it as they raped her.

Her shaking fingers brushed the top of her knife. As Sir Dirk raised up slightly to fumble with the lacings on his chausses, her hand closed about the hilt.

Another man heralded warning. Too late.

"Get up." Tamlyn wedged the razor-honed blade against her attacker's throat, forcing him to rise. "Else I'll split your gullet and watch your blood water the earth." Pearls of blood beaded from the pressure.

Another knight came up behind her. His rough hands wrapped around her wrist. The sudden movement jerked the knife tip to gouge into Sir Dirk's flesh along his jaw.

"Leave go, bitch, else I will snap your wrist like a

pigeon bone," Sir Geoffrey threatened. He squeezed until the knife fell from her grip.

Sir Dirk's countenance soured as his hand traced over his jaw, dragging the long fingers through the oozing blood. Black eyes narrowed on her, reptilian in their fury, utterly devoid of mercy. He roughly smeared his blood across her exposed breast. "Mayhap I shall kill the whore, then swive her."

He backhanded Tamlyn, so hard her ears rang. Blinding pain drove her to her knees. She lifted the back of her hand to her nose and dabbed at the blood trickling from her right nostril. More pooled in her throat, tasting coppery.

Weak, forced to remain kneeling, her other hand pathetically clutched the front of her torn sark. Swallowing fear, Tamlyn raised her trembling chin in defiance. She flashed hatred through unwanted tears, awaiting his next blow, damning him. She braced herself as he drew his hand back.

"Hold fast!"

A lone rider drove the magnificent black stallion across the dead-angle, bearing down on them, then reined the animal to a halt. It reared high, so powerful that its hooves slashed the air. The warrior dismounted with an inherent grace and recoiled power of a panther.

All five knights swung around to face him.

Hindered by their shifting positions, Tamlyn saw only glimpses of the sixth man. She held no hope for aid or mercy from one more of their breed. Just another dog of an English king, just another man to rape her.

Apprehension rippled through the guilt-ridden men as they fell back, creating room for him. Despite the heavy mail and plate weighting his body, he strode into the center of the group with regal bearing. Though a shade shorter than the others, he wasn't in the least intimidated by the taller men. His presence conveyed a raw, elemental power, the likes Tamlyn had never encountered. The hairs on the back of her neck prickled as she stared at him.

The armor covering his upper arms and thighs, the mail habergeon, mantle and surcoat were black. All black.

He removed his helm and pushed back the mail hood. His locks of the same unrelenting shade of pitch were not in the Norman style, but long, curling softly about his ears and brushing the metal gorget that covered the back of his neck.

Tamlyn's breath caught and held.

He was handsome—no, beautiful. The air surrounding this dark warrior seemed to stir as scorching energy discharged from him with the sizzle and crackle of lightning.

He handed the helm to Sir Geoffrey with no more regard than he would afford a servant. Aware of the men's unease, he clearly played on that. Stalling, he removed his black leather gauntlets with deft precision and then passed them off as well. With an arch of the black brow he conveyed disdain for the other men.

His keen attention fixed on Tamlyn. Heads bowed, the others let him through to her without one word uttered. Tamlyn trembled, knowing few men wielded such a chilling command.

His elegant fingers captured her chin, lifted it, forcing her to meet his stare. Eyes the shade of green garnets, they were ringed with lashes so long a woman would cry envy. When she stared into them, the world narrowed. Nothing else existed.

There was only this knight all in black.

His jaw was strong, square. The small mouth, etched with sensual curves, was seductive, though touched with a trace of what might be cruelty. Two black curls carelessly fell over the high forehead, a countenance sinful in ways no mere mortal man had right to be.

Tamlyn sensed a willful, razor-sharp intelligence

within this warrior. He was the *last* man she would want to face as an adversary.

Images possessed her, singed her with an ancient fire . . . of her hands on the bare flesh of his chest, how it would feel to be kissed by this black knight. Shocked, she nearly reeled backward. By what conjury did he put these visions in her mind? This warrior was dangerously beautiful, a killer angel with soul-stealing eyes. She trembled with fear, but could not take her gaze from him.

"My orders were not clear?" He turned to frown at the group, yet never wholly removed his focus from her. Angry green eyes encountered only downcast faces.

A mercenary blurted, "Bloody wench pulled a blade on Sir Dirk. She cut him." He flipped the knife tip first into the soil at the commander's feet.

"After he tried to rape her?" His voice was smooth as black velvet, compelling as the night. He smiled, warmth even flickered in the spellcasting eyes. Tamlyn sensed he was far from pleased by their actions. Had he been a cat, his tail would be snapping. "So, a mere Scots wench armed with a small knife held off five—*five*—of Edward's warriors who dared disobey my command. You were warned to handle Glen Shane's people softly."

"We . . . she . . ." Sir Dirk's words died under the glower of his liege.

"She's naught but a common wench." The second mercenary spit on the ground. "A castle worker or some swine girl from a croft."

Disdain flashed in the warrior's eyes, then they returned, roving over Tamlyn's curves in a way that missed few details. Nevertheless, it was impossible for her to scry his feelings. He kept them behind a will of iron, a master of the game.

"What is your name, lass?" his husky voice asked,

edged with impatience. He glanced at Bansidhe, grazing not far from them. "No serving wench has a mare of such quality. Yet your clothes are shabby. Do you work at Glenrogha?"

Tamlyn swallowed the dryness in her throat to force out the answer. "Bansidhe is mine, my lord."

"How many soldiers are within Glenrogha?" he demanded.

"I am a simple lass, my lord. These are men's matters." Tamlyn felt sick considering how few of the guard remained within the fortress' walls.

A faint lift of his brow signaled his doubt. "Simple? Not with unyielding audacity in those gold eyes. You grasp our language." The man observed too much. Grabbing her free wrist, he examined her palm. "Not the hand of a highborn lady or a commoner. How long can Glenrogha hold against siege?"

"I ken not, my lord. Winter just passed. Supplies should be hard pressed." No truth to that, the fortress could hold out for months.

His lips spread into a smile, slightly lopsided. "I repeat, what do they call you?' His soft voice belied the steel underneath. A voice, if he so chose, could hold dark allure.

"*Òinnseach*," she replied in a private jest at his expense, knowing he could not understand her godforsaken tongue.

He burst into a peal of laughter. "*Fool*? Your name is fool?"

Tamlyn's eyes widened with astonishment. She was more startled than he'd been when she spoke French.

"Yes, cat-eyes, I comprehend enough of your patter to keep my throat from getting split." He released the grip on her wrist. Bending down on his knee, he extracted the weapon from the ground and wiped the blade on the side of his thigh. "A *sgian dubh*—black knife."

Tamlyn watched him study the details, his thumb rubbing the runes carved into the hilt. As she struggled to rise, he lifted the hem of her faded kirtle, locating the hidden sheath for the dagger inside the edge of the right boot.

"Leave go," she snapped, skittish at being touched. This man terrified her in a manner she couldn't understand.

Tucking her knife under his belt, he eyed Tamlyn in appraisal. "You conjure riddles, my fool. I might presume you to be leman to the lord here, only it seems the Earl Hadrian gives the fiefs of Lochshane, Kinloch and Glenrogha to his three lady daughters. In this backward land men commit the unnatural folly of allowing women to rule fortresses."

"Hadrian MacShane is laird to the lands of Clan Shane, but he gives no power to his lady daughters. They hold titles in their own right through Clan Ogilvie."

"Blatherskite," he scoffed, raising a chuckle from his men, "women thinking they can control a fortress."

Tamlyn glowered. "Alba breeds women with strength and intelligence. No ease will you discover in the taking of the lands of the Ogilvies."

His sensual mouth lifted at the right corner. "Already I claimed Lochshane, my fool. We met little resistance."

Clinging to aloof pride, Tamlyn stood her ground whilst he rose, nearly pressing his body against hers. Blood thundered within her as heat from his body buffeted her senses. Yet she refused to be bullyragged by a man only half a head taller than she. Unblinking, she met his warlock eyes as his breath fanned across her face.

"Lochshane fell before alarm could be raised. Riders reached Glenrogha. You will find no ease in this undertaking."

"We shall see." With an arch of his brow, he swung

back to the soldiers. "I have little taste to find my men acting like a pack of rutting beasts. I shall deal with you after the fortresses are taken. Place her on Lasher. Fetch the palfrey. We rejoin my host."

Fires of Bel! Tamlyn faced the terrible Black Dragon! She should've guessed by the midnight armor, mail and mantle. She'd pondered why the English called this lord the Black Dragon when his standard was a green dragon on a field of deepest black. One glimpse of the imposing warrior and she knew: it was not the colors of heraldry to which they referred, but the man himself. Awe filled her as she stared at him, trying not to gape.

Tales of Welsh villages leveled under the Dragon's command were whispered so they didn't carry to the ears of bairns. Worse were the rumors of the sack of Berwick, over a fortnight's passing. Scots feared thousands had perished in a nightmare of slaughter and flames.

As she fumbled with the sark's drawstring, tightening it to close the ripped front, her eyes strayed to the imposing figure of the knight in black. Tamlyn felt torn, unable to believe that this man with the angelic countenance was capable of slaughtering all in England's path, putting them to the sword and scorching the very earth.

She jumped when hands took hold of her arms. Sir Dirk's glower chilled Tamlyn's blood as he obeyed his liege's bidding. He shoved her toward the midnight charger of the Dragon.

The black saddle rested upon material of dark green, covering the animal from withers to flanks. Recoiling, she knew her fears were valid. This man was no ordinary commander, but the king's champion, Julian Challon.

The earl mounted with lionesque grace, seating himself against the high back of the creaking saddle to leave room for her. Resisting for an instant, her heels dug into the soft ground.

The stallion reared slightly, bouncing upon hooves. "Beware, fool. Lasher is unaccustomed to carrying two. I hold no desire to see you trampled under his hooves. He is a trained killer," the earl cautioned.

The knight picked her up and deposited her atop the horse. From above the knee, her legs were bared. Worse, she rested against the leather and metal covered thighs of this Norman. She blushed hotly at the intimate position.

Tamlyn turned in the saddle. He was so close. Too close. His warm breath feathered across her cheek. Even so, she challenged and held his eyes.

The most beautiful eyes she'd ever seen.

"Like his master?"

"Aye. A truth you would do well to remember." A strange, almost poignant light flickered within those mysterious depths, then vanished as if never had been, displaced by the fierce determination in the set of his jaw.

The Dragon spurred the horse to rear, throwing her back against his armored chest. He placed his hand on her waist to anchor her. In reaction, her muscles tightened under the pressure. She couldn't seem to breathe.

Tamlyn looked down to see his thumb rested on the bare skin exposed by the rip in the sark. The thumb burned, a brand on her flesh.

She was still dizzy from the fall. That little compared to the way this warrior's touch sent her blood to thrumming. She turned to study his face. No emotions played in those green eyes, yet their force rocked her to the core.

"To Glenrogha!" he called.

Chapter 2

Reaching the road, Tamlyn viewed the great Dragon's host. Knights, so many knights! Mounted upon heavy horse, they were shock troops, and with their long lances served as a moving battering ram. Outnumbering them two to one were the hobelars—lightly armed and protected cavalry, used for quick, flanking maneuvers. Welsh archers were equipped with deadly longbows and protected by shields as tall as a man. Infantry were comprised of mercenaries, while conscripted Kerns from Ireland marched under the Harp Pennon, trailing behind foot soldiers belonging to Edward's war-seasoned troops from Flanders.

She breathed in dread. So many. Too many.

Facing reality, her heart sank. Despair was an emotion Tamlyn had never felt. Her world had always been safe, secure. She feared there would be no standing in the path of this ruthless earl.

What was to become of Glenrogha? Of her?

Lightheaded, she slumped, her spine hitting the metal of the Dragon's chest plate. The strong fingers flexed on her waist, a reminder of his control. Looking down, she

noticed the horse's gait caused her breasts to sway per-
ilously close to that invading thumb.

She shut her eyes, trying to will it all away.

Feeling the woman before him sag, Julian drew her
against his chest. The shock of what he'd prevented must
be hitting her mind. Concerned she'd slip from the
saddle, he held her close. Sensations evoked by her nearness intrigued him, pleased him. Having her in his
embrace pleased him.

Damn their eyes! Hadn't he given orders how he
wanted Glen Shane's people treated? *Handle them softly*,
he'd stressed.

After Berwick, Julian had little stomach to witness the
Dragon Standard raised before another town. The image
arose within his mind, of the flag bearer waving Edward's
new pennon—the one meaning no quarter given. It had
come just before a thousand Heavy Horse hammered
down the curtain walls of the Scottish city and madness
ensued.

The green dragon on black was long the standard of
the Earls of Challon. Spurred by rampant rumor, the Scots
now confused it with Edward's new dread banner. A slur
to his family's honorable name. Umbrage flared, but he
reined in futile emotions and tried to banish the memories.

Julian choked, oily nausea rolling within him. Wales
had been bad enough, a festering nightmare that plagued
his soul. Only Berwick had been nothing more than a
demonstration to the Scots of the force of Edward's might.

Breaking the English encampment at Hutton, the king
had ridden forth, leading his army of ten thousand. At
the gates of Berwick, he demanded immediate surrender. The foolish, prideful Scots jeered and called for
Edward to do his worst.

He had. His very worst. A horror unimaginable!

In a wave of fire and blood, the English had rolled through the defenseless town. Twenty thousand men, women and children came under the English sword in the killing frenzy. So many, they'd need burying in mass pits once command finally came down. Now, several sen-nights past, Edward's decree meant the putrid corpses remained where they had fallen, hacked down in the streets.

A terrible image that would haunt Julian until his dying days.

Returning to his sense of self, he realized that his arm tightly clutched the woman before him, almost as if to absorb her heat, hoping to banish the chill within his heart. He forced his muscles to relax, not wanting to alarm her after the rough handling by his men.

Julian breathed a sigh of relief when Lochshane came over with little more than words exchanged. It was the first of the three fiefs within Glen Shane controlled by the daughters of the Earl of Kinmarch. When the captain of the guard received news of a host under standard of the Black Dragon, surrender came quickly. There they informed him their lady, Rowanne MacShane, was not within the curtain wall, but was at Glenrogha this day.

By all, Julian would soon face that daughter of The Shane along with her younger sister, Lady Tamlyn. Then he'd deal their fates.

Only where did the female in front of him fit? He moved his thumb ever so gently on her bare skin, felt the warm flesh contract in reaction. His groin stiffened at her response.

Her clothes were thin, near ragged. Fanning around her hips, her long hair was a shade rare. Julian was used to the pale blondes so favored at English Court, or the black-haired beauties of his native Normandy. This

Scotswoman was neither. Nor was it the red so common in her land. The luster and hue of aged bronze, an image of it spread across a bed as she lay beneath him flooded his mind.

Her eyes fascinated him. As a rule Julian would be hard pressed to tell a woman's eye color—even those he bedded. Intelligent, penetrating, hers held a power, a pull. She rarely blinked. That directness would spook most men. Julian was *not* most men. To him they held a challenge, one his hot warrior's blood would be driven to conquer.

When he'd held her knife and looked into her amber eyes, he lost sense of time. A crippling jolt of lust racked his body. He'd just berated his knights for attacking her. Yet, had he been alone with this woman, he'd have lain her down on the cool earth and taken her. Nothing and no one could've stopped him.

Despite the overpowering, physical response, something elusive brushed against the back of his mind, a haunting feeling he couldn't place. Frissons of awareness had rippled up his spine as he stared, bound by both the knife and the woman. *A feeling . . . something from long ago*? With certainty, he knew when he was old and gray, and memories dimmed, he'd still vividly recall the image of her kneeling, those haunting eyes staring up at him. Nearer gold than brown, they possessed aspects of a cat having assumed human form.

Legends whispered throughout these heathen hills warned of the Cait Sidhe, witches royally descended from the Picts. These fey women held powers to transmute nine times into large cats. He'd scoffed at such superstitious drivel. No more. One now sat in front of—and upon—him.

As his thumb stroked the soft skin just below her

breasts, the corner of his mouth twitched. He pondered what it would take to make this strange one purr.

Without command the knights shifted, allowing their liege to pass to his personal guard. His brothers glared at him, but he ignored them. For several deep breaths Julian held the stallion in place, studying the fertile land stretching before him.

Some ghostly voice whispered to his soul that this pagan glen was rare, different. A sense of coming home filled his heart, as if he were born of this rich black loam. The feeling of welcome had haunted him since entering the pass of Glen Shane, and increased as the approach to the fortress neared. When first viewed, the sister's domain of Lochshane failed to touch him as strongly. The fey pull was for and to Glenrogha, which now belonged to him. By the rood, take and hold it he would, and no one could stop his course. Impatience pulsed heavy within his blood to reach the fortress.

Taking point, he raised his left hand and signaled the host to advance to the Scottish stronghold . . . and his waiting destiny.

Lasher's prancing shifted the woman side to side, her long legs rubbing his thighs. Worse, the position of their bodies in the deep seat of the war saddle set his mind awhirl with dark, erotic images of them together, naked. Heat flooded his flesh with potent cravings. The strength of his reactions to this Scots female were disturbing. Muscles along his jaw flexed as Julian did his best to dismiss them.

On the far tor a wooden cross burned. The height of seven men, its black pitch smoke curled high into the loch breeze, rising and spiraling into the heavy Highland fog.

Julian leaned his head close against hers. His chest

tightened, as all around him seemed to fade to gray. There was only her. Inhaling her haunting fragrance, he fought the urge to bury his face in the bronze tresses. Blinking to resist against the spell, he asked, "Pray, what is that, my fool?"

"Cross Tàradiach—the Fiery Cross. Even if your knights intercepted the rider dispatched to Kinloch, they see the cross burning on the tor. So does Clan Ogilvie."

"For all it serves Glenrogha. The fortress will not stand," Julian stated with complete assurance of success. Reining Lasher at the rise of the knoll, he stared upon the flanking towers surrounded by the vitrified stone walls of Glenrogha. "God's teeth, what means of bastion is that?"

"My ancestors—the Picts—built the battlement."

His smile held a trace of feline as the green eyes appraised the curtain wall, searching out strengths and vulnerabilities. "The gates are wood. No portcullis. Strong ramparts serve naught if the gates can be shattered."

He glanced to the left and nodded once. The high-ranking knight put golden spur to his steed, setting the animal to a lope to the outer wall.

Stirring on the bastion was evident. Nevertheless, the soldiers remained behind the protection of the wall, afraid of the deadly range of the Welsh longbowmen.

"Who answers for Glenrogha?" The messenger rode forth and called for all to hear. Full of barely controlled spirit, his white charger pranced sideways in a flashy display, the flag of truce snapping in the spring breeze.

A woman wearing a plaide strode to the edge of the rampart and stepped up on the platform. "Rowanne of Lochshane speaks for Glenrogha."

"A woman?" The knight scorned the notion. "Where is the captain of the guard?"

"Knave, in Glen Shane women hold the lands of our birthright." Her blonde hair swirled in the breeze like a warrior's pennant.

"Then I need parley with the Lady Tamlyn MacShane. I carry a message from the Earl of Challon."

She scoffed, "It is said the king's champion rides an ebony stallion, darker than your Devil's soul. I will speak with the Lord Challon, not his page."

Julian shifted hands. The left one gripped the reins now also pressed against the soft curve of the woman's belly, leaving his right free to rest on the hilt of his sword. He nudged the mount forward, guiding the pitch destrier with his knees and clicking of his tongue. The animal danced from the ranks of the advanced guard and to the curtain wall.

"Greetings, Lady Rowanne." His voice rang clear in the hushed stillness, all eyes upon him. "We missed your lovely presence at Lochshane yestereve."

"Why has Longshanks sent his mighty dragon to Glen Shane? We are a small fief and are no trouble to such a powerful king."

"But not thy sire at Kinmarch. The laird of Clan Shane supports the Scots king, Balliol, in his rising. A most unwise choice."

"My lord father follows his own path. The three sisters hold the titles in their own right, separate from Kinmarch."

"No longer, my lady. I now hold charter. Henceforth, all lands and titles within Glen Shane are forfeit. I rule here now as new lord and earl."

"You stray far past the Marches, Lord Challon. Your English king holds no power here."

"As Lord Paramount of Scotland, Edward's word

becomes law. Learn to accept this. Your sire rose to Balliol's standard so all lands and titles are now seized."

"No decree concerning Kinmarch can include the three fortresses in Glen Shane. These are held by the sisters. Look around, Lord Challon. None are in rebellion here," Rowanne countered, clearly refusing to be cowed. "Daughters of The Shane rally to the standard of no man."

"That aside, I seek audience with the Lady Tamlyn to see the transfer of rule is done in peace. I hold no wish to spill Scots blood," Lord Challon persisted.

Tamlyn watched her sister Rowanne shift her attention from the earl, the brown eyes finally locking with Tamlyn's. The silent question in them nearly made Tamlyn flinch. The earl was too observant. Surely he would notice. Scared, Tamlyn quickly looked away, glancing to her side.

With a tilt to her head, Rowanne answered in a level voice, "Our Tamlyn is not within these walls."

"May I suggest you permit our entry? A runner can be dispatched with word to your lady sister," Challon offered, mischief filtering through his deep, melodic voice.

"You, and you alone, Lord Dragon, may enter Glenrogha," Rowanne replied. "Come, we shall bid you one hundred thousand welcomes."

With a lift of the raven's wing brows, he cautioned, "I am no one's fool, Lady Rowanne. It is unwise to bait a dragon."

"I decline your generous offer, Lord Challon. Tamlyn kens your trespass. Only she may grant leave to reopen the gates. Until she says different, you and your grand fine knights must remain without."

The heavy rise and fall of his armored chest pushed against Tamlyn's spine. Impatience surged through his body—she felt it pulse with his every breath. The shortness of temper was reflected in his demand. "Where might the mistress of Glenrogha be found?"

"No one was informed where she went. Like our lord father, she has a mind of her own." Rowanne paused, but only briefly. "May I, Lord Dragon, beg a boon? I appeal for release of the lass held before you. Though garbed as a serf, she is of noble blood. It would prove muckle difficult if anything happened to her."

"It is hard to turn down a request from so beautiful a lady. Still, I think it best this fool remains under my protection." As if emphasizing his possession, his arm flexed about her.

Rowanne's eyes flashed fire. "Even from this distance I see the degree of your noble care."

"Not by my hand. Ask her," he granted.

Rowanne sought Tamlyn's eyes. Inclining her head slightly, she indicated to her older sister that the earl spoke the truth.

"Naught shall happen to her. This I so swear upon my oath as the Earl of Challon."

"Take heed, Lord Dragon, if the lass is harmed in any fashion, one night you shall waken with a *sgian dubh* cutting your gullet . . . take that as my bond."

"Shall I send in my brother as a hostage to guarantee her safety?" Caprice flashed in the arresting eyes, as he nodded to the knight immediately to his left. "Sir Guillaume of Challon would gladly offer himself as surety. Is that not so?"

The brother's eyes raked slowly over Rowanne. A smile curved his sensual mouth. "Indeed. It would be my pleasure, my lord."

Rowanne tugged the plaide snugly over her breasts, clearly rattled by the arrogant Norman's stare. With a tilt of her chin, she dismissed him as beneath notice.

"Gracious thanks for your grand offer, but the answer remains no. I prefer all your bonnie knights remain on that side of the curtain."

"I grant you until the morrow to summon your lady sister. If she is not here to empower the gates to swing wide, I shall commence siege. The force within—sorely depleted by your lord sire—shan't hold against my host. Take that as *my* bond."

Not lingering for a reply, he spurred the horse into a prancing trot back over the knoll to his waiting guard, followed strides behind by the handsome brother. He spoke to the messenger. "Food and rest is needed by all, Sir Guillaume. See the troops stand at ease. Give orders for the tents to be set and a hot meal prepared. Put the squires to care of the cattle."

With a nod and flashing grin, the man set to see the Dragon's orders carried out.

Clutching the high square pommel of the saddle, Tamlyn turned to glance back at Glenrogha, terrified what the future would bring now the Black Dragon had come.

Chapter 3

Tamlyn's hands gripped the saddle's pommel for balance as Julian Challon spurred his charger to the rear of the long columns of heavy horse and soldiery. Once out of sight, the earl reined the animal beside a small burn. He swung his leg back over the high cantle, descending easily for a man in heavy armor and mail.

Reaching up, he placed his hands about Tamlyn's waist. He paused, his eyes narrowing on her flesh exposed by the tear in her sark. Almost transfixed, he brushed his thumb against her flesh. Her skin quivered, scorched by his warlock's touch.

The kenning often permitted Tamlyn to read feelings in others. But his thoughts were suddenly so clear. Some fey cobweb brushed against his mind, warmth both exciting and discomforting to him in the same heartbeat. Then that steel shutter within him fell and she no longer shared the connection. Withdrawal of that bond left her bereft, alone as she'd never felt before. Tamlyn blinked back tears.

He swung her free of the saddle. Bringing her body close to his, touching, rubbing in places, he let her slide against him until her feet hit the ground. Her heart slammed in her chest as her eyes locked with his. She was breathless. The instant spun out as they both seemed unable to move. Gradually, he lowered his head, as if he would kiss her. She saw the muscles flex in his jaw as he fought the impulse. Irritation flashed in the green depths of his eyes, then he wheeled away from her.

Flipping the reins over the horse's neck, he permitted the animal to drink. Pulling a cloth out from under the black breastplate, he dipped it into the water, then strode back to her. Fingers deft, compassionate, he took hold of her chin and dabbed at the blood crusted around the edge of her nose. The gentle contact hardly seemed fit for a warrior, let alone the mighty Black Dragon.

Tamlyn stiffened, fighting pressure to shrink away from this dark earl. Odd. Though he terrified her, it was not precisely fear. She struggled to prevent him from witnessing how her body trembled due to his warmth, his closeness, his scent. The raw, palpable power exuded by this unusual man was more daunting than all his tall knights together. Small wonder he stood as a legend amongst men.

His eyes met hers with indifference, proclaiming her no more than a riddle that plagued him only in passing. Mayhap the arrogant man wondered if she had scales upon her belly. She shrugged. Indifference hadn't lit his eyes a few heartbeats ago. He *had* wanted to kiss her. Tamlyn didn't need the kenning to tell her that. Counter to all logic, she wished him to do so, to close his mouth over hers with a deep, driving hunger.

Freed from the weight of the mail hood, the black hair pushed away from his skull in thick waves. Bluish glints highlighted the locks stirred by the gentle breeze.

Despite what his coming meant, she found Lord Challon

compelling. That angered her. Curse this beautiful warrior! Why had the Fates been so cruel to send this intriguing man to face her as foe? With regret, Tamlyn could merely wonder how meeting him as friend instead of enemy might have been. Wisps of a dream. They were enemies. Nothing could alter that simple reality. Only, hating him would be easier if he weren't so . . . gorgeous.

Swallowing, Tamlyn summoned courage to speak. "Thank you for rescuing me."

He gave a slight nod, then changed subjects, as if he didn't wish to dwell upon the incident. "The Lady Rowanne is beautiful. Seems for once court gossip did not exaggerate. Edward oft encouraged matches for the sisters to English nobles. One incentive for resettling northward, entailing more taxes, was tales of the ladies' beauty."

"Aye, she is a bonnie lass." Jealousy fluttered in her chest at this man deeming her sister beautiful.

Challon paused from cleaning her nose. His dark green eyes skimmed over her features, pausing at the faint cleft in her chin. His thumb brushed across it as though he thought it a smudge of dust. When he found it wasn't, he rubbed the pad across the tiny dip several times. "And the Lady Tamlyn . . . is she as comely in face and form?"

Panic rippled through her as he said her name. "The daughters of The Shane are different. Very different."

"They say the baronesses are twins."

"In their faces such is apparent. Raven is Celtic dark, whilst Rowanne is fair."

"Then that was the darker sister, standing behind the Lady of Lochshane?"

Tamlyn felt the pull of his ensorcelling eyes. She had

to blink to concentrate upon his words. "Aye, that was Raven of Kinloch."

"The Lady Tamlyn? Is she as pleasing to the eye?"

"Whether she is swart hag or lovely maid, you come to steal her holding. If she was humpbacked and have warts on her nose it would make no difference," she accused, scared of his quest for knowledge of Tamlyn. Did he suspect? Was a big cat playing games of illusion with the doomed mousie?

"The lady has warts?" A hint of a smile played at the edge of the sensual mouth.

"Aye, three and a big hairy mole on her cheek—the mark of Satan, some folk whisper."

She'd heard Normans feared the Auld Ways. Twaddle! Lucifer was their invention, a bogeyman to keep gullible minds from straying from the kirk. Still, if these ignorant English were so easily spooked, then such was their lot and an advantage to exploit. A woman wisely used whatever weapons were at her disposal.

Searching his bonnie features, Tamlyn tried to fit his male perfection and sensuality to the name of the Dragon of Challon. Her heart thudded, erratic, as he lured her senses with his dark magic. She had trouble masking her unwanted reaction to this enigmatic lord.

Sooty lashes batted over his devilkin eyes. "A hump? She is so afflicted?"

"No, but her spine is twisted, so she hipples. It is sad."

"Strange," doubt laced his tone, "Jongleurs boast that the third daughter of The Shane is as lovely as the elder two."

"Folk at Glenrogha love her. They would never shame her pride. No looking glass is permitted within the fortress. The poor lass doesn't ken her homely state." Tamlyn was piling lie on top of lie, and it would return later to haunt her. Even so, she couldn't leash her wayward tongue.

"Such loyal subjects." He pressed the cold cloth against her reddening cheek. "I hope these tenderhearted serfs serve me as true."

Anger flared within Julian's mind. Nothing as finely molded as this woman's face should be touched in such harsh disregard. His knights would pay with the skin off their backs and count themselves fortunate he'd caught them in time. Had they raped her, he'd have seen them hanged.

"Such tales of her ugliness . . . I sense you play games, my fool. Mayhap you are jealous of the lady's appeal, hmm?"

"She has little for me to envy, Lord Challon." Unable to look in his eyes, she blushed and glanced away. A frown shadowed her face as the darkened sky over Kinmarch drew her attention. "May I beg an answer from you? Word came of the siege and that the earl was dead."

Julian's hand holding the cloth dropped slowly as he studied her reaction to his words. "By Edward's command, they dismantle the castle as we speak. Nothing shall be left standing, but a pile of fine Scottish stones."

"And The Shane?" Moisture formed in the large eyes, threatening to spill.

There was a strange pressure in his chest as he watched her fighting tears. What was it about those damnable gold eyes that had such power to reach him? Julian found it hard to look away. "So, you care for the earl." Not a question, just a flat statement of his inference.

"Please," she beseeched.

Ah, the puzzle was unriddled—she was the Lord Hadrian's lover. Foreign sensations invaded his body, increasing as he recognized he resented her feelings for the Earl of Kinmarch. He was jealous. Why now, why summoned by this fey Scots lass, a stranger who for some reason did not feel like a . . . stranger?

Nothing felt the same since coming into this pagan glen.

"He lives." Wishing the man didn't, he informed, "Edward ordered him made prisoner and transported to York. The governor shall hold him until the king crosses back over the River Tweed and onto English soil. The Earl Hadrian and the Lord Douglas, former governor of Berwick Castle, shall be carried to Westminster to stand trial, accused of treason. Edward intends to make examples of all nobles fool enough to support Balliol in his blear-witted rebellion."

She forgot about clutching the ripped sark. Folding her hands together, she dropped to her knees. Her lips moved in a singsong chant, but his grasp of Gaelic was too limited to understand.

Julian observed her madonna pose for several breaths, until he could abide it no longer. Sensations burned as quicklime, eating away at his innards. Never had he known jealousy was physical as well as a plague of the mind. Damn the bones of saints! He little liked this queer, possessing madness, a distemper that made him a stranger to himself. Unable to endure watching her shed tears for another man, he stalked away.

Weary of it all, he leaned back against the trunk of a silver birch tree. By all holy, he wished matters done. He was so bloody tired of war, fed up to the gills with Edward's insatiable greed and uncontrollable rages.

Julian knew he had lost the warrior's edge. The taste of battle was now rancid and with each day's passing grew more unpalatable. There had been too many wars, too many friends or relations dead, food for ravens on some foreign field of battle. Their lifeless faces haunted his memory.

Then there were the poignant eyes of his brother Christian . . . pleading. He squeezed his eyes tight to block out the image.

This strange disease of spirit was killing him from within, slowly. Agonizingly. Atrophying his very soul. After decades of unquestioning allegiance to Edward, never raising word whether his king was right, the cause just, Julian could endure the charnel house of war no more.

Wales had been bad enough. Only it grew worse. In his hatred of the Scots, Longshanks was poisoned. His virulent Angevin temper—rivaling that of Henry II— had morphed into a black malignancy, as if he were an apostate of Satan. No telling where it'd all end.

Julian wished his eyes had been closed at Berwick. Instead, it served as an epiphany.

War should be honorable, but all the Round Table's chivalry had been put asunder. What the Plantagenet let his army do in sacking Berwick bore only shame. Sights, sounds and smells lingered vividly, unwanted within Julian's tormented memory. Hideous visions persecuted his sleep. His dreams were made hell.

If Julian could find some measure of peace in this mist shrouded land, he'd ask for nothing more and count himself favored indeed. Let Edward be done with Balliol, depart this north country. Hurry to challenge the will of France, go far away . . . forget Julian Challon exists. Allow the legend of the Black Dragon to fade into fable.

When someone addressed him now as the Dragon he almost laughed. Nonetheless, it was a shield, a mask he'd don to reach simple goals. The name of Challon had panicked the garrison at Lochshane to surrender. If he remained in luck's fickle regard, he'd see the same at Kinloch and Glenrogha. After securing both, he'd use the legend to scare off those who might try to take any part of his new holdings. Only a fool would dare to reive cattle from the great Black Dragon.

Relief filled him when Lochshane came over without the first arrow being loosed. None were hurt. His occupation was bloodless. If the two sister domains followed suit, in time he might be able to sleep once again.

Guillaume and Simon galloped up. He smiled at his father's sons. More importantly, they were his friends— something he didn't call many men. Born to his lord father's leman before his own birth, neither was able to inherit lands or titles due to their bastardy. Julian was protective of them. None dared insult the openly acknowledged brothers of the Dragon of Challon and live to boast of it. Steadfast at his side, they stood against all, shielding his back so he fought with no fear. Their bastard birth had not embittered them; never had either gainsaid him.

For their loyalty, he'd reward one with the fief of Lochshane, the other Kinloch. Julian's plans were to claim Glenrogha for himself, unite the holding with the lands of Kinmarch and take the Countess Tamlyn MacShane as lady-wife . . . twisted spine, hairy mole and all. Anything for peace!

No more Edward and his spiraling greed for bigger kingdoms and greater glories for the First Knight of Christendom. No court intrigues. No war. Julian's time had finally come.

"Your tent awaits, Lord Brother," Simon informed him with a grin, leading the two stallions to the water beside Lasher.

His expression the opposite, Guillaume Challon

frowned. "You should seek rest, Julian. Your head aches when you push hard as you have this fortnight past."

He was tired, mentally more than physically. "We may all take rest. Time enough before my next move."

Pushing away from the tree, he strode to the kneeling woman and lightly touched her shoulder, hoping not to startle her. Her skin burned like a brand through the thin baize. In desperate hunger, he wanted to pull her to him, absorb that heat into his being. He'd been cold for so long.

Despite his care, she flinched, the large cat-eyes widening in alarm. Julian's mouth pressed into a hard line, not caring for her reaction.

In a soft voice he commanded, "Arise, my fool," and offered his hand to her.

Since she no longer clutched the front of the torn sark, it gaped, affording Julian a tantalizing view of her breasts. His gut clenched painfully in response. Desire rolled through his entire body like thunder.

He was surprised when she accepted his hand to help rise on unsteady feet. She wobbled. He caught her upper arms to lend balance. The haunting amber eyes slowly lifted, and in an instant frozen in time's fabric, they locked with his, ensorcelling him with pulsing, ambient power. A witch's power. A dark fire that burned straight to his soul.

Affixed by her cat-eyes, he was lured into the fathomless depths. So many extremes eddied there . . . almost as if echoes from the distant past. Julian felt time suspend, bend in on itself. The world narrowed to only this woman before him. All he could hear was the erratic pounding of his heart, the rhythm echoed by hers, and the cool air stirring through the new leaves of the silver birch trees. It hurt to draw breath. Lightheaded, he felt the whole world spin out of control.

He tried to resist the peculiar spell she cast by apologizing. "I regret the harm inflicted by my knights. They were under orders not to touch the females in this glen. Sadly, when nations make war, women suffer most. Rest assured, they shall be punished for disobeying."

Tamlyn nodded. She found it upsetting that the great Dragon of Challon apologized. Dragons didn't act contrite. They roared and breathed fire. No matter how breathtakingly beautiful, dragons were . . . *dragons*.

Chapter 4

Julian sequestered his captive within the waiting tent and placed a guard outside. The front flaps were tied back so all could watch her movements. And move she did. She paced with the restlessness of a cat trapped in a cage.

With feigned innocence she glided to the far corner, checking if she could slip under the edge. Julian raised his hand and signaled the soldier on station. The man leaned in and cautioned her to step to the middle. Julian choked back a laugh when she stuck out her tongue at him, then flopped down with a frustrated thud upon a large chest.

He admired her inner steel. Most women would be cowed given her situation. Not this female. She met their eyes with that witchy stare, not flinching, never backing down. A woman of fire.

Jealous, he felt certain she was the Earl Hadrian's leman. What man wouldn't covet her, kill to own her . . . protect her with his very life?

At the English court two years past, he was introduced to the flamboyant laird of Clan Shane. A striking Scotsman with arresting, ice-green eyes, he appeared much younger than his five and two score years. His wife, countess in her own right, had died nearly a decade past, making him a target of the husband hunts. He seemed disinterested in acquiring another mate, and oddly, the laird displayed a similar attitude in arranging marriages for his lady daughters. Balladeers sang how his marriage to the Countess Deporadh Ogilvie of Glenrogha was a love match. Julian found it hard to believe the man old enough to have sired three grown daughters.

The MacShane women attracted hordes of suitors. Worse for them, they had become an obsession with Edward. Zealous to see them leg-shackled to loyal English nobles, the monarch haughtily called it his *Seeding of Scotland Campaign*. Longshanks was vexed in his dealings with Hadrian MacShane and his daughters. In the king's eyes, they were a symbol of all that was wrong with Scotland.

These females held titles and lands through matriarchal lineage. In keeping with their ancient Pict laws, they held the right to select their husbands. The sisters refused all alliances proposed by the Plantagenet. Peculiar circumstances that provided fuel for Edward's volcanic rages.

Eventually, the earl saw the twins wed to Scottish barons, though both were now widowed. The Baroness Kinloch had lost her husband to a bout of lung fever, whilst the Lady Lochshane's spouse had died mysteriously. Scandal spread that the woman played a role in the man's untimely death. Having witnessed the lady's poise upon the rampart, it was within Julian's belief.

These Scots females were such a strong breed, unlike any he'd encountered. It didn't bode well for him in his upcoming dealings with them.

The striking coloring of his "fool" repeatedly pulled his attention to her. The bronze tresses made a man yearn to fist his hands in the silken mass. This fey lass drew him, fascinated him in dark ways he scarcely understood. He studied his captive, half listening to his brother's words, detailing their next move against Glenrogha.

Julian was medium height for a Norman, still she reached to the level of his nose. It was disconcerting. He was used to shorter, frailer women, not one who carried a knife in her boot or rode a horse astride with chivalric skill.

She jumped to her feet and once more took up the agitated prowling. He could watch her do that all night, the graceful sway of those curves. Not only was she taller than most females at Court, her hips were wider, rounder. Conceivably why these Scots' numbers seemed endless— their women were formed to cradle a babe with ease. A man's seed would find fertile purchase within their strong bodies.

As she paced, Julian envisioned her belly swollen, heavy from his life within her. She'd wear motherhood well, breeding second nature to this sturdy Scots lass. A surge of possessiveness spiked in his warrior's blood, engulfing him with a yearning to see her carrying his seed, bearing him strong sons.

Mayhap Julian would claim her as his mistress. He'd plant his child deep in her belly, then she'd forget to shed tears for the Red Laird of Clan Shane. His lower body pulsed agreement.

It would be intriguing to see a child resulting from the mix of their bloods. Was her golden coloring strong enough to influence the black hair and green eyes that so marked the Challons when no woman before had altered their ancient line? Heat crawled under his skin as he contemplated whether she coupled with a man as fiercely as she'd fought his knights.

Admiration filled him when he first saw her, kneeling,

but not humbled. She'd looked his men in the eye with
the strength and power of a warrior. Those haunting gold
eyes were so furious, so vulnerable, though trying not to
show it.

Could that intensity be bent, turned into another fierce
emotion—passion? His blood quickened as these questions possessed him. Julian glanced away, shaking the
lust clawing his thoughts. Or miming he had. He little
cared for this lack of control. No woman before held the
power to bind his senses so.

"Guillaume, place a second guard outside my tent.
Have drink and food sent." He paused, the long fingers
of his right hand stroking his chin. "Make known under
threat of losing heads that none save me touches the
Scottish demoiselle."

Guillaume grinned. "Growing territorial, are we?"

"We?" Julian shrugged, a mask to cover that Guillaume's well-aimed arrow found its mark. "Glenrogha is
mine. All of it."

"What say you, Lord Brother?" Simon called Julian's
attention back to the drawings scratched in the dirt.

"It is sound. I shall send forth a messenger in the
middle of the night, when exhaustion dulls their minds.
With their attention is on the front of the fortress, they
shan't spot men flanking their lochside. You still wish to
attempt this, Simon?"

"Attempt? I enjoy rising to a good stiff challenge.
Makes one's blood surge." His smile salacious, Simon's
green eyes flashed to the woman in the tent. "Amongst
other things."

Inclining his head, Julian altered the command.
"Choose three and ten. I want none harmed—especially
you, Simon."

"The flanks are their weakness. The Picts were renowned

for pegging the best defensive locations. Foolishly, these Scots trust the cliffs. Chance of the lochside being scaled likely never entered their heads. My Lord Brother, you shall warm your boots in Glenrogha's Great Hall before dawnbreak," Simon assured, the Challon reckless streak showing.

Finding pretext to linger near the campfire, Julian spoke to his squires. Truth be told, he was avoiding going to her.

His unyielding warrior's mind was in conflict with mating instincts over how he should handle his Scottish fool. Without hesitation, he would claim her. It was his right. Why deny himself when he craved her as he never wanted a woman before? Too long denied, his soul hungered for the warmth she could bring him.

First, he needed to ferret out something to call her. A smart man simply did not command, "Fool, you shall warm my bed." Not with expectations of her obeying! Women liked to think they had a choice and rarely did any appreciate being called a fool.

When he found no further excuses to delay, he walked toward the tent and the arousing, yet perplexing problem housed there.

Julian felt as if his soul were being placed in the balance.

His squire Moffet set coals in a brazier to dispel the penetrating chill. Working to get the flame to catch, he pretended to ignore the pacing woman.

She stopped, put her hands on her hips and gave him the sharp edge of her tongue. "Why not just ask the bloody Dragon to breathe fire on them?"

An eager lad, he'd never speak to a prisoner without Julian giving leave. He saw Moffet's suppressed smile. The lad liked her, admired her spirit.

So did Julian.

Moffet was at that awkward stage of growth—four and ten. Nearly as tall as Julian, he'd transmuted from child to man within the passings of a few moons. One could almost hear bones creaking. Rushing to please his liege, he often tripped, unused to his new, larger feet. Kinsman, he was bastard son of Julian's second cousin, Damian St. Giles, Lord Ravenhawke.

Moffet was the image of Julian's youngest brother, Christian. The Challon blood showed in the young man's midnight hair and vivid green eyes. At times it pained Julian to look upon him. The resemblance was that haunting.

Blessed with a rare talent, Moffet could conjure a smile from him even when Julian's mind was in the blackest of malaise. Since Christian's death, Julian found smiling difficult, thus he treasured these quiet times they shared. He was glad Damian had sent him for training.

Julian ached for a son of his own.

"My lord, I fixed all as Sir Guillaume bade," Moffet informed with adoring eyes.

Julian patted him on the head. Pangs of wanting a son twisted in his gut. "As do you always. No lord is blessed with a better squire. This I said to your father less than a fortnight ago."

He beamed. "I try, my lord, though I fear the Scots will die laughing at hearing my accursed voice."

"Time will solve the problem, then you will not fight foes, but comely wenches. Aid me from my armor. Eat, then rest while you may. I shall require you later."

Julian's eyes settled upon his fool in a predator's gleam. He never took them off her the whole time the lad unbuckled plates, mail and his aketon—arming jacket.

The dark gold hair curtained her shoulders with the texture of silk. It took his last shred of sanity not to march over, fist his hands in it and drag her to the ground. He swallowed the hard knot of desire choking his throat, lest she rank his character as low as that of his men.

To distract himself he tried to focus on other details about her. The drawstring of the ripped sark had been tightened again so the wool in front met. The thin material did little to mask her full curves. Blasted female didn't even wear a chemise! Small wonder his knights had disobeyed his command.

Her pagan earthiness hit a man hard as a fist to the center of his chest. Heat spiraled in his blood, his lust feasting upon her full, sensual form. As if she sensed his musings, her nipples pebbled, clearly defined under the threadbare fabric.

The corner of his mouth tugged in a slow, feral smile as his eyes sought hers in unspoken communication—man-woman responses. Ancient. Elemental. The honey-colored eyes flashed in anger, causing the twist to his mouth to deepen. He couldn't suppress it.

Anger implied awareness. Awareness could be bent into arousal. In the right hands—his hands. Yes, his fool and he would deal well together.

Moffet rushed to complete his tasks, only tripping thrice. Before scurrying off to comply with his lord's instructions, the lad pulled the tent flaps closed.

Tamlyn's eyes watched the young man lowering the tent sides, leaving her alone with the Dragon. She resented the Norman's smug grin and lecherous eyes. His aura conveyed he was master of all and there was nothing she could do to change this. The male arrogance provoked her, drove her to want to slap that expression off his face.

Oddly, instead of woolen hose as most men wore, his were made of soft leather. She'd never seen the like.

They molded indecently to his body. Dressed in only them, boots and a short under tunic—the hem tucked into the wide belt—he should present a less imposing front without the mail and armor. Yet an indefinable air made him seem more dangerous. The drawstring of the tunic rode loosely about his shoulders, revealing the honed muscles.

A vital force pulsated from this man in hot waves.

With casual grace he strode to the large trunk where the repast waited. With precise movements he poured wine into the ornate cup.

Burning eyes lifted from the golden goblet to her. "Wine, demoiselle? It is French."

Tamlyn shifted, ill at ease under the earl's scrutiny. With the flaps down, the tent muffled the noises from outside. It felt as though they were alone rather than in the midst of an army preparing for a siege. His radiant virility lent the enclosed space a suffocating sensation. Tipping up her chin, Tamlyn eyed him without flinching. A bluff.

She was forced to reassess the Earl Challon. He exhibited kindness and affection for his young squire where often knights did not. As well, he'd displayed softness toward her. Legends said dragons breathed fire and were never benevolent. Challon's gentleness didn't fit the fables. How could she remain indifferent toward a man who patted a lad's head, reassuring his pride? A man who had rescued her as a Knight of the Auld Code?

"I wish to return home." Tamlyn tasted panic. The kenning warned her to get far away from this beautiful warlord. He threatened her in ways she barely understood.

"You shall . . . soon." He raised the cup. "Wine?"

"You likely poisoned the bloody stuff," she huffed,

trying to create distance. Being detained by him in the tent seemed too intimate. She felt exposed, vulnerable.

Half smiling, Challon carried the cup to his lips. His mouth closed upon the golden rim and took a deep draught. His Adam's apple undulated as he swallowed.

Unable to meet his penetrating gaze, she looked away—had to for the sake of her soul. With the pull of a warlock's lodestone, Challon drew her against her will. Her eyes were compelled by his comely features and superior masculine form. Sighing, she admitted she liked—no enjoyed—watching the Dragon. Curse his black head! She shivered, hugging herself. Her body trembled with a chill, though felt hot in the same breath. How could that contradiction be?

His stare never left her, the compelling eyes sending frissons of awareness up her spine. Tamlyn was disturbed by his dominating presence. Every aspect of this warrior was daunting, humbling.

"It is damp. Have you a plaide?" A cover would offer a measure of protection from his branding gaze.

"If you feel a chill, come closer to the brazier."

"I'd rather have a plaide, if you don't mind."

"But I find I do," he said calmly. "I prefer you where my eyes can see you. All of you."

She muttered, thinking he couldn't hear her, "*Chomh dana le muc.*"

Eyebrows, dark as his midnight hair, lifted in amusement. "I do believe you just called me a pig."

"A wee distinction, Dragon, I said you are as bold as a pig." Tamlyn fought against the escaping smile.

His eyes danced with humor. Pure green, scorching fire. "I know nothing about swine. I've been called worse. And I am bold—a man who dares much. Are all Scots females like you?"

"What do you mean?" Skittish as a fawn, she edged toward the flickering coals.

Or was it toward him, Julian wondered. "For one, you're rather tall." He'd spoke as though he found that distasteful.

She flashed him a haughty glare. Ah, touchy and prideful was she? He smiled to himself, strangely pleased.

She tossed the goad back at him, "You're small for a Norman."

"Actually, I am average height for men of my country. Men—and women—often err in judging by such trifling standards. My size lends me speed and quickness," he answered, unruffled by her taunt. He traced his eyes down her body and then back, pausing to linger on her breasts. It set her to blushing. "Also, better for other . . . er . . . activities."

A faint frown crossed her face as though she didn't comprehend his double meaning. Julian found the puzzled expression fascinating. The corner of his mouth twitched, he could feel it, but was sure the tic didn't show.

"Also you're . . . stout," he said offhandedly.

Outrage flooded her cheeks. "*Graineil peist!*"

"I gave no insult with my humble observances. I doubt, demoiselle, you can say the same when you just call me an earthworm . . . loathsome, at that."

"I suspect, Lord Challon, you've never been humble in your whole bloody life!" When he said nothing in reply, just stared impassively, she stomped her foot and snapped, "I am not stout!"

"I merely point out your hips are wide and round. Do females of your clan handle breeding easily?"

"It is not fit for you to speak of such matters."

"Oh come, my fool, playing the blushing virgin ill becomes you."

Confused by his jibe, she countered, "Do all English warriors behave as you?"

"And you mean what?" Challon removed the small knife from the sheath at his belt and carved the wedge of cheese.

"Arrogant."

"I am. Others vary."

"Greedy," she snapped.

He shrugged. "All men are greedy. They lie if they say different. Some men are greedier than others. A few have simpler wishes and are direct in getting what they want."

And he wanted this woman. Nothing would stop him from claiming her.

"You come to our lands as thieves and rapists." Fury bubbled in Tamlyn as this strange manner of man took no insult. Still, she found it easier to wield ire, a shield against other emotions the lord conjured within her.

"I never steal nor commit rape. There's need for neither." His smile was devastatingly sensual, leaving little doubt his claim was true. He stuck the blade into the cheese, then held it out, almost beckoning her to come close. "Would you like cheese, demoiselle?"

Tamlyn glared at him as if he presented a dead rat.

After several blinks of the thick lashes, he shrugged and carried it to his sinful mouth.

A mouth she again wondered how it would feel pressed to her own. Aye, she longed for this man to kiss her. Raw desire slammed into her with a force that was alarming. She hated herself for it. Never had any man affected her so. Oh, why did he have to be a Norman earl, the king's champion?

"As I said . . . arrogant. Herds of scrawny English lasses toss themselves at your big feet."

Breaking off a hunk of bread, he held it out to her. "Oh aye, I weary of stepping over their prostrate bodies."

She saw Challon wasn't surprised she spurned the offering. He almost seemed to smile at her indignation over his calling her stout, as if he had used the word to provoke her. The Dragon was proving to be a most vexing man.

"Do you know the Lady Tamlyn?"

"In Alba we set no great store in rank. Her people call her Tamlyn MacShane or Tamlyn of Glenrogha. She has no use for English airs."

"Then you share her confidence?" Skepticism was clear in his tone.

Mischief flickered in her eyes as she met his challenge. "Aye, I ken, better than most."

"They say she is a bit long in the tooth." His level stare collided with hers.

The power slammed through her and lodged painfully in her heart. Flustered, Tamlyn sucked in a hard breath. "I do not use your tongue often, but I take you to mean she's old, not her teeth seem a muckle length."

"We both know you have a good grasp of my language. As for my tongue . . . you are free to make whatever use of it you will, as often as you will." Challon's eyes moved over her, burning with a jeweled gleam of craving. "Aye, I speak of age, not condition of her teeth—provided she still has any."

"How old is the mighty Dragon?"

"Five and thirty next Michaelmas. And I have all my teeth." He flashed them before biting the cheese.

"Och, the Dragon also has teeth a bit long."

His half-raised eyelids over the haunting eyes appeared little more than a sleepy countenance. Even so, Tamlyn sensed a deadly, recoiled power within him—when Lord Julian Challon was at his most dangerous. Few likely recognized this until it was too late.

His brow lifted, mocking. "Aye, all the sharper for it, my fool."

"So he comes northward to take a bite out of Alba?"

He settled back against the edge of another trunk, stretching out the long, muscular legs. In a careless pose, he crossed his boots at the ankles, gold spurs gleaming. The leather chausses lovingly hugged the iron thighs and hips. Julian Challon projected the lazy air of a big cat sunning itself on a rock. So relaxed, yet ready to strike in the blink of an eye. Tamlyn's heart thudded in her ears as she stared at him. The soft leather was taut over his loins, drawing her attention to that part of male anatomy, which a lady's eyes should never linger upon.

She caught him watching her, one side of his mouth quirked up knowingly. Smug. Arrogant. Uneasy around him, she moved closer to the brazier and held her hands to its warmth, trying to ignore him.

Julian drank the wine to cover his amusement over her appraisal of his body—and most interestingly, his groin. He was pleased how he affected her. "Edward means to subdue the Scots. He shall."

"Ages ago, Merlin foretold of *Le Roi Coveytous*—the covetous king. To save all, he set an ancient spell to bring defeat upon his head."

Julian scoffed. "Mere fables."

"Was not your king at Glastonbury in years past for entombing of the bodies of Arthur and his queen?"

"Aye, Edward paid homage to hanks of hair and a few bones. Men bending fables to further pale aims. The abbey faced crumbling, their coffers empty since their flock had strayed back to the Auld Ways. The convenient discovery of the bodies reversed that. As for the Plantagenet, he was there to press the claim that he's the right and true king, heir to these isles by blood of Arthur."

"Another fable."

Lifting the chalice, he smiled. "Precisely, my fool. I was there for the ceremony in all its pomp and splendor. Arthur likely rolled in his real grave that day. Edward proclaimed he is Arthur's heir by direct line. Shall the ancient warrior-king and his all-powerful wizard stand and be counted alongside the Plantagenet?"

"Twisted logic from a king's champion, his creature," she hurled the insult. "Longshanks covets all. Following that overreaching trail he shall find Merlin's prophecy awaiting."

"Did you know the Welsh boast four score years past this so-called spell caused the downfall of *Le Roi Coveytous*— King John, Edward's grandsire." He grinned at her. "It is the nature of Plantagenets to covet. They covet as they breathe, they know no other way. It is the way kingdoms are forged. Females hold no understanding of the realities of warfare."

"Aye, we just see to the holdings whilst you males traipse off to the Holy Lands, fighting an enemy we women only hear tales about. No Scotswoman ever faced rape at the hands of those barbarians, unlike the English."

"Would you see the Holy Lands in the keeping of foreign devils?"

"Och, you knights of the sword rush to the standard of king and kirk and leave females to keep the wolves from the gates, nurse the sick and see to the harvest so we do not starve. We collect rents, sort out clan disputes, rule law and hang reiving scum. When you highborn knights return from your grand fine adventures, you weary of fireside, so you create wars close to home. Then we lasses must fear facing slaughter—or worse, left with the seed of the enemy growing within our bodies. Aye, you are right, Lord Challon. We ken nothing of these weighty matters."

Julian's eyes raked over this unusual woman. Surprisingly, he enjoyed the banter, even the upbraiding of his male superiority. He'd never spoken with any female on subjects of such consequence.

Most would be fearful to repeat these beliefs since the church could prosecute the words as heresy. Women were for serving, bedsport to relieve male humors and for breeding heirs. The clergy debated if females were even endowed with souls. Men, they held, found equals only amongst other men. Women weakened them, lured them into temptation.

Nonetheless, he relished this spirited wordplay with his fool. Enchanted by her vibrant face that expressed her every thought, he was eager for more. Her intelligence only sharpened his desire for her.

"So, they permit the daughters of the clans to work their tongues?" Julian's tone was provoking.

"Aye, they have and they shall," she snapped.

"Do they not also beat their women?" His brows arched to add emphasis to his rejoinder.

"None have raised a hand to me. No husband shall but once, else some night he might waken to a *sgian dubh* being buried in his heart."

"A black knife for a black heart?" Julian raised the cup in mock salute. "Is that not the fate that befell the Lady Rowanne's lord husband?"

Her mouth tightened. "Stories carried afar by bards."

"Tales are a way to pass long nights. They say winter

nights are endless in this heathen land, so one surely needs diversions."

"Heathen? Oh aye. Here the Auld Ones whisper ever so softly from shadow and mist."

Her gold eyes had a feline look, sending a shiver up Julian's spine. He ignored the reaction. Little triggered fear in him. No female would—even if she possessed eyes of a cat. "A cowardly lot forsaking their children in their dark hour . . . just as Arthur sleeps undisturbed. No supernatural being, be it blue meagre hag or swart faery, no divine intervention changes our fates, my fool."

"Not even your Christians' one true God?"

Challon exhaled, suddenly exhausted. "Not Him especially. He must be a warrior-god, if He takes a role a'tall."

He wondered if those cat-eyes saw the bone-deep fatigue within him, a weariness of the mind as much as the flesh. Characteristics of a man, not a legend. Would she even care? After all, he was her enemy. Why did that make him feel very old, very tired?

"Must I continue to call you fool?" he regarded her, wanting something in response, not sure precisely what. "Since we have shared so many thoughts, shall you not tell me your name?"

"Why should you care, Lord Challon? Am I not just part of Glenrogha you seek to take and to hold?" She trembled, though clearly trying to maintain her defiance.

To take and to hold. Aye, Julian would love to do those things to her and more. So much more. He'd bury himself so deep in her woman's warmth she'd dispel the unyielding cold plaguing his warrior's soul.

He'd lie upon a sunny hill with this fey lass, feel the kiss of the summer sun as he lazily stroked her luscious body. Close his eyes and listen to the serenades of sea gulls, peewits and curlews. He wanted to watch his growing children chase butterflies and kittens. Simple pleasures of life little valued by men of war now filled his being with a gnawing hunger.

Julian wished for a home. He desired a wife and children . . . a son. He longed to sit by fireside, his arms around his woman as she leaned back against his chest. He wanted—no, needed—peace.

And in those tranquil visions, Julian saw himself holding the woman staring at him with amber eyes. He blinked several times, disturbed by how vividly he saw this.

His mental malaise was staggering. He ate because his body would sicken without nourishment, not because of hunger. Food tasted like wormwood. He slept what few tormented hours he could for it was night and there was little else to soothe his restlessness.

His lust demanded periodic release—just another physical function, bringing only fleeting gratification. Hasty, dispassionate couplings left him empty. The hot throes of green youth no longer ruled and were barely more than faint remembrances. Desires dimmed with each year's passing. Sometimes, Julian wished to close his eyes and never wake up.

So much of his life, his soul, had been forfeited for niggardly gain. Even that was less, now he'd drawn Edward's enmity. This pocket of the Highlands might be pagan, untamed. Even so, the moody, near forgotten valley would be his last bastion. If Julian found no peace here some part of his soul would be forever lost, leaving naught but the cruel, hard-bitten warrior. A man who had witnessed scores of battles, endless scorched villages and far too many dead men staring up at him with cold, sightless eyes.

Edward had been right to send him away. The Black

Dragon needed to slip into the mists of these Scottish hills, lick his wounds and hopefully heal. Find something in life worth living for. Find a reason to go on.

When no reply came, Julian rose to his feet. "Then, my fool, the pallet of furs is at your disposal. I have tasks to sort out."

"Such as building siege engines?"

Her eyes signaled bravado and resentment—a bad mix. Despite that, hidden in the gold depths were emotions calling to him with a witch's craft. Emotions too new for him to name, feelings as ancient and enduring as these purple hills.

Almost as if echoes from the past.

Shoving these strange notions aside, he straightened and raised his chin in a condescending tilt. "Hardly, my fool. Glenrogha's defenders are feeble and ill-trained. I foresee no need to waste time and scarce timber. Matters should be settled soon."

He saw her jerk. "Meaning?"

"By lightbreak my host shall enter the dun with or without Tamlyn MacShane's consent."

"That you shall never get."

Her haunting eyes revealed panic. Julian's warrior instincts warned as soon as he was out of sight she'd try to escape, possibly end in harm to herself.

"My fool indeed." He laughed softly. Raising the lid of a trunk, Julian removed two thin leather thongs. "I promised the Lady Lochshane you'd come to no harm. You shall be less distraction to me if not left to your own devices. Your wrists, hold them out."

"Och, how obliging you are." Tamlyn backed up as he advanced, stalking her.

Her movements provoked his predator's instincts. "I try. Come, I shan't harm you, my fool." In that breath he recognized when he called her *my* fool he spoke the word with the stress of possession. The surge of ownership pulsed in his blood—and painfully in his loins. He was unsure when he'd begun to regard this woman as his property. It just felt . . . right. "I simply wish you to stay put."

"You don't want me to slip away and warn them in the fortress," she charged, skirting backward with trembling steps.

"Glenrogha knows that we plan to attack should they contest my right to enter. Come, my fool, trouble me no longer."

He pounced, grabbing her. A quick minx, she dodged, though his fingers caught the sark's edge, the soft material tearing again. "Sorry. Surrender before more battles with the English see your bountiful charms fully displayed. Not that I'd complain."

"Let go of my hands, Norman *muc*."

"Back to calling me a pig, eh?" He jerked left in feint, then cat-quick to the right, trapping her.

Seizing her about the waist, his force carried them down. Half on the pallet, he pinned her under his solid weight. Hands freed, he manacled his fingers around her wrists, shoving them above her head, compelling her body to bow to his. He shifted, stretched until he was hip against hip.

She snapped at him, trying to sink teeth into his flesh, but Julian bore down, applying his warrior's strength so it was impossible for her to catch a breath. She had to weaken. There was nothing else she could do, her surrender a foregone conclusion.

The urge to dominate washed through his body and congealed painfully in his groin. He wanted her. Agonizingly. As he'd never wanted any woman. It was exhilarating to experience such raw desire after endless months of apathy.

"Fine set of long teeth you possess, my fool. Much like my charger," he taunted, laughing. By damn, it felt good to laugh again. "He bites, too."

"You compare me to your bloody horse?"

"You called me a worm and a pig. Besides, I happen to be quite fond of that horse. Go ahead, my fool, bite me. I shall bite back." Julian easily countered, struggled with just enough exertion to keep her pinned. "Ah, demoiselle, keep up that wiggling. I enjoy the feel."

She stilled, eyes wide.

His gaze traveled down her body and gradually returned to her face. The line of her jaw was squarish, stubborn, though not so strong as to detract from her earthy sensuality. The effect was softened by the faint cleft in her chin. Her features were strongly defined, enchanting. Her mouth was small, though the lips were full and shaped with high double peaks. A mouth begging for kisses.

But it was the eyes that reached into him, held him with their power. They clashed with his, demanding something from him. He drew in a measured breath, trying to slow his thundering heart. Everything about this she-cat called to him to take her, resonated with a violence within him, the likes he'd not experienced in so long. Mayhap never. More so, he sensed she possessed the ability, the art to reach him, affect him, *change him* in ways he scarcely began to identify.

Julian's sexual appetites were animalistic, strong. Only of late, his soul cried out in indefinable hunger, yearning for more.

So desperate for something more.

She remained motionless, golden eyes searching his wearily, questioning. Frightened, yet intrigued, she was drawn against will as her body felt the call of instincts older than time. He saw it.

His nostrils flared, picking up her heady female scent. A witch's potion. His heart lurched hard against his ribs, sending his blood thundering. He lowered his head to hers, his lips brushing the curve of her neck where the blood throbbed strong. Reveling in the sensation, nearly frightened by its intensity, he lifted his head to watch her reaction.

She drew in a breath and held it. The pounding of her heart thudded erratically against his chest.

To Julian, she smelled of spring grasses, sea-kissed Highland mists and lavender. So soft, her skin seemed to shimmer with a touch of golden faerydust. It invited a man's caresses, his lingering strokes. Julian nibbled on her unstable pulse. It thrummed under his mouth. He sensed a tangible radiance . . . as if he drank her life essence. The aura spread through him, burned him, overwhelming his senses.

In gentle nips, his teeth traced the column of her throat. He fought the spinning, yet savored the exhilaration. Careful not to bear down against the faint reddening where his knights had slapped her, he relished the sweet, piquant taste of her skin.

For an instant, outrage over her treatment reared its head. A savage possessiveness declared this woman belonged to him and none other had the right to touch her. An all-consuming lust supplanted such thoughts.

His mouth hovered over hers, catching her warm breath as though he needed it to survive. Mayhap he did. Slowly, he fit his mouth to hers. So perfect . . . so right.

The world spun as whirling leaves in a storm.

She didn't resist him. Breaking the kiss, Julian gasped for air. His eyes searched hers before closing to taste her once more. Slanting his head for a better angle, he pressed. Hungry. Deepening the contact, he issued the primitive male demand for her submission.

Control shattered as the kisses went on. And on. He heard a low moan, felt it through his skin and every drop of blood. Even so, he was unsure whether the sound emanated from her or him.

Kissing was foreplay, youthful sport in which Julian had rarely indulged or enjoyed. Until now. Lost to the lure of this pagan Scot, he wanted the kisses to last forever. Never had he experienced such searing satisfaction in sampling a woman's mouth.

His tongue slid along her lips, seeking, near begging entrance to her honeyed warmth. The tip touched the sharp teeth, outlining their edge. He did nothing to compel her to open for him. He wanted—no, needed—her to share the turbulent desires raging in him. She answered. Soft, sweet lips moved under his, matching, mimicking his lead. Finally, she gave in, allowing his tongue to dart into her.

He released her wrists, his left hand slid down the back of her head, fisting in the dark gold tresses. The other palm spread over her shoulder, tugging the thin wool of the sark down, vexed by the knotted drawstring that prevented him from pulling it farther unless he tore it. He settled for cupping his fingers to cover her fullness.

Announcing the depth of her arousal, her nipple thrust against his palm. Julian wished to close his mouth upon that supple flesh and suck hard, coax her to join him in this madness. He craved to see her arch to him with burning passions. She shifted, her rounded softness fitting his body to perfection. Yea, this Scots lass was made for a man's pleasure. His pleasure. Julian doubted she was aware her arms twined around his neck, or her legs parted so he could push his thigh between them, riding high against the apex of her female heat.

God's blood, she drove him to folly, the quickening drowning all reason. Was she a witch to bind his senses, ensorcel him with only simple kisses? Sweet, honey-mead kisses. As his hand slipped into the rip in the sark, the scent of her arousal clouded his brain. She moaned in shaky need as his thumb circled the distended nipple. Encouraging.

Yea, his fool followed the dance. Her breathing was hoarse, as her thighs locked hard about his, gripping with amazing strength, near desperation. Shudders ripped through them both, as their pulses beat as one.

It was more than he ever dared hope, everything for which he could dream.

Never, even in the hot throes of his youth had such a primal urge to mate torn through him. If he didn't take this woman he'd die from the yearning. Exquisite, voracious magic encircled him. Suffocated him. Terrified him.

Witch's spell or not, he would take her, possess her— own her. It wasn't his intent when he kissed her. Fires of damnation! He never planned to kiss the wench! It just . . . happened. But nothing on this green earth would deter him from joining his body to hers.

"Julian, Simon wishes to know—" The man entering the tent pulled up short. "Beg pardon." Just as quickly, he ducked back out.

They jerked apart, staring at each other, barely able to draw breath, bewildered by a sensual haze.

Julian's hands shook as he shoved away from this Highland enchantress. By the black rood, never before had he lost his wits over a female. Dark witchery!

He had to get far from her, clear his befuddled mind of her pagan magic—tricks to ensnare a man's soul and weaken him. He was the Black Dragon of Challon and no woman brought him to his knees.

He searched for the narrow strips of leather. Before she thought to struggle, he bound her wrists, then her ankles, leaving the witch trussed up on the pile of furs.

At the opening of the tent, Julian paused to glance back. Not once had he believed fables about faery queens, witches or Cait Sidhe, nor the mysterious enchantments they wove around mortal men. Yet that, and only that, could account for what had possessed his body and banished his mind. He still wrestled against the siren's call, evoking the pagan pulse in his boiling, traitorous blood.

His mouth compressed into a frown as he stared down at his trembling hands . . . rough hands, callused from years of wielding a sword. Hands of a veteran warrior, the Black Dragon of Challon. A man once the king's champion. Hands suddenly made weak by a mere woman.

In that instant, he hated her as much as he wanted her.

Chapter 5

"Awake, my lady."

The soft, cracking voice slid through the velvet sleep. A touch—a small shake to the toe of her left boot. Then the words were repeated.

Tamlyn's lids opened to see the squire of the Dragon—the one, oddly enough, with a Scots name—leaning over her. He wore a bemused expression.

His smile came easily, lighting his eyes so like Lord Challon's. When she first laid eyes upon him, she'd jumped to the conclusion the young man was likely lad of the Dragon. The age was right to be his son, so were the comely features, the same wavy, blue-black hair and penetrating green eyes.

Once more his fingers worried the tip of her boot. "I touched you farthest from your heart, my lady, so not to frighten you."

She struggled to sit up before recognizing the awkwardness was due to being trussed at wrists and ankles. Exhausted, she fell back onto the furs, listening to the erratic thunder of her heart.

Kneeling on one knee, the young man sliced the

leather thong about her wrists, then the one binding her ankles. "My Lord Dragon ties a wicked knot." He blushed from having touched her bare legs. "You must arise, my lady. The Dragon commands it. We leave."

"To where?" she asked, waiting for the wool in her head to clear.

"The fortress, my lady." He set about to gathering his master's belongings.

One word escaped on her harsh gasp. "Glenrogha?"

He nodded. "It is what my lord ordered."

Not pausing for blood to flow in her tingling legs, she exited through the tent flaps, then froze when she spotted Julian Challon across the encampment. His back to her, he stood by the campfire talking with his knights.

All wore full battle gear, girded for the coming engagement. Words concerning her were traded, for the Dragon swung around, his unsmiling stare one of indifference. The sensual mouth thinned under the raised, disdainful brows. His warlock green eyes glowed with an incandescent power as they danced over her body.

Strangely, he acted as if nothing had occurred between them, as if he'd never lain upon her body and kissed her senseless. His expression clearly said her presence angered him for some reason, that he now viewed her as the enemy. Her heart felt saddened by that.

The muscles of his jaw flexed, but he displayed no other response.

Shame flooded her, coming on a tide of recollections so acute it was painful. Her traitorous body throbbed to the pagan magic he'd awoken within her. Her heart tightened that he now viewed her in such a hard way. She nervously licked her lips. Furious at him, more so with herself, she straightened her spine, intending to beard the Dragon.

With a faint arch of one brow, Challon turned his back on her, dismissing her from his attention. His hands clasped behind his hips, as he rejoined the conversation with the other men.

The two men flanking his sides studied her with keen intensity. The one on the right she thought was the man who had entered the Dragon's tent, yet she couldn't be positive. Only Challon stood apart.

But then, legends did.

Tamlyn hesitated, unsure, having received no sign to what the Norman warlord expected her to do. As if she had intention of complying!

Still, his reaction tweaked her pride. He could ignore what had taken place in his tent; she'd yet to confront her body's betrayal of mind and will. Only his attitude pushed her toward peevishness. The Dragon seemed so unstirred by this dark craft he wielded effortlessly, ruthlessly, robbing her of all will to fight him.

Whether in laughter or temper, her emotions were on the surface for all to see. More than once that lack of guile had landed her in trouble. Yet it was honest. Never had she fathomed the games women and men played to gain advantage over each other.

This warrior shunned her as though hoping she'd vanish and cease to vex him. It was hardly what she imagined from the arrogant Norman. A smug grin, surely. Most men tended to strut peacock proud when they tricked a woman into surrender.

For spite, she meandered about the camp. None spoke to her, let alone challenged her movements. All eyes went to their liege to take cue from him.

They were busy dousing fires and organizing weaponry, stirred with hushed urgency by the commands of the Dragon. Careful to stay clear of the squires readying the magnificent Frisian warhorses, she observed the soldiery and knights of the combined troops of Plantagenet and Challon moving off into the night toward Dun Glenrogha.

She felt certain if she attempted to slip away, the Dragon's indifference would alter in a blink. The temptation rose within her to mime escape just to get a rise from the haughty earl. Exasperated by his detachment, she felt like screaming at him. Challon wasn't indifferent so much as demonstrating his mastery, letting Tamlyn see how far down on the scale of importance she ranked. He was forcing her to come to him in a display of male audacity and conceit.

It taxed her not to march over and kick the Dragon in his leather-clad arse!

Finally, he deigned to turn around. The devilkin eyes raked over her form, the near apathy shifting to fierce calculation. Odd emotions. Despite the icy, controlled air, his sexual response betrayed itself in the slight flaring of the nostrils of his aristocratic nose.

Her fires of anger abated.

Another heat quickened within her body, fed by those unearthly green eyes. Head spinning, she lost sight of all surrounding her. The world narrowed to the dark warrior . . . a man whose color was that of the sacred ravens.

Save for the imperceptible reaction, Tamlyn might think the burning passion that just a short time ago had consumed them both was nothing more than mists from a dream. His detachment stung. It was obvious these feelings so new, so surprising to her, held small value for the earl.

She swallowed the knot in her throat. Just as well. They were enemies, could never be anything more. Tightness went down to lodge in her heart at that finality.

With a faint nod, he contemplated her with the wariness of a hard-bitten fighter facing a foe. Obviously, their minds worked on the same level, Tamlyn mused.

He straightened his spine, as if bracing for her reaction. "Shortly we move out, my fool."

"Your squire says to Glenrogha. How?" Her hands fisted at her sides, trying to hide the trembling. Her nails dug into her palms. Fearful of drawing blood, she forced them to unclench. The action not missed by his all-seeing eyes.

"The gates of Glenrogha are open." Challon studied her. "Daybreak nears. I see no reason to wait for full light to take possession of my fortress."

"Lies!" Tamlyn shook her head in denial, fighting for her next breath.

"Nay, demoiselle. Whilst you slumbered, my men slipped over the east loch wall and met only token resistance. Hardly astonishing when you consider the citadel is under the command of a woman. An absent woman, at that."

Tamlyn struggled against fear threatening to claim her. Wanting to inquire about her sisters, she bit her tongue. Mayhap it was childish not to reveal her name to the arrogant Dragon, but she held onto the tiny advantage. In some manner it might still serve her.

"Time to mount," Challon announced, seeing the squires leading forth the stallions. "Sir Guillaume, take my fool before you."

"If that's your wish, Julian." Wearing a half grin, the taller man looked at his brother, eyes flashing in communication.

Not bothering to reply, the earl turned to mount his black destrier.

Smarting from Challon's rebuff, Tamlyn lifted her chin. "You are brother to the Dragon?"

"That surprises, demoiselle?" he asked, the grin spreading into a dazzling smile. Aye, the men of Challon were born lady-slayers.

"I did not ken dragons came with brothers."

"Julian is just a man, though oft he convinces one to think otherwise. I am Guillaume Challon. My other brother, Simon, waits within Glenrogha. We are Julian's bastard half-brothers." His face was guarded, waiting for her reaction.

The blunt admission made her blink. Not due to the bastardy, as Scots never looked upon this the way the English did, just that few men were so forthcoming.

"Yet you serve him as liegemen?"

"Eagerly, as knights bannerets. My lord brother is a rare man. Never once has he treated Simon or me as anything but beloved siblings. It is a high honor to serve the great Dragon of Challon."

More facets of the man that did not fit a legend. Julian Challon had two bastard half-brothers, yet love, loyalty and respect rang clear in Sir Guillaume's words.

The handsome knight mounted a gray horse, kicked his foot out of the stirrup and then leaned forward to offer his hand. Tamlyn paused, wanting to run away from what lay ahead. Only she was no coward. She was the lady of Glenrogha. It was up to her to protect her people. Carefully, she took his strong grip and stepped into the stirrup, not struggling as he settled her before him.

Foreboding gnawed at her insides as Tamlyn watched the massive force fall into formation. In the cloudless night, he maneuvered into the line of horses, streaming down the tract to Dun Glenrogha.

Tamlyn rocked to the rhythm of the stallion's gait, fretting over why Challon ordered her taken before his brother for the ride to the fortress. Not that she wished to travel with the earl. The farther she was from the man, the easier she breathed. It was nothing more than feminine curiosity, and though she was loath to admit it, a wee touch of wounded pride over him calling her stout.

She frowned over her confused reactions to Julian Challon. He was here to steal the holdings of Glen Shane, an invader, the enemy to her clan. How could she have permitted this Norman warlord to embrace her? To her shame, she'd kissed him back, her body relishing his dark touch.

When the vile Sir Dirk had put his hands upon her, she hadn't felt the same. His contact, his crude actions, made her feel ill. She'd had only one thought—to see her *sgian dubh* buried in his foul heart.

Why hadn't she reacted in like fashion when Challon caressed her? Instead of revulsion, her traitorous nature warmed to him with hungry instincts.

He'd stolen dominion of her soul. All will to resist fled, leaving her with the fires of craving. The need to feel the dark lord's hands upon her flesh, to caress him in return, pulsed within her. Against all reason, she'd wanted him to take her. Desperately.

A trembling hand brushed away the tear trickling down her cheek.

Her vanity was bruised still. Mayhap compared to delicate English beauties a healthy Scots lass seemed, well . . . stout. Men from four countries spoke of the MacShane sisters as grand lasses. Her father bragged in highest praise that his daughters represented the breed. That did little to ease the sting that Julian Challon didn't find her comely.

Glenrogha's gates were swung wide. Torches burned along the bastion's battlements and within the inner ward. A spectacle beautiful to behold, it was reminiscent of the tors lit by balefires on Beltane Eve. So terrifying, the images burned into Tamlyn's mind as a sense of helplessness washed over her. Never in her whole life had she felt so forsaken.

Her existence at Glenrogha was rarely exciting, often grinding. Yet her days remained fulfilling. She drew satisfaction from seeing Glenrogha run well and her people prospering. Now, as she neared her beloved stronghold, every aspect would be altered.

The feared Black Dragon had come as conqueror and nothing and no one would ever be the same.

The armored knights, long shields slung over their shoulders, shifted the prancing chargers into precise formations of threes, passing through the predawn landscape. The metal helms and plates covering shoulder arms and thighs reflected the flickering glints of breeze-stirred torches. Dancing over them, the glow gave the long flow of Englishmen on warhorses an eerie skeletal outline. It was as though a host of the Unseelie Court—malevolent warrior-faeries—descended on the Scottish holding.

People gathered in the shadows of the Pict broch as if the ancient stone tower shielded them magically. Braver souls milled near the center tower to glimpse the mighty Dragon of Challon. They observed the ward filling with the limitless numbers of English chivalry, girded in armor and mounted upon monstrous stallions of war. Obviously, Julian judged, Glenrogha had never witnessed such an awe-summoning spectacle.

Standing in the stirrups, he rotated to glance at the formidable assemblage. Raising his hand, he halted the imposing force. He projected a pose of resolute power, a man born and bred to rule, the precise impression he wanted branded into the Scots' minds.

"Sir Dunstan, see the troops bed down in the outer ward. By noontide, the force should be ready to push on to Kinloch." Julian's deep voice shattered the strange stillness reigning over the bailey.

He climbed the stone steps of the lord's tower, pausing at the top to permit his personal guard to catch up. Making use of the interval, his attention swept over the fortress and its people. A shiver snaked up his spine. Once again, ghostly feelings of belonging brushed against his mind.

The ostentatious display of his armored knights would serve him to bring the stubborn Scots quickly under his control. The shock and worry upon the haunted faces pleased him, would work to his favor. He wanted peace here. If it came through fear instead of respect, so be it.

His eyes casually took in Guillaume as his brother gripped his fool around the waist and swung her to the ground. A hand at the small of her spine propelled her forward, guiding her toward the staircase. Julian's teeth set as jealousy speared through him. The emotion knotted his gut. Trying to mask the reaction, he nodded to his guard. It was time to enter Glenrogha.

Torches in iron sconces lit the long corridor leading to the Great Hall. The black oak doors were open wide and the fireplaces within blazed in a manner bordering on festive.

A smirk tugging at the corner of his mouth, Simon stood, awaiting Julian's arrival. Thighs wide apart in a balanced stance, the blade of his great-sword rested tip down, halfway between the space created by Simon's booted feet. Both hands clasped the leather-wrapped hilt. A careless pose, yet Julian knew it was one of coiled anticipation, ready to strike before anyone could draw the first breath.

Before turning his attention to the people gathered behind his brother, Julian tarried to survey the hall. In that fleeting instant, he took full measure of the great chamber, the heart of the stronghold.

The lord's table was dominant and would remain in place whilst the trestle tables below-the-salt were broken down and put aside each night. A mark of prestige. Only high lords had such in their halls. A triple fireplace covered the greater portion of the far wall, providing light as well as warmth. A recent addition, he deduced. Oddly, no rushes covered the floor. The stone slabs appeared scrubbed clean and not a home for fleas and rats attracted by food scraps. No tapestries covered the stone walls nor were they plastered and painted, not even a simple covering of limed whitewash.

During his travels he'd been a guest in scores of castles more richly appointed, yet Glenrogha possessed an understated elegance that pleased him. This place showed potential. His mind already seeing improvements to be made, his coinage would be well spent here.

The Great Hall felt . . . familiar. This inner sense of coming home didn't reflect upon his countenance. He kept his stare impassive. None could guess whether he was impressed or found fault with his surroundings.

Raven of Kinloch, Rowanne of Lochshane, several foster women and three men-at-arms—without weapons—waited in front of the trestle table on the raised dais.

Challon's eyes sought Sir Guillaume. "Deploy soldiery on the bastion. Double the guards at the gates. Send out scouts toward the remaining dun. Then set a detachment to thoroughly search this place and spare no corner torchlight. Since daybreak nears see the meal fetched."

"It shall be as you bid, my Lord Brother," the knight

replied. Before leaving, he paused to run his hazel eyes over the twins, lingering on the taller blonde. The glint in his brother's eyes warned that their personal skirmish was far from finished.

Julian inclined his head at the remaining Challon. "Compliments on a task flawlessly executed, Sir Simon."

With a mocking half bow, he said, "You expected less from your humble servant, my lord?"

"Never." Julian removed his leather gauntlets, using the pause to study the people flanking his taller sibling.

Expressions were an odd mix. Defiance from the females. Grudging acceptance laced with fear from the rest. Julian suppressed a smile. In spite of the emotions, all were curious. It wasn't everyday they faced a legend. Good. Let that impression linger in their minds.

"So, Rowanne MacShane, has the Lady Tamlyn been twigged or is she still missing?"

"Our Tamlyn has not made herself kenned," came Lady Rowanne's evasive reply.

The woman lowered her eyes. Odd reaction. She was as defiant as before. It was as though she lied and had trouble meeting his stare. He also noted several of their people exchanging questioning expressions, then quickly masking their faces to echo the Lady of Lochshane's lead.

He frowned. "Playing seek-and-hide with the Sisters MacShane wearies me. I demand answers, not half truths. Where is the mistress of this fief?"

"When we broke slumber yestermorn, she was gone. No message why." Again, the woman had difficulty meeting his eyes.

He controlled his breath, as anger pulsed through him. "And could you say where one might begin the quest for the elusive lady?"

Lady Raven, the darker twin, offered, "Perchance our Tamlyn sighted your host coming through the passes and retreated to Kinloch."

Unlike her sister, this woman met his stare. Few could gaze into the gray eyes with the long sweeping lashes and not accept every word from her as truth. Despite, his warrior's instinct warned she tried to divert his attention from her twin.

"Mayhap." He scowled, patience waning. "I think she has not wandered far. Since Tamlyn the Absent isn't here to greet her new lord, Lady Rowanne, you may see to readying the lord's quarters for my possession. Order a bath drawn. Once the fast is broken, all of your people shall come forth and swear fealty to me as their lord, the new Earl of Glenrogha."

Lady Rowanne swallowed hard at his command, then flashed a look of annoyance just beyond him. Over his shoulder. Julian noted his fool stood trying to hide her shaking. The gold eyes shifted repeatedly between the other woman and him.

"Shall you require . . . aid with the bath, Lord Challon?" the lady inquired, panic barely veiled in the soft brown eyes.

Julian stepped close to her in a move of intimidation. Taking measure of the mistress of Lochshane, his eyes roved over her lush body in the blue côtehardie. A silver girdle encircled her waist, the heavy chain hanging down to the hem. Her graceful neck was adorned with a Pictish torque, whilst wide cuffs banded both wrists.

Gads, these Scots bred sturdy women, Julian thought! The Lady Rowanne stood nearly as tall as he and with an opulent form similar to his fool. Same proud carriage, same square shoulders. Rounded hips molded for the bearing of babes. Breasts men dreamed of fondling, sucking. Aye, this daughter of the Red Laird of Clan Shane might be seven and a score, and no longer a virgin, but no man with half sense would kick her from his bed on a rainy night.

Her wheat-colored hair fell over her right shoulder in a braid, across her breast and past the curvy hip. Not a hair out of place. Her appearance would serve her well at the English court. Despite the mien of a lady proper, sexual heat radiated off her. Aye, he could imagine those strong hands with long aristocratic fingers caressing a man while she slicked soap over his burning flesh.

Inclination aside, he meant this hellion to be taken to lady wife by either Guillaume or Simon. Temptation to tangle with the long-legged beauty was best resisted. Besides, he noted with pleasure, his fool's jealousy bristled over his interest in the Lady Rowanne. A few heartbeats and his Cait Sidhe would unsheathe her claws and begin hissing. Her strong reaction satisfied him. After his previous loss of control with her, this placed him on a better footing.

"My fool shall be put to the task." His smile was arrogant, provoking, his eyes possessive as they skimmed over the woman in a declaration of ownership none present could mistake. He wanted the whole fortress to understand she now wore his brand.

Rowanne nodded, her face showing relief. As she turned to go, her eyes lingered on his fool in a silent question. Lady Rowanne's escape meant the other woman would be pressed to that service in her stead. It was apparent she felt a measure of guilt.

What Rowanne of Lochshane expected to twig in his fool's witchy gold eyes he couldn't fathom. Fear, resentment, rage most likely. Aye, those emotions were reflected upon her arresting face. And jealousy possessed her mind. There was no doubt about it.

He saw Lady Rowanne blink in disbelief, unable to cover her surprise. With a nod, the astonished Rowanne rushed to remove herself from the Great Hall.

Chapter 6

Shivering, Tamlyn sat perched on a stool in a dark corner, watching the flurry of activities. She wasn't cold. She was scared. Life would be different from this point forward. Very different.

Feeling distant from it all, she observed the steady procession as the three squires of the Dragon toted his belongings into the lord's chamber. Swerving, they dodged the maidservants carrying buckets of steaming water to fill the huge wooden tub.

Ignoring the comings and goings with obvious disdain, Challon stood next to the bench. Moffet unbuckled and unlaced the auguillettes, arming points of the plate and mail. Setting them aside, he pulled the padded aketon, which protected the Dragon's skin from the metal, off his master's broad shoulders.

The women cast furtive glances at the Norman lord, then to her, questions clear on their faces. None risked speaking to Tamlyn. All waited to take cue from their lady. Curious, their eyes shifted from their chores to the body of the earl. Some held fear, worry, others an appreciative glint—especially the half-Irish Elfine.

As if the squire and he were the only ones present, Challon leisurely undressed. The arrogant earl acted unaware of their eyes upon him. Tamlyn decided that this was a pose. He was mindful of the females buzzing around him, drawn by his virile perfection. Shards of jealousy ground within her, just as it had when the Norman considered having Rowanne assist him with his bath.

Her mind was befuddled. She couldn't unriddle why she experienced such a burning possessiveness toward the warlord. The emotion had a life all its own and increased with each heartbeat.

"Moffet, take the armor and mail to the barrack's tower to be sanded and oiled. Settle the horses into the stables. Once done, break your fast and afterward find a quiet corner for a long nap. This day you earned your keep." Challon spoke softly, yet all understood the signal to withdraw and did so without his command.

The squire set the plate armor outside the room, so not to disturb his liege when he'd return for them. Hefting the weighty habergeon, Moffet departed the chambers. He paused, flashed a smile at Tamlyn and then pulled the heavy door closed.

Once more, she was alone with the Dragon.

Challon's eyes skimmed over the oils and scented soaps awaiting his pleasure. As if her presence was forgotten, he tugged his under tunic over his head and tossed the garment to the floor. Sitting on the bench, he removed the cross-garters and boots. Each dropped with a thud in the hushed chamber. Movements unhurried, he loosened the lacings on the leather breeches and removed his braies, stepping from them.

Not once taking her eyes from him, Tamlyn stared as Challon stripped away his clothing without a shred of modesty. So enrapt, she nearly forgot to breathe. She'd seen men without garments before, especially after the Floating of the Sheep—when the men tossed them into the creek to clean the wool before shearing. Only none as beautifully formed as Julian Challon! His unclothed body put to rest the Scots' belief that Englishmen had long tails like dogs.

As naked as the day he was born, he strode to the steaming tub and climbed in. Lowering his body into the hot water, he heaved a sigh.

The man had no shame about his naked form. To the contrary, he was quite comfortable striding in the all-together to the tub. Whether nude or in mail and armor, he moved with born-to-rule grace.

Tamlyn couldn't deny the warrior possessed bonnie arms and square shoulders. His hips were narrow, his waist lean, lithely corded with hard muscle. His buttocks were rock-firm, sloping into granite thighs that controlled his mighty stallions of war with ease.

It meant nothing to her. No more than her next breath—which came with difficulty!

Tamlyn fought the confusion that threatened to claim her. Her brain must have been bruised in the fall to sit contemplating—no, ogling—this knight's sleek body with such wanton hunger. She couldn't even muster a degree of shame. Tucked in the shadowy corner, she prayed he failed to recall she was in the chamber.

His head dropped back against the rim of the tub, so still he might be asleep. Shattering the thick silence, his deep melodic voice called out, "Come, my fool, you looked your fill. Now I require your assistance."

Lord Challon hadn't moved. He remained facing away, yet he spoke as if he read her thoughts. Did these

Normans possess eyes in the back of their skulls? Perchance he was indeed a warlock!

Too exhausted to protest, Tamlyn rose to do his bidding. At least being tired was the excuse she afforded herself.

Picking up the pot of softened soap, her lips curled into a wicked smile. Gentled with worts and oils, the lye soap smelled of lavender, heather and verbena. The Dragon would exit his bath reeking not as a knight but a lady fair.

Cupping it in her palm, she embraced the sense of purpose. "Lean forward, Norman, so I may scrub your back."

He inclined, resting his body against his bent knees. "I wager you love ordering me about."

"The Auld Ones grant small wishes. Lets them believe we are not greedy."

"All men are greedy. I presume women to be the same. The lie through their teeth if they deny this. Some men thirst for more than others. Some hungers are different."

"Some covet what belongs to another," she snapped.

Hands shaking, Tamlyn steeled herself to place them upon the Dragon's flesh. She flinched, almost jerking back. Challon burned hot as a brand. Spellbound, she rubbed the soap across his broad shoulders. Disturbing sensations twisted her stomach. His back was taut. It was . . . beautiful. The muscles were knotted, rigid.

She kneaded them, not pausing to wonder why she cared. "Your muscles are tight, Norman."

"It has been a hard moon's passing. First, the armies mustered at Newcastle, then we moved into Scotland. So bloody cold and wet. Does the sun never shine here? Then we took Berwick—"

Tamlyn stilled. "You came from Berwick?"

Rumors had spread throughout the Highlands of the

sacking of the ancient city. She knew of this, but his words gave reality to the whispers, making clear Glenrogha's situation. It sent shards of terror into her soul.

Lord Challon went on as if she hadn't voiced the question. "I've lived in mail, even slept in it more nights than I care to remember. Likely, I'm as filthy as that pig you called me."

"Och, poor dragon. And on the morrow, you ride to Kinloch. A knight's reiving never sees end."

"My brother Simon shall sort out Kinloch. I hold their lady so I foresee no troubles."

Tamlyn stroked the length of his bonnie back. Contours pleasing to the touch, the finely honed warrior's muscles rippled beneath her hands. She swallowed hard. Even so, she'd eat an apple with a worm in it before she ever confessed she drew satisfaction from touching him.

He sighed. "My fool, you conjure paradise on earth for my aching body. What other tricks can you perform to soothe a dragon?"

"Were I not tired, I would duck your black head under and hold it," Tamlyn muttered under her breath.

He glanced over his right shoulder, teeth flashing in a seductive grin. "Then I must see you stay fatigued to assure my safety."

His words sounded as if they held a hidden meaning. Not twigging this Norman double-speak, she shrugged. "Bob your head under and wet it for scrubbing."

Challon's eyes assessed her. "After you just said you would drown me in my own bath? You may call yourself fool. I never shall."

"Och, I said I was too tired."

Leaning back, he took his upper body under, soaking his head. Water sluiced off his sleek chest when he sat up and trickled down to his stomach. And below.

Tamlyn's eyes were unblinking. Her heart thudded slowly, almost painfully.

Finally forcing herself to move, she lathered the midnight hair, scrubbed for a long time. Too long, her inner voice mocked. Angered with this growing weakness towards the earl, she ignored suds sliding into his eyes. Lye soap stung, she knew, yet he said nary a word.

Leaning back, he submerged and shook his head until it was free of the foam. After he broke the surface, he kept his eyes tightly shut. Holding out his hand, he snapped his fingers. "Rag."

She considered prolonging his agony a wee bit, only she regretted the petty action. Irked that she thrilled to touching him, she'd taken out her anger in this shameful way. In contrite sympathy, she placed the sun-bleached cloth in his waiting hand.

Stepping to the front of the tub to soap his leg, she waited as he dabbed his eyes. It gave her a chance to study this sensual warlord up close without feeding his arrogance. With the wet curls pushed back, he appeared less dangerous.

Compelling.

"Evil stuff. What is it, second cousin to Greek fire?" he barked, staring at her through red-rimmed eyes. Raising his leg, he propped it on the rim of the tub. "I do not rebuke you for it *accidentally* finding the way into my eyes. I detect lavender, berries and something odd . . . haunting . . . I cannot place."

Half closing his eyelids, Julian cast his mind inward to embrace the vague, yet poignant memory. The same fragrance had been on her warm skin when he held her on the ride to Glenrogha. Again, that ghostly touch brushed against his thoughts. Of remembrance. It caused a strange pressure in his chest. One he wasn't sure he liked.

"It is heather. We even brew ale from it."

"Ah, the Picts' heather ale, alleged to have magical powers so its secret is jealously guarded. And do these other extracts possess unnatural qualities?"

"Lavender attracts love—of a man. Wild berries soothe a woman's pains. Heather summons rain and prevents rape."

His green eyes flashed with amusement as his long fingers tapped a rhythm on the side of the tub. "Attracts men? Soothe female miseries? Prevents rape? This witch's concoction was brewed for a female? You created this?"

"Aye, I learnt the ways of worts from Evelynour, Oonanne and Auld Bessa."

"Three crones who chant incantations over a cauldron?"

"Just elders who live in the sacred wood of Glen Shane. They treat both clans' miseries."

"If you say." His bored dismissal sounded as if he didn't believe her, but didn't care either. "I charge you to create a batch with scents for a man. I shall instruct you in the ways to please me, cat-eyes."

Julian watched her soap his thigh, aware she hadn't used the rag, wondering how high her hand would go. Wanting her not to stop. He bit his tongue to keep from begging her to touch him, though he burned with need. *Soon, my fool.*

Fatigue lined her face. Nonetheless, he knew her lethargy came more from her fascination with his thigh. She ran the foam up and down its length in near bliss. Delighted by her reactions to his body, he drank in the sight of her witchy eyes glowing by firelight. Never could he recall a woman's eyes enthralling him so.

A dark shadow tinged the skin where she'd been struck. He reached out, his thumb faintly tracing the discoloration. He half expected her to slap his hand away.

She would've before. All the resistance had ebbed from her. The only reaction to his touch was a sharp inhale and widening of the eyes. Her responses put him in control.

She'd been through nightmare enough, or he'd do as his body urged and finish what they started in his tent. That didn't keep him from playing at the edge of seduction. As she leaned closer, he blew across her neck where the throb of her blood was visible. His warm breath caressed her soft skin.

When he repeated the action, she snapped at him, "Stop that." Her tongue darted out to moisten her lips.

Did she know how that small action twisted his gut into knots? With a mix of innocence and wickedness, Julian inquired, "Stop what?"

"You are aware, Lord Dragon."

With a smug smile, he settled back against the tub resting his head on the rim. "How now, my fool. Safe?"

In that position, she could see those beautiful arms stretched along either side of the edge. So lean, so powerful. Dark images swirled in her mind as she inhaled the intoxicating male scent. A clear scent belonging to only him and not overwhelmed by the fragrance of the soap.

The right scent, the kenning whispered.

She envisioned those bare arms wrapped around her naked body, pulling her hard against his unyielding form, of him burying his mouth in the valley between her breasts. Her hands fisted in the silken hair, black as midnight. She shook, petrified by these flashes of foretellings. A wanting that went counter to all reason clawed at her insides.

Uncomfortable from heat pooling in her loins, she leapt to her feet, kicking over the stool. To cover the abrupt action, she walked to the other side, dragging the footstool as though it had been her intent. Glaring longingly at his left arm, she denied herself, instead started on his leg.

"With the Earl Kinmarch made prisoner, you shall need protection, my fool."

"I thought all here are now under the protection of the great Black Dragon," she sneered.

"I speak of personal matters." His countenance held a trace of calculation.

Tamlyn couldn't untangle what he implied, her thoughts too foggy, witched by this Norman's male sorcery. Also, it was the damned lavender! The wort was at the center of any love-drawing ritual, its scent stimulated emotions, opened them to erotic lures. Her smugness in making him smell as a woman came back on her triple fold.

But then, she doubted few women could resist this man even straight out of sweaty mail and smelling of horse.

As she washed his arm, he searched her face. "Your eyes are like amber. Striking. Bespelling."

Challon brought the back of his wet hand against the curve of her throat, allowing soapy bubbles to slide down her neck and under the sark. Her lids lifted as the foam crawled across the sensitive peak of her breast. Judging the glint in those penetrating eyes, he was aware what sweet torture the silky suds worked upon her. Blushing hotly, she jerked away from him.

His right hand shot out and caught her arm at the elbow. He'd moved so fast she had no time to react.

Challon's words were a husky incantation. "You shy from me like a fawn when she scents a stag. My scent causes you to shy?"

She forced a laugh, terrified by the dark magic he wielded so easily, so ruthlessly. "You smell as I do when I bathe."

"Join me. We can both smell of lavender and heather."

Challon tugged her toward him, his spell weaving around her. Tamlyn leaned back, trying to break the physical hold. This man was her enemy. He scared her—yet drew her as no man ever before.

"See . . . you tremble. You fear me."

Emotions paralyzed Tamlyn, but not as when she faced his knights. "I fear no Englishman."

The corner of his mouth lifted as his hand brushed against her neck where her blood throbbed. "*A cushla mo foil*, if you have no fear . . . prove it. Kiss me."

Pulse of my blood, he'd called her in Scots.

"Why would I wish to kiss you?" Oh, but she had from the very first.

"Curiosity? Desire?" His eyes held hers bound. "Prove your words as a warrior true."

Yea, she wanted to kiss that bold sinful mouth, had from the instant she locked eyes with his. Even so, she hated herself for the yearning, knowing she'd give away a small piece of her soul if she let this dark earl too close.

Still, she couldn't allow his challenge to go unanswered lest he cry her a coward. She had been maneuvered by a master strategist, she suspected, but it now was a matter of Pict pride—or so she convinced herself. Feeling she had nothing to win and everything to lose, she leaned to him and pressed her lips against his, hard and quick. Her mouth firmly closed. Even with that fleeting brush, she tasted him. With a satisfaction of passing Trial by Ordeal, she sat back.

"You see," she said, almost to silence her taunting inner voice as much as him. The flavor of the earl remained on her lips, made her yearn for another sample.

He laughed, the musical sound ringing against the

stone walls. "Is that what passes for a kiss to High-landers? My horse could kiss better."

"You kiss your bloody beastie often, Norman?"

Laughter died as his eyes burned into her soul, searing as a brand. "As I said—you are afraid."

"Never!"

He yanked her nearer, the front of her woolen sark getting soaked. "Then kiss me. Really kiss me. Kiss me like before."

So under his dark thrall, she had no choice. She could only obey. Against her will, her eyes drifted closed as she waited for the brush of his lips.

"Open your eyes." The command was low, seducing, holding a power, a pull. *"Is miann leam, a cushla mo foil."*
I desire you, pulse of my blood.

She did as he asked—no, bid with a conjurer's voice—unable to resist any more than she could stop her heart from beating. Green eyes, as deep as the forest in spring, glittered before her. The room shifted, seemed to spin, but he held her moored with his sensual magic, plundering her will. Devouring her unprotected soul.

First contact was light. Gradually, agonizingly, he put his mouth full against hers. Coaxing, his soft lips slid over hers, yet sent bolts of lightning arcing through her body. His tongue stroked in velvet textures until she parted for him, then speared into her, making her taste madness. This time she wasn't so maidenly shocked.

Never had she kenned men liked putting their tongues into a woman's mouth. Mayhap only Normans used this tool of sorcery.

At that, she tried to jerk away. This man was her enemy! How could she permit him to handle her, caress her as a husband did his wife? Engulfed by awakening female instincts, her hands smoothed up those bonnie arms and snaked around his neck. She gripped the wet locks and hung on for her very soul.

His arm caught her body and pressed her to his wet chest. Water splashed over the tub's edge and onto the stone floor. The kiss consumed them with hungry flames as they were lost to all.

Julian felt drunk. This woman captivated him as she had in the tent, drowning him in kisses of mead and sweet witch's brew. He wanted to kiss her endlessly. Even so, he broke away to draw air. There wasn't enough.

The strength of his craving for her frightened him. It roared through his body until the pounding was agony. He neither knew nor cared who claimed whom. As a man starving, he kissed her again and again, unable to stop himself. More. Julian needed so much more from this pagan witch . . . more than he needed blood or air to survive.

Julian's teeth nipped the column of her neck, wanting to spin her around and sink them into her soft, pale shoulder— claim her as a stallion would a mare. His hand slid into the rip of the sark, his thumb tracing invisible circles around the baby-soft areola. It tightened as he stroked it. He pinched the engorged nipple lightly. Then firmer. Spreading the fire in her pagan blood, he caught the jumping pulse point under his ravenous mouth.

Tamlyn arched in the embrace of his unyielding arm, reveled in the touch of the elegant fingers. It was madness. Sweet madness. In a shard of sudden lucidity, she understood why women so willingly gave away their few freedoms, wanting to yield to a man . . . even an enemy.

Challon spoke between kisses, smatterings of words, which floated away on the smoke of the peat fire. ". . . so you need not worry about the Lady Tamlyn."

At least she thought he murmured that. "Tamlyn?" she echoed, confused.

He laughed, then kissed her shoulder in a stinging nip, soothing the spot with his oh so clever tongue. "I said you should not fear my taking the lady to wife. She cannot come between us."

Her mind screamed, listen, but his caressing her breast muddled her thoughts. A strange burning ache burned between her legs. The yearning cut like a knife.

"Take to wife? I do not understand."

"I see." Laughter rumbled deep in his chest. "I must marry the lady to secure the claim to Glenrogha. I shall claim you as mistress. With the Earl Hadrian gone from Scottish soil you need someone to care for you."

"Tamlyn—to wife?" Words floating in the air gained substance and crashed with a resounding thud. "Mayhap she will not wish to marry you, Norman."

"The choice is not hers. When Edward granted the charter for the four holdings, he made the daughters of The Shane his wards. I must wed one. I decided upon the Lady Tamlyn. Edward received dispensation for my brothers to take the other two as their wives."

"You have not laid eyes upon the woman."

"No matter. I shall wed her, twisted spine, warts and all," he stated flatly.

Glancing down, she saw his hand still inside her sark. Jerking it out, she flung it back at him. "Mayhap Tamlyn shan't feel the same!"

"She shall be taught the way of things." His strength was terrifying as he forced her close and kissed her roughly.

Panic bubbled in her throat. Fury drove all passion from her system and not even his dark magic could conquer it.

She shoved against those broad shoulders. "You want me for your whore?"

"Never use that word," he growled. "We suit. You cannot deny it. As for the lady's objections, she has no say. Edward spoke his will."

"Then, Lord Arrogant, you need to learn a lot about your supposed lady bride."

"The lady is my concern. I shall handle her."

"Handle? Like a hound?" She jumped to her feet, sputtering indignation. "What if I do not want to be your whore? Shall you handle that as well?"

"Your objection against becoming my lover rings hollow. Your body wishes it. Taking the Lady Tamlyn to wife is duty—"

"And since you require heirs and not bastards, you shall lay with your lady wife at the same time you lay with me?" She spat the words.

"I must marry. You I shall enjoy taking to my bed. I want to plant my seed in your body. Watch you breed my sons." The words sprang from his deepest longing, and just as suddenly, Julian experienced the knife of regret that their children would carry the taint of bastardy as his brothers had. Ignoring it, since there was no changing the reality, he reached out, grabbing her hips to guide her back to him. "I shall keep you on your back so you soon forget the touch of the Red Laird of Clan Shane."

She gasped in umbrage. "You think I am The Shane's whore?"

"There is no shame in being a lord's leman. A lady wife is taken for wealth, land or political alliances. A duty. It does not mean a man must endure a cold body in bed."

"Cold?" She closed her eyes and let out with an ear-piercing scream.

Julian blinked, surprised. The door swung open and

the guard stepped in. Lifting his hand he signaled them to back out. With a nod, the guard closed the door.

This was hardly the reaction he expected. Her body wanted him. Why was she raising a fuss?

"The lady has refused all offers of marriage for nearly a decade," Julian said. "One with such a temperament likely must fear the lures of bedsport. Likely, she is near a hag at her age and will thank you for keeping me away from her side most of the time."

"Hag? Most of the time? Ooooo . . ." she growled, her head snapping around, looking for something.

Julian feared it was something to hit him with. He shrugged. He'd enjoy a battle with her. Enjoy her surrender. "As you pointed out, I need heirs."

"You steal Glenrogha, make prisoner of my—her lord father, plan to force her into a loveless marriage, yet feel you can claim me as your whore? Contemptible. So English."

"My head aches with all this prattle." He held out his hand to end the discussion. "Come, sweetling, finish washing me. The water cools."

His seductive voice curled around Tamlyn, trying to trap her with its fey magic. It did little to cover his imperious manner. Lord Challon was so used to having everything his way.

Nothing could dissolve the wrath boiling within her. Tamlyn vibrated with frustration and not even knowing what distressed her most. That he assumed he could take Tamlyn to lady wife, just because an English king decreed it? Or the gall of the swine to presume she was Hadrian of Kinmarch's whore, and thus, spoils of war he was entitled to claim.

"I am no whore for The Shane!" She slapped the water, creating a splash into his face. "And you can scrub your own private parts, bloody Lord Dragon!"

Stalking away, she pulled open the heavy door. Faces impassive, the guards turned and stepped together, blocking her. Lips pursed, she slammed it in their hateful English faces. On a turn of the heel, she stormed past Lord Challon.

As he stood to climb out, water streamed off his lithely muscled form. She tried to ignore the perfect body of a warrior-true. Tried, but failed. He was so flawlessly created she nearly walked into the wall.

Too bad he was such a . . . a . . . pig!

Not thinking, Tamlyn rushed to the solar, then rotated in a semicircle. She'd forgotten there was no exit. She stayed, hugging her arms around her trembling body, fighting to keep from falling apart. Returning meant facing the earl in all his naked beauty. She quaked, the sense of being cornered fluttering in her chest.

Smaller than most solars, it was a bride's gift from her father to his young wife. The outside wall had a real window inlaid with precious glass. The clear panes of the center were bordered on each side with narrow, alternating panels of pale yellow, green and deep amber, similar to the stained glass used in kirks. The window had made the passing of gray winter days more cheerful for the Lady Deporadh.

The sun lifted over the tor, spreading a glow through the foggy, dawn sky. Exhaustion prevented appreciation of the pagan beauty of the awakening land. Too many emotions raged within her, desire, fury, helplessness. So exhausted, she could only stand shaking, trying not to cry.

For three nights, she had found no rest. A dream tormented her into breaking slumber. She'd awoken covered in sweat, heart pounding. The dream faded, but wisps lingered: the sound of ravens screaming, then thunder of a coming storm.

Yestermorn the sense of looming danger had been so pressing she had sought distraction in harvesting the violets. The first violets of spring had a power. One could make a wish upon them and it'd come true. Too bad she'd forgotten to cast a wish upon them. Surely a whole basket earned her at least one wish granted.

So much had happened since and little would ever be the same.

She wanted to find some overlooked corner, curl up with a soft plaide and sleep for days. Wanting to blot everything from her mind, she was afraid to do more than draw breath or she might crumble. A tear trickled down her cheek. She swiped it away.

On panther feet, Challon came up behind her. Tamlyn became aware of his presence when he placed his hands upon her shoulders, sliding the sark to the right. His voice was low and husky. "It is a view to inspire bards."

She nodded. "Once the sun peeks over the tor, the colors of the panes flood the solar."

"I spoke neither of hills nor window, but what is before them." His voice sapped her will, weakening her to surrender again.

Not as a last choice, but the only choice.

His body edged closer. Hard curves pressed, molding to her contours. Snaking his strong warrior's arms around her, he flexed the unyielding muscles to draw her back against his chest.

"Please, do not hold me like this." She whimpered her plea.

"I cannot stop myself." Challon's whispered words came against her right ear. "You enchant me, pagan."

His right hand swept the long hair over the opposite

shoulder. Light kisses chained their way across her bare neck, ending at the ear's shell. His tongue traced its swirl, then flicked inside. Shivers rippled through her body.

Words clamored inside her head, but she couldn't battle his temptation. His fingers tilted her chin, then his mouth covered hers. He deepened the pressure. He plundered. Devoured. His hands skimmed over her breasts, belly and hips, the rough friction igniting the fire to flare. Winning her surrender. Her soul.

Julian knew she was so tired, nearing collapse—physically and emotionally. Despite that, he couldn't prevent himself from holding her, touching her, fondling her softness. If he couldn't he'd go insane.

Not playing fair, he used that fatigue against her. Never before had he drawn such pleasure from simple gestures of lovemaking. Every touch, each kiss was special, seeming to warm his cold warrior's soul.

He'd been cold for so long . . .

This stubborn Scots lass was passion embodied. He cared little if it were heathen enchantment or if the price was his immortal soul. Julian could no more fight her allure than will his heart to cease beating. When her lips parted for him, male ascendancy flooded through his entire being. He entered, not with the thundering force raging in his blood, but in gentleness, coaxing to draw her to a final acceptance of him.

Turning her within his embrace, he pressed her into his body, reveling in the perfection of their fit . . . as if their bodies were two parts of a whole. His hands cupped the curves of her derrière and raised her weight, rubbing his aching groin against the luscious torment of her woman's heat.

Mews rose in her throat as she arched into his body.

Grasping his shoulders, her nails all but drew blood. Her tongue touched his, then went into his mouth . . . willingly. His warrior's drive thrilled in his conquering of this wild Highland lass.

Someone cleared his throat. Guillaume stood in the shadowed archway between the two rooms.

Bathed in the halo of the rising sun and the brilliant golds and green of the windowpanes, Julian's eyes blinked, trying to focus. "Not again, Guillaume, if you value your hide."

"My Lord Dragon, it is of import," his brother insisted.

"What is so pressing you cannot sort it out?"

Blushing, she eased from his embrace and leaned against the stone of the wall for support, almost trying to melt into the shadows of the far corner.

"You have my attention," Challon bit out. He was wrapped only in a short sheet of linen about his hips and it did little to hide the arousal defined against the dampened material. "Out with it."

"I presumed you would wish to know that the Lady Tamlyn has been located."

Challon nodded. He wanted to set eyes on the sister who was to be his lady wife. Yet he felt strangely discomforted discussing her in front of the woman he wanted so desperately. "Where has the lady been hiding all this time?"

With a faint smirk, Guillaume's eyes moved from Julian to the woman in the shadows.

Julian frowned. For an instant jealousy exploded within him, blinding him from comprehending what his brother imparted. Then he caught Guillaume's flashing eyes and insight dawned.

"Julian, I present Tamlyn MacShane of Glenrogha,

lady daughter to the Earl of Kinmarch." He tacked on, "Your betrothed."

Julian's face hardened. "So, it seems I should be calling myself fool after all."

Chapter 7

Julian struggled to rein in his spiraling temper, spurred by the frustrated mating drive. By damn, he'd held Tamlyn in his possession the whole time! Small wonder she was so offended when he assumed she was Kinmarch's whore. Also explained was her ridiculous insistence that he call her fool. He'd been so caught in her web, enthralled by her pagan charm, he never pressed the blasted woman on the issue.

Evidently the daughters of The Shane considered baiting dragons a grand sport.

Not liking any aspect of this, Julian frowned. Never before had he thought with what was in his braies, a mistake that saw many a warrior in their grave. He stalked away to where her scent couldn't cloud his mind. The fury refused to abate. Nor did the ravenous hunger vibrating in his blood.

Swinging about, he glared at her. "So, Tamlyn of Glenrogha or Tamlyn MacShane, but *never* Lady Tamlyn, where are the warts, hairy mole and twisted spine? Sorry my brother spoiled your game. Has no one warned you dragon baiting is risky? Dragons eat maidens, flesh and bone."

In a move to intimidate, Julian leaned into Tamlyn, letting her burn in the scorching heat that rolled off his body.

Tamlyn. The name echoed in his mind. A charming name. One he'd never encountered before coming to this pagan glen. He could hear it falling from his lips as he took her in the deep of night. Tamlyn MacShane. Soon to be Tamlyn Challon. His lady wife. Despite the black fury that bordered on uncontrollable, a spark of pride flared within his chest.

His groin throbbed hard as he considered she'd bear his son. The craving was so intense it flooded through Julian's muscles until it was physically painful, pushing him to take her. Here. Now. Standing as they were.

By all, Edward had exiled him to this forgotten pocket in the Highlands as punishment. When he learnt the news, Julian hid his reaction, not wanting the king to suspect he welcomed the chance to get away from war, away from death. Glen Shane then became his last hope for peace, for sanity. Never had he thought he might be so blessed as to have this woman as his.

The violence of his rages of late scared him. Attempting to channel the foul temper, he focused on Tamlyn. With no mercy, he used how she reacted to his body as a weapon against her. His eyes bored into hers. He trailed his hand down her neck, then to the tip of her breast and watched the nipple pucker under the damp fabric, begging for his caress. How her traitorous body arched into his touch.

With the tip of his finger, he faintly traced circles around the taut nub. Her breath hitched, provoking a mirror reaction within him. Driving lust racked his body and it took the last measure of his willpower not to go down on his knees and suck that distended peak into his mouth. Teach her the ways of being a woman. His lids lowered, as he was lost to the pull of that image strong in his mind.

He saw her arousal shudder through her. Likely, her mind screamed for her to slap him for the too familiar touch. But she craved it. Giving her what she really wanted, he used the edge of his fingernail, pressing it into the engorged nipple. Testing the depth of her awakened mating instincts. It would have been uncomfortable for an unaroused female. Her chin tilted, defiant, yet she held still, letting him increase the pressure, rolling it against his nail.

Guillaume cleared his throat, reminding they were not alone.

Turning her head, Tamlyn tried to hide from the smug gaze of the Dragon. Tried to shrink away from his branding touch. She wanted to laugh or project haughty insolence, but she lacked the grit to stand against the redoubtable power of this terrifying warrior.

Her breath grew faster, matching the cadence of his, her fear waxing in measure to his wrath. Both of them were caught in sensations that seemed to have an existence all their own.

Tamlyn still tasted him, recalled how it felt to be held in those bonnie arms when in his tent. Her core throbbed, branded by this warlord with the Selkie beauty. She stood in dread of this mighty Black Dragon, so aptly named. Only fools and blind men wouldn't be. Never had she sensed such raw power. She felt wonderment at his mysterious, possibly more dangerous craft, the ability to touch her as no man before. A touch she craved.

His hand lifted to her face. She flinched, shutting her eyes, afraid if he put his long, strong fingers on her body again, she'd be unable to resist him.

"Open your eyes, Tamlyn." He waited until she obeyed. Clearly, his frown said he'd mistaken her response. He thought she was afraid he planned to hit her. "I strike no woman or child, no matter how they provoke me. What did you hope to do with this game, other than playing me the fool before Glenrogha's people?"

Tamlyn tried to answer him. The enslaving eyes of this warlock earl held her mind, destroying simple thoughts. She could only stare at him and swallow the dryness in her throat.

"Seems the cat has your tongue. More's the pity. I could find a use for it." He stared at her, the focus of his thoughts humbling. Then the steel shutter within his mind fell, and once again, Tamlyn was left cold, empty, as the kenning could no longer touch his life force. With a lift of his brow, he turned his back on her and asked of his brother, "Has food been prepared for breaking the fast?"

"The fortress is well run." Guillaume's eyes slid past Challon to Tamlyn. He inclined his head in a salute. The intense eyes lingered, running over her disheveled condition.

Challon glanced over his shoulder at her. Then the two men locked glares. Finally, the earl stalked out of the solar and into the lord's chamber.

Tamlyn finally exhaled as she saw punishment was no longer imminent. Still, she couldn't quell the quaking in her legs. The Lord Challon was overwhelming.

From where she stood in the shadows, she could see only part of the adjoining chamber. The Dragon crossed to the bed, dropped the small sheet and then pulled on black hose, which molded to his muscular legs. Next came the leather chausses, the black under tunic, followed by a black leather jack. He donned the garments with deft and precise movements.

Rarely had she seen a man of such lionesque bearing. So beautiful to watch. A man who would totally alter everything she'd ever known.

Tamping down on foul humors roiling in his warrior's soul, Julian fastened the ornate buckle about his hips. This Scots female pushed him past the pale—in more ways than one. It was best if he walked away until this violent disposition curbed, until his body no longer ruled his mind.

"Mayhap it would be wise for the people of Clan Ogilvie to swear their oath to me without their lady there wearing an expression worthy of Boudicca," Julian decided.

"The lady's defiance might set a torch to rebellion," Guillaume concurred. "So what are your plans for the willful countess?"

"It would serve her if I tossed her into the oubliette." Hands on his hips, Julian closed his eyes and tilted his head back, trying to regain control of his overheated body.

Of late, when his temper spiraled to the point of losing control, intrusive memories flashed before his eyes, to where he often had a hard time seeing what was about him. As a warrior this terrified him. What if this happened on the field of battle where the hesitation of a heartbeat could cost him his life? He had to fight from being sucked back to Wales, him kneeling over Christian's gutted body, of the festering hell that was Berwick.

"Julian, fare you well?"

Hearing his brother's concern, Julian opened his eyes and forced a smile. "Keep Lady Tamlyn under guard until my black temper cools. Let no one in. Fatigue numbs me so it is difficult to think. My head aches and

I've much to do before I seek my rest. I dare not go near her. I might put my hands around that perfect throat and squeeze until bones snap."

Arching a brow at Julian's aroused state, Guillaume chuckled. "Long-range plans, Julian. You still intend to take her as lady wife?"

Jealousy erupted inside him. Territorial where his fool—Tamlyn—was concerned, Julian exhaled. Opening his eyes, he studied his brother. Did Guillaume harbor hopes he'd change his mind? "If I manage not to murder her first . . . aye."

Julian's head snapped around as Tamlyn entered the chamber. His glare colliding with hers, he noted her chin was in that now familiar tilt of defiance. The effort was undermined by her shaking. He frowned. He wanted Tamlyn submissive, not cowed, though he feared it might come to that before he gained control of her.

"Lord Challon, I wish to go to my room on the level below."

Julian saw it galled her having to ask his permission. His chest rose and fell several times before he deigned to answer. "You remain here."

Clearly incensed at having to beg leave, she complained, "I wish only to withdraw to my own quarters."

Julian's hand motioned toward the door, signaling his brother to depart. With nod of assent, Guillaume left. He paused at the threshold to judge Julian's mood. Satisfied, he closed the door quietly.

Her amber eyes watched as Julian walked toward her. "These rooms are now your quarters, my lady."

"I presumed you claimed them," she stammered, his physical magnetism clearly flustering her poise.

"I do, as the new Earl Glenrogha."

She gasped. "Surely you do not mean us to share?" Tamlyn's steps moved backward as he drew close.

Male dominance sang in his blood, bringing a smile to his mouth. Indulging in the arrogant display, he continued the advance as she retreated. Cat and mouse. His fury transmuting into another fierce emotion. "It is precisely what I expect."

Her spine jarred against the stone wall. "It would not be seemly, Lord Challon."

"By Edward's decree we are betrothed. Think of it as bundling, I believe you Scots call it." Placing his hands on either side of her shoulders, he pinned Tamlyn against the wall. Leaning to her, he nuzzled the soft hair at the side of her temple. "The long nights, while we await the banns to be called, shall afford us time to become acquainted."

"I shall not wed with you, English dog." Her threat sounded hollow.

"Back to calling me animal names? Lady Tamlyn, you shall do as you are told." Grabbing her wrist, he spun her across the short distance to the bed, the high frame hitting the back of her hips.

"I will do more than call you names," she warned.

Placing a knee on the bed beside her right hip, he brought his body down against hers, forcing her back on the flat plane. Julian indulged in a flexing of animalistic superiority, and by God, he enjoyed it! Physical domination was the fastest and most pleasurable way to demonstrate to her there was no fighting him.

"Silence," he ordered. Closing his mouth over hers in a rough, possessing kiss, he proceeded to conquer Tamlyn. She pushed against his chest to no avail. No gentle wooing, he laid siege to her, staking his claim. When he pulled back, he left her gasping. Her hands now clung to his upper arms. "Glen Shane is mine and I shall hold it. Just as I shall take and hold you. Get used to it—to this—Tamlyn."

He kissed her again, longer, harder, savagely devouring her lips. Sucking her lower lip twixt his sharp predator's teeth, he bit down, not enough to draw blood, just enough for her to feel his mark. To brand her.

At the nip, Tamlyn once again shoved against him. He took her wrists, pinning them over her head with the grip of one hand. The position left her arched, helpless. Exposed. What he intended. It was imperative he had Tamlyn MacShane subdued and under control before Edward arrived.

He feared the king would likely show up here within the coming weeks, wanting to gloat over sending Julian away to what he considered a Scottish hellhole. Julian's eyes traveled over her, knowing her full value. A value beyond measure. Edward wouldn't be pleased with the prize he'd so carelessly given Julian.

The thought of Edward seeing her this defiant nearly made him shudder. His mentor, his king had changed since his beloved queen's death. His soul was poisoned. For too long Edward had been vexed by the refusals from the earl's daughters. If the three sisters came under Edward's fist . . . well, Julian would do what he must to prevent that.

He had to bring Tamlyn to heel, and quickly, for all their sakes. He had no time to woo this wild Highland lass. That left power and intimidation as his only weapons.

Fingers of his free hand splayed over the slight swell of her belly, the place he would plant his seed. Where she'd breed his black-haired, green-eyed sons. Sliding down, he cupped the apex of her thighs, pushing the material to mold between her legs. Her body jerked as he increased the ungentle caress, allowing her no quarter.

The corner of his mouth tugged as he watched her struggles, useless, for he manacled her with the grip of his sword hand. His strong thigh banded across her legs so all she could do was buck. His lady was a she-cat, a fighter. Rage drove her when reason should tell her to surrender. Smiling, he permitted Tamlyn to wear herself out.

Soon, Julian would enjoy taming his Cait Sidhe. "Are you tired yet?"

"Not a'tall." The defiance failed as the reply came through puffed breaths.

"You lie." He laughed.

Slowly, he lowered his lips to hers, only this time in softness, wooing. She fought him. He expected it. Her body was rigid, her mouth flattened and closed. With supreme arrogance he ignored her opposition, plying her with tender kisses to court her wild Highland spirit.

By all that was holy, Julian knew he was blessed with this union, more than he dared hope in the darkest nights of the soul. Now he knew her to be daughter to the laird, he recognized her responses as untutored, making them all the more arousing. His blood surged when he considered he would be the first man to be inside her body.

He wanted nothing more than to toss up the kirtle and push his aching male flesh into her heat. She wouldn't resist. He could feel her female dampness on his fingers through the fabric. Still he held back, exerting every scrap of his iron control.

This pagan witch needed to learn he was master here. He meant to start as they would go in this marriage. Tamlyn was his property. He was overlord of Glenrogha and nothing could alter that reality. She could only accept and bend to his will. In fact, she wasn't losing anything, but gaining his protection.

His fingers worked against the fabric as he brought her to a shallow climax, her body bowing off the bed as fire undulated through her. His dragon's fire. Tamlyn's gold eyes flew wide in shock at her first taste of passion.

She'd be easier to handle now. He released her wrists and leaned on his elbow, enjoying the awe in her tawny eyes. Nearly his undoing. His body thrummed with need so strong it nearly crippled him.

Kissing her once—hard and quick—Julian shoved away, leaving her there. It was imperative he distance himself before he lost control. It was vital Tamlyn comprehend he was the conqueror, master over her and his emotions, that she held no craft to bind him with pagan spells.

There'd be no repeat of what happened in his tent.

At the door he paused, commanding, "You remain here until I return, my *faidhaich.*" Without a backward glancing, he strode from the room, the great door slamming behind him.

"I am not your wildcat, Dragon," she said to the empty room.

Sensations pulsing in her woman's place reminded Tamlyn of the warrior's touch, his total domination. Never had she met anyone like him.

Tamlyn had tried to resist being sucked into the eddying pools of his dark green eyes. There was no escaping when the scent of his male heat rolled over her.

The man smelled . . . right. She ignored the kenning.

Rolling to her side, she trembled. A tear slid down her cheek.

Wallowing in self-pity was futile, so she rose and went to the chest belonging to the Dragon. Pushing open the lid, she rummaged through his clothing until she found a simple green sark. By all, she figured the earl owed her. Unlacing her kirtle, she slid out of her clothes and dropped them.

Looking down, she saw they landed atop Challon's discarded garments. Dismissing any significance, she climbed into the cooling water, her shaking knees barely holding her. Taking a handful of the soap she began scrubbing the scent of the warrior from her skin, rubbing until her flesh was bright pink.

Her head dropped in despair. A sob welled in her chest as she acknowledged defeat. She could rid her body of his musky male odor, but the taste of his lips lingered.

Paying no heed to the cold water, she pulled her knees to her chest, leaned forward and released tears she'd fought so hard to hold back.

She was losing the battle against this arrogant warlord. She fought not only him, but also her own nature. And by the Auld Ones, she hated him for it.

Hated herself even more.

Chapter 8

Flames of the peat fire flickered low as Julian entered the chambers. Its warmth and scent brushed against his mind with that odd sense of coming home.

At first glance, he feared Tamlyn had somehow escaped, possibly through a secret passage from the lord's chamber. On the morrow he'd check out that likelihood. After his heart lurched, he saw she slept curled up on the far side of the curtained bed.

Pulling aside the half-closed drapes of plaide, his eyes lingered on the slumbering form of the woman who was to be his bride. A smile molded his lips when he saw his tunic covered her lush curves. A sign of his possession.

So weary, Julian's body screamed for sleep. Yet he hesitated to surrender to the need, only to face the nightmares waiting.

Instead, he stared at the rise of her hip under the green silk. His eyes hungrily traveled to where the leather lacings crisscrossed over her full breasts. The nipples puckered, pushing against the soft material.

Lust racked his body as he stared at those soft mounds, rising and falling with the cadence of her breathing. Images swirled through his brain of him holding them, testing their firmness, of his mouth on one while his fingers gently toyed with the nipple of the other. Or seeing their paleness above him, shadows caressing their naked flesh as he drove upward into her body.

God's teeth, he tried to dispel the pull. These flashes felt more like memories . . . as if he'd already lived and loved Tamlyn before.

Julian blinked, fighting the coming flashes. Oddly, instead of seeing his brother dying or walking through the ugliness of Berwick, other scenes came. Of Tamlyn under an apple tree, the white petals falling about her until they appeared heavy as snow. Of balefires and people dancing. The most bizarre tableau that flooded his mind was a creature—half-man, half-stag—walking toward him.

Mayhap the feeble hold he had on the threads of his sanity was finally slipping away. He closed his eyes for a moment, listening to the buzzing inside his head. The noises grew louder . . . sounding like the strident cries of ravens.

Shaking the peculiar fit, Julian reached out and slowly traced the lacing back and forth across Tamlyn's breasts. Regretfully, he dropped his finger, knowing he had to stop or he'd end up taking her.

Sighing, he blamed exhaustion for his weakness for this Scots lass. She could not stir him so otherwise.

Pulling the jack over his head, he tossed it on the trunk. His tunic followed. Then he unlaced the chausses and boots, the effort nearly more strength than he had left. Clad in only in hose that tied about his waist, he strode into the solar and added a peat brick to the fire, still bewildered how these Scots burned dirt.

He paused at the table to pour a goblet of mead. Swallowing the sweet cider and fermented honey, the flavor was pleasing, satisfying. Like kissing Tamlyn.

Tamlyn.

Setting down the empty cup, he padded back to the bed on the raised dais. He unlaced and removed his hose, then slid under the black-wolf throw and tartan cover, pulling it over them. Tamlyn's skin radiated heat, dispelling the coolness of the bedding. He shifted closer.

Her hair, like heavy silk, was irresistible. Lightly, so as not to waken her, he ran his fingers over the gold mane. When she remained untroubled in her slumber, Julian shifted his body, molding against her.

Thankfully, he absorbed her calming radiance, praying her potent witch's craft could hold at bay the coldness tormenting his soul. If only he could steal just a few hours of rest.

His lids drifted shut as he breathed in the intoxicating lure of wild berries, purple flowers . . .

And Tamlyn.

Within the dark dreams Tamlyn stirred, comforted by a welcome warmth. The swirling images strengthened. As it had for three nights previous, the haze held the distressing sounds of a great storm nearing the sacred passes.

Thunder shook the ground as her bare feet trod the soft, rain-soaked earth. Mists veiled the Highlands and Lowlands alike with impenetrable grayness as she waited, barely able to draw breath. The sense of foreboding was oppressive, stifling.

Something comes.

Bumps skittered across her chilled flesh. Aye, something dark and unearthly approached, shrouded by the shifting fog.

The silence shattered as a jet stallion broke from the eddying fog. Nostrils flaring, the beast expelled streams of hot vapor into the moist air. The horse tossed its head, the heavy mane undulating. It set the metal fittings of bit and bridle jingling. Faery bells tinkled in the silence. This was no goblin steed. Upon its back sat a knight.

He wore an unadorned breastplate, black leather breeches and studded jack. The color of a starless night, his mantle rippled heavily behind him. The material seemed restless, almost imbued with life.

Thousands of unseen ravens screamed within the fog. Their cries increased to a deafening cacophony as the raw energy of both rider and steed held Tamlyn in awe. Paralyzed, she was unable to flee as the black knight and his terrifying horse of war bore nearer. Fearful they meant to run her down, she shut her eyes.

At the final instant the knight controlled the horse, halting so she stood by his right leg. He inclined in the creaking saddle and held out a white rose. Tamlyn reached for it, hesitant to accept the offering.

A tear-shaped bead of red hit the bud. Then a second. Still another, until the whole bloom was sanguine from the blood where the thorns had lacerated the warrior's palm. She blinked. The color changed again and was now black. Black as the crying ravens of death and fore-telling, hidden in the fog.

The warrior removed the helm, revealing the face of Lord Challon. He stared down upon her, the dark green eyes so empty. Tamlyn sensed pain so crippling it nearly drove her to her knees. Moved by empathy, she touched him, stroking her finger along the wrist of his right hand

and down the first finger to the ring of gold. The seal of Challon. The mighty dragon rampant.

As Tamlyn touched the metal, a bolt of lightning seized her. She was carried to a place unfamiliar . . . a huge town.

Hordes of people ran, pushing and shoving, fleeing something terrible. Their desperate cries filled the cool spring air. They slammed into her, propelled her with them along the narrow, twisting alleys. Fire-blackened buildings. The acrid smell burned her throat and turned the noonday sun to midnight.

Bodies were everywhere. Hanging from windows. Streets were impassable—men, women and even children hewn down where they'd fled the heavy horses of war. The air was suffocating. Some corpses were older, beginning to rot, drawing blueflies, maggots and ravens. Blood ran into small rivers, swirling with the soft mud into a foul black miasma.

Tamlyn stared in revulsion, the taste coppery in her mouth. So vile, it pushed her to retch, over and over, until dry heaves left her body bruised from the force. Her mind echoed with the words of a man, *the pearl of Scotland* . . .

Julian caught Tamlyn's tense body in his arms, holding her as a silent scream ripped through her mind. Trapped in a nightmare, she couldn't break free. Julian knew the experience only too well.

She struggled weakly against him, but soon settled in his embrace. He whispered assurances. She was safe, he'd protect her. Surprisingly, she accepted the security of his arms and pressed her face to the curve of his neck.

Her soft hands slid around his waist and clung as if she couldn't absorb enough of his heat.

Julian leaned back and draped her across his chest. His hands traced circles along her spine to give her ease. Oddly, he found the action soothed him as well. Soon his lids drifted closed. There was satisfaction in this simple embrace. Not with sexual intent—though that was never far from mind and body when this Scots lass was near. This solace was meant for her, yet it seeped into his soul. Having her next to him, offering her comfort, was one of those seemingly insignificant things his heart craved.

Dawn must be near. Strange. For the first time since Berwick Julian slept with no hellish visions haunting him. He'd forgotten rest could be so peaceful, so healing.

A piteous whimper came from Tamlyn, as words fell from her sleeping lips. "The pearl of Scotland . . . lies . . . crushed . . . beneath my heel . . ."

Julian's blood chilled.

He'd heard those words—spoken by Edward. Agony poured through his soul as he recalled kneeling in the bloody mud, retching out his guts. Nothing could've prepared him for seeing that vile well and the desecration of those helpless women.

Berwick . . . by damn, would there never be an end to his torment?

For three days the unholy bloodbath had raged. When Edward, mounted upon his mighty warhorse, rode up along with his commanders, they happened upon ugliness unimaginable. An English soldier hacked a woman to death as she gave birth.

With heartless ennui, yet ever mindful of his self-professed piousness, the king had ordered his dogs leashed. The cold blue eyes flicked over the woman's lifeless, child-swollen body and drawled, "The pearl of Scotland lies crushed beneath my heel."

How had those words come to be in the mind of Tamlyn nearly a month's passing? She would know that Berwick was called Scotland's pearl due to its important commerce with Europe, but naught of Edward's sick jest.

On this eve he'd lain beside her, and for the first time since the sacking of the town, not been tormented in the hot coals of Berwick's everlasting Hell. Had she by some strange spell taken the dreams from him and suffered the torment in his place?

Having no answers left him uneasy. Mayhap she was indeed a witch. How else could she possess such knowledge?

A violent wave of nausea rolled over him.

Shoving her away, he rolled to the bed's edge, sat up, fighting the bile rising in his throat. Panic gripped him. What else could this fey lass twig about him if she knew this much already? Could she see that he had killed his own brother?

Oh, Jesus, have mercy upon him!

Sensing loss of warmth and protection, Tamlyn opened her eyes. Naked, Challon sat perched on the bedside, his strong back to her. She sucked in her breath sharply. By the Auld Ones, the man was beautiful . . . everywhere! Something in his tense position evoked a poignant note, compelled her to offer words of comfort.

She came fully awake. Offer solace to the Norman? Was she daft? She grabbed the wolf throw, clutching it to her chest. Her movements caused him to start.

For an instant he looked at her with haunted eyes, his emotions a strange mix of perplexity, sadness and abhorrence. Grabbing his hose, he dressed.

"You slept with me, Lord Challon?" she asked, heat flooding her face.

"Your place is with me now, Tamlyn." His tone was unbending.

"It is unseemly. I was a maiden."

His laugh was harsh, condescending. "And still are, my fool."

Julian wielded anger as a shield for his sense of vulnerability. Twice she'd disarmed his warrior's nature. The first time with the witchery of lust, now by stealing his mind, his innermost secrets.

He leaned across the bed, grabbed her wrist and yanked her to him. So close, he could feel the warmth of her breath. He had to fight to keep from closing his mouth over hers. It wouldn't do to kiss her whilst in this mood or the raging beast inside him would devour her.

"What sort of man do you take me to be?" he snarled, a wounded beast.

Tamlyn trembled, yet spoke her truth. "The kind that would force a woman to marry him and yet would seek to claim a whore for his pleasure."

"Permit me to enlighten you, dauntless virgin. Had I taken you during the night—and it would not have been just once—you would not be able to walk this morn. Rest assured, when I claim you as my lady wife you shall be very aware of my possession. Not an event a person sleeps through—or would want to."

"Rape, you mean," she retorted.

"Not between us. Never between us."

"You demand I marry you without my consent. It is not fair." She trembled under his hand, tears glimmering in the corners of her eyes.

"Show me where it is decreed that life is fair, my fool. Never have I found such. There are no golden rules, no Auld Code," he scoffed, as if speaking to a child.

She tried to jerk away from his iron grip, but he held

her firmly. "I have done nothing to earn such enmity from Edward Longshanks."

"Your existence angers the Plantagenet. You are a Scot, first liability to him. Never have you tended fealty before him, a second wrong in his eyes. And your final offense—you are a woman holding fortresses through an ancient charter in your own right and title. All those spurned offers of marriages return to haunt you. Before heading back to English soil, Edward shall garrison soldiers at every fortress throughout Scotland. All nobles will be forced to sign instruments of fealty before Edward Plantagenet, King of Britain, not to a new King of Scotland. Accept this. Learn to live with and make the best of it, for there is no changing our path. Heed my words, Tamlyn."

She lifted her chin pridefully but it quivered. "Never shall I swear to an English ruler."

He bent her back, his bare chest pressing her flat to the bed's surface, demonstrating she couldn't fight him. He hovered just above her. Touching. Yet not touching. "The lady of the Black Dragon need not endure such a humbling before the king. You shall speak your vows to me as your lord husband when we proclaim our union. I am Edward's man."

"You may lick his boots. I never shall."

"Tamlyn, no one gives you a choice. After calling banns, we shall marry. You cannot fight me and win. Accept—yield to me. Your match is made."

"My match is not made."

Julian inhaled, then closed his eyes to seek patience. "Surrender. There is no alternative—for you or me. I am the lord of Glenrogha. Your people understand the way of it. Even your knights forswore you. Yield to me and let us begin a life together in peace."

Disbelief and hurt flickered in her eyes. "They forswore me?"

"Five knights refused. They are held in the oubliette."

"You cannot force me to accept you as husband," she countered.

"Do not make threats you cannot keep, *faidhaich*." Lazily, his thumb stroked the slender column of her throat, finding her pulse. It jumped erratically under his touch. "I doubt force shall ever be necessary between us. Your body already accepts me, warms to me as master, desires me. Only your mind battles uselessly. Your blood jumps from my nearness. I see the throb here."

Julian rubbed the pulse point.

Tamlyn put her hand to his chest as if to push him away. She glanced down to see her palm rested against his heart. Her eyes dilated, staring at the hand magically fused to his burning flesh, then lifted to meet his.

"Fear me, *faidhaich*? Or are you terrified of your body and its hungers?" he mocked.

"I do not fear you, Julian Challon." She lied. They both knew it.

Challon's eyes traveled slowly over her body, then back to her face. "I enjoy spirit and I loathe anything cowardly. I can accept the same in a lady wife—provided she is smart enough to surrender. Yield to me. We both bring much to this union."

"I see nothing I do not already possess."

"You attain the protection of my name and sword. I hold great wealth in the care of the Templars. I shall spend it to improve Glenrogha. I shall give you fine sons. Ah, Tamlyn, think on it. If I had not taken Glenrogha, another warlord would have come in my place. Edward will not stop until Scotland is under his fist. You saw the mettle of his mercenaries. Instead of leading a host of vassals, they are now little more than a pack of rabid animals that do as they are told—anything they are told—as long as they receive coins. As much as you abhor my taking of your precious fortress, stop and consider. You were nearly raped. I prevented that. That is just a taste of what happens when Longshanks sacks a town or holding. I shall stand between you and the king, protect you and all in this valley. In time, you may even view this union as a blessing."

"You want a wife who will never love you?"

Julian shrugged, releasing her as he slid off the bed. "I never voiced one word about wishing love. A word overused by silly bards. You shall rule as lady of my holdings, warm my bed and breed me strong sons. What need have I for foolish words with little value? Do not mistake in replacing reason with useless Scots pride."

Wearied with trying to make her see his position, he shook his head. With quick movements, he finished dressing. "We shall see in the long run." With that, he stalked to the door, not looking back.

"Am I to remain here as prisoner? Dawn is upon us. Many chores require my attention below," she called.

"You remain. Later I shall return to take you below stairs, at which time you shall declare your acceptance of me as lord here." He paused, hand on the door. "Or your men in the oubliette will starve until you see reason."

"How vile! To starve prisoners—"

"Ah, they shan't face that grim fate unless you prove obstinate. Think hard, *faidhaich*, before my return."

He slammed the door with a resounding finality.

Chapter 9

Guillaume smiled, satisfied over the fine meal, a pleasant night passed in a soft bed and prospects of the future. "I love you, Julian, and willingly would follow you into the very jaws of Hell. But I'm weary of war and more than ready to settle down to fireside and a wife. A quandary you force upon us humble servants with this choice. Both women are so hard upon the eyes."

The jesting comments addressed Julian's question concerning the fate of the remaining daughters of The Shane: which one did they want? "Both holdings are rich in lands and resources," Julian said. "That leaves the ladies as the deciding factor."

"No reason to rush, Julian. Mayhap you were bitten by the peculiar need to lay claim to Glenrogha—even before you sighted the fortress or its lady. Neither Guillaume nor I go forth under such an enchantment." Simon smiled, clearly seeing no need to settle matters in haste.

At the mention of enchantment, Julian flinched inwardly. All that morn he'd pushed aside Tamlyn's strange utterance, but Simon's words summoned forth the odd memory and the persistent unease behind it.

"No witchery holds sway over me," he snapped. Too harsh to sound casual.

"Only a jest, Brother. Though even you must admit it is odd how you fixed your sight on this holding without prior knowledge of it or the maid. You're a man of incisive judgment. Yet, from first breath after Edward granted the charter, you were determined to claim this fief, as if you twigged Glenrogha was fated to be yours." Failing to notice how his musings soured Julian's mood, he raised his chalice. "What say, when I return from taking Kinloch, that Guillaume and I joust for the hands of the fair ladies? Neither of us walks under spell."

"Only knaves and lackwits joust with you. Last time I proved dimwitted enough to accept a challenge, you cut the girth on my saddle." Guillaume slapped Simon on the back as they rose. "Come, Julian and I shall bid you away to Kinloch before one of these witchy sisters casts evil-eye upon you, Simon."

Julian stood with Guillaume, observing Simon leading the knights away, followed by the hobelars, archers, soldier of foot, and lastly the loaned mercenaries from Edward—a grim, hard-bitten bunch with hungry eyes and empty souls. Julian knew his brother shared his apprehension for Simon striking off alone to take Kinloch.

That and more weighed upon their minds. Julian felt the sadness hovering between them, as if a ghostly presence lingered at their shoulders.

Eyes skimming over the high hills ringing Glen Shane, Guillaume spoke. "It is sad Christian is not here. He would have liked these purple highlands. Kinmarch's lands could've been his. We could rebuild the castle to guard the entrance to the passes."

Julian stared at the ground, swallowing the pain constricting his throat. "An irony. He deserved to be here whilst I, his murdering brother—"

"Silence! I shall hear no such words from you," Guillaume barked. Julian turned away, only to have his brother grab his arm to restrain him. "Christian found God's peace. It is a shame you cannot do the same. Mayhap speaking of him and his passing will finally put these misreckonings into the grave with him."

"Leave me be," Julian snarled, jerking against Guillaume's hand.

"Christian would not allow you to carry this burden of guilt. He loved you. You loved him. Simon or I would have made the same choice had we been there. Bloody hell, Julian, it is a sin to never speak his name. To do so keeps him alive in our hearts. His spirit follows us in all we do. His gentle soul watches over us."

"Even more, since entering this heathen glen—I feel him. I catch myself turning to ask his thoughts on our new lands." Julian stared at the flock of ravens taking to the sky, flushed by the troop's movements, as if he sought their answers or mercy. "Christian always protected my back. The one instance he needed me, I was not there."

"By God, Julian, the wound of his death festers in your soul. Grant yourself absolution. Has it not occurred to you how driven you were to claim Glenrogha from the first? You never considered the other holdings. It was always Glenrogha. A near obsession. Mayhap it is why you feel his presence so strongly. His hand guided you here where the Fates offer you the chance for the peace you desperately seek. You cannot continue to let our brother's death and the nightmare of Berwick to rot your soul."

Closing his eyes, Julian squeezed the lids tight. "My mind bends inward. These black tempers grow more uncontrollable, as do pains accompanying them. I pray to find some measure of solace here in these mist-shrouded hills."

Guillaume's eyes roved slowly over the purple ring of high peaks, seeming to embrace and protect the whole of Glen Shane. He paused, listening to the screeches of the ravens. "I am not one given to imaginings, but I must agree there is something . . . different about this valley. It is a queer, moody place that bespeaks of witchery. These Scots, even their females, possess a stubborn streak I think our king woefully underestimates. Do you think you shall find healing in this pagan land with a lass like the Lady Tamlyn. She might fight you in all you hope to achieve."

"Something pulls me to this place. I feel . . . I belong." He shrugged, embarrassed to speak so to his brother, who'd likely think him mad. "As for being content, I only know I cannot go on as I have and survive. This may be my only chance to salvage something of myself."

"Then make haste. Take the Lady Tamlyn to wife, see her quicken with your seed and name your son Christian."

Julian nodded. "Can you forgive me for losing our holdings?"

"Challon was always yours, never in part Simon's or mine." He raised his hand to stay his brother's argument, knowing it well. "It could never belong to your father's bastards, though you did everything in your power to make the world believe otherwise. Simon and I were satisfied being your knights bannerets. It was not necessary to offer us Lochshane and Kinloch. I know it cost you dear to procure papal dispensation for our marriages."

"Not so. Edward finally has revenge upon the Sisters MacShane for scorning his matchmaking efforts this decade past. He sent them dragons for husbands. I wish each of you to be lord of your own fortress and lands.

Saints' blood, for far too long we have lived, slept and even ate warfare. Here I sense there is a promise of something better for the weary Dragons of Challon. I am eager to see heather in bloom. My secret hope is to breed horses, the best stallions any knight could crave to possess. Most of all, I want children. Sons, if God wills it. I wish to dandle them upon my knee, kiss them, tickle them silly, tell them stories of their uncle Christian. I so need . . ."

His muscles clenched, knotting in the coil of black, empty hunger. Julian feared the cracks in his sanity widened with every breath. Tremors racked his body as he fought against them with his warrior's will, this dark malaise tearing him apart.

Guillaume stood, frustrated at his inability to help his brother. "Cry, by damn! Cry for him! Cry for yourself! You have carried this foul burden too long. Christian would never want you to hurt so for him."

Julian drew himself up, summoning control over the raw despondency. "Allow time. As we build lives here, you shall see me heal." He spoke the words for Guillaume's comfort, not with any real conviction, though mayhap with a spark of hope. "Come, let us inspect these Pict vitrified walls. See if they are as ugly up close as they were from afar."

Tamlyn stirred in her dark sleep, disturbed by the noise.

Dulump . . . dulump . . . dulump . . .

Pounding hooves sounded in the fog. It swirled around Tamlyn to where she couldn't see anything. Turning full circle, she sought her way, but the heavy mist shrouded all.

Dulump . . . dulump . . . dulump . . .

Suddenly, the black steed broke free of the mist, the bridle jingling as it tossed its thick mane. The rider was without helm. The beautiful face of Julian Challon became clear. He repeated the action of offering her a rose. The instant she touched his ring, lightning flashed and she was spirited away.

As before, she was carried to the horrible town of death. Smoke and stench of burning flesh nearly made her gag. Choking, she fled, running down the narrow wynds. She broke from the avenue into an open area. Feeling exposed, she pulled up.

Ravens screamed as she spotted Challon on his knees beside the public well. His body shuddered from dry heaves. When she approached, he looked up, tears in his eyes, startled and confused. As she neared the well, he rose and stepped before her, but not before she saw it was stuffed full with the bodies of women. He pulled her into his arms. His hand pressed her head to his shoulder, holding her tightly so she couldn't see the hideous sight.

Lightning cracked. Blinking, she gazed about an open moorland. By the looks of the countryside, she assumed it was not Scotland. A man knelt beside the prostrate form of another. Others hovered nearby, whispering. Her steps carried her closer, the soldiers moving aside at the ghostly touch of her hand.

On his knees, his body jerking from choking back tears, Challon's arms cradled a body. She blanched as she saw he embraced a young man. So very like him, it could have been Challon ten years earlier. Tamlyn knelt on the other side of the corpse, tears of empathy flooding her. Her shaking hand reached out and brushed the curls off the forehead of the young man held in the curve of Challon's arms. The kenning told her the boy had found peace. The Sidhe had encircled the loving soul as they prepared to carry it on the final journey to Annwyn—the Otherworld.

Intense sorrow pressed inwardly upon her mind and heart. This lad, so beautiful, was too young to die. She looked up into Challon's face, saw the madness of grief in the green eyes. Aching for him, she placed her hand to the side of his face, wishing desperately to have some sway to ease his crippling pain.

"His last thought was worry for you, my lord. He wanted to thank you for being so brave and doing what you must to spare him," she offered in solace.

Challon blinked in shock. For an instant hatred clearly roared through him at her daring to speak the young man's thoughts. Then he reached with a bloodstained hand and pressed hers tightly against his cheek as if her touch could soothe the anguish.

The ravens' screams grew deafening as they took to the sky, turning it black.

The standing stone circle loomed on the far tor, visible from any point in the small protective wood. Here the earth was dark and fertile, cool beneath her bare feet. She always felt restored by the hallowed place of the Auld Race. Toward the far end of the enchanted ring of apple trees was a small pool at the base of a narrow waterfall.

The rushing water whispered soothing promises, luring Tamlyn with its sweet, healing sound. If she could reach there and dive below the crystalline depths, she knew the peace she sought would be hers.

Pausing at the water's edge to slide her soft woolen chainse and sleeveless tunic over her head, she draped them on the tall ferns.

In respect, she knelt by the rippling waters, arms opened and extended, whispering the dark words of the charm of blessing, offering thanks to Annis, Lady of the Pool.

With the spell cast, Tamlyn stepped into the water and sighed as the coolness slid over her hot skin. The pool wasn't deep, scarcely over her shoulders at most points.

Floating to the falls, she stood under the pounding spray to allow the water to soak her long hair. Her breasts tightened in response to the cold and a shiver crawled over her body with the sensual pleasure of a ghostly lover's caress, wakening an aching hunger.

The snorting of a horse broke the stillness. The sound drawing nearer within the swirling, thickening fog, alerting her she was no longer alone in the sacred circle. Bridle fittings jingled with the tinkling of faery bells. Rare. A horse's fey sense usually stopped it from entering the enchanted forest.

A black stallion materialized from the shifting mists, rode by a knight in black mail. She knew him, her mind spoke the hushed warning. A great lord.

Her eyes searched about her as she treaded water. She expected to see more knights in his wake. Only the sound of unseen ravens calling from the fog followed the warrior. The horse danced closer, tossing its heavy mane in ripples, the head flung in barely contained energy.

Tamlyn pushed through the water, hoping to reach the bank where her clothes were. As she neared the edge, she judged the horse and rider would intercept her. Turning in panic, she swam back to the opposite side.

The man never took his warlock eyes off her. With a nudge of a golden spur, the knight sent the majestic beast to rear, the hooves slashing high in the air. The horse landed, dancing, sidestepping to keep measure with her progress to the far side. Again, it arrived there just ahead of her.

Frantic, Tamlyn spun once more, going back toward her clothing, just to have the knight steer the black warhorse to her destination. She was barely able to gasp for breath, forced to stop in the middle of the pond and admit defeat. The horse and man could play this game until dark and never grow winded.

The warrior all in black dismounted, holding the rein in his right hand. Green eyes flicked over her nakedness, unhidden by the clear waters. Cool insolence was all she read there.

"Never run from me," he commanded.

Dropping the rein, he marched into the water, ignoring clothes, mail habergeon and mantle. His long strides brought him to stand waist deep in the pool before her. His eyes ignited with a demon's glow. Knowing he could see into the crystalline liquid, she wrapped her arms about her to shield her breasts from his lust.

He reached out and pulled her arm away, hauling her toward him as he moved forward. For several breaths, he just stared at her body, swirling emotions blazing in his eyes.

Long fingers slid up her arm to her shoulder, as he grabbed the back of her neck, preventing any attempt to resist. With equal determination, Tamlyn tugged against the hold, but he followed. He permitted her small retreats until she felt the waterfalls against her back.

"Never run from me. *Tha sibh liom.*" *You are mine.* His husky declaration was uttered close to her face.

Dragon-green eyes claimed her soul as his head lowered, his hot mouth opening on hers. It was not a gentle kiss, but one of branding. Giving no quarter, he would accept only her complete surrender. He tasted wild, as intoxicating as summer mead.

Her heart thundered with fear, pounded with wanting, a longing the likes she never knew could exist.

Filled with rebellion, she held back for an instant. Wanting to resist. Wanting to protect herself. Soon her arms clung around his neck, her body softly arching to his. Her lips molded under his with all the passions he evoked. Her trembling hand fisted, weaving in his silky blue-black curls . . . and held on for dear life.

His hard mouth slashed across her willing one, taking her lips. Spellbound, she followed his sensual lead. She wanted to learn all the forbidden secrets of this rough magic. She would sell her soul to have him.

Tamlyn pressed against his solid chest. Wet chain mail was cold against her bare breasts. She didn't care, disappointed it was mail and not his flesh.

As if he fathomed her urgency, his left hand slid down her back, moving lower, lifting and fitting their bodies hip to hip. It was still not enough for Tamlyn. Not enough for him. The waterfalls flooded over them, anointing their driving passion with the blessing from the goddess Annis.

The flowing water shifted, changing, as the crystalline streams of the falls transmuted into yellow-orange flames that engulfed them in a sea of fire. Never breaking the kiss, he seemed unaware of the change. She was. The wall of sizzling heat consumed them, embraced them.

Alarm mounted until she wanted to scream. She must scream. She had to scream or die! Yet, breaking the bond with this dark warrior would also feel like dying.

Suddenly a cacophony arose about them. It was not Tamlyn who screamed, but a thousand hard cries of frantic ravens taking wing and filling the sky until it was black.

Chapter 10

The slamming of the chamber door yanked Tamlyn from sleep. Resting on her belly, she pushed up on her palms and blinked. The soft tartan covered only her hips and legs, but she welcomed the coolness of the dark room. Her flesh burned.

The dream washed over her, nearly sucking her under. She yearned to close her eyes and go back there to the waterfalls . . . back to him. Her body pulsed from the warrior's touch, as if she had actually lain with him. The images scared her. Terrified her.

Her heart pounded out erratic rhythms of fear. Only was it truly alarm?

Then she sensed *him*. The kenning reached out and brushed against his mind.

"Good." Challon stepped from the shadows. "You awaken."

How long had he been there watching her? Her fuzzy mind struggled to break free of the dream, but Tamlyn finally understood the Dragon had slammed the door on purpose.

Maidenly modesty should have made her clutch the

plaide to cover her body. Yet some vague impulse, a feeling almost feline, drove her instead to arch her spine and stretch as a cat lazy from soaking up the afternoon sun. Strange, she wanted Challon to gaze upon her body. To provoke his lust. Womanly instincts coming to life within her guided Tamlyn, whispering there were ways to control a man that had nothing to do with fighting him.

Tamlyn eyed the Dragon, judging his mood. After dawnbreak she'd awoken to find Challon wasn't within the chamber. Evidence of his presence lingered with a pulsing vibrancy, almost with the twinkling of faerydust. His stimulating male scent clung to the pillows, bedding—on her skin.

Then there were the dreams . . . dark dreams so acute, so achingly real her body throbbed with unfulfilled need. Images so vivid, sharpest to the smallest detail, they now seemed memories of actual events. Echoes of something long ago?

Steeling herself, she reached out with the kenning, trying to see into Julian Challon's his mind. She wanted to know this complex man. Her fey gift brushed against his inner force, so strong, she almost flinched. A shiver skittered up Tamlyn's spine. Their eyes met and held, guarded.

Julian smiled. Aye, his Cait Sidhe just assumed human form and sheathed her claws. For now. Her long supple spine was arched, allowing Julian the tantalizing view of the shadowy curves of her breasts.

He looked his fill.

It was a vision that left Julian's mouth arid as the deserts of the Holy Lands. Instead of scurrying under the covers, Tamlyn remained balanced on her palms, her rich gold hair spilled down her back.

Before he found his tongue, the door pushed open and

Tamlyn's maid entered. Several pages trailed after the woman, fetching pails of heated water. Tamlyn gathered the tartan to her breasts whilst the lads emptied the buckets into the tub. "I ordered you a bath," Julian informed her.

As this parade of servants passed between them, neither Julian nor Tamlyn spoke.

Strolling to the table, Julian picked up some shelled hazelnuts and popped them into his mouth, but barely tasted the treat. His action was a cover for how she unsettled him. Should Tamlyn find her full power as a woman, he'd be lost. So odd, each time he saw her, he found her more pleasing to his eyes, as if her beauty increased with familiarity.

Or was it her spell coiling tighter about him?

His gaze never left her as the servant came to hold up a blanket, so she could climb from the bed unmolested by his stare. Julian rested against the table and crossed his booted legs at the ankles. His brows lifted in provocation as he displayed no intention of quitting the chamber.

He noticed the strong emotions in her golden eyes. She half expected he would stay, wanted him to. This side of her nature asserting itself scared her. He saw the confusion.

Tamlyn asked with disdain, "You stay, Lord Challon? It is not proper."

"Julian."

"Pardon?" The huge eyes batted, puzzled.

"I would hear my name from your lips, Tamlyn." His expression had to be predatory. He couldn't help it. His arms crossed over his chest to emphasize his resolve. "And aye, I stay."

A blush flooded her as she wrapped the cloth about

her form, leaving it loose to hang about her hips in the back. "You plan to watch as well, Lord Challon?"

"Julian," he corrected, one side of his mouth quirking with a wicked twitch. "Aye, again."

He saw her swallow, flustered by the warring emotions within her. She was tempted to play siren, yet the beautiful virgin was scared of him, scared of her own womanly power. Sucking in courage, Tamlyn crossed to the tub and unwrapped the wool. Holding it until Roselynne, her maidservant, took the ends to create a curtain against his hungry eyes.

Stepping into the steaming water, she sat with her back to him. He almost laughed aloud as Roselynne winked at Tamlyn, before folding the fabric and setting it on the bench. The wink was one of encouragement. He had an ally, it seemed.

Roselynne brought the rag and pot of soap to her lady. "Shall I stay?"

"Aye," Tamlyn gasped, obviously wanting a buffer between them.

Julian growled in the same breath, "No." He raised two fingers and motioned toward the door in dismissal.

Roselynne looked from Julian to Tamlyn, her lady's defiant glare silently ordering her to remain. With a twinkle in her eye, the maid curtsied before him. "As you wish, Lord Challon."

As the door closed, he heard Tamlyn mutter, "Traitor. What about my wish?" but it was spoken without rancor.

A flush crawled over her beautiful skin. Tamlyn leaned forward against her knees to shield herself.

The door jerked open and Moffet rushed in. Used to entering Julian's chambers without knocking, he pulled up short when he spotted Tamlyn in the tub. Turning red, he backed up a few paces.

"Beg pardon, Lord Challon," his voiced cracked. "I came as ordered."

Julian grinned unrepentantly at Tamlyn, wondering who was more flustered, Moffet or she. "So you did, my young squire. The Lady Tamlyn is sufficiently hidden. Come, remove my mail." When the lad hesitated to go past the tub, Julian snapped playfully, "Moffet, the lady is soon to be my wife. You need to accustom yourself to her presence within my chambers."

Blushing, the squire jumped to follow Julian to the long bench. Mounting the three-legged stool, he unlaced the aiguillettes and released the buckles on the heavy hauberk.

Tamlyn allowed her long hair to fall forward as a shield. She needn't have bothered. Too embarrassed, Moffet never took his eyes from his master. Just the opposite, Julian wore a grin saying nothing could veil her from him. Peeking through her hair, Tamlyn covertly watched Moffet unbuckle and remove his master's arming jack.

Taking it with him, Moffet seized the chance to escape. "I shall carry the mail to the sand barrel, my Lord Challon."

Julian absently waved permission.

Stretching his back, Julian ended the motion by pulling the tunic over his head and tossing it to the bench. He liked how Tamlyn stared at him, though she'd loathe admitting she did. Her keen eyes roved over the lines of his broad shoulders, his honed warrior's chest and waist, as he sauntered to the tub and picked up the pot of soap.

She tensed as he reached out to gather her long hair, the bottom half wet from dragging in the water. He carefully separated the locks to plait them. The way Tamlyn tilted her head, almost in a lull, he could tell she found the rhythmic pull of his hands weaving the stands soothing.

Her voice was husky. "Are you planning to bathe, Lord Challon?"

He almost laughed aloud. She'd tried to sound so casual, yet her knees trembled. "An invitation, Tamlyn?" His hand stroked over the back of her head, savoring the sleek softness of the deep gold hair. "By the lack of response I take it the answer is no. Pity. I have too much work this day—though you tempt me. Another time, mayhap. A promise for a rainy day? I merely wished to visit you and I removed the tunic so it would not get soaked."

"A dragon playing lady's maid? Surely it is forbidden in the Dragon's creed?" She glanced over her shoulder at him.

His hand slid down her neck, then across her shoulder, his thumb tracing a hard trail. She shivered. Julian laughed, mimicking her accent, "Och, a dragon is a mystical beastie and may do as it wishes with none to gainsay."

"Assistance from a dragon might prove dangerous. They are not thought to be gentle creatures."

His laughter increased as he saw the prickles raise on her sensitive skin. "My lady, you have much to discover about dragons."

Her gold eyes stared at him oddly, poignantly. A tear glittered at the corner of one.

"What is it, Tamlyn?"

She shrugged, hugging her knees tighter to her chest.

"Speak freely to me. We have much to learn about each other."

"When you laughed, the sun broke through the clouds in your eyes. I do not think you laugh enough, Lord Challon," she answered softly, blinking away the tears.

"I am a warrior, Tamlyn, have known little else my whole life. It is not cause for laughter. I want peace here and perhaps with encouragement I shall find a reason." He ran the soap rag over her back, creating foam.

Julian's blood thrummed when he saw the responsiveness of her soft flesh. Restraint, he cautioned himself. He moved the rag over her gently, wishing the cloth were his hand. "By royal decree, we are betrothed. A betrothal contract binds us in the eyes of the church, even more than marriage vows. We are man and wife in all but act and deed."

"My people have always permitted our women to choose their own husbands, Lord Challon. I cannot be commanded to marry a stranger."

He watched as she swallowed the emotions rising within her, that stubborn chin tilting in an effort to control them. At the set of her jaw, Julian knew her rebellious blood was coming to a quick boil over his declaring they were betrothed. Tamlyn was too spirited, too beautiful in her wild pagan ways to be broken, but he had to gain her acceptance speedily before Edward took a hand in matters.

"You say that as if I force this decision upon you. I have no choice either. Edward decreed I must marry one of the daughters of the Laird of Glen Shane." Julian pushed the point. "Would you rather I wed either of your sisters?"

He smiled when she didn't reply. Gad, she was stubborn. "This morn I visited the kirk and spoke with Sir Priest." He allowed the foam to slither over her shoulder and down to her breast. A frisson shook her as she slumped deeper in the water to prevent the suds from reaching her nipple.

"How did you find Malcolm?"

"Malcolm?" Julian heard jealousy tinge his voice. It

was surely a sign of madness—being jealous of a man of the Cross. Aye, but that particular priest had fathered seven sons.

"Aye, Malcolm Ogilvie, my uncle. My mother's brother."

Julian considered. "Why does he not rule Kinloch or Lochshane?"

"Morag and Caitrona, my aunts, held those fiefs. Since neither bore daughters, Rowanne became lady at Lochshane and Kinloch passed to Raven. Titles and lands pass through the distaff side of the Ogilvies of Glen Shane. In the Culdee Church—the Celtic Church—the priesthood passes from father to son. Malcolm descended from the Culdee line. His eldest son, Jamie, shall lead the kirk next."

He swirled the rag down her arm, allowing his knuckles to brush against the side of her breast. Her breath sucked in and held, but she didn't challenge his advances. First step in gentling a horse was to allow it to become used to its master's touch, his scent. Julian employed this principle with Tamlyn.

All Julian wanted was to fling the rag aside and allow his hands to slide over every inch of her golden skin. His eyes were drawn to the pale breasts bobbing just under the water. Their seductive sway made a shiver to crawl up his neck and across his scalp.

This pagan witch just might kill him.

Fighting the dizziness brought on by her scent, Julian exhaled. "The visit to a church full of pagan carvings was . . . ah . . . enlightening."

Tamlyn's lilting laughter burst forth. "Och, the sheila-na-gigs. Aye, it was surely that."

Julian thought back upon the carvings of females exposing their genitals, and shook his head, still having a hard time accepting it. "Aye, I am unused to seeing pagan fertility symbols within a Christian church."

When the rag roved to the front of her shoulder—and nonchalantly downward toward her breast—Tamlyn's hands locked on his wrist to prevent farther encroachment. "I can manage the rest, Lord Challon."

He leaned close, whispering against her ear, "Consider all the delights you deny us."

When she didn't relent, he dropped the cloth into the water with a plop and moved to pour himself a goblet of wine. Leaning back against the table, he sipped the drink and studied her. She had no idea how she provoked him.

Julian wasn't a patient man. Used to command, rarely had he ever bent his mind to compromise.

He wanted her. Now.

His life had been stagnant this past year, guilt over Christian's death eating at his soul. For the first time since Wales, he was forward-looking, eager to begin his life here. The reawakening of his desires for a home and family were so strong that the need for self-control was almost painful. He had made mistakes with Tamlyn already, so he reminded himself. No more.

"Are you going to remain?"

Julian could tell Tamlyn waited for him to leave so she could get out of the tub. Suppressing a smile, he almost laughed at her dark glower. Tamlyn was not passing fond of patience either.

Julian smirked inside, yet kept his expression indifferent. "You shall prune and shrivel like an old woman if you stay in there much longer."

She put him in mind of a wet cat ready to hiss. "If you would hand me the drying cloth." She indicated the blanket of baize on the long bench.

Acting as if he saw it for the first time, he held it up. "This?"

"*Amadan.*" When he didn't move, she snapped, "Bring it to me."

Julian moved closer. Still out of her reach. Holding it chest high, he let the large sheet unfold. Her flashing eyes spoke her fury, but he liked baiting her. In that instant, he realized being with Tamlyn made him happy. The sensation was so foreign, he almost failed to recognize it.

"Hand it to me . . . please." It hurt her to tack on the please.

The right side of his mouth pulled into a sensual half smile. "Shall we compromise, Tamlyn? I come halfway— you come halfway."

He stood holding it as she considered outwaiting him, her stubbornness biting at her. The chill of the room caused her to shiver. Spring might be upon them, but even so, it was unseasonably cold. Giving up the pretense of her modesty, she rose from the tub. The water sluiced off her skin. She didn't shrink, but threw her shoulders back, proud of her body, and just now beginning to understand the power it could hold over a man.

Julian felt gut punched.

His game of playful torment now came back on him as she turned the tables, her sensual beauty nearly driving all reason from his mind. He wanted her. Badly. The pounding within his body was blinding. Even so, Julian knew this wanting went much deeper than mere urges of the body. He *needed* her. Yet, in some fey fashion, he sensed she could be his salvation from the darkness that consumed his mind.

He would kill for this woman. He would die for her.

She stepped from the tub and walked to the sheet of

wool, allowing him to wrap it around her. He did, ending with her in his arms. He leaned close, letting her feel the heat off his skin, the scent of his male body. He was visibly aroused. She arched into him, so close.

He wanted to reach out and claim what was his, take her in a hundred ways. He dare not. She had to accept him. If she didn't come to him freely, in mind and heart, something in him would die. The darkness would claim him and there'd be nothing left.

Part of him feared becoming like Edward. Since the death of his beloved Queen Eleanor, that spark of humanity she instilled in the king had turned to cold ash, leaving nothing but hard-bitten cruelty. Julian would rather die than continue life headed down that same path.

Tamlyn held the power to drive away the blackness of night devouring his soul. She was the beacon by which he could try to find something better in life, the sun at daybreak.

Their bodies close, almost brushing, he let the confused jumble of sexual desire and emotions spill over him, warmed by the magical radiance she exuded. After feeling so dead inside for the last year, all these violent extremes were almost too much to bear. He closed his eyes against the way she stirred his senses and let her power storm through him. The muscles in his jaw flexed, struggling for the control, giving her this chance to accept his nearness.

Oh, please accept me, his soul whispered.

He swallowed the dryness in his throat, the muscles so corded it was hard to speak. "You need to sit by the fire. You shiver."

Tamping down the deep hunger, he helped her into the solar to sit on the bearskin throw before the fire. She watched him warily as he added more peat, the blue flames spreading quickly.

"You have met my lord father," Tamlyn began. It was not a question, but a statement. "Before you . . ."

Her voice broke, unable to finish the sentence, an arrow that pierced Julian's heart. Pushing down the reaction, he concentrated on the chore of building the fire, forcing his mind to only that. The black emptiness still raged within him, howling for her light, her warmth. He paused from adding the peat and glanced at Tamlyn staring at him with those luminous cat-eyes.

"Several seasons past." Their meeting just struck him, one of those forgotten fragments of memory really. Only now did he see the import. "He said I should come to the Highlands for a stay, that I would find peace here. Did you know that?"

Stunned, she said nothing, the importance of his reply not lost on her.

He had delivered her father, a man she obviously held in great esteem, to Edward. How did one overcome that obstacle? Feeling pressure, regret, Julian jumped up and searched for something to do, to keep his emotions under control. He tried not to read too much into The Shane's asking him to visit him and his family. The conclusion was unavoidable.

Nausea rolled in his stomach at the irony.

Well, he'd come, but not as The Shane expected. How different life would have been . . . he swallowed the pang of anguish in his soul. Tamlyn and he would have met in fellowship, instead of the strife of war. Without doubt, he would've been captivated by Tamlyn, wanted to possess her. They might have a son by now.

Instead, he'd followed Edward to Wales and Christian had died. He wanted to throw back his head and howl his madness.

His throat was parched, yet he dare not drink more wine. His emotions were just too unstable around her, too rattled by this new turn of the screw. He required all his wits.

Concentrating on the moment, he fetched a comb for her hair. Figuring his mind was best occupied, he picked up his knife and a whetstone and carried them in as well.

Tamlyn accepted the comb without word and quietly began working tangles out of her hair. A safe distance away, he settled in the chair and pretended interest in sharpening the dagger, keeping at bay all these wild thoughts. A quiet moments like this might chafe most men, not him. They both seemed content in the companionable silence, leaving Julian to draw some small measure of hope from this peacefulness.

Tamlyn stared at the dark lord, while working the tangles from her long hair. She tried to come to terms with what Challon just told her. Her lord father had sought him out and asked him to come to Glen Shane. Since both of her sisters were in deep mourning, there was only one conclusion she could reach—Hadrian had been contemplating a marriage for her to Challon.

It was much to absorb. She loved her father dearly. He was a constant joy and so handsome with his red hair and pale green eyes. All the ladies twittered and blushed in his presence. Fear over his fate ripped at her heart.

Despite all, Challon drew her. Oh, how much simpler it would've been had he come seasons ago! Instead of arriving as friend, he came as conqueror and delivered her lord father to the hateful English King.

She forced herself to speak. "My men . . . the ones in the oubliette . . ."

"They were never in the oubliette, Tamlyn," he said quietly.

"But you told me—"

"I merely prodded your mind. They are held under guard in the barrack's tower. They fare well." He regarded her with those hooded eyes. "I am not an ogre."

"Just a dragon." She offered him a faint smile. There were questions in her mind, but it was hard to think clearly around him. "Your brothers—you say they are to marry with my sisters. Will they make good husbands for them?"

He answered frankly. "My brothers may be bastard born, but none dare speak it to me. They are good men, ones I put above all others. I paid dearly for dispensation for the marriages. Guillaume is calm and steady. He should suit the Lady Lochshane. Simon is reckless in spirit, loves to laugh, but when needed he is a rock. The Lady Kinloch is serene, sensible, a good balance for him. I owe my brothers much in life. They chose to follow me. Your sisters could not find better husbands, Tamlyn."

She lowered her eyes to the comb in her hand, not seeing it, listening to what could not be heard. She loved her sisters and wanted their happiness ensured. The kenning was at peace with this. Accepting, she gave a small nod.

"You and I must to seek resolve. You have a duty to your people. They look to you for guidance. There comes a time when we choose for the whole, not for ourselves. Edward means to crush this rebellion and his manner can be most foul." Closing his eyes, his face turned ashen as he seemed to walk through the hell of his memories. "Pray God, Edward does not do to Glen Shane what he did at Berwick. Tamlyn, you have no idea how ugly that can be."

Tears welled up at his words. Aye, she did know. She was coming to understand this man as she, too, walked through his memories. The town of dying—it must be Berwick. What Challon had lived through.

That they shared this fey bond told her much.

Her mind saw the lad who died in his arms. His brother. She choked on a sob, her heart mourning as she recalled his horribly mangled body. No man so beautiful, so pure in spirit, should suffer such an end. No brother should have to face what Challon did to ease his passing. She shook with the pain of that image now forever burned into her memory.

Challon surged from the chair, coming to his knees before her. The freshly sharpened dagger was in his hand. Obviously, he mistook her tears for his young brother as ones shed over sorrow for her own situation.

"You do not understand. I will stand between Edward and Glen Shane. I will be your shield." He grabbed her hand and pushed the knife in it, wrapping his fingers around hers. Forcing her to hold it. "You wish to be rid of me, Tamlyn? Then do it! Here is your chance."

Tamlyn stared into Challon's eyes, drowning in his pain, knowing she'd sooner take the knife to herself than to harm this man.

So much had changed with his coming. Her father's destiny hung in the balance. The betrothals of his daughters, decided by a man not even their king. Knowing she felt things for Julian Challon, their dark bond.

She needed time.

His voice was harsh. "Go ahead, Tamlyn. Use the knife! What stops you?"

She could barely see through the tears as she tried to drop the knife. He wouldn't let her. His hand around hers squeezed tightly. His body vibrated with the raw emotions as he tugged her hand and the dagger toward his bare chest, pointing the tip at the spot where his heart beat.

"Do it!" he barked.

Tamlyn gasped as she saw into his pain, understood that Challon almost hoped she would use the knife to end his torment. His wounded soul had rotted with this fetid blackness for too long. But now, his thoughts were so clear. His desire for a home, a son. To show him glimpses of this possible future, and then to snatch it away, was just too much for his shattered heart to bear.

"Accept me or kill me. Now."

She tried to blink away the tears. "You do not care?"

"If I cannot have some measure of peace, a home, a family . . ." The words lodged in his throat. For the longest time, they remained frozen. His eyes beseeched her, seeming to ask something of her. Something only she could grant. He finally pleaded, "Say it."

"My lord—what must I say?" Tamlyn struggled to comprehend his words, too stunned by the depth of agony coiling within him.

A man so powerful, a king's champion. Yet, it was as if he believed only she could heal him.

"My name," he replied hoarsely.

She reeled as visions flashed through her mind. The dark knight and the rose. The town of death and ravens. His brother's dying. So many things. Too many things. The blackness of his despair sucked at her and she had to fight against the paralyzing anguish tearing this man apart. Her body trembled, his agony hers.

"Is that so much to ask?" he begged.

Tamlyn tried to answer. The images still came, nearly drowning her. His young brother, so like Challon, them laughing together. Challon crying over the crumpled body. Him raising his sword high and driving it into the chest of the young boy, saving Christian from an agonizing, lingering death. The howl of madness that seized him as life departed the body on the ground.

"*Baoth smuain.*" Foolish thought. Julian jumped to his feet. He closed his eyes tightly, as if he struggled to gather the frayed threads of his sanity.

So shaken by all the painful glimpses into his soul, Tamlyn shook free of the lethargy. She grew aware he'd pulled on his tunic and was leaving the room.

Through the tears, she called out, "Julian!"

Too late. The door closed.

Chapter 11

Jerking up, Tamlyn took several breaths before she could accept the reality of being in the lord's chamber at Glenrogha.

Growing bored, while waiting for Challon's return, she'd fallen asleep. The dreams had come again. Stronger, more detailed. More arousing.

The door opened and Auld Bessa came in. "I fetched your supper, lass. Sit and eat."

"My head aches, Bessa." She frowned at her teacher as the pain increased.

"You dreamed. Dark dreams. Ravens carry messages from Annwn, the Otherworld. Messages for those wise enough to understand. Your soul kens him."

Tamlyn frowned, hating Bessa could read her thoughts about Challon so easily. She shrugged indifference. "I do not ken who you mean."

A cat-after-cream smile touched Bessa's lips. "The braw one. It is time, Tamlyn, to speak of the dark earl. This Norman warlord is worthy of reflection."

"Bessa, he vexes my mind."

"But not your body?" Bessa clucked her tongue.

"Through the long days of my life I have seen the faces of many a warrior, looked into their hearts. Lord Challon possesses courage and fire. His coming is the will of the Auld Ones."

"The kenning whispered this to you?

"Evelynour has seen him for many months. Dressed all in the black, he comes in fog, riding a stallion of war. He holds out an offering—"

Tamlyn gasped. "A white rose!"

"Aye, blood from his hand spills onto the bloom, changing the color from white to red, then red to black. Ravens scream unseen in the fog, foretelling death and a great coming. His coming. Only you have power of the craft to exorcise his bloodstained soul. By the balefire of Samhain, Evelynour predicted his coming a year ago. Blood of the Sidhe pulses within his veins. He is their chosen one, though he does not ken it. Your destiny travels the same path as his. This you cannot escape."

Tamlyn dropped the chicken leg to the plate, suddenly not hungry.

Bessa mixed a potion and handed it to her. "Here, lass, this shall ease the pain in your head."

She took the goblet, staring at the dark mixture. None of Bessa's tansies tasted good. Hesitating, she admitted, "The dream visits me. But, how can I not stand against the man who destroyed Kinmarch, made prisoner of my lord father and now reives the holdings of both clans? He seeks to force me to the marriage bed. What of my sisters? Challon says his bastard brothers will take them as wives."

"Lord Challon has sent your sisters back to their fortresses. You cannot smooth their paths. They must fight their own battles, as shall the laird."

Hearing Bessa out, Tamlyn downed the thick brew,

then grimaced at the taste. Feeling the effects almost immediately, she had to concentrate on Bessa's words as the potion sped through her.

"I warned your lord father that John Balliol and Clan Comyn would never unite Scotland, not while the young Bruce draws breath. The seer True Thomas foretold the same. Was he not right about the death of our King Alexander? He stood before all and prophesied of Alexander's death and that Scotland would be torn in two."

"Robert Bruce is nearly as Norman as the Dragon." Tamlyn scoffed. "You ken what Highlanders call the Earl Carrick—Edward's Lordling. Small wonder, he was raised at the English's knee. Some say Longshanks loves him more than his own son."

"Aye, Norman blood from his father flows in him. And not blood of a warrior such as your Challon. Carrick's title and blood come from Lady Marjorie. Pure Celt. That binds him to this land and her ways more than even he kens. Robbie's soul belongs to Alba. The day shall arrive when he seeks to claim what is his. This Bruce is born of fire. Your sire should have heeded these warnings and stayed within the safety of Castle Kinmarch. Waited for the right time to fight. He should have considered his actions might come back on his daughters. Scotland soon will be ripped asunder, from within and without, and through those flames of destruction one man will raise his head in defiance of Edward Longshanks."

"This man, do I ken him?"

"You shall. A man of simple blood. He shall destroy much, for much has been taken from him. Everything he holds dear. This man faces a trial by fire that most could not pass. Yet in his betrayal, he shall give Scotland what she has never had—a true sense of herself. Just as your dark lord arrived on the wings of spring, the wind in autumn shall carry this man's name. He will touch both your lives with the coming storm."

Dizziness assailed Tamlyn. Her skin shivered with a frisson, but it was a cold of the soul. "Evelynour has seen more? You said she saw Challon."

"Seven seasons past, the laird sought auguries about a man. A man he called the Dragon. The man he thought would make a braw husband for you."

Tamlyn gasped. This confirmed what she feared. Her father had sought to know about Challon, with an eye to a marriage offer. How much easier it would've been had Challon come to her as a suitor instead of her conqueror. A tear formed in the corner of her eye.

"Evelynour predicted he would come with the first flush of spring. A dark warrior, a fearful man armored in black. Her prophecy is now revealed as truth. Challon's life threads are entwined with yours, Tamlyn. There is no turning back for either of you."

"What else did Evelynour see?"

"Dark shapes through flames. Blood, great famine, sorrows . . . and death. Two lovers with a love immortal, whose souls have touched before." Bessa stroked Tamlyn's cheek. "In this time of the troubles, do you not see that living under the Black Dragon's standards serves Glen Shane? Listen to the cries of the ravens, Tamlyn. Listen with the craft and not your pride. It is fated by the Auld Ones. You cannot fight their will."

"He confuses me, Bessa." Tamlyn fought the tears welling in her eyes.

"A woman learns to handle her man. The Dragon warms to you. All saw this in the Great Hall. Instead of resisting him, learn to reach his heart. Think. If something befell your Challon, would Longshanks not just

send another? Mayhap one filled with hatred for all
Scots, the same hatred that eats at this king. Mayhap an
ugly one in body and soul. Julian Challon is not so hard
to gaze upon, eh? Swallow that fool pride and listen with
the kenning. Hear what the ravens tell you about your
dark lord."

Ignoring Bessa's assessment of the Dragon, Tamlyn
pressed, "This man, the one who shall rise for Scotland?
How shall he be kenned?"

Bessa lowered her head, drawing upon her fey powers.
A shaft of light from the solar illuminated her glowing
amber eyes, seeing what could not be seen. "A tall man
is he, man above many. Brown hair streaked from the
sun, he wears the braids of *ceann-cinnidh*—a chieftain—
at his temples, though he is chief to none. Eyes bright as
jewels, the color neither blue nor green, as only a true son
of Auld Alba can own. His life will be a shooting star, but
in Scotland's darkest night, and for ages to come, sparks
from his wake light the fires of rebellion."

Bessa picked up the plate and goblet.

The potion sent its dark tendrils coursing through
Tamlyn, causing her to slide down on the bed. She fought
the sleep, fearing the dreams would come. Suddenly, she
wished she were next to the warmth of Challon's body,
sensing he could protect her. She could not to keep her
eyes open, as she gave in to the effect of the words.

She heard Bessa croon, "Sleep, Child of the Stones.
Sleep and dream of the man wrapped in the shade of
ravens. Sleep and dream of a love you have kenned
before. Sleep, Tamlyn. Sleep and prepare."

Several times Tamlyn roused.

The night grew long, and still Challon didn't return.

Exhaustion claimed her mind. Despite her fears, there were no dreams of the town of death. No knight on the black steed.

No Challon.

Dawn broke and the first rays peeked over the tor, flooding the solar. Tamlyn stirred, her hand reaching out, seeking something. She froze. She sought him. His warmth. Leaning forward, she rubbed her nose against the spot where he should have lain. The bed seemed cold, empty. Had he even been there?

Tamlyn quickly dressed in the clothing Roselynne had fetched, a soft kirtle of woad blue. Wrapping the plaid ruanna about her shoulders, she went to the door, expecting the ever-present guards there to block her way. She was surprised when the hall was empty. Was this Challon's way to say she was no longer a prisoner?

The hour was early. Only a few of her people were about their chores. They nodded in respect as she passed. She returned the greeting, sadly sensing a distance that hadn't been there before. Things had changed between them.

Oddly, Tamlyn felt apart from everyone and everything, as if a stranger in her own fortress, a place she'd lived all her life. With a newfound determination, she headed to the lady's tower and gathered her basket. Gathering herbs always brought a sense of peace. Mayhap it would again—provided the Dragon's men didn't stop her from leaving the bailey.

"Good morrow, my lady." The guard at the gate greeted at her approach. "You seek Lord Challon?"

She tried to smile. "I go to collect herbs and worts for healing."

"I will summon one of the Dragon's squires to accompany you."

"I shan't be out of sight—"

"Lord Challon would have the hide off my back. I cannot permit you to venture beyond the curtain wall without a guard."

Tamlyn opened her mouth to argue, but figured there was little use. Resigned, she waited until one came. Not Moffet, he was one of the older squires nearing the age of knighthood.

"I am Vincent, my lady. I shall accompany you. My liege would want it."

Exasperated at not having her wishes made orders, the first time since she became Countess Glenrogha, Tamlyn glared. "If I must endure a guard, remain two score paces behind me."

His dark eyes twinkled as if he understood her frustration. "Ten paces?" he countered.

She felt churlish, especially when he seemed so polite. "Ten and five."

"Very well."

She trod on at a brisk pace, doing her best to ignore the squire. The Highland fog swirled, thickening at some points to swallow him, but she could hear his steps keeping pace with her.

Odd noises in the fog drew her attention. Cautious, she paused to identify them. Ready to protect her with his life, the young squire drew his sword and moved to stand before her.

His stance eased. "Lord Challon."

The mist eddied, revealing the black horse and the man upon its back. Astride the monstrous destrier, Challon obviously had worked the animal for some time. Foam lathered the beast's neck and flanks.

Tamlyn was spellbound by his mastery of the great horse. Never had she seen a man so at one with an

animal. Using only spoken commands and his knees for
control, he had it sidestepping at a rapid pace that
brought them near enough for her to almost reach out
and touch the beast. On his whistle, it spun on its hind
legs and danced off in the opposite direction.

Shivering from the damp, she pulled the ruanna over
her head and turned away. The scene unsettled her,
though Tamlyn had trouble understanding why. Mayhap
it was the fact the horse gave its all to please the man,
and not through fear, but devotion. Few men spoke to an
animal's mind as Challon did.

Rattled, she strode away at a swift clip. Not running,
but with purpose. Only when she could see it in the distance did she realize where she'd headed—the sacred
grove, the Ring of Oaths.

Patting the horse's neck, Julian walked the charger to
cool him down. He'd worked Dragon's Blood hard. Not
battle seasoned like Pagan or Lasher, still his youngest destrier showed great promise. He hoped the three stallions
would sire the herd he planned to breed at Glenrogha.
Knights would pay dear to have mounts of their caliber.
His respect for the value of the beast was why he walked
the animal, instead of racing like the wind after Tamlyn.

Upon return to Glenrogha, he'd received word that
she'd left the fortress and gone toward the wood suppos-
edly to gather herbs. Only knowing his squire trailed
after her stayed his panic. She wasn't trying to escape,
he kept repeating in his head. Giving into the pressing
urgency, he put spurs to the horse.

He needed to see her, reassure himself he'd not put her
off by revealing too much of his pain, his hunger.

He'd stayed away last night until she fell asleep, know-

ing if he came back he'd muddle the situation even more.
The emptiness in him gnawed at Julian. He wanted to
take her in an effort to bind her to him, brand her as his.
A woman could be controlled through physical intimacy.
Yet something in his heart whispered it would be a
hollow victory. He needed Tamlyn to accept him.

Some fey sense guided him to her path. Guillaume
had asked whether Christian's shade had steered him in
seeking Glenrogha. Was his brother's ghostly hand
trying to direct Julian to find some measure of peace?
He'd like to think it was Christian's spirit. He sensed a
sentient consciousness behind the force. In England,
such thoughts might cause him to question his sanity. In
this valley steeped in shade and mists, untouched by the
ways of the world, it seemed natural.

As he entered the circle of ancient oaks, a murder of
ravens took wing, startling Dragon's Blood into shying.
Those damn birds again. They seemed forever close, as
if they watched his every move. Spotting a flicker of
blue ahead near the pool, he nudged the horse's flanks.
After a strange refusal, the beast entered. The animal's
fear was palpable.

Carrying a basket, Tamlyn moved from one small
shrub to the next in the manner of a butterfly, flittering
from bloom to bloom. Giving sway to the passions
riding him hard, he spurred Dragon's Blood, reaching
her in a few strides.

Her stubborn chin tilted, causing him to pause. He
knew the news he brought would likely provoke Tamlyn's
rebellious spirit, but mayhap it'd also put an end to Scotland and Edward being bones of contention between
them. His king would soon wish to return to England and
take up preparations for the campaign against the French.
With Longshanks gone from Scotland—and his greedy

eyes turned to the land across the Channel—dealing with Tamlyn might be easier.

Julian dismounted, his eyes noting Vincent discreetly keeping watch. The corner of his mouth twitched, feeling empathy for the young man. This woman was hard enough for him to deal with. Julian tried to polish his squires' courtly manners, but knew they needed instruction from a lady. That task would fall to Tamlyn soon. He didn't know whether to envy them, serving such a vibrant lady, or pity them. Nodding to the squire, he raised his left hand and flicked two fingers toward the direction of the dun, dismissing him.

"You rose early this foggy morn, Tamlyn. You slept well?"

"Aye, my lord," she answered nervously.

"Are you not curious how I rested?" Julian stepped close, his elbow brushing her arm. He savored even that smallest contact, hungered for more.

Questions flooding her eyes, Tamlyn watched him. Reaching out, she tenderly brushed a stray curl off his forehead. "Your face is drawn. By the time I fell asleep, you hadn't returned. Did you rest well, Lord Challon? Did you even sleep?" Shocked that she'd touched him registered upon her face. She blushed and turned away.

Julian caught her wrist. "I kept watch on the tower . . . all night."

Tamlyn blinked surprise. "Why? As lord you can order your men to such tasks."

"I needed to be alone with my thoughts. I was unfit company and dared not risk being near you," he replied, admitting more than he intended.

She looked puzzled. "I do not understand."

Using the hold on her wrist, he pulled her slowly

against him, wrapping his arm about her waist. "I am aware your mind does not. Mayhap your body will."

Pleased there was no resistance in her, only questioning, he held her. He saw the jump in her pulse as his breath caressed her face, her breathing rising in cadence to match his. "Our bodies speak to each other. With a woman it can be a strong driving force. In a man it oft overwhelms all reason. It is hard to recall there is need to pay court, to woo you. *Is miann leam, a cushla mo foil.*" *I desire you, pulse of my blood.*

And she wanted him, too. He saw it. Witnessed the fire spreading through her, unsettling her, but she couldn't back away from the challenge any more than he could. "I try to give you room, let your mind come around to the idea you will be my lady bride soon. But I am a man, Tamlyn, and I have been lonely too long."

He lowered his mouth to hers, brushing lightly, waiting until she signaled her acceptance of him. And she did. She pressed against him, twining her fingers in the hair at the back of his head. By all that was holy, he wanted her, with an ache that nearly drove him to his knees. Had he been surer of her reactions, he'd lower her to the ground and do as his body demanded.

Julian broke the kiss, knowing if he didn't there'd be no pulling back. He turned from her and walked away several paces. This desperate need for her unnerved him, and in some ways he resented it and the weapon it put in her hands.

He willed his body to calm and turned to her. "A messenger came at dawn. The Earl Warenne pressed the Scots into battle."

"And?"

"Warenne chased the Scots to Spottsmuir, near Dunbar. The Earls Mar and Atholl—long supporters of

Clan Bruce—failed to answer the call to Clan Comyn's standard. Cospatrick, Earl of Dunbar and both Bruces rode with Edward. Even with those powerful clans supporting the English side, Badenoch and Buchan rallied nearly forty thousand troops."

"What an embarrassment for Cospatrick! Lady Marjorie commands Castle Dunbar whilst he curries favor with Longshanks. She is daughter to Buchan."

"Battle took place, Tamlyn. Though outnumbered three times over, Warenne's troops are battle-hardened veterans from campaigns in Wales and Flanders. They held and repulsed the Scots. After that, the Scots crumbled. Lady Marjorie had turned Dunbar over to her brother and father so Edward ordered Cospatrick to invest the castle. The castle fell—"

"And the Lady Marjorie?"

Julian hoped Tamlyn wouldn't empathize too strongly with Marjorie Comyn, Lady Dunbar. "No one is sure. Some of Dunbar's people escaped using the tunnels to the sea. Possibly she slipped out with them and returned north to a Comyn stronghold."

Tamlyn shivered. "Or she was in the castle when it was stormed? Many dislike the Earl Dunbar. His persecution of True Thomas is legend."

A wary look came into her eyes. Julian saw she wondered if Dunbar had done away with his wife for her defiance. Well, hadn't he wondered the same?

"It is nothing to us, Tamlyn. Soon, as Edward brings the barons unto his peace, he will depart to England and take up his campaign against France. It shall leave us to build our lives here."

Tamlyn stared at him, fury spiking in her blood. No man told her what to do . . . not even her lord father. It was on the tip of her tongue to tell him there'd be nothing built together until she willed it. Only the wind swirled around her, playfully tickling the stray strands of hair about her face. A fey, ghostly caress.

Tame the Dragon, came the words of the kenning.

She glanced to the side to see if someone stood there, but saw nothing. A few rays of sunshine suddenly poked through the fog, the brilliant beams shining down on Challon, creating a halo around him. Her breath caught at his beauty.

The Dragon was a hard man. She thought back on the dreams, his dreams. The horrors of wars, of seeing his brother die. No man should suffer such torment. Challon breathed out power and haughtiness in equal measure, assured of himself and his ability to control the world around him. That arrogance made her want to slap him, wipe that expression off his face. Yet, some part of herself she didn't understand wanted to touch that face, try to reach past the hardness.

Tame the Dragon . . . once more, the words floated on the wind.

Her hand lifted toward him. She could see his spine perceptibly stiffening, eyes darken with a soul-deep hunger. Well, she'd show him he couldn't anticipate her. Softly, she laid her palm against the hollow of his cheek.

This man so needed healing. Needed hope.

His green eyes locked with hers searching, probing, almost as if afraid to accept the gesture for what it was. She wanted to flinch from that wave of intensity, from the heat radiating off him. His haunting male scent filled her head. It was all too much. She forced herself to remain still, her fingers curving to the contours of his much too beautiful face.

"Julian," she whispered.

Slowly, his hand lifted to cover hers, lightly at first,

still unbelieving, then tighter, desperate. Raw hunger flashed in those haunted eyes, the hunger of a mind nearly consumed with loneliness and despair, beset by an ache so strong it was frightening. His eyelids lowered and his head tilted back a degree. The gesture reminded her of one savoring something long denied.

In the distance toward Glenrogha trumpets sounded, shattering the spell, calling his attention to the need for his presence.

"Come. We must return." He moved to the horse, mounting with ease. Kicking his foot from the stirrup, he held out his hand for hers.

Hesitating for an instant, her eyes searched his face. He smiled a small victory when Tamlyn stepped in the stirrup and accepted his hand that he might aid her in mounting. Settling her crosswise on his lap, he nudged the destrier to make haste toward Glenrogha.

Approaching the dun, they saw the gates were closed and men lined the boulevard. The captain of the guard recognized the Dragon and waved. The gates opened and Julian spurred the horse through without slowing.

Moffet rushed out to take hold of the horse's bridle to steady Dragon's Blood to let them dismount. Tamlyn started to slide down, but Challon caught her upper arm. "My lady, whatever the trouble—we face it together. You by my side, I shielding you. I sense we reached pax between us?"

She glared at him for several breaths before nodding acceptance. "Oh aye, pax. You are lord here by the will of your English master and the choice of the Auld Ones. So be it."

Chapter 12

Tamlyn watched from atop the lord's tower as Challon led the garrison below. Her men-at-arms stirred to his orders with a speed that caused her a slight shock. For the most part, Glenrogha's soldiery obeyed her with never a gainsay. A few voiced the complaint she was a woman and ought to marry so Glenrogha would have a man to lead them. Now, she saw they performed the Dragon's bidding, all recognizing Challon was lord here now and a warrior true, one they could respect.

She was certain Auld Bessa had spread word that months ago her father, sensing Challon might make a good husband for his youngest daughter, had sought an augury from their seer to confirm this. None doubted Evelynour's visions. Her pronouncement that the Dragon's coming was the will of the Auld Ones saw Glenrogha's people resigned to their fate. Already, they accepted him as earl here.

Challon strode along the boulevard, mouthing words to reassure the men. His air said he was unconcerned, as if he expected her people to obey him without question, even if there might be Scots on the other side of the wall. His innate authority, his sense of control, made soldiers move to his command without pause. They drew on his calm, his strength. He patted a squire on the arm, praising him. The young man smiled at his lord, adoration clear on his countenance.

Challon stood out amongst the men. This force in him drew her.

As if sensing her eyes upon him, he rotated and looked to the top of the tower. Locating her solitary form, he stared at her for several heartbeats. Their eyes locked as dizziness spun through her. He inclined his head faintly in recognition, then turned back, focusing his attention to the fore of the curtain wall.

On alert, all nervously waited as riders emerged from the sacred passes and approached the fortress. Men on horseback looked hard-pressed, as if straight from combat. She knew Challon feared these might be fleeing Scots from the battle at Dunbar, evading pursuit of the Earl Warenne. If so, this would be a test for the force at Glenrogha. They'd have to choose to obey the Black Dragon when it meant they held the gates against their countrymen.

Reinforcing Challon's command was the long-standing feud between Clan Comyn and the Ogilvies of Glen Shane. Clan feuds often made for strange bedfellows. This now saw her people's willingness to fight with the English against Scots.

Tamlyn's eyes tracked the horsemen crossing the dead-angle. About two score. Even from this distance, she saw many were injured.

She shivered. It was the second time in a sennight the passes revealed themselves to Outcomers. Tamlyn had no idea what that bode. Mayhap they were like a woman— once breached, she was no longer virgin. She almost smiled at the notion, and yet, couldn't push the disquiet from her mind. The passes of Glen Shane had always shielded them before.

The riders pulled up when they saw the gates barred, halting at the edge of arrow range. Both men and animals labored for breath. One armored knight, mounted on a dapple gray, continued to the curtain.

"Open the gates in the king's name!" he shouted.

Challon stepped to the edge of the battlement, looking down from the crenellation to the lone rider. "And what king is that? Longshanks or Balliol?"

"Hail, Lord Dragon, has it been so long you do not recognize your kinsman?" The man laughed, removing his helm to reveal his face.

A face obviously of the line of Challon.

The earl made a small pass with his hand, commanding the gates to open. It set off a flurry of activity. He headed down the steps to greet the newcomers, as the bailey filled with the mounts lathered in sweat. The men appeared to be in worse shape. Arrows protruded from the shoulders of three men and another had two in his thigh. Several more bled from slash wounds from swords.

Tamlyn rushed into the tower proper, calling for Janet and Roselynne to set the pages to help boil water and fetch the baskets of bandages. Pausing, she issued orders for cook to move up the noontide meal, as these men would need food and drink. Not once did she stop to consider they were English. They were just men needing succor.

The whole fortress was abuzz. She reached the front of the tower in time to see the Dragon embrace the leader. It was startling how much the knight resembled Challon. This man stood a shade taller, mayhap a bit longer through the torso. Even up close, the two might be mistaken for twins, though Tamlyn had no trouble telling them apart. This man didn't provoke that frisson of alarm as he neared. The kenning remained silent within her.

"What happened, Damian? Are you all right?" Challon stepped back, running his eyes over his cousin to assess his state.

The other tucked his helm under his arm. "Hell happened, Julian. And aye, I am fine, though I fear half my men are not. They are sorely in need of a healer before arrows poison their blood."

As the men were aided to dismount, Tamlyn dashed ahead to see pallets put down for them. The men pierced with arrows were weak from blood loss, and if the shafts were not removed immediately, they'd die as wound-poisoning spread in their bodies. No amount of herbs or craft would turn the tide. She was a good healer, learning from the Three Wise Ones of the Wood. Still, she'd never dealt with this sort of damage. Relief flooded her to see Auld Bessa already standing in the Great Hall, waiting.

Julian kept an eye on Tamlyn while she settled Damian's cadre. She moved so gracefully, confident in handling her workers, keeping them moving with purpose and speed. Though these men were English, she just did what was necessary. He felt pride in this woman who would soon be his wife.

"Warenne charged us to pursue the Scots fleeing Dunbar." Damian set down his helm and removed his dark gray mantle from his shoulders. "Edward thought of it as killing two Scots birds with one English stone toss. I come to assume the holdings of Lyonglen from my grandsire. Our king thought we could press the remains of Clan Comyn as we made way here. These Highlanders know the terrain and caught us out in the open. They had cross-bows, Julian, and were not out to defend, but kill. Lucky we were. The fog rolled down from the hills, so thick we were able to slip away before they moved in to finish their black deed. Glenrogha was closer than Lyonglen, so we headed for your safety. I feared we would never find the passes, no matter how hard we searched we could not find the entrance. The fog was so thick it was unnatural. Then suddenly it parted, revealing the way in."

"Word of the battle reached us. Was the rout as bad as the messenger said?" Julian signaled the servant to fetch wine for his cousin.

"Outside of clans who supported the English side, most nobles were killed or made prisoner to Edward. Mayhap six score knights, the Earls of Atholl, Ross and Menteith, the son of John Comyn of Badenoch, the Morays and possibly a dozen magnates are all being transported South. Buchan's army was destroyed." Damian sat in the chair. "I am not sure when I've been more weary."

"Then it is over," Julian pronounced with relief. "What word of your grandsire? Has he been told you assume the title as lord of Lyonglen?"

"With the current state of the country, who can tell? My guess—Edward sent no word, so they shan't expect me. Still, news travels on swift wings through the Highlands." Damian leaned back in the chair, clearly exhausted. "I hear conflicting tales about his condition. Some say he is too ill to rise to Balliol's standard. Others claim he stays home because he is too busy swiving his young bride."

Julian arched his brow. "Sounds as if you are cut from the same cloth as the old lord."

"I shall see soon enough. Though I shall have trouble calling a woman grandmother when she is younger than

I." He rubbed his forehead, pain clouding his countenance. "For now, I pass on the offer of food. I crave a nice soft bed so I may sleep half the day away. Mayhap a pretty serving wench to soothe my . . . brow. I owe you a boon if you send that one my way."

Julian started to laugh until he saw Damian's eyes rested on Tamlyn. Rage erupted through him, nearly blinding his reason, though he recalled how easily he had demanded Tamlyn help him bathe as his right. As visiting nobility, Damian should be afforded the same honor. Only Julian knew, though he loved his cousin as a brother, he would kill him if he touched her.

"Tamlyn," Julian called, summoning her to his side.

Damian's green-gray eyes glittered with desire, his smile widening. "Now that is a woman, Julian, to spend your life making babies with."

Tamlyn hesitated, her eyes casting about to assure all the injured had received care. Only then did she answer Julian's summons. She stopped by the arm of his chair. "My lord, the wounded are well and resting. Auld Bessa says all shall make a full recovery."

"Tamlyn, I present Damian St. Giles, Lord Ravenhawke, my second cousin." Julian possessively took her hand in his. "Damian, this is Tamlyn MacShane, Countess Glenrogha. My betrothed. After banns are proclaimed we shall wed."

Ravenhawke's face blanked in shock. "Forgive me. A two-day ride without sleep slowed me. Beg pardon, cousin, if I erred."

Julian glared at him resolutely. "Aye, you did."

Damian had come to the Challon household as a page and stayed for training as squire, then knight to Julian's father. So like the Challon sons, everyone had assumed Damian was another dragon in Michael's litter. Julian loved Damian and never treated him as anything but a brother. Still, the tone of the reproof brought Damian up short. His cousin looked again at Tamlyn.

Jealousy burned within Julian, as he knew what his cousin saw. Tamlyn's kirtle was simple. She wore no jewelry, no ribbons in her hair. Yet her brilliant coloring and beauty would draw any man's eye. Her sensuality would hit them like a fist to the heart.

Damian's attention was easily captured by a beautiful maid. The result of that endless fascination had seen him father three bastard sons. Even so, no woman had ever held his attention for long. As he watched his cousin stare at Tamlyn, the hot sensation flared brighter within him. Julian had this odd feeling Tamlyn could have been the woman to change that, for his cousin stared at her with the same longing Julian knew was in his own heart.

"Welcome to Glenrogha, Lord Ravenhawke," Tamlyn offered with a smile.

Damian stared at her with a sadness that had her glancing in question to Julian.

"I thank you for your hospitality and for the care of my men, Lady Tamlyn, and wish you joy on your up-coming nuptials." He took her hand and brought it to his lips. "I am sure you will make all Julian's dreams come true. He is a very lucky man."

Resentment scalding his mind, Julian barely heard Tamlyn's reply as she mumbled a few words and then hurried away to see the meal was ready for those want-ing it. His eyes followed her departure, lingering on her with pride.

"I fear there is a need to explain, cousin. I am not so usually awkward in situations of this sort. It is just . . ."

Julian swung back to Damian. "Just what? Speak,

before I drag you out on the quatrain and use you for a practice dummy."

"No woman has ever had the power to make me care, because I always saw this vision of a woman before my mind's eye. That fey voice I oft ignore—and regret doing so—brings images to me. It is the Scots blood from my mother. Usually it proves right."

"And?" Julian stomach burned as he suspected what his cousin would say.

"The face in my mind—the face of the woman I felt was fated to be my bride—it is the face of Lady Tamlyn." Damian swallowed regret, staring at Julian.

"Over your dead body," Julian said quietly.

Damian nodded. "Of that I would have no doubt."

Tamlyn brooded whilst seeing to the wounds of St. Giles' men. How was she to proceed tonight? Did she just go to bed with Challon as if all had been settled? Did she demand they talk? Of course, she could say that she needed to stay and keep an eye on the injured, but all rested peacefully, thanks to Bessa's potions, even the men who'd had arrows removed. No coward, she would not wrap herself in that lie.

Challon remained engaged before the fire, talking quietly with his squires and two knights. Once she'd been close enough to overhear that they planned to ride on the morrow to rid the area of the Scots who attacked Ravenhawke's party, though their words were lowly spoken. The Dragon was unsure how the Scots now under his command would react to this news.

Checking the wounded once more, she girded herself to face Challon before others.

He slouched in the lord's chair, feet crossed at the

ankles. The gold spurs gleamed by the firelight, matching the glint in his eyes as he tracked her every move. She had felt him staring all evening as she tended chores. Oh, he pretended not to notice her, carrying on discussions and issuing orders. Only his mind constantly brushed hers, keeping her on edge.

Would they sleep together this eve? This proud man would not force the issue, fearful her Pict temper would flare and they'd clash before his men and her people. His pride was strong, as strong as hers. Yet, in some ways he had more to lose. A simple point in their lives: her wanting to retire and unsure how to proceed. A small choice, aye, but one that could have repercussions—for them, for their people.

Well, she was no child to tremble before the unknown. She must use all her cleverness and craft to ensure life traveled a path to where she could find some happiness.

Sucking in a deep breath, she approached the Dragon.

A hush fell as everyone turned idly to see, pretending nothing of import was about to occur. There was little doubt all waited to learn what Glenrogha's lady would do.

This was the third time today for them to play this game.

As the nooning meal was served, Challon came to escort her to the table. She knew it was more than courtly manners. He wanted Glenrogha's people to witness her at his side, accepting her role as his lady. She escaped that by insisting she needed to care for his cousin's men. Challon nodded, letting her win that round. He'd settled his cousin and then went on patrol with his guard.

The second time came as supper was served. The same silence descended earlier when he appeared at her elbow and took her hand, saying it was time for the evening meal. Her turn to give in. Squaring her shoulders, she allowed him to lead her to the table. Though he did naught to flaunt the small victory, all sensed his will ruled and that she was at his side, a signal of her acceptance of his new role here.

Well, she was no gooseberry fool. The path was clear. It was not her place to challenge the will of the Auld Ones. Even her lord father had recognized the Dragon as having a place in her life.

She desired Challon. Never one for games, she would be silly to try and pretend otherwise. No man affected her as he did. Not his brothers. Not Damian St. Giles.

She had to admit upon first sight their striking resemblance gave her pause. The visions foretold of the coming of a lord whose color was that of the ravens. St. Giles was so very much like his powerful cousin, and part of his device was a raven. Was Evelynour's foretelling in error?

She had only to stand before the two men to hear the kenning's answer. She found Lord St. Giles attractive. He bore the stamp of the beautiful men of Challon, same black hair and green eyes. Any faint response toward the cousin came because he was a reflection of Challon, enough to be his twin. There was only one man to touch her emotions so deeply.

It was up to her to curb her pride and learn to deal with the vexing man.

Mayhap giving into him wouldn't be so easy had she not glimpsed the pain inside the man, the hunger for peace. Desires so strong, her empathy disarmed her. That longing was a tool in her hands. She had the power to offer him what he craved.

She stopped, quaking inside as she always did when near Challon. "It is been a long day. I wish to retire."

When he just stared at her with that irritating air of

sangfroid, she wanted to kick his booted feet. He made no move to acknowledge her and it goaded her temper he let her stand there. Everyone watching. She kenned what he did, letting them all take notice that she came to him. Fine, she'd grant him that ploy.

When he still said nothing, she nodded and turned to leave.

"My lady," he called, stopping her in her tracks.

He waited until Tamlyn turned around. When she did, he held out his hand for her to take.

Her amber eyes flashed. This wasn't only a show before their people, but a test between them. He was a master at hiding his feelings, but she'd begun to sense the workings of his mind. He wanted a clear display of compliance, so none mistook her bowing to him as lord of Glenrogha.

Defiance flared, but for once she used her mind, not her pride, to react. Tamlyn went and put her hand in his upturned one. The tension she sensed in Julian, his fear she would be too willful to make the compromise, eased when she yielded.

"You worked hard to see Damian's men tended. I thank you." He used the hold to pull her nearer so she stood, her knee brushing against the side of his outstretched thigh. "You fare well?"

"Aye, but a wee bit tired . . . so I would seek my slumber." His glittering eyes bespelled her. She nearly smiled when the cool disdain shifted to heat at the idea of her going to bed.

"It is well you do so. Bid my squire to bank the fire in our chambers. I shall join you shortly." Once again, he used his hold to tug her close, so his mouth could brush her fingers.

* * *

Unbuckling his belt, Julian pretended not to notice Tamlyn. She shifted, restless in the far corner of the bed, drawing the tartan to her chest. Pretending ignorance of Tamlyn was not an easy task. She watched him undress and then slide into bed with her. He felt her eyes roving over his naked form, knew what she found in him pleased her.

Tonight was different between them. She knew it. He knew it.

Not confined to the room by guards standing watch, she was no longer his prisoner. Yea, Moffet's pallet rested just outside, but it was hardly the same. This night was the first time she'd had a choice. She could have put forth excuse she needed to stay belowstairs and care for the injured men. He smiled, pleased that she'd come to his bed willingly.

He was coming to see many things to admire in Tamlyn. She had the spirit of a warrior. While that vexed him now and again, it was a trait that would breed strong sons. He sensed she had little use for games and possessed a bone-deep honesty he rarely saw in women at court. There was an openness to her emotions that let him sense her mind's workings. As they came to know each other, built a life together, this would strengthen.

He smiled in the darkness. How could one woman affect his senses, raise his hopes so much?

"Tamlyn," he growled, tucking one hand behind his head, "lie down. Stop hiding in the corner like I am going to eat you."

She huffed. "Is that not what dragons do to fair maids? Eat them?"

He groaned at the choice of words. He doubted Tamlyn understood the torment they conjured. His body throbbed to life, complaining of how much he needed to find physical release with this woman.

Nevertheless, he was determined to do this right. Even if it killed him.

He'd give her time to adjust to him becoming her lord husband. He was a stranger, the invader, the man who'd made prisoner of a father she adored. No matter how painful holding back would be, he was determined to do it for her sake.

Mayhap upon their wedding night, his lady would look upon him with wanting, not just compliance. The priest had said he'd perform the ceremony a fortnight after May Day. He and Tamlyn could use the time to speak to each other's mind.

Provided it didn't drive him insane.

She wiggled again.

"Tamlyn . . ." he growled.

"Challon, are you all right? You sound in pain." She scooted over to place her ice-cold hand on his taut belly.

His body jumped in reaction—from her touch on him when he burned with fever for her—but more so from that icy hand. "God's teeth, woman, your hand—"

"Beg pardon, my hands get cold when I am nervous." She didn't remove it, though, instead slowly rubbed it over his corded muscles.

His groin bucked hard in reaction. "Ah! I would never have guessed." He closed his eyes, struggling against the overwhelming power surging within him.

"Touching you is touching fire," she whispered in awe.

Even in the dimness, he could see tears in her eyes. He reached up and swiped one away as it fell. Instead of dropping his hand, he held it there, his thumb brushing the softness of her cheek. Feeling . . . he wasn't sure how to reason what filled his heart. It was a haunting sense of something newfound and precious, and yet, as if the gesture was one he'd done before.

Under other circumstances, he would have relished her putting her hands, even cold ones, on his body. While it took the last shreds of his reason to keep from flipping her over onto her back and thrusting his body into hers—showing her just how hot he could burn—he sensed Tamlyn needed more. She needed reassurance.

"Lie down, wench." *Please, lie down before I get up and pound my head against the stone wall.*

She did, but her hand remained on him. For a moment, he thought he could control the driving urge, but then she wiggled again, scooting closer.

"Challon, this feels so good. When I get cold like this, it is hard to get rid of the iciness. Would you mind if I put my other hand—"

Julian moved so fast Tamlyn barely had time to blink. He yanked her down on the bed next to him and pulled the wool cover over them. "Not another word. Be still. Try to sleep."

"But I—" The words were muffled since he'd pulled the cover up to her nose.

"Wench, close your mouth or I shall stuff my glove in it." His chest vibrated with the suppressed chuckle.

She poked her face above the covers, then rose up on an elbow. "You always bark orders."

He sat up to glare at her, nose to nose. "And you disobey them." Putting a hand on her shoulder, he pushed her back to the bed. "Now obey me before I get angry."

Silence filled the chamber. Gritting his teeth, he fought his frustrated mating drive. His heart thundered out a tattoo of need that increased more with each breath, each ghostly caress of her scent. If they would just remain quiet, mayhap his body would cool and listen to his mind. No. Not in a hundred years.

As he thought reason might rule again, she moved.

First one foot, accidentally brushing against his calf as she straightened out. God's breath, her feet were as cold as her hands! Then she tried to roll so she wasn't lying on her left arm. She shifted again, then again, seeking the comfortable place to put it between them. Next came her hips, brushing against the side of his. Damn the woman. Did she not understand the ordeal she inflicted upon him?

"Tamlyn, if you place any value on having a sane man for a husband . . . stop wiggling!" he snarled, but a laugh exploded on the end of the statement.

"The Dragon is a grouchy dragon. Mayhap you have a toothache."

His control was rapidly fading. "Aye, I have an ache, but it is much lower."

"You do seem to be running a fever." She rubbed her face against his bare arm.

"Fever? Oh aye, I have a fever."

Tamlyn sprang up on her knees. "Do you have a wound? Fever comes if the pus rises."

"Something rises, Tamlyn—it is not pus."

Bringing him to the point of sheer agony, Tamlyn leaned over him as she checked his body for a wound he didn't have. By damn, there was only so much he could stand. He grabbed her upper arms and pulled her to face him. For several breaths, their eyes locked—his blazing with need, her golden ones with surprise.

"Don't move, don't wiggle," he ordered. Her mead-sweetened breath fanned out in short gaspy sighs, nearly sending him over the edge. "Here is what we shall do. Lie down, no squirming. You will close your cat-eyes and go to sleep or—"

She blinked in curiosity. "Or what, Challon?"

"Or we shan't sleep at all," he threatened.

"Oh," she whispered, understanding sinking in.

His mouth eased into a half smile. "Aye . . . oh."

That puzzled her. "Why?"

"You need time," he stated simply. "There still is much unsettled between us. I know your mind is not reconciled to our situation. If it were up to me, I would permit you time to know me better before our marriage. Edward will not grant us that grace. So I shall not take you until our wedding night. This I vow. I mean to honor you, Tamlyn."

There was a connection between them, a bond so strong it caused too many feelings. They threatened to inundate him. After Christian's death he'd just existed. He felt nothing, just a sense of emptiness. In some ways he welcomed that hollowness inside him. It was easier to be numb, not caring beyond the basic needs to survive. But with spring's return, some intangible force stirred inside him, as if his emotions had been frozen through dead of winter. Now it was time to live again. His spirit awakened.

Perchance this came with his growing older. He was no longer a green youth with his whole life ahead of him. The time had come for him to build a future, leave something of himself to survive his passing. He wanted it with a mind-devouring hunger.

Julian had seen the face of hunger. Men or women gone so long without food, with big eyes and gaunt bodies. If offered a feast they gorged themselves, only to find they sickened. Their bellies had shriveled from famine and couldn't stretch enough to accommodate the meal.

Julian feared his heart had similarly withered. Then Tamlyn brought feelings to him, filling his heart to overflowing. Though he tried to welcome all these new emotions, it was almost too raw for him to endure. He too needed time.

"Go to sleep, Tamlyn, before I truss you up and put my glove to use." When she stared at him with those luminous eyes, he stirred, catching Tamlyn off guard. Tucking her under the blanket, this time he turned on his side with his back to her.

Tamlyn must have believed him. This time she remained quiet. The peat fire died to a smolder, as coolness crept into the room. He forced his breathing to slow, pretending he'd fallen asleep.

As the chill increased, Tamlyn wiggled closer in soft movements, trying not to awaken him. Her hands were cold again. So were her feet. It took all his warrior's will to continue the sham of slumber, when she placed them on him. One hand against his back, the other on his waist. Then those icy feet pushed between his calves. When he didn't stir, she shifted even closer, until he felt all of her body, spooned against his.

She seemed to settle now that she stole his body heat. With a yawn and a sigh, she mumbled, "Dragons are excellent bed-warmers."

"Go to sleep, Tamlyn."

Her head nestled against his shoulder. "Aye, Challon."

Chapter 13

The clanking of Julian's sword against the baldric as he buckled it about his hips woke Tamlyn in the first light of dawn.

She'd slept on her side. She yawned, then stretched. Still drowsy, her hand slid over the bedding where Challon's warmth lingered. She'd slept but a few winks, yet she felt so content. She couldn't recall if her bed had ever been so warm. His heat, his scent, wrapped around her, tormenting her, tempting her throughout the night. Like a cat curling before the fire, she'd molded her body to his and soaked up his radiance.

If she were a bold, sinful lass, she'd have followed through on the provocative images swirling through her mind. Her hands on the Dragon, tracing the smooth skin over the steel muscles. Putting her mouth against that strong column of his spine. Instead, she'd lain awake and thought long on everything that had happened since his coming, all she learned of the man.

Whispers, followed by more movements, told her his squire was helping Challon dress.

She smiled another yawn. Not enough she must grow

used to one man being in her chamber, she had to accustom herself to the comings and goings of his four squires as well.

Light coming in from the solar was blocked as Challon moved toward the bed. It shifted under his weight. He was dressed in the heavy black hauberk with the aketon underneath. The metal was cold.

"Beg pardon, my lady, I did not mean to break your slumber," he said in hushed tones. "It is early still. You should rest."

"You wear mail." Touching the cool metal, she voiced her fear.

"We ride to hunt down those who attacked my cousin and his men. I assured Sir Priest the May Day celebration shall take place on the morrow. There is no way we can do so with Comyn men lingering in the shadow of Kinmarch. I am not sure how long I shall be at the task." His hands took hold of her shoulders. "Stay within the curtain wall until I return. No herb gathering, eh?"

Tamlyn nodded. She'd do as he asked, though there was little threat to her since they were Scots. They were just men trying to return to their homes.

As if sensing the bend of her mind, Challon stroked her jawline. "Warfare changes men, Tamlyn. You have no idea. High ideas of chivalry, of honor, are ground into the dirt. Do not harbor loyalty or sympathy for these men, thinking they shall treat you fair because you are a Scot. Right now, they are desperate. All is lost for them—their homes, their lands. Longshanks will see every castle and stronghold with a new lord—an English lord—before he is done. They know that. There is no going home for them. They lurk in the woods, living off the land and stealing from other clans. These men live on hatred to survive and hope to fight another day. This turns their minds inward. They would not hesitate to kill, rape or make prisoner of you or the people in this glen. You have too much. You retain all through my being lord here. They will resent that. Resent you. Do you understand?"

Tamlyn nodded, unable to voice her sadness. Men fighting, dying—this was something that never touched her world before. She didn't understand it, didn't want to understand it.

"I know you view my coming as punishment, but you will still be lady of this holding. Other than marriage to me, you shan't suffer because of the Scots' rebellion. You are to be the bride of the Dragon of Challon. There are many who would seize you and try to use you against me. It is important you accept that."

Tamlyn sensed he spoke the truth, but it was too much for her to think on. In just a few days, her life had been put on its head and spun about. Glenrogha's gates had always been open in welcome to her countrymen. Now those same men were to be eyed with suspicion, even fear. The gates would remain closed and the enemy she so dreaded was their protector.

"I know this is strange to you. Give it time, Tamlyn. Once we wed—"

She tried to pull away from him. "There will be no marriage between us until you offer true compromise. I ask two things. I will not marry you unless you wed me in our ways, not just the Christian ceremony, but in the rites of the Auld Faith."

"Agreed," he laughed, "though I have no idea what I just consented to. And the second?"

"You will help see my lord father is freed."

"Tamlyn, despite once being the king's champion, I now hold little sway with Edward. No one does," Challon admitted.

"Surely, he would listen to you?"

"I would grant this if it were within my power. You ask for something beyond my control."

"I do not ask for much, Challon. Meet these conditions and I will not fight you about the marriage," Tamlyn reasoned.

Sounds of his squires outside the door signaled he was out of time. "We shall discuss this further when I return—"

"You say compromise. I have. Now I say you compromise. Please, Challon."

He grabbed her arms, yanking her so his mouth could cover hers. Not in gentle wooing, but in a hot demand, as if he could change her will through a kiss. At first she held back, hurt at his continued refusal to help her father, but Julian's magic swirled around her in a heady storm of sensations.

He broke the kiss, pressing her tight to his chest, so tight it hurt to breathe, his hand fisting in her hair at the back of her head. Then he released her, stalked to the door.

He paused in the deep shadows to glance back at her. "We shall speak again upon these matters." Sword rattling, he was gone.

Tamlyn slid beneath the bedcovers where he'd lain, absorbing his remaining heat. Running a finger over her swollen lips, she tasted Challon's kiss.

Julian stood beside Lasher, impatient as Gervase adjusted the long shield on his left arm. The fog was thick, blanketing everything. He was coming to learn this was typical for Glen Shane. Haar, the Scots called it. The gray mists hovered low, shrouding the landscape until the sun finally rose over the tor and burned it off, only to creep back at the approach of gloaming.

Off toward the passes, he heard those bloody ravens screeching and raising a fuss. It was odd so many of them flocked together, staying close to the entrance of the Glen.

Lasher was antsy, shifting nervously from hoof to hoof. Then he saw why. Tamlyn's mare was stamping in the barn. He wondered if she were coming in season. If so, he might breed her with Lasher or Dragon's Blood, though he feared Tamlyn would likely raise a fuss.

He slid his hand down the stallion's muscular neck. "Keen to mount your lady, my fine steed? I sympathize with the feeling."

He put his foot into the stirrup. As he swung into the saddle, he caught a glimpse of Tamlyn at the window of the lord's chamber. She watched him preparing to leave. For a brief bend in time, their eyes locked and he saw little but her. It took all his willpower not to dismount and storm back into the tower and take her.

He patted his horse again. "Aye, I know the feeling well."

Damian reined his stallion before Julian, his eyes taking in what his cousin saw. "Strange morn, eh? Those bloody ravens seem to nest in the passes. Like guardians."

"Aye, I never knew so many to stay in the same place, outside of the ones at White Tower."

"Odd, they are carrion birds, but the Scots consider them sacred," Damian said. "My lady mother spoke of them as bringers as omens of great import or death. Likely why she designed the Ravenhawke crest for my lord father when they first wed."

Julian nodded to Tamlyn, but received no show of recognition. He supposed she was still upset that he wouldn't agree to help her lord father. If only he could.

Returning the man from Edward's prison would go a long way to put his upcoming marriage to Tamlyn upon the right footing. He couldn't very well explain Longshanks had ordered his marriage to Tamlyn not as a reward, but punishment. That reality would not set well with his Highland lass.

As he turned Lasher, he noticed Damian's eyes lingered on the woman in the solar window. His cousin hadn't made prisoner of her father. He'd not bear that taint in her eyes. Irritated, he spurred Lasher, leading his men out of the bailey.

Damian finally caught up, keeping pace at his side. They rode across the dead angle, their silence companionable, albeit cool. They'd grown up as brothers, thus Julian found it hard to remain angry with his cousin.

Soon, Damian would lay claim to Lyonglen. Edward could have awarded the holding to anyone, but this way, the man to seize control would be the estranged grandson Lyonglen had never seen. Lyonglen would still be held by the family. With Damian baron of the ancient holding in the glen beyond, Glen Shane's position would be all the more secure.

Damian broke the solitude with a question. The wrong question. "Is the Lady Tamlyn resigned to this forced marriage?"

Julian looked to his side, sizing up Damian's mood. "Tamlyn consented. She spoke of wedding preparations upon rising this morn."

Damian watched Julian with hooded eyes. "She seemed resigned enough last night, but did you really give her any choice?"

"Neither of us had a choice. Edward decreed it. I am satisfied. She shall make a good lady wife," Julian snapped.

"I see your understanding of the gentler sex has not improved."

"Gentler?" Julian snorted, "The females of Glen Shane are a hazard to the English male. Simon took an arrow to his leg when they stormed Kinloch, a bolt from a small crossbow shot by a female not yet marriageable age. So even you, with your St. Giles charm, might find them troublesome."

"Troublesome or not, handle Lady Tamlyn softly." Damian's gray-green eyes narrowed on him. "I love you as a brother, Julian, but if ever you raise hand to Lady Tamlyn, I shall kill you."

"Cousin, we have traveled long, hard roads together. It would be a shame your misplaced regard for *my* betrothed would come between us."

There was plenty to occupy Tamlyn whilst Challon and Ravenhawke hunted the rebels from Clan Comyn.

She reflected on how everything in her life had changed so quickly. No one at Glenrogha voiced concern that Challon chased Scotsmen. Respect of the Dragon as a powerful warrior was part of that. Bessa's fine hand was also at work in this acceptance. That The Shane had once thought to make a match between Challon and Tamlyn, supported by Evelynour's visions and foretellings, went a long way to easing his approval in Glen Shane. She'd asked old Angus about this. As an elder of Clan Ogilvie, his word held great sway with the opinion of the other men.

"Lady Tamlyn, if our laird sought a marriage for you with Lord Challon, it was with knowledge the man would make you a braw husband. Aye, he is English. When he weds you, he becomes a man of Glen Shane.

He will fight for Glen Shane, not for England. You'd do well to heed Evelynour's foretellings," Angus advised in fatherly fashion.

Challon and Ravenhawke rode to protect the people of this valley. Her people understood.

Reinforcing the fact, the Scots they sought were Comyn men. The Comyns came from ancient bloodlines through Pict heiresses. This usually drew respect amongst the Scots. Animosity arose with their constant greed, which now saw two-thirds of Scotland under their control. They were powerful, holding thirteen Scottish earldoms. Still, bitter feelings were held by some due to the actions of a cadet branch called Quhele. To cement their hold in Dunkeld, the Quheles invited the MacIains, their rivals, to a gathering. At given moment, the head of a black bull was brought in on a platter—an ancient symbol of killing of an enemy's chief. It was a signal to rise and kill all the Mac-Iain visitors. The incident demonstrated their ruthlessness.

That long held enmity now worked in the favor of the Dragon. *The enemy of my enemy is my friend.*

Tamlyn pushed away from the table in the Great Hall, intending to set her fortress to order. The Beltane festival was upon them and much needed attending. First, rooms for her sisters and Challon's brothers need to be readied. Then she should check with cook about the May Day cake. She conferred with the alewife about the brewing of extra ale, and left instructions for the casks of wine and mead from the cellars to be carted to the stone circle. Also, the wounded men required their bandages changed and potions given to keep their blood pure.

As she came from the kitchen, Rowanne and Sir Guillaume arrived. Happy to see her sister again, she rushed to embrace her. Strangely, when her sister hugged her back, Tamlyn had the urge to break down and cry. Most unlike her.

Rowanne's expression showed her shock at feeling the small tremor through her sister's body. "Tamlyn, how fare you? You never needed anyone's strength before. Has the Dragon done something in my absence?"

Tamlyn smiled. "I fare well. I am just happy to see you." Her gold eyes moved past her sister to the tall knight, soon to be the Lord of Lochshane. "And matters are well for you, Ro?"

"Well enough. I and the people of Lochshane shall all come through, I believe. I thought you would need help with the Beltane preparations. We heard there had been trouble, news about Comyns attacking Glenrogha." Rowanne's face reflected her concern.

"They did not attack Glenrogha, but men under Lord Ravenhawke. Challon and he led a force out at dawn to rid the area of Comyn men."

"My cousin was unharmed?" Guillaume asked.

"Tired, but fine." Tamlyn drew herself up to a stance proper for chatelaine of her fortress. "Come, I shall tell you all as I show you to your rooms."

Worn to the bone, Julian fell into the lord's chair. He wanted to see Tamlyn, to hold her, but the hour was late. She was likely exhausted from May Day preparations and caring for the wounded. He accepted the tankard of mead from the servant.

"Thank you," he said, so exhausted he didn't even take notice if the serf was male or female, before closing his eyes.

"You are most welcome, Lord Challon," the young man replied, then his steps carried him away.

Julian opened his eyes to watch the servants rushing around to see his men fed. It pleased him to see this almost seamless fitting together of his men and Tamlyn's folk. They worked together well and with purpose.

Damian eyed his cousin over the tankard of mead. "Julian, have you noticed how the people of Glen Shane accept you so easily as the new overlord here?"

"Tamlyn's approval makes the difference."

Julian sighed, setting the tankard down, untouched. He was tired. They had ridden for a full day, tracked the Scots rebels all the way to Lyonglen, until they'd vanished into the Great Mountains. Scouts said they'd moved on, likely trying to make it back to Comyn territory, but Julian had concerns if that was the case. In the morn he'd send a detachment to ride the hills to assure they'd not double back.

He'd slept little the night before with Tamlyn keeping him awake with her constant wiggling and her cold feet. Sighing, he just wanted to fall into his bed and sleep. He'd go up in a moment, but the fire felt good seeping into his bones. His age was showing. Once he could spend days in the saddle with little concerns. Now he ached to the marrow.

"It is more than that." His cousin's pale eyes studied him with a predator's intensity. Damian's words brought Julian back to the present. "Someone spreads rumors The Shane had already entered into negotiations with you, planned on wedding you to the Lady Tamlyn. Is this so?"

Julian chuckled, rubbing his forehead. "There is some truth to it, though mayhap someone stretches facts a bit. The one they call Auld Bessa carries the tales, I wager."

"The crone speaks facts then?" Damian pressed.

Julian stretched and yawned. "Let us say it is not a lie. The Shane suggested I come for a visit to Glen Shane.

With all that has happened, it slipped my mind. The earl had just married off the two baronesses at that point, so one can see where his thought headed. Why?"

Damian shrugged, staring into the mead as if to find the answers there. "Just wondered if you were aware of the rumors."

"I met the Red Laird several times. He discussed this valley and his daughters, especially the youngest. Quite proud of her. Earl Hadrian vowed Lady Tamlyn represented the breed. Mayhap it is why I set my mind to marrying Tamlyn even before I laid eyes upon her. If Auld Bessa seeks to smooth my path here by saying negotiations had begun, and it sees my acceptance here easier for these Scots, then so be it."

He studied his cousin. Damian had been in a peculiar mood since arriving, more reflective, so unlike the carefree knight he knew.

Damian's expression deepened. "Julian, I was not raised in the Highlands, but I recall my lady mother speaking about the women of Clan Ogilvie. They cannot be forced to marriage. They have to give consent."

"I know you set great store in the visions you say come from your mother's Scottish blood. But I advise you to fix your mind elsewhere, Damian. Despite whatever dreams you have—where you think you see the face of Tamlyn—you are mistaken in this. Look for another answer to your question." Julian rose, his hand touching his sword's hilt. "It is not Tamlyn's face you see. Tamlyn is mine. No man shall come between us."

Chapter 14

When Julian entered the lord's chambers, he discovered Tamlyn on her stomach, sleeping. His breath caught, eyes drinking in the sleek curves of her bare back. A plaide blanket covered her hips, while the shimmering mass of gold hair spilled over one sultry shoulder. Blood surged in his exhausted body, and suddenly he didn't feel quite so tired.

He carefully removed his sword and baldric so their clanking wouldn't disturb her. With her constant wiggling last night, he doubted she'd found any more rest than he had.

As he undressed his gaze never left her still form. Her pagan beauty moved him, in a way words failed to express. He just knew he needed her. His life had been cold, empty before her golden presence came to bless him.

As youths, he'd become aware his cousin Damian often experienced feelings, warnings he couldn't explain. Especially vivid in Julian's mind was the incident a year ago in Wales. As they approached a pass, Damian abruptly reached over and yanked the reins on Pagan, bringing their mounts to halt, insisting they were about to ride into an ambush. He'd been right. Flanking the passes, they outwitted the Welshmen lying in wait for them. There was no way Damian could've known. With a shrug, he'd chalked it up to his mother's Scottish blood.

Now, Damian insisted that fey ability conjured the face of the woman he was fated to marry—Tamlyn. Julian had known his cousin right too many times to doubt Damian believed this assertion. Regardless, Julian knew he'd never let her go. Glenrogha and Tamlyn were his and hold them he would.

His dark side spurred him to take her tonight, brand her body, inside and out. Claim Tamlyn, bind her to him so she'd never leave him. With a mind muzzy from exhaustion, he had trouble remembering why that wasn't the path to travel.

After disrobing, he felt the penetrating chill in the chamber. Wearing just his braies he walked to the hearth and added a brick of peat, still finding humor in the Scots burning dirt to stay warm. It caught quickly, flaring to life. The heavy, earthy scent filled the chamber. Closing his eyes for several breaths, he inhaled the mysterious scent and just listened to his heart thud out a plaint for Tamlyn.

The corner of his mouth twitched as he whispered to himself, "Fool, stop thinking about the wench and go lie next to her, hold her."

Quick steps had him dropping his braies and carefully easing under the cover. Oh, what he wouldn't give to roll her over and push his throbbing flesh into the slick heat of her woman's warmth. A glow filled him. He envisioned the many nights ahead, when after a long day of exhausting work he'd come to bed and do just that. Tamlyn waiting for him was heaven in his mind.

Drawing a ragged breath, he edged closer, needing

Tamlyn's nearness as he needed his next breath. Her scent hit him like a potion. Gently placing his hand on her back, he savored the coolness of her skin, its softness.

He drew his hand down the column of her spine, hesitated when he reached the tartan. The darker side of his desires held sway, so he slowly edged the material away exposing her rounded derrière. His palm traced over the curve. Unlike her back, the flesh was warm. Unable to stop himself, he leaned against her and kissed her shoulder. She sighed, then a small shudder rippled over her. She turned, leaning into him. Seeking his body heat.

And he had plenty to spare.

Tamlyn had no idea just how he burned for her. Those beautiful breasts tightened under the cool air of the room, the soft areola puckering. Her nipples jutted high and taut. With one finger, he faintly circled the darker tip, watching it respond. Even in sleep Tamlyn was so utterly sensual. Unable to resist, he edged down the bed, just enough to use his tongue in the same action.

Her breath sucked in, her body arched against his mouth, wanting more. His trembling hand sought the tip of the other breast, stroking, circling, then finally gave it a small tug and rolled it, as he greedily drew the first nipple into his mouth. He kept up that rhythmic pull on them both, her raspy sighs rising in strength as craving seared through her body and mind.

Male instincts rose within him, provoking him to take what was his. Edward's betrothal decreed she was his in all but deed. None would gainsay should he take her now and wave the bloody proof of her virginity as a pennon from the lord's tower. He wanted to claim her, first with his hands, then his mouth and tongue—wanted to lap at her scalding honey—then ride her hard, her under him, over him, up against the wall, mount her as a stallion did a mare, and a thousand other ways.

"Yea, Challon. I . . . cannot . . . run from you," came the faint breathy words.

His heart slammed against his ribs at the avowal, seizing them as near salvation after doubts from Damian's pronouncement had rooted in his mind. At first, Julian thought she'd awakened and spoke to him, but he saw she remained in the darkness of her slumber. It thrilled him that her dreams were of him, fed his hunger she that knew there was no escaping him.

Bending his knee, he pushed his leg between hers, forcing his thigh up against her female mound. Her thighs locked around his leg, rubbing against him as a cat. It was nearly his undoing. He craved to kiss her, kiss her all through the night and until dawn. Slow and soft. Hard and ravenous. He wanted to kiss her as the first shafts of morning speared into the solar, watch her golden beauty under him, and then slip into her body. He envisioned her eyes opening as she awoke in the throes of a shattering climax, letting him take her, understanding that he owned her and no man but him had right to touch her . . . ever.

If he kissed her, the fantasy would be made real.

Instead, he wrapped his arms about her body, pulled her tight against him, and helped her rock out her urgent need. A strangled cry escaped her throat as the faint thrusting of her hips stilled. Leaning to Tamlyn, he lightly brushed his lips over hers, drinking in her release, sharing it. Using all his restraint not to devour her mouth with the hunger clawing at his insides.

Julian leaned against the headboard, hugging her to his chest. He shook from the force within him, the blind yearning, unable to fathom the depth of what she caused him to feel.

In all his years, he'd never needed much. He loved his brothers. Loved his father. Loved Damian as a brother. His chargers were necessary to protecting his life in battle. Yet, as he sat holding Tamlyn tightly, he couldn't recall ever needing anyone, that his happiness rested on the whims of another.

He needed Tamlyn.

If he couldn't bind her to him, make her breathe for him as much as he needed her, he feared for that final shard of his sanity. He was a hard man, had to be to survive and live to this age. But he was so weary. He desired more than fighting, had to know his life counted for something other than an instrument to further Edward's pale aims.

He put his hand to the back of Tamlyn's head, cradling it with a fierce possessiveness. Silently, Julian called himself a fool for placing so much hope on Tamlyn. He might be casting his lots, only to have all his dreams crushed.

Panic rising in him, he pushed her aside and left the bed.

Tamlyn roused slowly. She'd dreamed of the black knight, of the pond again, how he took her under the falling water. Every detail had been so real. This time the dream didn't end with the waterfall turning into flames and the screaming of ravens, but moved past, to him taking her on the banks of the sacred pool.

Her body still pulsed with the sensations.

With a smile, Tamlyn stretched like a lazy cat. Reaching out, her hand stroked the bedding, still warm from where Challon had lain. She rubbed her nose against the coverlet and allowed his special scent to flood her mind, summoning the dark erotic images of her dreams, of the warrior all in black. A wall of heat roared through her body, excruciating. Her breasts sensitive, the tightness in her womb clenched like a fist.

Her eyes glanced about seeking Challon, wondering where he'd gone. Gray light filtering into the chamber from the solar told her dawn neared. She listened for sounds. All was quiet, yet somehow she sensed Challon's presence. Rising from the bed, she wrapped the soft ruanna around her, then padded quietly into the other room.

Tamlyn paused under the archway. She blinked, trying to adjust her eyes.

Challon stood motionless, silhouetted against the stained-glass window, an air of sadness lingering about him. Tamlyn wondered if he was recalling his brother Christian. She wanted to go to him—hold him. Offer this man solace.

The rhythm of her heart quickened, fluttered, as Tamlyn fought the emotions warring within her. How could this man conjure these responses from her, while St. Giles—so like him—did not? Standing still, she thought Challon remained unaware of her presence. Respecting his desire for solitude, she started to turn away.

"It is peaceful standing here, watching the world come awake." He spoke softly. "They say your father gave your lady mother this window as a bride's gift, that she set great store in it."

Unsure, she crossed the room with silent steps. "Aye, my mother loved it. She died here, you know. My father had them fetch his chair from the Great Hall and placed here. He carried her in, held her in his lap, rocking her frail body. They watched the sun rise together."

Even after all this time, the image of her father holding

the woman he loved more than life, humming to her as
she passed over, brought tears to Tamlyn's eyes. The
sorrow was as strong as if it were yesterday. Tamlyn had
thought Hadrian would go mad. She'd never forget that
insane howl that tore from him as he sensed his wife's
spirit no longer lingered.

A blanket hung around Challon's shoulders like a
mantle. Lifting his arm, he partially opened the cover, a
silent invitation to share the warmth of his body. Tamlyn
didn't hesitate, but rushed to that promise of comfort.
His intense heat dispeled the coldness of the heartrend-
ing memory.

Challon enfolded the wool about her and pulled her
near. "You still cry tears for your lady mother. How old
were you?"

"Five and ten." She wrapped her arms around his
waist, greedily seeking his body's heat.

"You were lucky to know her that long. I barely recall
my lady mother. She died trying to give my father another son. I was only five. After her death, Guillaume
and Simon's mother raised me. She was a kind, gentle
woman." Challon lifted her chin so she would look at
him. "What is it? I felt your heart miss a beat."

When she didn't answer, he stroked his thumb over her
cheek. It was difficult to imagine a warrior so used to
wielding a sword being that gentle. She looked up into
his eyes, sensing so many contradictions within this man.

"Tamlyn, you must learn to speak your thoughts. How
else are we to know each other?"

She nodded. "My father loved my mother deeply, honored her above all others."

"Go on."

"I asked two conditions in our compromise . . ."

Challon drew a frustrated breath. "I promised I would

wed you in your rites. As for your father, I shall do what I can, Tamlyn. If it were within my power I would see him released. These days, Edward hardly listens to anyone."

She swallowed her tears. "It is not that."

"Then pray what?"

"I would add another condition."

He exhaled. "Let it be the last, Tamlyn. I want your agreement after this. We need to move forward."

"If you speak your troth with me, I expect the vows to be kept. I shan't accept a lord husband who keeps a leman."

Challon moved so fast she had no time to react. He pushed her against the wall beside the window, his mouth taking hers. The stones were cool to her back, but Challon was all fire. He used his lips, his teeth, his tongue, working her mouth until she gave him what he wanted. Head spinning, sensations eddied through her blood until it was painful. He wasn't rough, but he devoured her, kissed her with a hunger that was terrifying.

Tamlyn shoved against his shoulders. Challon was strong, the muscles of his beautiful arms rock hard, unyielding. He refused to break the kiss, but finally sensing her panic, gentled his demand. The slow, tender siege of her senses made her fear dissipate. Instead of pushing against him, she clung to him, fearing her legs wouldn't hold her. His hand snaked over her hips, then the fingers of his left hand shifted through the soft curls. She squeaked in the kiss, as his middle finger slipped over her mound, along the wet crease and then into her body.

He broke the kiss and lightly nipped her lip. Moving the finger in and out slowly, he spoke low husky words. "Feel how your body weeps honey for me." He chained kisses up her jaw, then nuzzled her ear. "I want to taste that honey."

Her eyes widened as she understood what he meant. "But that is—"

"Is what, sweet Tamlyn?" His chuckle rumbled in his chest.

"But surely men do not—"

"Aye, they do. Think on it, my *faidhaich*. My mouth moving on you . . . my tongue thrusting in you." He moved his finger slowly, agonizingly, making her body tremble in response.

Tamlyn was shocked by his suggestion, thinking it not proper. Then Challon's hand worked magic and her mind instantly conjured the dark image, of him on his knees before her, doing everything he promised. And she wanted that, ached for that.

Her thighs clamped around his hand, holding him as lightning arced through her. The world seemed to vanish . . . then slowly put itself together again.

"Sweet mercy." Julian sagged against her, his forehead dropping to her shoulder as his whole body tensed to steel.

Tamlyn listened to his labored breathing. Not moving, she feared he might fall since he leaned heavily on her. Just as she grew concerned, he straightened up. Putting a hand above her shoulder, he loomed over her.

"Give me that—any time I want, *faidhaich*—then there won't ever be a question of a leman."

Chapter 15

As dawn kissed Glen Shane, Tamlyn joined the women and left Glenrogha, heading to the sacred orchard of the Silver Bough to keep the rites of Beltane—May Day. Gnarled apple trees twined high to form the entrance to the ancient grove. Beneath their arched branches, Evelynour waited for them.

Muted shafts of light filtered through the spring leaves, haloing her long white hair. It lent her the appearance of an angel descended to earth. Named after the goddess of the orchard, no elder recalled a time when she wasn't there serving the members of Clan Ogilvie. Despite that, she appeared ageless, her years scarcely marring her face. Pale lavender edging toward gray, her eyes were so translucent many oft mistook her as being blind. Her milky skin burned easily under the sun, so few ever saw her except at dawn or in the gloaming. She seemed most at ease in the haar, as if her grayness made her a part of it.

Gowned with fragrant blossoms, the silver-limbed trees held the promise of a good harvest. Tamlyn laughed as petals fluttered from overhead, raining down on her hair and then to the ground, blanketing it as thick as snow. The ghostly fog shifted and swirled around their gray trunks, embracing the grove and rendering it a faeryland of white and silver.

As she entered the orchard, Tamlyn was imbued with a sense of peace. There was a harmony, a balance about this sacred place. She wore a plain white kirtle, same as the other women, at accord with the foggy wonderland.

On Beltane morn, the women and young girls came to wash their faces with dampened apple blossoms. It was believed the dew and blooms worked magic to make them beautiful.

To renew the life of the orchard they'd plant three rows of apple seeds. Thirteen in each. Come summer one tree would be marked for death, and at Samhain the wood of the apple tree would burn in their sacred balefire. A symbol of the wheel of life.

For as long as she could recall, Evelynour welcomed them to the grove on Beltane. The Three Wise Ones of the Wood were the mothers of the two clans in the truest sense. They taught lessons needed for life, guiding the clans with the ways of the stones. They were charged to keep the oral history and advised through aid of their special gifts.

After the death of her lady mother, each woman played an important role in molding Tamlyn. Yet in some ways Evelynour was closest to her. Their embrace was more like mother-daughter than teacher-disciple.

Lighthearted, the women gathered hands and wove their way through the apple trees. They sang a chant to Evelynour, goddess of the apples, asking her to bless them with a plentiful harvest. When they were done, they gathered fallen flowers wet from the morning dew and brought them to their faces.

The scent was heady. Breathing deep, Tamlyn let the essence wash through her being. Apples were magical.

They provided delicious treats in late summer, cider come autumn, and with careful handling, slices could be dried and stored for winter. Apple petals were at the center of any love-drawing spell, so the blossoms were valued and gathered for sachets and possets.

Kneeling on the ground, Tamlyn brought handfuls of blossoms to her face. She inhaled the sensual aroma and cleared her mind of all thoughts. "Oh, Goddess Evelynour, please guide me on the right path and help me choose my fate." She whispered, "Is Challon the one?"

Julian reined Pagan to a halt. The powerful stallion fought the bit, craving to run. Instead of letting the prancing destrier have his head, he turned him in a circle as he tracked Tamlyn.

He'd seen her enter the sheltered area under the boughs of two ancient trees. All the women wore the same simple white kirtles and silver girdles about their waists. Still, he had no trouble singling out Tamlyn. She shimmered, her aura golden.

Julian didn't stalk her to spy, but for protection. Last night after hearing of this ritual, he left orders for several knights to discreetly follow in the ladies' wake and guard them. They'd chased the miscreants who'd attacked Damian from the glen, but it didn't eliminate the possibility of stragglers missed in the sweep. He wouldn't permit the women of the four holdings to be at risk.

Protective streak aside, Julian admitted to a pinch of male curiosity about this female-only start to their day of Beltane. He'd spotted the old woman waiting for them. By the white hair, he presumed her near the age of Auld Bessa. As he maneuvered Pagan closer to the grove, he was surprised to notice she was comely. Despite the youthful face, something about her manner bespoke a wisdom of the ages.

Tamlyn nodded her head in deferment, then received a kiss of peace upon her forehead from the woman. They linked arms and leisurely strolled into the grove, nearly swallowed by the fog.

The haar was disquieting, and so thick, it shrouded the area around the orchard. Pagan shied. Julian's head whipped around as he could swear he heard tinkling of bells off to the right. The horse was sweating, spooked, an unease Julian almost shared.

It was odd. No chirping of birds. Not the first stirring of breeze. This place was touched with otherworldliness, ancient mysteries. A stillness that was unnatural. Julian found disquiet that Tamlyn was a daughter of this primeval land. This glen held a claim on her soul, owned some part of her he could never touch.

His blood surged, resenting that. Julian closed his eyes for several breaths, willing his anger to still, until the thud of his heart was the only thing he could hear.

You belong to Glenrogha . . . the ethereal whisper brushed against his mind.

If he listened hard enough, he could almost hear furtive voices speaking. The words were foreign, but not the emotion behind them, reassuring him in some strange manner that he was also of this land. Whether these shades were Tamlyn's Auld Ones murmuring to him, or mayhap, as Guillaume suggested, the presence of his brother Christian, he couldn't decide.

Julian embraced the feeling of rightness. This rich dark earth and the golden woman touched him. Not once had he tasted this sense of being a part of a place, of knowing this is where he was meant to be.

Of coming home. The sense of belonging was water to his parched soul.

"Where is our Aithinne?" Rowanne asked, pausing from pared twigs from the low hanging branches and dropping them into the basket. "Our cousin loves the festival. I cannot imagine her missing this day for any reason. It seems odd her not being here, sharing this special morn with us."

All heads turned to Evelynour for the answer. The pale, iridescent eyes looked in the direction of the hills far behind Kinloch, as if seeking knowledge. "She will not come. Matters press her. You will not see her until summer."

Raven inquired, "She ails?"

"Her presence is needed there." Evelynour turned away, signaling that was all she'd say concerning their cousin, who closely resembled Tamlyn.

"Come, there is much to do this day," Raven called.

As they approached where the ancient trees arched and grew together, the fog parted and revealed the warrior upon the black destrier just beyond. In the world of white and gray, he was clothed all in black. The apple blooms swirled around him like a snowstorm, ruffling the blue-black hair, and covering his head and shoulders.

Tamlyn's breath caught and held. He was beautiful, as powerful and majestic as these Highland hills. The kenning whispered he belonged here. Just as she belonged to him. As their eyes locked, she accepted her destiny was twined with his, that Evelynour's visions of the coming of the dark lord were true.

He was the one.

Petals rained upon him, the Goddess Evelynour giving Tamlyn the sign for which she'd asked.

Slowly, he held out his upturned hand, beckoning.

As if still needing affirmation, Tamlyn glanced to the pale woman, almost materializing from the fog. Evelynour's witchy lavender eyes met Tamlyn's and she nodded.

Tamlyn ran to her and hugged her. Evelynour squeezed her tightly, as a mother would a daughter. "Och, lass, you are special. The fate of the whole clan rests with your happiness. The most chosen daughter, the child conceived under the Silver Bough on Beltane. Listen with your heart. Show him the way."

Tamlyn nodded, a sob catching in her throat. Lifting her eyes, she saw tears of joy mixed with a bittersweet sadness in her teacher.

Evelynour leaned her head to Tamlyn's and whispered against her hair. "Go to him, my bonnie lass. Trouble looms ahead for you both. But take him, make him part of us, a part of this land. Remember, that which is worth most is what you must fight for. Fight for him. The Lord Challon is your soulmate. Never forget that, my child. Never."

Tamlyn kissed Evelynour's cheek. In some ways, she'd rushed to Evelynour as a child seeking assurance. Her eyes now sought the Dragon, waiting upon the midnight charger. The horse snorted and stamped its impatience. After a hesitation, she went forward—a woman ready to accept the changes he made in her world.

Willing to take him, as Evelynour said, make him a part of her life, a part of this glen. Willing to fight for Challon.

Julian's jaw clenched as Tamlyn sought the assurance from the witch. His gut tightened, fearing what the woman might do. Relief flowed through him when Evelynour nodded to Tamlyn, almost seeming to encourage her to go to him. He met the fey woman's eyes. Pale, almost dead, eyes that saw more than others. She nodded to him.

Warmth filled him at her acceptance, her blessing. She was clearly happy to see Tamlyn set upon the path of her life. Then the expression altered to sadness. Julian almost flinched at the change.

Though the urgency to snatch Tamlyn away from the old woman was strong, some invisible aura stopped Julian just outside the entrance to the coppice. The unseen barrier warned both male and beast they were intruders in this female place and unwelcome. Even so, he was ready to set spur to Pagan, violate that sanctity and swoop down to carry Tamlyn back to a sphere of his control should the crone call her back. She didn't.

The witch's crooked half-smile made Julian feel as if she looked into his dark soul and found him wanting as a mate for the young woman she so clearly loved, yet recognized there'd be no stopping him from claiming Tamlyn. Her white head drooped slightly. Then she moved back, the mist beginning to rise around her angelic form to enfold her.

Impatient, Julian observed Tamlyn kiss her sisters on their cheeks. Raven clutched at Tamlyn's shoulders and leaned to whisper words to her ear. Turning, Tamlyn picked up the kirtle's material on either side of her knees and then ran to him.

Until that instant Julian hadn't realized he held his breath, for what seemed so innocent held much portent, for Tamlyn . . . for him.

Julian's knees controlled the steed, dancing its edginess at the entrance. He wasn't making Tamlyn come to him, but sensed his black presence wasn't welcomed in this white and silver world of the orchard.

He kicked out of the stirrup so Tamlyn could use it, and leaned over to reach for her.

Tamlyn's face was so open, as she placed her icy cold hand into his. All her emotions were etched there, all the hope, trust and faith. All the wanting. He lifted her and seated her crossways on his lap, feeling her shiver.

Julian swung the heavy black mantle around her, and for the first time since coming to this grove, felt secure in his possession of his lady. Tamlyn was now surrounded by his color. His left arm slid around her and she leaned into his warmth.

Once again, he heard the tinkling of bells and then laughter off in the distance. Then it struck him, his shoulders and hair was nearly white from the apple petals. In an odd way, the whiteness of this fey grove was touching him with its color.

Julian closed his eyes and leaned his head back for an instant. For a man who abhorred tears from a woman, and saw them as a weakness in a man, he felt much like shedding them. In his life, he'd not cried many times. Once, when he was sent away to be page to the Warrior Prince Edward at the age of seven. Again, over Christian as his brother lay begging for death.

And this morning as he held Tamlyn in his arms. Julian wanted to say a prayer of thanks, knowing somehow in his dark, empty life he'd been granted this blessing.

He could force Tamlyn to wed him, force the people of this glen to accept that act and him. It was the way of the world, the way of the sword, yet to travel that road would kill him in a manner he lacked words to explain. He needed Tamlyn as he needed air. The ravenous plaint was as fearsome a power as any he'd ever encountered. He was incapable of controlling it, any more than he could put name to it. It scared him, more than facing the Infidel in the Holy Lands, more than the horrors of Berwick. Terrified him. If this consuming need wasn't satisfied, it would destroy him beyond time's healing.

Tamlyn buried her face against the curve of Challon's neck, nestling against his heart. She inhaled the heady male scent off his flesh. So right, whispered the kenning. She'd been so cold, felt she might never be warm again. Then she put her hand into his and he pulled her against his body and wrapped the thick mantle around them both. Sharing his body's fire, she felt safe.

Other knights materialized out of the fog—Sir Guillaume, St. Giles and Sir Simon. Then other men-at-arms moved forward. They'd been on guard the whole time, yet the women remained unaware.

The way of men, she thought, reaching up and dusting some of the petals from Challon's black locks. It scared her, being lady to this powerful, complex man. Even so, it was a fate she'd embrace. A fate she'd fight for.

The gentle rocking gait of the prancing destrier, coupled with the soothing energy from Challon, nearly lulled her to sleep. Batting her eyes, she resisted. She didn't want to lose one precious moment of this magical day.

She leaned to him and kissed his jaw.

Surprised, a small smile tugged at the corner of his mouth. Pleasure warmed his dark green eyes. "What is that for, my lady?"

"A Beltane kiss, my Lord Challon," she whispered, once more burying her nose against the soft skin of his throat to drink in that wonderful scent. She could stay like this forever, absorbing his dragon's fire, the magic aroma that was his alone.

Aye, she was Challon's lady.

And tonight, she'd make him hers.

Chapter 16

In the gloaming, Challon joined his brothers and cousin to watch the kindling of the balefire of Beltane. The Scots considered this a sacred fire, he'd learned. Within Glenrogha, every candle, each fire had been extinguished, and they would be lighted once again from this blaze at dawn.

Men and women formed seven rings. In opposing directions, each circle revolved about the balefire, its pitch-fed flames shooting high into the twilight sky. Their pagan invocation to the god Bel, Lord of Light.

"It is difficult to tell the women from men." Damian laughed, referring to the Scots males wearing their *feile-beag*—kilts.

Arms folded across his chest, Julian's eyes took in the festive spectacle, but shifted to judge his cousin. He was uneasy. Damian downed yet another tankard of mead, as if seeking to escape some inner demon. Julian feared the trouble stemmed from Damian's increasing preoccupation with Tamlyn.

He tried to make light of the situation. "Sorry to hear

you are so sorely afflicted, cousin. Fortunately, I do not suffer the same problem."

Guillaume laughed. "A first—Damian having troubles differing between males and females. Mayhap you indulge in too much mead, cousin?"

"Normans," Tamlyn huffed, coming to stand next to Julian. Her amber eyes glowed in the light cast by the bonfire as she smiled up at him. "In the Highlands it is said any man can appear manly in trewes and chausses. Only a real man can wear the plaide. Lasses ken him virile."

"Then mayhap I shall wear one for you." Julian breathed the words against the side of Tamlyn's hair, meant for her ears only.

Her blood thrummed, visible in her neck. Julian felt the same pulse echoed in him.

She leaned, rubbing her shoulder against the back of his arm. "You would be bonnie in one, Challon."

"Bah, it is too drafty in winter," Damian snarled. The mead letting his guard down, his eyes flashed in raw jealousy. "A man could die of exposure." Realizing his jest, he howled in near drunken laughter.

Behind his cousin's back, Simon pantomimed the motion of downing cups. His brother's arched brow asked Julian if he knew the reason why. They all recognized this sort of behavior was unlike St. Giles.

Julian shrugged, ignoring Damian's troubled spirit. Reminding his cousin of the realities, he placed a possessive hand on the small of Tamlyn's back.

Noticing the heavy gold torque about Tamlyn's neck, Julian ran his thumb over the intricate design. The workmanship was strong, with subtle artistry, bordering on the mysterious. The flattened torque would fetch a king's ransom on any market. The gold's patina meant it wasn't new, yet it shimmered just as the woman who wore it did.

"The Romans wrote about the Picts and their skills with gold and silver. Yet so little is known about your race. What happened to your ancestors, Tamlyn? Where did the Picts go?"

"Go? Nowhere. They remain here in the blood of their children." Pride flared in her eyes, her words containing a small barb. "What generally happens when invaders come? In this case the Irish—called Scoti—came and formed a kingdom on the southern shores of Alba. It was called Dalriada. Then Kenneth of Alpin used his mother's Pict blood to claim the double crown. He rose and slaughtered all the royal houses of the Picts, uniting Alba under one Scottish Crown."

"Then why do the holdings of Glen Shane still passed to the distaff side?"

Tamlyn swallowed hard, distracted, as he continued to glide his finger along the figure of a wildcat etched into the heavy metal about her neck. "A special charter granted by Malcolm Canmore—in return for another Lady Glenrogha saving his life—keeps the three holdings in the matriarchal line, as long as there is a woman with Ogilvie blood."

"Beg pardon, my lord." A small girl bobbed an awkward curtsy, trembling before the Dragon of Challon. Holding up the basket of small cakes, she smiled. "For you. A May Day cake."

Julian studied the oatcake, then glanced to Tamlyn. "It is some custom concerning this?"

"Everyone gets a May Day cake. Once we baked one large cake and handed out slices, but there are so many people it is easier to bake small ones."

When he reached for one, the child squealed, "Och, not that one!"

His brows lifted. "No?"

"I . . . I touched that one. The one to the right, my lord. It is a grand cake." She tried not to giggle.

Suspicion caused hesitation, but Julian read no change in Tamlyn's expression, so he took the child's suggestion. It was faintly warm and smelled deliciously of spices and honey. Biting down, his teeth grated against a solid object. "Christ's blood! What affront is this? There is a piece of metal in the cake." Anger—and oddly, hurt—exploded within him. "Someone shall pay for this insult."

Tamlyn grabbed his arm, as he went to fling the cake away. "Wait, Julian."

Her using his given name reached through the ire as nothing else could. He paused, his chest rising and falling in fury. He couldn't say why the incident upset him so. Mayhap because he'd been lulled into thinking he could actually belong here and these people could come to accept him as their lord. "Was something purposely put into the cake?"

"Aye, I suspect it was." She took the cake from him and broke it apart. As the cake crumbled, she revealed a small gold ring of a twisted weave design, similar to the one on her torque. "The Beltane cakes all are the same, save two—one special cake for a man, one for a woman. Inside each is a ring. That is how the May Queen and the Lord of the Glen are chosen each year. In this instance, I think you had a bit of help from a pixie." She winked at the child.

"And what happens to the chosen lord? Clan Ogilvie tosses him onto the balefire, a sacrifice to your Auld Gods?" he asked with edged sarcasm.

"Mayhap, long ago, in darker times when the crops

failed, such happened," she replied with a dram of humor. "For the next four seasons, the May Queen and her Lord of the Glen are royalty. If peat is needed for winter fires, then all men pitch in, cut and stack it for him. If the roof needs thatching, he does not work alone. Women sew for him, bake bread and brew heather ale for him. The tanner makes him fine boots. The farrier shoes his horses, and they receive extra oats and apples from the sacred grove. His fields are plowed and reaped with help of the whole clan and he gets the second portion of everyone's harvest. Come spring, they clip his sheep and his cattle are driven to shielings—high pastures in the mountains—and then back to the glen in autumn."

One side of his mouth twitched, the tension in him easing. "Ah, I see. For a year and a day, this man shall be treated as a king. What happens after the calf is fatted for four seasons? Then you toss him on the bonfire next Beltane?"

She laughed, actually laughed. It was the first time Julian had seen her do so, and he was entranced by the pulsing vibrancy rising off this beautiful woman. His lady. No resentment, anger or pain clouded her heart, for only growing adoration was reflected in her witchy eyes. She scintillated with awareness of him.

Compelled, his left hand touched her face, stroking the soft slope of her high cheekbone.

Taking the hand, she glided the gold ring onto his pinkie finger, her eyes almost shy in meeting his. "There, Challon, you are our Lord of the Glen for a year and a day."

"Answer me, Tamlyn, what happens after the year and a day?" His voice was husky.

"The rites come from dark times. They cared for the

human king-god, felt if he prospered, so did the clan. When the harvest thrived, then he remained safe. If famine gripped the land, they made the horrible sacrifice to the wicker man. Those days are gone from memory. Now, it is only a privilege. My people worry about this coming year, Challon. The May Queen chosen last year ran off with a lad from a clan three glens away. It was viewed as a bad omen. The coming of the Dragon changes many things. My people are saying they grant you a year and a day to prove yourself a good lord to Glen Shane."

"And what of their lady?" Julian pressed his advantage. When she lowered her lashes, he lifted her chin, forcing her gold eyes to meet his. "Does she grant me a year and a day to prove I can be a fit lord and husband?"

Tamlyn smiled softly. "You ken what I asked in compromise."

"I granted you the right to wed in the traditions of your people. I shall honor that. As for the laird, I will do what I can, Tamlyn." Julian watched her face register relief. He swallowed the bad taste in his mouth, knowing it was a false promise. Edward would hear no plea from him for leniency for the Earl Kinmarch. "As for the third condition—I told you what you must do to ensure I comply."

Even in the firelight he saw her blush, recalling how they greeted the dawn in the solar. Heat exploded in his blood, and he leaned toward her planning to kiss her, but was interrupted as Raven whirled to a stop before them.

The frantic dancing halted, long enough to give everyone a chance to regain their breath.

The darker twin picked up the explanation. "Lord Challon, The May Queen is revered in same fashion as the Lord of the Glen. All her weaving and spinning is done for her. That thrills Tamlyn. You will find Tamlyn *hates* those chores. She reigns as May Queen tonight because that mooncalf Jenna ran away with Ian Campbell. Special gifts of sweets and apples are left at her door. Of course, it is a very special blessing for the clan if the Lord of the Glen begets a bairn upon the May Queen. It is thought the child is favored by the Auld Gods. Tamlyn is such a chosen one."

Tamlyn's color turning a deeper shade of crimson, she glared at her sister. "Our Raven is usually the quiet daughter of The Shane. Mayhap she should recall that."

Julian gently rubbed his hand at the small of Tamlyn's back, wanting this nearness. "It seems some of your pagan customs contain fine sense."

Another young girl carrying a basket bobbed before them. Raven's gray eyes flashed with mischief as she plucked one off the top. "Your turn, sister," she insisted, before biting into hers.

Tamlyn selected one to the side. Instantly, Aggie jumped back two steps so the cake Tamlyn had been about to grasp was beyond her fingers. Frowning, she reached for it again.

"Och, Tamlyn of Glenrogha, not that one. Auld Maudie touched it. You ken how dirty her fingers are." Aggie giggled.

"Likely no one has ever seen Maudie's skin under four score years of grime. It is a standing joke amongst the men. Each year they threatened when we hold the Floating of the Sheep to toss Auld Maudie in along with the sheep, for it is the only way they will see her clean," Tamlyn explained. She lifted her hand to reach for the next one, watching the eyes of the freckled-faced girl for a reaction. When the child shook her head, Tamlyn said, "Not that one either? She touched it as well?"

"Aye, I am certain she did." The child chuckled.

Sighing, she moved to the back. "This one, wee Aggie? Shall I select it or has Maudie ruined it, too?"

"It is a fine one." Aggie grinned triumphantly.

Tamlyn carefully bit down and chewed, clearly disappointed she didn't find the ring after the little game. By the third bite, Julian feared Aggie erred in her game of biscuit switching.

She bit down again. "Och, what a surprise," she announced dryly. "I think I found the queen's ring."

Raven laughed, snatched another cake, and tossed it to Sir Simon, who rested in a chair due to the leg wound he received in the seizing of Kinloch. "Can anyone doubt the workings of the Auld Ones?"

"You are getting up in years, sister dear." Tamlyn pulled a face at Raven. "Only I would hardly call you ancient."

Julian took the band from Tamlyn's fingers, eager to see it on her hand—a visible symbol of her bond to him. He should have gifted her with a ring before now, showered her with a queen's ransom in jewels.

Her eyes lifted to his, and then back to her trembling fingers, as he slid the ring on the little finger of her left hand. The woven circle matched his, but was more feminine. Possession and need swelled within him to where he wanted to crush her hand to his heart. Instead, he raised it to his lips reverently and placed a kiss, a promise, to the soft skin on the back of her hand. Their eyes locked, speaking in a language that needed no words. Words were too pale to convey the power that rose between them.

Rowanne rushed up and whispered into Raven's ear. Both Raven and she linked arms with Tamlyn, tugging on her. "Apologies, Lord Challon. We must spirit Tamlyn away, but promise not to keep her any longer than necessary," Rowanne called over her shoulder to him.

As Julian watched the three beautiful women rush off, he twisted the ring of Pict design on his finger. The gold band moved easily, but when he tried to tug it off, he found resistance. The metal band seemed crafted just for him.

The breeze swirled around him, causing the balefire to shoot sparks high in the night air. On that playful wind were whispers that once more called to him, telling Julian this was where he belonged.

"Has anyone seen where our ladies vanished?" Julian searched the crowd, trying to locate the three women. He hungered for Tamlyn's presence and fretted at the separation, wishing to share this magical night with her.

Malcolm, their priest, joined them. The handsome man smiled, the glint in his eyes mysterious, as if he read Julian's thoughts. "You shall see Tamlyn shortly, Lord Challon. First, enjoy the pageantry."

The music changed, oddly haunting, the pipes sending chills up Julian's spine. Not the usual tunes of war, but a low, slow droning that enthralled the mind. A hush descended over the area as the people settled down to wait.

The music wrapped around Julian and held him. His eyes followed the priest as he walked to the bonfire.

From a pouch hanging about the man's waist, Malcolm removed an object, molding his fist around it. Raising his arm straight out at shoulder level before him, his mouth chanted some words that didn't carry. Then spoke out so all could hear. "Lo, behold how it has been from the dawn of time, since the Daughter of Anne formed our clan."

Finished with the heralding, he flung gritty powder into the fire. Flames jumped and hissed, flaring white hot for an instant, before settling down to a blue flame. It sent out a curl of thick smoke. Instead of rising, it spiraled outward, rotating around the balefire in an ever-widening circle.

Julian felt unsettled, almost alone in the strange smoke. Guillaume either sensed Julian's warrior unease, or shared it, for he stepped closer, placing a hand on his shoulder. Glancing over to check on Simon where he sat in the chair, Julian's eyes were drawn past his brother.

Damian stood talking with strangers. Having accepted oath of every vassal and serf of this glen and Kinmarch's, Julian knew they weren't of his holdings. He blinked twice, for the small group was more than passing strange.

One, of Viking descent judging by the white-blond hair, stood a head taller than any man present. He wasn't someone you'd forget. A warrior, he stood in a position of deference and as protector behind three younger men.

In earnest conversation with his cousin, the middle one offered Damian a horn of mead. Dressed too fine to be anything but high-born, all three were the exact image of the other—same light red hair and narrow faces. Triplets?

Julian knew he hadn't drunk anything to affect his senses, for fear of losing control around Tamlyn tonight. Mayhap the herbs the priest tossed upon the fire affected him. He blinked thrice, yet the trio remained with their pet giant.

Suddenly, a feral war-scream jerked Julian's attention back to the balefire.

A man soared over the flames of the sunken fire, almost seeming to split the smoke. Clad in doeskin breeches, they molded to his legs by the lacing of leather thongs up to his midthigh. He wore nothing else, though upon his head sat a mask with antlers of a large buck. He executed several high leaps, kicking to fly through the air. Then with the grace of a cat, he landed before Julian, stopping to stare at him. Vivid lavender eyes glowed from behind the animal mask, locking with Julian's. With a magician's pass, the man extended his hand. Between his thumb and first finger was a single fresh-picked violet.

Julian glanced at the purple flower, a shade similar to the eyes of the masked man. Unsure of the significance, Julian sensed he was supposed to take it, so did.

"Your first gift as Lord of the Glen." Malcolm materialized, just behind Julian's shoulder. "On the first violets of spring, one may make wishes and they come true. What will you wish for, Lord Challon?"

Julian lifted the flower to his nose. There was no scent. The delicacy of the bloom belied the endurance of the plant.

What did he wish for? He thought of touching Tamlyn, her scent, her heat. He wanted to plant his seed within her body, for them to create a son.

"Wish, and it will come true, Lord Challon," the masked Scot entreated. Then with a small half smile, touched with a hint of wickedness, he spun in a circle and vaulted away from Julian.

He continued to leap, capering around the bonfire with a vertiginous force, the jumps rising higher and higher. It appeared he almost gathered power from the bluish smoke, until his bare chest glistened with sweat. His arms flung open and closed with each turn, his head snapping about.

So absorbed by the nimble display, Julian failed to

notice four men stepping out of the shadows. Unlike the leaper, they dressed in the green garb of hunters.

They began a fascinating mime—the four hunters chasing the male stag, pursuing, spinning and leaping through the smoke. The hunters drew closer and closer, until they finally brought the man-stag down with "an arrow from a bow." So spellbound by the mummers, the crowd groaned in agonized empathy as the stag suffered death throes. The four hunters bent down, each taking a leg or arm, then lifted his form to their shoulders. In solemn respect, they circled of the balefire, while the pipes wailed a dirge. The smoke grew thicker, until it finally swallowed the hunters and the fallen prey.

Then a skirl split the lull as a man leaped through the flames, to exultations of the people of both clans. The stag was reborn as a young Highlander—the Lord of the Glen. No longer clothed in the leathern chausses or wearing the animal mask, he dressed in a plaide of black and green and carried an ornate claymore.

Instead of performing high leaps and turns, he moved in fluid motion, demonstrating the skill of the man and the Highland great sword as one. He slashed the air and parried with power, force and control, turning the weapon into an extension of his body.

Before, Julian had sneered at the Scots claymore as too long and clumsy. The fluid swings, thrusts and parries meant for offense and defense he now witnessed were anything but cumbersome. The magnificent sword, nearly as long as the height of a man, seemed a part of the warrior. Julian envied the artistry. Awestruck, he watched, memorizing the sinuous, elegant movements of the Scotsman. Julian knew that on the morrow he'd seek this man out to learn this mastery.

Then the melody slowed and lowered, stilling to only

two pipers playing a haunting refrain. Whispered hushes descended over the gathering, followed by the crowd drawing in a collective breath. All eyes left the braw Highlander and shifted to the opposite side of the hill in anticipation.

Then Julian saw what pulled them.

Two men in long green robes, bearing torches, approached the south entrance to the tor, solemnly promenading down the long avenue. Behind them was a smaller female figure shrouded in a fine net of spun gold. The metallic fabric captured glints from the firelight, twinkling as if anointed with faerydust. With an air of a mock wedding march, Rowanne and Raven trailed behind a woman, each holding a corner of her train. As the music fell to a lone tin pipe playing slow, poignant notes, the robed escorts stopped at the edge of the circle, and in unison they stepped aside giving way the veiled woman.

Julian's eyes were riveted to her.

Stepping into the balefire's light, she took hold of the long veil. Drawing her arms up before her, she then raised them skyward. Everyone seemed not to breathe while she remained in that position of supplication. Gradually, she allowed the netting to slip down her arms.

Tamlyn stood bathed in the amber firelight. Her kirtle was gold, spun from Highland magic. It clung to her body, with splits up both her thighs. A chaplet of apple blooms crowned her unbound, honey-colored hair, rippling in the soft breeze. The heavy golden torque was about her neck, but she now wore matching cuffs on her wrists, the only thing on her bare arms.

A Pictish princess conjured from the Scottish mists.

A second pipe joined the first, playing the haunting tune, as Tamlyn rose up on her bare toes. She swayed, rocking to the accent of the drum. The heavy, throbbing beat of the bohran provided cadence for the wanton roll of her hips. When the music swelled, the bagpipes joined in.

Her body undulated in a dance so carnal, so profane, that a blinding wave of lust seized Julian's whole being. Flames of desire roared through him. The pain tripled as Tamlyn circled the fire. Her lithe, feline movements gained force, matching the power of the melody as she kicked her legs out, spun, arched and leaped. She flung the net about, trailing it behind her, so it appeared she had wings. The Cait Sidhe—Cat Faery.

Julian stared, incapable of thought. Tamlyn held him utterly spellbound. The pounding of his heart echoed the bohran, his blood thickening until he felt lightheaded. Unable to take his eyes from her, he watched as she danced on air, lifted by the strange music. A music that had a life all its own.

The Highlander stepped back into the light, swinging the claymore. Tamlyn spun around him, and almost in pantomime he followed her, his circles turning inside of hers until they finally came face to face. The music lowered as the pair slowly began to move in unison. The sword and the net symbolically worked as counterpoints in the blatantly sexual dance.

They drew closer, Tamlyn's body arching toward the Scotsman, each feeding off the radiant sexuality of the other. Voices here and there began to hum the music, adding to the potent brew of this magical enchantment.

A fine sheen of perspiration coated Tamlyn's golden skin. She glowed with an inner light. And the force with which Julian wanted her nearly drove him to his knees.

Julian wanted to howl. No man should dare dance in such a manner with his lady. He took a step toward them, but Guillaume grabbed his arm to stay him. Shaking his head, he silently cautioned not to interfere.

Once more, the music lowered and three couples entered the circle of light. Soon their sinuous movements mimicked Tamlyn and the Highlander. All eight pranced around the fire, swaying, almost touching at times, only to have the females twirl away playfully, taunting the males to follow their lead. Another three pairs joined the dance. They revolved about the fire, yet almost seemed a part of it. The scene enthralled his senses.

But Julian could only see Tamlyn.

The other dancers were vague, faceless figures, mere moving shadows next to Tamlyn's glistening presence. He burned for her. Jealousy ripped through him with talons every time the Highlander accidentally brushed his arm against hers. Each time Tamlyn looked into the man's eyes, Julian wanted to march over and claim the woman that was his. Guillaume's cautioning grip held him in place, bidding him not to interfere.

Each time the pairs circled, three more joined the swaying and spinning, until they numbered thirteen. They wove, first the men around the women, then the females circling the males. Teasing. Luring. Taunting.

And it was slowly killing Julian.

The music rose, driving the dancers onward. Then it would fall again and slow as the couples drew closer together.

Abruptly, the Highlander plunged his sword deep into the earth before Tamlyn. The meaning was not lost on Julian. Hot rage, jealousy and lust surged through him to the point of madness. He flung Guillaume's hand away and stalked into the circle of light.

The music dropped and then swelled to the crest again, sending Tamlyn spiraling away from the man who was the living king-god. The music lifted Tamlyn, carrying her along, but some element wasn't right. Still she danced, furiously, sensually, obeying the refrain and the pulse of the bohran. Even so, her body pined for something demanded of her.

She'd danced as the May Queen twice before. Never had it affected her in this manner. Her body throbbed with need, the pressure increasing. With dizzying force she twirled, casting the netting behind her as a warrior's pennon.

Suddenly, the net seemed to catch. A jerk yanked her around, causing her to slam into the hard wall of a body. Disoriented, barely able to breathe, she stared into the chest covered in black. Slowly her eyes lifted to the burning green eyes.

Challon.

Her chest rose and fell, heaving from the exertion, but also from his nearness. Aye . . . oh, aye . . . this is what her body craved. She danced for *him* this night. Ached for him to come dance as the true Lord of the Glen. The power exuded by this dark warrior made her wonder which emotions were strongest in him. Anger? Jealousy? Desire? Did his need match what pulsed in her? Would Challon dance with her and summon the powers of this special night?

Her mouth crooked a little. She decided to test if her Dragon would play. She took two steps preparing to spin away, but Challon used his hold on the netting to reel her back, forcing her to arch into him. Their bodies close, their mouths almost touching so they shared each other's breath, her hips began to rock to and fro, seeing if he picked up the rhythm.

Slowly, he did. Tentative at first. But then his hips rocked against her with surer movements as the bohran spoke to his blood. She turned, moving around him so they nearly touched, rubbing her back against his. He followed, woodenly the first time, his eyes never leaving her. As they continued dancing circles around each other, he soon mirrored her steps.

As if he'd done this a hundred times before.

The music rose pushing them onward, their sexual need spiraling within them as their bodies swayed together.

Voices joined with the music's crescendo in near exaltation, proclaiming the rightness of what they witnessed, the clan seeing their May Queen accepting the Lord of the Glen in rites that meant life, meant the clan would endure strong and healthy.

The music slowed, but not the chanting voices. She heard a man male murmur *yea . . . yea . . . oh, yea*, while others were a soft feminine sigh.

Challon swung the net around her and used it to drag her closer, until she was hard against him. The deep breaths pushed her breasts against his chest. The thinness of her kirtle did little to shield her from his arousal. Releasing his hold on the netting, his hands slid up and down her hips.

Unexpectedly, Challon seized her about the waist, and lifted her high, spinning around and around, carried on the music and the elation of the people watching. He gradually slowed. Her dizziness was nothing compared to the windswept emotions storming through Tamlyn. Challon let her slide against his body, down to the ground, the friction both agony and ecstasy.

Tamlyn had never felt stronger, never felt weaker. She wanted to provoke him. Wanted to surrender. She wanted their bodies joined as one.

Had the music stopped or had she just ceased to hear

it? All she could do was stare into the dragon-green eyes. Drown in them. This man was her destiny. Nothing else mattered.

Hunger burned in his eyes, robbing Tamlyn of breath. Yanking the netting from her grasp, he dropped it and then lowered his head as his mouth took hers. Lightly at first. So poignant, it brought tears to her eyes. He deepened the kiss, desperate, more demanding. The primitive male need to mate had been let loose within Challon.

Yet beneath that driving force, Tamlyn sensed the desire was for *her*. This powerful man, a king's champion, needed her in ways she knew he didn't begin to understand.

Lost to him, Tamlyn wasn't aware of the hundreds of other people around them or their celebrating. To her the world stood still, narrowed, until there was nothing but the star filled night and Challon.

The cries of people from both clans filled the night air. Their dancing around Tamlyn and Julian grew more frantic, expressing the joy at the bonding of these two people. A good omen for the glen. Some whispered they witnessed something very rare, a coming of a love that was timeless—a love that had been before. How ages ago, another woman and a warrior danced on this high tor before the Beltane balefire on a night such as this.

The Elders recognized their coming again.

Chapter 17

In some ways, Julian was like a cat—drop him and he always landed on his feet. Yet, as Tamlyn took his hand in hers, Julian followed until his sense of direction completely disappeared. Spiraling down the hillside, she drew him away from the gathering on the tor. The music grew faint, as did the laughter echoing through the night. At first, he assumed she guided him back to Glenrogha, but she turned from the path and headed deeper into the darkness. Only when they paused, and the heady scent of apple blossoms filled his head, did he realize she'd brought him to the orchard of the Silver Bough.

Tamlyn paused, leaning against him as if seeking his warmth. He wrapped his arms around her and took her mouth, kissing her slowly, thoroughly, nearly drowning in emotions this woman brought to him. She broke away, laughing musically. Reaching up, she dusted white petals from his hair.

Julian glanced overhead to notice they stood under the natural arch formed by the two ancient apple trees, entrance to the sacred grove. The tug of her hand told him to follow. He hesitated.

Julian recalled how the grove hadn't welcomed his presence before. It held him outside the opening with an unseen barrier, reminding him he was male and thus not part of this female bastion.

He stopped and studied the lay of the land, how the hills rose on either side of this mound. In some ways, the land reminded him of a woman as she lay on her back, her thighs open, waiting, fertile. Warm air stirred through the apple trees and rushed out to swirl around him in welcome. This morn, he'd felt warded against entering. Strangely, he now sensed the grove embraced him, opening itself to his male intrusion—as his body craved Tamlyn to open to him.

Mayhap the wanton rites had addled his thoughts, but he suddenly understood the Scots worship of the May Queen and the Lord of the Glen. There was something very feminine about the day, the softness of dawn with its pale colors. Then the night came, and with it the sensuality of the male.

The grove drew him now because he was a part of the force of life, part of that balance.

He didn't know when Tamlyn's ancestors created the grove. Ages ago, judging by the long rows of trees. He wondered if they laid it out with purpose, or if the power of the land moved her people to plant the two apple trees—a male tree and a female—for there would've been no apples otherwise. The limbs intertwined to create the arch to the grove of the Silver Bough, the natural gateway to the womb of the orchard.

He let the sweet, redolent scent and the warm air eddy around him, intoxicating him with a sense of belonging to this pagan land. In a spinning blend of reality and fantasy, he saw the pageantry of the stag-man play through his mind. Julian sensed the connection, why the masked

Scot had stood before him and offered the single violet. As the images floated in his head, Julian envisioned the man leaping through the flames, reborn. Only, this time he wore Julian's face.

As he passed beneath the archway of the two trees, the whole world shifted. Suddenly, the night, the land, the ritual told him that Tamlyn and he were meant to be together, as if this scene had played out before.

"Come, Challon," she entreated softly.

Apple petals fluttered in the breeze, raining down upon them. Off in the distance he heard the light tinkling of bells, just as he had this morning. Everything felt mystical, as if unknown powers rose from this spot in the earth, as if all in his life that came before were mere guideposts leading him to Tamlyn and Glenrogha. As he drank in the scent of the earth and the apple blossoms, he felt the force moving through him, renewing, healing.

Glenrogha. He knew glen meant valley. "Tamlyn, what does rogha mean?"

She paused, smiling at him in the moonlight. "Choice, best if you like."

Tamlyn was the chosen daughter of Glenrogha—the chosen fief.

The warrior in him should feel exposed, moving away from the crowd and into the darkness. The hills might harbor some of the lingerers from Clan Comyn. He'd been oddly fortunate in that the Clans Ogilvie and Shane harbored deep resentments toward the Comyns. Also, his path was easier since the glen was so far removed. They'd never witnessed the horrors of war. So far, the people of Clan Ogilvie seemed to accept him, welcomed his presence in Tamlyn's life. Still, he knew it only took one or two malcontents to cause trouble.

Despite his warrior instincts being on guard, he sensed

peace and safety in this grove and was pleased Tamlyn had brought him.

He tugged on her hand to slow her. "Why have you led me here, Tamlyn?"

She turned back, the shadows wrapping around her. "To show you my tree. This way."

"Your tree?"

"Aye, my lady mother planted the seed for my tree on May Day a score and six year ago." She paused, going to a nearby tree. Putting her arms around the silver trunk, she hugged it. "This is her tree, planted on the day she was conceived. It no longer produces apples. It stopped flowering after she died. My father tells he took her under its boughs on Beltane and nine moons later I arrived."

Once more, she took his hand and drew him deeper into the orchard, finally coming to a stop near the end of one row.

"This is your tree?" he asked.

"Aye, planted by my lady mother. As I planted one earlier today."

Julian's body pulsed to a dull throb. The music from the tor filtered down to the orchard, making him recall how she'd danced with him before the balefire. "I should be wary of us being away from the crowd. The stragglers that attacked Damian and his men may still lurk near. Yet . . ."

"Yet?"

"I feel protected within this grove."

"All here are protected. The sacred mists shield this glen. None shall find their way into Glen Shane."

"What mean you? The sacred mists shield the glen?"

Tamlyn hesitated, then finally spoke. "The mists of Glen Shane were a warding set long ago by the Daughter of Anne, the first lady of the glen. They protect us. The passes remain hidden by a fog so none may see the entrance. For centuries no invaders put foot on the soil in this valley."

She turned away unable to meet his direct stare. Julian granted her no quarter. Taking her arm and pulling her back around, he asked, "If that is so, then why did I see them?"

She gazed into his face, her answer a whisper. "Because the Auld Ones willed it so."

"Your gods willed my coming to this glen? They opened the path for me?" Julian paused, trying to fathom the knowledge she imparted. "I saw the mists swirl, then lift so the passes were revealed to my eyes, I felt . . . a sense of coming home." In a soft voice, he asked, "How can I feel welcome in a land I have never seen before? How, Tamlyn?"

A tear glistened in her eye, but he wouldn't permit her retreat. He still held her by the elbow. The first finger of his right hand curled under her chin and lifted it so she was forced to meet his eyes. "How, Tamlyn, tell me?"

Her lip quivered, as she drew in a shaky breath. "You are guided by the kirk. You will not wish to hear our heathen ways."

"Tell me. This night I find myself believing in many things."

"You have been here before. Long ago."

"I would remember if I ever came to Glen Shane before. Never could I have met you and forgotten." He took a step closer, compelled by the glittering tears in those haunting eyes.

A weak smile tugged at the corner of her mouth. "But you have forgotten me, Challon. My mind recalls you . . . you came on a black steed wearing black mail—"

"Never. I say never." His thumb traced over her chin,

feeling the hint of a clef. "Never could I forget you, Tamlyn."

"It is so. Why do you think the people of the glen accept you so readily? They are brave. They would fight for their lands, their home."

"My troops are too many."

"They would not be mooncalf enough to face your English might on a field of battle. They would come from the mists, strike at your weakest points, your flanks. Pick at your troops like a carrion bird on a carcass. When you gave chase, they would vanish into the mists and shroud themselves from your eyes. Instead, they accept your coming. My lord father recognized you. He sought Evelynour's foretellings. She said you were him come again."

"Him?" A shiver shuttered up his spine.

"The warrior-king came and took the Daughter of Anne to wife. They came to this glen and founded our clan. It is why the Auld Ones showed you the way into our valley."

He felt the fine tremors racking her body. He stepped closer, not in intimidation, but in succor. "Shhh . . . why do you tremble so, Tamlyn?" Logic told him this was naught more than a dream spun of Highland mists, but one he could use to bind her to him.

Then why did his soul hunger to believe her words?

Some part of him wondered. His scouts had hunted for the entrance from Kinmarch that led into Glen Shane, searched for nearly half a day. When he tired of their failure, he spurred Lasher away from the troops. No sooner than he'd ridden a few rods, the mist became so thick it swallowed his soldiers and heavy horse. For a space, time seemed to bend in upon itself and he seemed so alone.

Except for the cries of ravens.

Their cacophony grew louder, almost deafening, causing Lasher to shy. He had trouble making the charger
move forward. The horse refused to obey the signals of
his knees, and was sweating and showing clear signs of
fear.

Then suddenly the mist swirled and slowly lifted,
showing he stood at the mouth of the passes to Glen
Shane.

He leaned toward her, brushing his lips over her
cheek. "If your gods will it, who am I—a mere mortal—
to defy them? By the same token, my lady, you must
heed their will as well."

A tear slipped over her cheek and he caught it with his
lips, drinking in the healing nectar. She trembled against
him. Her hands grasped his upper arms, her fingers digging into his muscles. He had an idea she'd brought him
here for more than to show him her tree. Yet the skittish-
ness told him she was still frightened of being with him,
giving herself to him.

He forced himself to pull back and set her from him.
"We need to return to the tor, Tamlyn."

Her face reflected her confusion in the moonlight.
"I—I thought—"

"Tamlyn, soon we will be wed. Then as your lord husband I shall claim you. It is not that I do not want you.
You know I do. After this morn, there can be little doubt
of how I desire you. But I told you, I grant you the time
until the wedding."

She lowered her head shyly, then glanced up at him.
"What if I do not want to wait, Challon? Some things are
just meant to be."

The breeze shifted, carrying notes of the pagan music,
floating down to them. The throb of the drum beat out a

tattoo that seized his heart, almost beating for it. Tamlyn tossed back her hair, a feline smile curving her small, full mouth. Picking up the beat of the bohran, she rolled her hips, her whole body rocking to the sensual melody.

Tamlyn leaned into him. Like a cat, she brushed against him. Held breathless in her thrall, he felt the friction send heat spiraling through his body. White hot, it exploded within his mind. She placed her hands on his hips and swayed, encouraging him to follow her rhythm. Arching on her toes, she brought her mouth to his in a slow kiss, dragging her lips over his. Vaguely, Julian was aware that her hands tugged at the chain across his upper chest, unhooking the fastener. His mantle fell away from his shoulders; the black splashed across the white blossoms under the tree. He stared, transfixed by the symbolism.

She knew. This was meant to be. Somehow, it seemed right he should take Tamlyn on a bed of apple blossoms and his midnight mantle.

Her hands unbuckled his baldric. When it separated, they both moved quickly to catch the sword before it hit the ground. Her witchy eyes glowed as Tamlyn pulled back with only the sheath.

The image flooded his memory of Tamlyn dancing with the Highlander, how he'd driven the sword into the earth. That act nearly crowded him to madness. For a long instant they remained transfixed, the music curling around them. Then, sensing what she wanted of him, Julian raised the sword and drove it into the ground beside the mantle.

Tamlyn smiled. He was held in her spell, couldn't break away from her. Nothing could stop this. The questing hands moved over his chest to help pull off the surcoat. Next came the sark. Julian tossed them to the ground with little thought.

Once more she kissed him. He tasted the sweet oat-cake on her breath, yet as he sought to deepen it, she slithered down his body. The vision of this pagan princess on her knees before him set Julian's blood thundering to the point he felt faint. Her nimble fingers undid the lacing around his boots so he could kick out of them. With a heady mix of pure innocence and raw wickedness, Tamlyn snaked her hands up his tensed thighs, agonizingly over his groin. Then her body followed the same path.

Sheer torture.

Running her hand over his chest, she kissed him lightly again, then whispered, "Dance with me, Challon."

Julian's body seemed to know what she wanted, for he began the slow rocking, his hands on her waist, mimicking the pagan rhythm. Tamlyn rotated so her back was against his chest, her rounded derrière pressing, rubbing against his hard groin. She placed her smaller hands over the top of his, sliding them up to her breasts. He swayed with her, grinding his body to hers while he squeezed the full breasts until she moaned. She took her hands from his, pulling at the golden gown until her breasts were freed.

His Highland enchantress became a wanton as he controlled their dance. Her nipples hardened as he stroked them, using his thumb to circle around and around. A moaned rose in her throat, urging him on, encouraging him to squeeze them, roll them.

Suddenly, he spun her to face him. His arms went around her hips, then lifted her. In rising hunger, his mouth feasted on her breast. Sucking it hard, he drew on it in a rhythm he knew would echo inside her body. Her head fell back, her long hair cascading behind her. Carefully, reverently, he lowered Tamlyn to the black cloak. Hands clutching his upper arms, she arched to him.

For an instant out of time, Julian paused to stare at the beautiful woman under him. He wanted to capture this image in his mind. When he was old and gray, he'd conjure its power and recall Tamlyn, so beautiful, her golden hair pooling about her on his black mantle, the white apple blossoms raining down upon her.

Julian wanted this to last, to go slowly with her, make the beauty of this joining perfect for her. Only she wouldn't let him. He kissed her as he undid his leathern hose and pushed out of them and his braies, then his hands ruched up the golden gown to her hips.

He slid his fingers through the soft curls, finding them wet with her body's desire, preparing her for his invasion. He moaned as he slid a finger in her, hoping to stretch her there, then two. She was so very tight. He didn't want to hurt her.

"Julian . . . *please* . . ." She seemed unable to gasp anything further.

Taking her hands, Julian interlaced his fingers with Tamlyn's and pushed them up beside her head, his body aligned to make them one. His erection nudged against her opening, moistening the tip with the honey of her body. He knew virgins felt hurt, but wished pain to be no part of her memory, so he held back, kissing her breathless. Just as he flexed the muscles of his hips and slid into her, ready to breach the maidenhead, she jerked her head back from his, gasping.

"Wait . . ."

He blinked, nearly blind with the quickening. "Wait?" came his strangled reply.

"Aye. You must . . . make a wish."

Julian echoed the words as if they were foreign. "Make a wish?"

"Aye, it is important. Wish for what your heart desires the most, Challon." She kissed the column of his neck.

Julian forced his eyes to focus on the woman beneath him. She lay on the mantle—so black in the midst of the snow-white petals. Her lustrous hair spread out around her, her cat-eyes shining. He knew he belonged to this woman. Aye, she was likely a witch, but then maybe it was a witch's charms he required to heal him, to exorcise the black miasma claiming his soul. No price was too high to own her, possess her.

Tamlyn sensed his hesitation. "Our joining is special. My people call it *deas-ghnath mòhr*."

"Grand rite," he repeated.

"Aye, it is magic. Wish for what you want most, Challon."

Tamlyn looked up into the face of the man who was about to claim her and had never seen anything more rugged, more terrifying as his male power. Never seen anything more beautiful.

She hoped in her secret heart he'd wish for her to love him, for she knew she loved him and always would, no matter what lay ahead of them. Likely, she'd loved him from the very first, when she'd been kneeling and her eyes met his. She'd been too unused to the ways of emotions, desire and love to understand what was happening to her.

Now she knew.

"Make a wish, Julian."

A crooked smile touched his lips. "What about you? Do you not make one as well?"

"Oh aye, I wish for your wish to come true." Her replying smile was all woman, mysterious and born of the cat, confident of the man who was about to make her his.

Warmth left his face, replaced with seriousness, a yearning so deep it caused her to blink. "My wish . . . I want a child . . . a son born of your body."

Not the words she wanted to hear fall from his lips, but then a child—their child—was a bond between them. She saw how desperately Julian desired a son, and hoped one day he'd desire her, love her with the same intensity.

"So be it," she intoned. Tamlyn turned her head into the shadows to hide her disappointment. She wanted to hear Challon say he loved her. Wanted it with the same burning ache she heard in his voice when he asked for a son of her body.

"Tamlyn, look at me," he commanded his voice soft, deep. "I want to see your eyes when I take you."

She blinked, staring into his shadowy countenance. She felt him stretching her. Then felt that hot, pulsing flesh push against her barrier. Her body was magic, conforming to accept him within her. Confused, she felt Challon pull back, but then he plunged forward. A cry escaped her lips, but he caught it, kissing her until the pain passed. She was amazed how deep he was within her, how joined their bodies were.

He raised up slightly and then moved inside her again, causing her to cry out her need.

He whispered against her lips, "Dance with me, Tamlyn."

Chapter 18

It was nearly nooning when Julian entered the lord's chamber to seek his rest. The tower remained eerily silent. Besides men of the guard, no one was up and about their chores, likely sleeping off remnants of the Beltane revels, too much mead and *uisge-beatha*—whisky.

Overwhelmed by so many conflicting and indefinable emotions, he felt frustrated with himself, impatient.

God's teeth, last night had been so good. Tamlyn burned out all memories of anyone else—there was only her. Never had he known the pleasure he found with his Scots lass. Never had he wanted to give so much. He'd taken and then taken more, seeking to use her warmth to exorcise the chill lodged in his soul. Well, she had. Blazed as bright and hot as the sun, scorched him to the very core with her pagan fire.

What surprised him was his need to give. He had to fill her with himself—not just the flesh—with a radiance that branded every inch of her body, her being, her mind, with his complete possession. Julian had wanted to own her, dominate her, bend her to his will.

Somewhere along the path, all that control had been ripped from his hands.

She now owned him. Possessed his very soul.

On his long journey to Glen Shane, he'd mapped out plans for the future in his mind. On the steps of their ancient kirk, he'd take Tamlyn to lady wife before all of Glenrogha. The pomp and the circumstance would be formidable, as befitting a man formerly the king's champion. Already, he'd planned the details, down to what they both should wear. Raven sewed a dress for Tamlyn, copied from a drawing he'd done.

Long ago, Julian learned the value of appearance. A formidable weapon in life. So much of what people thought, how they treated you, hinged on how they viewed you. The lavish wedding and the feast to follow would be talked about, praised, envied. Julian's possession of the Lady Glenrogha would spread through the Highlands. The tides would be upon the lips of bards throughout these Isles. Nothing less would be expected when the Dragon of Challon wed.

Men feared his persona. He'd spent years polishing and perfecting that invisible shield. Being the Black Dragon was as strong a weapon as his lance or sword.

He intended his marriage with Tamlyn to follow that exacting creed, serve to enhance the legend of the Dragon. After they spoke their vows and reigned jointly over the wedding feast, fusing in the minds of the people of both clans that he was her lord husband and that she came to him willingly, then and only then, would he lead her to their chambers where he would instruct his virginal lady in the pleasure of their marriage bed.

Instead, he'd lost his head and taken her as a common wench beneath the apple tree. What would Glenrogha's

people think of him? That he dishonored her? How
could they not?

Before he had time to organize his thoughts, the door
flew open and Tamlyn pranced in carrying a tray of
food. She hummed the same song they'd danced to last
night, a satisfied smile upon her full lips.

Suddenly, memories roared through him, how their
bodies swayed to the pagan melody. He sensed there was
a deeper meaning to their rites. He'd been correct. As the
music flowed around them, enfolding them in the erotic
madness, the muscles of his body seemed to know the
sensual movements. After that, he recalled nuances,
essences, details. The overpowering, intoxicating scent
of the apple blossoms. Her glowing cat-eyes. The soft
feel of her body as she danced close against him. The
taste of oatcakes on her breath.

The whole night had been magical, so perfect, he
could almost believe it a dream. No, not a dream. A
witch's enchantment.

This loss of control angered Julian. Her humming the
same melody seemed to taunt him. Reminded him he'd
taken his betrothed, as if he had no restraint or respect.
Point of fact, there was very little that didn't irritate him
at this moment. What rankled most, he was close to
losing control and taking her again . . . on the floor,
against the wall . . . in a hundred ways.

"Good morrow, Julian." Tamlyn danced on faery feet
to him, then brushed a faint kiss across his unrespond-
ing lips

She stared up at him with those witchy cat-eyes. His
blasted body sprang to life from just her scent, the light
brush of her small warm mouth.

Tamlyn wore the look of a woman thoroughly loved
and not in gentleness. There were marks on her shoulders

and neck—and likely other places. He hadn't been careful with her as he should. She'd been a virgin. Oh aye, that was very clear in his heated memory. When he broke through her maiden's veil, she hadn't reacted with fear or pain, but embraced his burning need.

"You seem rather cheery after such a long hard night, wench." He'd meant it as a reproof, instead it came out in a tone that was playful, teasing. Damn him! He needed to get down on his knees and beg her forgiveness.

Tamlyn eyed him saucily, as she fed him a slice of dried apple. "Wench? Och, the man has no respect."

She teased, but Julian cringed at her words, reminded how it must appear to all at Glenrogha. Surely they'd see this as an affront.

His eyes softened as he took the hand, that fed him the apple piece, and kissed it. "Lass, you understand there will be no waiting for the crying of the banns. I shall ride out and speak to your uncle this day. With everyone still reeling from May Day, I suppose it will be too much to arrange the ceremony for today, so we will speak vows on the morrow."

"Julian, you set my head spinning. Why must we wed so soon?" Tamlyn laughed.

The door pushed opened and two pages brought in pails of heated water. They emptied them into the wooden tub in the corner, smiling at Julian. "Good morrow, Lord Challon. You enjoyed our May Day?" one asked.

"Hush, Connor Og." Tamlyn winked at the lad. "Hurry to fetch the remainder of the water before your lord grows impatient."

The two boys dashed off, chuckling.

"I ordered you a bath, Challon. You can relax in the steaming water, and I shall feed you. Then we can discuss why you think it necessary to move the day for our wedding." Tamlyn went to the cabinet and took out a clay pot. She sat on the edge of the heavy tub, slowly poured in some sort of powder, then lazily stirred it with her hand.

"I must make amends whilst the damage is still fresh in everyone's minds."

Tamlyn frowned at him, rose and steered him to the tub. "Undress, Challon, then you can tell me what sort of damage you think you have wrought. I think I shan't like what you have to say."

"Blast it, Tamlyn, I took you on the ground as a common trollop. Honor demands that the slight done you—"

Her laughter filled the chamber.

"You dare laugh?" He sucked in his breath trying to stare her down.

"Hush and get into the tub, Challon, before you ruin my good spirits." She helped him undress, efficiently as a squire, then guided him to the tub.

The boys returned with more buckets, which they sat beside the tub before scurrying off again. Tamlyn crossed to her wardrobe and pulled out a simple white chemise. "Let me get out of my Beltane gown. Then I shall assist you with the bath. Whilst I do that, I shall answer your questions and mayhap ease some of your foolish concerns."

"We should marry as soon as possible."

The golden kirtle dropped to the floor and she stood naked before him. He swallowed hard, his pulse jumping. Tamlyn lifted her hair back and pulled on the chemise, so thin it did little to hide her beautiful body from his hungry gaze. Placing the tray with the food across the tub, she pulled up a stool and sat.

"You soak and chew while I explain, for if I hear more nonsense about damage I might push your head under."

He caught her arm as she brought another slice of apple to his mouth. Holding her wrist, he allowed her to feed him. Chewing slowly, his eyes devoured her. "I recall another time you helped me with my bath."

"Behave, Challon." She fed him a chunk of cheese. "I rather thought you smart enough to understand what happened last night. First, there is no affront by your taking me on Beltane night. No one here thinks less of you. They shall, in fact, view our bonding as a grand omen. Underneath our rituals there are traditions, meanings going back to the dawn of time."

He frowned. "I am not stupid, Tamlyn. I understood the meaning of the swords plunging into the earth."

"Beltane is a very sacred day to us. Our ways—"

"Pagan heresy," he muttered.

"Do hush, Challon. You want me for your lady, then you must accept that I am pagan. You say compromise. I compromised. Now I say you must do the same. My ways are the ways of the people here. You do not have to embrace our beliefs, but you have to be tolerant. You can wed me tomorrow or in a fortnight, it shan't matter to my people. Our bonding last night was a joyous occasion. You are now Lord of the Glen. As the sun rose, you greeted the morn as their Lord of Glenrogha, and none— save mayhap some of your small-minded Normans—will look upon it any other way."

This took some of the wind out of Julian's worries.

She removed the tray, took up the pot of soap and began to lather his back. "Our marriage before the Christian church shall unite us in your eyes. To our people, what took place last night is just as binding, if not more. So there is no need to rush forward the ceremony. The only affront my people will see is if you persist in treating our bonding as shameful."

"Tamlyn, I meant no shame to your ways, but I was raised to believe an honorable man does not take his betrothed under the apple tree in the dirt. A virgin needs—"

"First, it wasn't in the dirt. We had a soft cushion of apple blooms and your soft mantle. Secondly, we Scots do not value virginity the same as you Normans. In fact, the Picts considered all unmarried women virgins."

"What nonsense," he scoffed.

"Not nonsense. Equality. The Picts granted women the same degree of freedom and respect they did men."

"Blatherskite."

Her eyes assumed a catlike glint, as she held up the little finger that bore the May Queen ring and wiggled it. By damn, the teeth of the hydra were upon him! His need to take her resonated within his blood, ignoring all his teachings. Tamlyn splayed her hand down his chest, her finger circling the flat male nipple in torment, imitating how he'd touched her in the same manner.

"I wanted to take my virgin wife in bed," was all he could muster as a rebuttal.

Tamlyn smiled, nipping his chin with her sharp teeth. "Och, then your wish is mine to fulfill. There is the bed, my Lord Dragon. And until we wed before the kirk, I am considered virgin by Pict ways."

Julian grabbed her with a quickness, a ferocity that should have frightened her. His power, so many times stronger than hers, was now barely held in check. Tamlyn should have been scared. Tamlyn—his wild Tamlyn—wasn't. She gasped as he pulled her into the tub. Her chest heaved with the quickening as he set his mouth roughly on hers, possessing hers. Water spilled over the edge of the tub, but neither cared as he grabbed the front of her chemise, ripped it down the middle and filled his hands with her beautiful breasts. With some awkward shifting, he finally had her sitting astride him, and with a quick flex of his hips, he was inside her. She came instantly, her internal female sheath rippled along his shaft, squeezing him, milking him.

Riding the crest of this terrifying power she unleashed within him, he met the force head on, taking the raw desire and giving it back to her. Her release made her sigh, but he gave her no measure. Breaking the kiss he commanded hoarsely, "Again, Tamlyn."

He pulled her head back so he could suckle her breast, drawing hard until she keened. Bucking into her, he forced Tamlyn to ride him hard, his hands roughly skimming over her wet skin and raising her body as he drove up into her repeatedly.

Julian wanted it to last forever, but he knew he had no more control than he had last night under the apple trees.

"Aye, Challon, again," she purred. "Oh, again."

Julian was nervous as he led Tamlyn belowstairs to the Great Hall, facing Glenrogha's people for the first time since the Beltane ceremonies. The bath had gone on until they were both wrinkled as prunes, then they fell into bed, laughing. They finally slept, though the sounds of the castle came alive around them. He should have felt sated. Never had he found more pleasure in a woman. Tamlyn made him feel alive again. So alive, he wanted to take her, again and again, touch the golden fire that was his Tamlyn. He'd held back, concerned she might be tender after their strenuous activities.

She was dressed in a new green kirtle Raven had sewed for her. She wore the wide Pict torque at her neck.

Across her forehead was a thin gold circlet. Still the Pict princess, but this Tamlyn was a more sedate version, the true Lady of Glenrogha.

His lady.

Julian felt pride at having her hand on his arm as they entered the Great Hall. Despite her assurances the people of Glen Shane would view their bonding as a grand omen, he still had fear there would be glares of condemnation in their eyes, hushed whispers about how he failed to show Tamlyn the respect due her rank. His step paused, assessing reaction. Even with Tamlyn's guarantee, he was surprised and relieved to see only bright eyes and wide smiles.

Tamlyn smiled and nodded as they passed to the lord's table.

Julian was a little uneasy at her confidence. She seemed so relaxed in this new stage of their relationship. As he'd seen in the bedchamber, dealing with her was going to be all the harder. Tamlyn was coming into her full power as a woman. He grinned foolishly, thinking he was glad his surcoat was long, for just watching her sent his damn tarse to throbbing.

The servants were quick to serve him, saw his plate never empty, his goblet full. It done with grins, and requests to know whether he was pleased with the food, the wine.

His hand closed over Tamlyn's, giving it a small squeeze. In response, her eyes flashed her happiness as they silently said, *see, my people accept you as I have*.

As his gaze roved around the Great Hall, he found all faces were happy, watching Tamlyn and him preside as lord and lady. At least until he paused on the countenance of Sir Dirk. The expression he saw there turned his blood cold. The man's hawkish eyes watched Tamlyn with emotions that unsettled Julian, a mix of desire, loathing, resentment. A dull thud pounded in his eyes as he watched his knight.

On the morrow, he would send word to the Baron Pendegast that Sir Dirk should be recalled. It was time he moved on to his own holding. He knew Pendegast hoped Julian would settle a fief on Dirk, one in Mortain. That was no longer an option since Edward stripped him of Challon holdings in Normandy and his English holdings of Torqmond.

Wondering how Damian would react to the clear sign of Julian's possession of Tamlyn, he leaned to look down the table. His cousin wasn't present. He'd indulged in too much mead the night before, so mayhap he still slumbered.

Julian smiled at Simon and chuckled. "I see Damian is not ready to rejoin the land of the sober."

Simon carried a piece of the roast pig to his mouth and shrugged. "I have not seen him since the dancing started. Mayhap he took his wounded heart away and drank himself into a black stupor."

"Damian is gone," Guillaume informed them.

"Gone? Gone where?" Julian and Simon exchanged a quizzical look.

Guillaume shrugged. "I had Moffet search for him, fearing he might have fallen into the loch. I saw him go off with those men last night. At the time I paid little heed, but this morn I grew concerned. I do not think they were of this valley, Julian."

"Not of this valley?" Tamlyn echoed. She looked pointedly at Julian, reminding him of the Sacred Mists warding the valley.

"They shared a horn of mead, then he went off with them in search of heather ale."

"Moffet said his belongings are here. His destrier is in

the barn so I would presume he shall show up later than sooner."

Julian pressed, a little concerned about his cousin's mood. "Was it the men who looked the same—triplets— with the tall Viking that Damian left with?"

To his left Tamlyn choked on a bit of food. "Triplets?" she finally managed to get out, through him patting her on the back.

"Aye, three men, same faces, same builds, around a score in age. The taller man was clearly of Viking ances- try." Julian noted at his description, Tamlyn exchanged speaking glances with Raven and Rowenna. "Who are these men? Obviously, they are known to you."

"The three are Hugh, Deward and Lewis. Our cousins, and aye, they are triplets. The big man is a Viking. Through an ancient trust, the Vikings send an honor guard to protect the Lady of Coinnleir Wood, our cousin Aithinne."

A laugh erupted from Julian at her naming her cousin. "Aithinne? *Firebrand*? Lord save me if she is as willful as the other ladies of Clan Ogilvie."

Tamlyn laughed, then took a drink from his goblet when he offered it. "Actually, fate smiled upon you, Challon. Edward might have sent you to claim Coinnlier Wood. My cousin is redheaded, and has quite the temper. Count your blessings, my lord, and light a candle for me and my fair hair."

Raven chuckled. "Oh aye, our Aithinne has freckles and a temper that goes with them."

"Then I am glad Coinnlier Wood is not of my hold- ings. I have all the Ogilvie women I need for one lifetime. Let another deal with this troublesome female with freckles." Julian raised the golden goblet in salute to the Sisters MacShane. "Where is Coinnlier Wood?"

"About a half day's ride north of Lyonglen."

Julian shrugged. "Mayhap your cousins merely escorted Damian to visit his grandsire. If he doesn't show on the morrow, I shall send a messenger to inquire if he arrived there safely."

"I am sorry, Lord Challon. They say at Lyonglen they have never heard from Lord Ravenhawke and were not aware he traveled north to assume control of the holding," Gervase informed Julian.

Tamlyn came over to where he sat slumped in the chair before the Great Hall's fireplace. She put her hand on his shoulder and gave it a small squeeze. Glancing up at her, Julian took her fingers and laced them with his. On impulse, he tugged her into his lap. He adjusted her so she leaned back against his shoulder and they could just enjoy the warmth of the peat fire. He leaned and brushed a kiss to the side of her head.

Beneath her rounded bottom, his body throbbed with desire for her, and her wiggling to get comfortable was excruciating. He smiled. Not due to the physical reaction to Tamlyn's nearness. It was strong, so strong it overrode nearly all within his mind. Everyone around them receded to a blur, to where it felt Tamlyn and he were alone. He rested his head against hers, soaking up this contentment, the need just to hold her. This was one of those tranquil moments his soul hungered for. Even when he had seen this image in his mind, he'd never realized just how fulfilling it was to hold Tamlyn, know she was his.

Chapter 19

Tamlyn sat upon a black mare, name of Goblin, a bride's gift from Challon. At her left side, he rode upon the prancing Pagan. A restless energy possessed the charger, reflecting the same impatience in his master. While Challon had gone to great expense to see the wedding take place in a manner befitting a man once the king's champion, she sensed eagerness, an urgency to have the ceremony over, as if wanting to make sure of his possession of her and Glenrogha.

Challon wore black, though the edge of his surcoat was trimmed with thin gold braid. At his throat was a gold torque, a heavier version of the one she wore. A smile formed her lips as she recalled giving it to him this morn. The reverence with which he touched it, stroked it, told her just how humbled he was to receive the gift to her husband, the new Earl of Glenrogha.

Her eyes glanced down at her black kirtle trimmed in gold braid, designed to match Challon's surcoat. The heavy golden chain, another bride's gift, encircled her waist and hung down to her feet. It went well with her gold Pict torque and cuff bracelets. Her final present from him was a wide gold circlet, adorned with a large oval of green garnet, fit for a queen. The stone reminded her of Challon's eyes. An exact match sat upon Julian's brow.

Raven told her Julian had designed the wedding gown, down to the smallest details. Such finery wasn't her style, but she understood his need to strike a statement with the marriage. Challon's lady would only be wed dressed in a manner befitting a princess. While touched by his care, these beautiful adornments caused her to feel as if she were in the body of another.

Though she couldn't define why, butterflies flittered in her stomach as Challon dismounted the steed. Mayhap it was that he stayed away from their bed for a full week. Oh, the man offered excuses. Yet, she couldn't wonder if she'd displeased him in some fashion, that he had second thoughts about their union. As each night passed and he hadn't come to her, these nagging doubts had grown. The bed had been cold and lonely without him.

Moffet rushed forward to take the horses' leads. Pagan rubbed his nuzzle against the mare's neck, murmuring to her. Challon lightly smacked the nose of the randy horse and pushed him back, so he could lift Tamlyn from the sidesaddle.

As Julian set her upon her feet, his eyes locked with hers. The breathless moment spun out long threads, as he seemed to want to speak something of grave import. Her heart swelled as she hoped he might finally say he loved her. Instead, he placed a kiss to her cheek. "You are beautiful. A bride worthy of the Dragon of Challon."

He took her hand and led her to the steps of the ancient kirk. The throngs of people lining both sides of the road fell in behind them, following. Malcolm, dressed in his robes of the Culdee, stood on the top step, waiting.

As her uncle began the ceremony, Tamlyn nervously glanced about her. So many people had gathered to witness the union of the Chosen Daughter of Clan Ogilvie to the Black Dragon of Challon, their new lord. Everything around her had a pall of unreality. She trembled, though failed to know what spurred the reaction. Trying to calm her fears, she concentrated on the faces of the people of Glen Shane. Even so, most remained a blank in her mind. To her right were her sisters. Likewise, Challon's brothers stood at his back, and behind them was their kinsman, Lord St. Giles.

Though she'd convinced Challon there was no need for an immediate wedding, he'd still insisted. Through the kenning she finally sensed he just wanted the wedding done to put their seal to their bonding. She'd asked him to learn to become accustomed to their ways, so she had to accept his as well. They reached their compromise and Malcolm agreed the wedding could take place within a sennight's time.

With all the preparations, the days passed in a flurry of activities. Despite the busy days, concern over the continued absence of Ravenhawke had cast a dark note. Challon sent out riders in all directions, but none had seen the handsome black-haired man dressed in gray.

Much to their surprise, he'd shown up at the gates of Glenrogha early yestermorn. His clothing was neat, he was clean, but he seemed slightly disoriented, spinning some tall tale about being captured by the Faery Queen.

The way he stared at her set Tamlyn to unease. Before Beltane, he'd watched her, but it was with a coveting, a sadness, knowing his feelings weren't returned and could never be. Now . . . well, she wasn't sure what she saw in his eyes. A question? Tamlyn had no idea what that question was.

Those challenging eyes continually stared at her. Not dark like Challon's, they were a gray-green—neither one color nor the other, yet both. Their lightness was emphasized by the trappings of gray in which he clothed himself. She had a feeling his continual dressing in the pale shade was his way of emulating Challon, calling on the hint of gray in his eyes to create his own declaration about the Lord Ravenhawke.

The long, thick lashes lifted and Damian's eyes collided with hers.

Emotions lived within him that had no right to exist. His eyes seemed to speak to her. But what? Regret? Reassurance that all was for the best? Envy?

She pondered his disappearance after Beltane. Where had he really gone?

Her question was pushed aside as Challon turned slowly, catching his cousin's attention fixed on Tamlyn. Worse, her eyes and mind had tarried too long on Ravenhawke.

Challon lifted a warning brow at Damian, who had the grace to lower his eyes to the ground. Turning the glowing dragon-green eyes on his betrothed, Julian sent her a cold stare of reproach. Clearly, the censure said he wouldn't brook her looking upon another with favor.

Tamlyn quailed inside at the silent admonishment. One earned. It was unseemly for her to be staring so long at another man whilst words of union were spoken. She felt dizzy, the trembling worsening. Why she felt so off kilter she couldn't define. She sought this marriage, knew in her heart, despite everything, Challon was the man she wanted. They'd already lain together, so it wasn't virginal jitters. Mayhap it was the finality of how different her world would be from this point. She was placing her life into his keeping.

She'd no longer be Tamlyn, Countess Glenrogha. She'd be Challon's lady.

He would fight for her, protect this glen, but could he come to love her?

The words from Malcolm droned on, having no form or substance, just a constant hum, and she found it hard to keep her eyes open. She turned her gaze to the beautiful face of the Dragon, soon to be her lord husband, seeking assurance from the man to which she bound herself.

Challon glared back at her, his eyes flashing angry fire. At first, she assumed it was because he caught her staring at St. Giles. Then she became aware of the stillness, the silence increasing the depth of Julian's ire. She glanced around and saw all faces were staring at her. Waiting. Confused, Tamlyn edged toward rising panic. Trying to shake this strange mental whirling, she fought the odd spell possessing her. Julian's hand squeezed hers, hard, sending a message. The action only spurred her bewilderment.

Malcolm repeated words asking for her consent to this marriage. Only then did she realized he'd asked for the response before and this long silence had been his waiting for her reply. Her eyes flew wide as she again looked to the man to her left. His mouth pressed into a thin line. Tamlyn saw that he thought she hesitated in defiance, as if she would refuse to plight her troth. It was only confusion, but he wouldn't understand that now. She opened her mouth to apologize, but immediately stopped. This was not the place.

The question was repeated by her uncle. Tamlyn swallowed. So much rested upon the simple one-word response, so many extremes warring within her. She hated that Challon had come to her as a conqueror, that her lord father still faced imprisonment at his hands.

Oh, why could the Fates not have woven a beautiful spell? Lord Challon should have accepted her father's invitation and come to the Highlands as an honored guest. They'd have been introduced, and their attraction, the passion would've been instantaneous, then soon a betrothal. Such a scene would've had Tamlyn giddy, forward-looking to the day he claimed her.

Instead, he'd rode into the glen as conqueror, claiming all, destroying Castle Kinmarch, and taking her just as he took the three fortresses. No wooing, no soft words of desire, just demands.

Oh, to have known he *wanted* her, chose her, instead of being commanded to marry her, her heart cried.

Challon's spine straightened, his head tilted back. Black was his anger, his dragon's fury. Never would he think she was capable of this. He was prideful. Well, it mattered not if she might prefer St. Giles's courtly ways and Scottish blood. The choices that would shape their lives were already made. He'd thought Tamlyn made hers the night she led him to the orchard. Her refusal to reply to the priest obviously was some final act of rebellion.

For the third time, the Culdee called for Tamlyn's consent. When he finished the question and Tamlyn's silence continued, a buzz fluttered through the masses. Come to witness their joining, murmurs asked why Tamlyn withheld her consent. From the corner of his eye, he saw Tamlyn turn toward him, wearing, oddly enough, an expression of confusion and pleading in her golden cat-eyes. He was exasperated, to the point of answering for her. Just as he drew a breath and opened his mouth, her voice rang out.

"Aye, I take this man as my lord husband. To honor him above all others, provide him comfort, support him in times of the troubles, and give him daughters and sons."

Julian turned toward her, startled by the lengthy declaration. He would have danced a Highland jig just to hear the word aye. Never did he expect her to make such a clear assent before all.

Tamlyn smiled up at him as he took her hand to lead her into the church. That smile was like the brightest sunshine, dispelling the shadowy corners of his troubled soul.

"Surely you jest?" Julian glared as Malcolm explained the rites of the second ceremony soon to take place—the pagan one. "I see now why you waited until just before we departed for the stone circle you saw fit to explain the rites to me."

The day had been long. First the wedding at the church. Then his bride and he reigned over the lavish marriage feast, lasting the whole day and into the night.

This past week he'd stayed away from his bed—away from Tamlyn—continually finding excuses for his absence. First, he traveled to Lochshane to inspect the fortress and decide what improvements were needed. He'd stayed the night, then rode on to Kinloch to check on Simon, see that his wound was healing. Once more, tarrying until the next day. He knew Tamlyn didn't understand his distance. After they'd agreed on holding the wedding in a sennight, he wanted to give her the time to fully adjust to the idea of being his bride. Had he slept with her, he would've been unable to resist touching her, holding her, taking her.

"The ritual of the Sword and Ring goes back to the dark times, Challon. When the Lord of the Glen—the willing king-god sacrifice—was offered to the Auld Ones, it fell to the lady to choose his fate."

"So I am to offer Tamlyn a ring and a sword. She either takes the ring or lops off my head?" Julian laughed, but found no real humor in the prospects of being a sacrifice, willing or not.

"I am sure Tamlyn explained these are just rituals that echo the dark ways. You offer the ring. Tamlyn will take the ring, then you drive the sword into the ground by the plaide."

"Then I take my lady wife before all?" Julian rolled his eyes.

"No, your guard screens you. Can you say our ways are so different than English ceremonies, where the king, priest and family members sit and wait in the bridal chamber for the bloody sheet to be tossed from the bed, afterward the poor groom did the deed in a curtained bed not far away?"

"I am a Christian. These strong pagan beliefs are unsettling," Julian admitted. "You as a priest, do these ceremonies not trouble you?"

"You will learn, Challon, the Scots tend to accept both. Christianity is still new to us. The Auld Rites are our ways since the dawn of time. Change is best served when it comes slowly."

Julian recognized his willingness to observe their ways would provide mortar to strengthen his position here as their new lord. His people would respect him for honoring their ways. "The moon has risen. Let us get this over with."

Still dressed in his wedding garb and wearing the golden torque and circlet, Julian felt a nervous tension at facing the pagan ceremony, though unsure why. Malcolm had explained it all, and he was right, it was not so different. Actually, he couldn't imagine anything he would like less than having Edward witness his bedding of Tamlyn.

Julian hadn't visited the huge stone ring that sat upon Lochshane Tor. Oh, he'd seen it. The ring was hard to miss, visible from nearly all points within the glen. As he followed on foot behind Malcolm, up the spiraling path of the tor, he was amazed to see just how large the stones were. There was a vibration in the air as he neared them, an almost tangible hum that resonated from the ancient gray stones.

There were two entrances. One to the south, where Tamlyn would come from, another to the north where Julian now passed. He'd seen the magnificent complex of Stonehenge, but this ring seemed older, more primeval—powerful. The sense he drew from these ancient giants humbled him. Their mocking whispers said they'd been here forever and would be here long after he was dust.

Julian trailed seven steps behind Malcolm, garbed in a green woolen robe. Seven paces behind him came Guillaume, then Simon, Damian and finally three of his squires: Vincent, Michael and Gervase. In single file, they made an inside circle of the stones, the men taking a position before a sarsen.

The chanting and singing of the merrymakers outside of the ring died down as a great horn was blown. A single bohran thumped out a slow, repetitive beat announcing Tamlyn's approach. Her entourage entered from the south. First came, the braw Highlander—the stag-man at the Beltane rites—carrying a torch. Next came Auld Bessa, then the angelic Evelynour.

His eyes hungrily awaited his lady.

Shimmering in the torchlight, Tamlyn's hair flowed down her back. His circlet upon her brow. She was gowned in a simple white kirtle, the one Raven had worn for her own marriage within this stone ring only two years before. His bride's gift, the golden girdle, circled her waist. Heavy, the chain swung from side-to-side with each step. Her ornate Pictish torque hung about her graceful neck and in her hands was a small bouquet of blue violets—a handful of wishes for the future, she'd told him.

Each part of her dress bespoke something old, something new, something borrowed, something blue. Old for her to remember the past, her heritage. New, a promise of life to come. The something borrowed was from someone she loved to give her luck. And blue was the color of the Auld Gods. All summoned a blessing on their union.

Never was Tamlyn more beautiful. She robbed his breath. She set his heart to thundering. As he looked at her all else faded to gray.

He'd married the woman once already today, but despite his Christian teachings, he was suddenly eager to make Tamlyn his bride by her ways.

Dressed in gowns of saffron linen, Rowanne and Raven came behind their younger sister. At the interval of seven paces trailed the five men from Tamlyn's guard. They each stopped before the remaining sarsens.

Where the Christian ceremony had been conducted by Malcolm, the pale Evelynour clearly would reign over these rites. She took a position before the small fire lit in a pit, Bessa behind her to her right, while Malcolm moved to her left. Before her was a plaide spread on the ground.

"We bid good cheer to all who come to celebrate the sacred joining of our Tamlyn to Challon, the new Lord of Glenrogha," Evelynour intoned in a clear voice.

"Tamlyn, Chosen Daughter of Clan Ogilvie, will you have this man as your lord and husband, by the ancient ways?"

Tamlyn smiled at Julian. "Aye, I shall." She took a step forward and handed Evelynour a strip of tartan, the black and green of Glen Shane.

Evelynour then turned to him. "Julian, Lord Challon, will you take our Tamlyn as lady wife in the ways of the stone, with your men standing and wearing iron?"

"Aye, I shall." He leaned to hand her a swatch of fabric cut from one of his shirts.

The pale woman took the two pieces of cloth and tied them into a loveknot. Raising her hands over her head, she held it up for all to see. "So be it. Let none raise voice against this holy union."

The people outside of the circle joined hands and began slowly circling the stones. They hummed a slow melody, haunting as Raven and Rowanne moved to Julian. Already prepared for this part of the ceremony, he knew the two women would undress him as a squire would. Used to servants coming and going, accustomed to having highborn women help him bathe, this part shouldn't have bothered him. Notwithstanding, as they removed his clothing, he felt an unease crawl up his spine—his naked spine.

He presumed this part of the ceremony was similar to the bedding rites of the Christian counterpart. Where the groom and bride were disrobed by the wedding party and then inspected to see if they were without flaws. Forming his face to show no emotion, he permitted Raven and Rowanne's hand to unlace and untie his clothing until he wore nothing. Evelynour brought forth a folded garment. Tamlyn's sisters slid the black, sleeveless robe over his arms, then to his shoulders.

He'd kept his gaze on Tamlyn the whole time, flashing

silent words of retribution for this. As he looked at her amber eyes, drank in her beauty, he found everything about him receded to mute and he was only vaguely aware of all going on around them.

Evelynour stepped to him. She pressed her oily thumb to his forehead, then to his heart. The scent of apples rose up around him, filling his head.

Malcolm came forward carrying a green velvet cushion. Upon the pillow was a golden ring and an ornate claymore—the Sword of Glenrogha. "The Lord of the Glen has in tradition offered the bride a choice. The sword or the ring. Do you come to this place of your choice and of free will?" He passed the pillow to Julian.

"Aye, I choose." Walking to Tamlyn, he held the cushion out to her, the long claymore balanced across his arms. "My lady, my bride." Julian swallowed to moisten his throat so they didn't crack on the words. "I offer you your heart's desire. I am the willing Lord of the Glen. Do you accept me? Do you reject me?"

Julian stared at her, knowing she would choose the ring. The rite of the Sword and Ring went back to dark times, when a woman could choose the sword. If that was her will, she'd ritually kill him, sacrificing the willing king-god to ensure the survival of the clan. He understood the ceremony, but it still troubled him that such things once actually took place, that Tamlyn's roots sprung from such a bloody ground.

Tamlyn watched as Challon knelt before her. She cupped her hand to the curve of his cheek then leaned forward and kissed his mouth gently. When she pulled back, she held the ring in her palm. Setting aside the cushion with the sword, he waited as Tamlyn took his hand and slid the ring upon his first finger. Like the smaller Beltane ring he wore, it fit as if it had been crafted for him. Tamlyn raised his hand to her lips and kissed it.

Julian rocked back on his haunches, then leaned to place a kiss to the top of both of her feet. As he stared at her, he saw how sheer the simple kirtle was. He could see the dark shadow of her woman's mound, the two dark orbs of her areola straining against the fabric.

She trembled as he placed both hands on her hips and kissed the dark triangle at the apex of her legs. Next he kissed her belly, where she would carry his sons. Continuing upward, he pressed his lips in turn to each breast, where she would suckle them. Lastly, he kissed her mouth, not gently, for this ceremony was raw and pagan as these wild Highlands, and it provoked a response in his blood. He wanted this woman with a force that was terrifying. He suddenly craved to take her, bind her in this primitive manner.

He barely had enough reason left to break the kiss. Rising, he took up the sword and stood with it, tip down, as Rowanne and Raven undressed Tamlyn. They slipped on a robe of the same sleeveless style as his, but hers was in red. The music of the tin pipers and bagpipes rose, but underneath that, Julian heard the tinkling of wind chimes or bells, just as he had in the orchard.

Tamlyn came and took his hand. Turning to face Evelynour, they knelt before her. Behind the witch, Malcolm chanted in words of the dark tongue. With a flick of his wrist he tossed herbs into the fire. An odd green smoke slowly rose filtering around the stones as Evelynour held a golden plate before her. On it were slices of dried apple and two small oatcakes. Julian took the cake and fed it to Tamlyn. In return for the symbolic offering of succor, she fed him the other one. Next, she fed him the slice of the apple, then receiving a second slice from his hand.

Evelynour returned with a golden goblet etched with Pictish symbols. She held the cup for Julian to take a sip. Ensuring Tamlyn put her mouth precisely where he had, she gave Tamlyn a drink.

"Shall the Lord of the Glen take our Lady of May?" Evelynour intoned.

Julian's his head spun. Either the cake or the drink was drugged, laced with some love philter. His groin throbbed and he wanted Tamlyn—now!

"Oh, aye, I shall take her as my bride."

The greenish smoke strengthened as Raven and Rowanne began to sing. All he could see was Tamlyn. Only through force of mind did he recall what he was to do next. He offered Tamlyn his hand and they rose together.

Picking up the sword, he intoned for all to hear, "Let no man touch what is mine." His eyes locked with Tamlyn's as he plunged the claymore into the earth next to the plaide.

Screams of exaltation split the night as voices rose outside the circle. The twelve men took a step, spun on the heels to face away from the fire. Each man in armor moved into the space between the upright stones and put their swords tip down, standing guard.

Tamlyn's sisters, the crones and Malcolm stepped backward until the strange greenish smoke seemed to swallow them.

Oddly, it felt as though Tamlyn and he were alone. He breathed deeply, smelling peat, apple, wild rose, lavender and heather, taking in the aromas so they filled every drop of his blood.

Tamlyn stepped against him, arching her body to his. He lowered his head to meet the kissed as her hand wrapped around his shaft, already riding high against his stomach. He muttered against her lips. "You and those cold hands."

"Take me, Challon, fill me with your fire. Make me warm."

He followed her down to the plaide, feeling everything about them die away. There was only Tamlyn and him in the greenish fog. All the trepidations over the ceremony were gone and he felt so blessed that Tamlyn had wanted to share this special bonding with him. The black robe flowed around him with a sentience, cloaking them.

Julian kissed her lightly, "Tamlyn . . . I . . ." Words failed. Couldn't begin to express the passion, the emotion flooding him, so he just said, "My wife."

She kissed his throat, then arched against him, receiving his body as he plunged into her, just as he'd plunged the sword into the earth.

Chapter 20

Tamlyn wiggled in excitement, standing atop of the lord's tower. Three days ago, Challon had led his men off, escorting Ravenhawke to see him officially installed as Lord of Lyonglen. The first time they'd been separated in the three sennights since they were married. Challon as earl was to be Damian's overlord. He was pleased to have his cousin as baron there. It would only see Glen Shane more secure.

She had wanted to accompany him, but Challon stubbornly insisted she remain at Glenrogha. He was still concerned about stragglers from the Battle of Dunbar, lurking in the hills outside Glen Shane.

It was strange. Challon's time in her life was measured in sennights, yet already his presence only served to tell her how empty it would be without him.

She spied the long column of riders approach, crossing the dead angle. As they neared, she saw they traveled with a woman. She might kick Challon. It was not safe for *her* to accompany him, but all right for another woman?

Gathering her skirts, she dashed inside the tower and down the steps, rushing out to greet the riders as they filed into the bailey. A quick sweep saw all fared well and seemed unharmed, and the woman was, as she assumed, her cousin Aithinne.

Her eyes went to Challon as he dismounted. He looked tired, needed to shave. This was the first time she'd seen him with any amount of a beard, as he followed the Norman way of keeping a clean face. Heat flooded her as she wondered how it would feel to kiss him. Would it tickle her nose? She wanted to run to him and jump into his arms, but she was still nervous enough to fear he might not like that sort of welcome before all.

He passed off the reins to Moffet, then looked up to see her standing, waiting for his notice. Typical Challon, he hid his emotions behind that shutter within his mind. She could not tell if he was happy to see her, or displeased because his lady wife bounded down the stairs like a harridan.

Well, if he could play games, then so would she. She composed her face into the lady proper and greeted him. "Welcome, Lord Challon. I hope your business was settled to your liking and the ride was not too tiring."

For several breaths he stared at her, then burst out laughing. "The mantle of proper lady does not rest well on my *faidhaich*."

"Oh, Challon, hush." Tamlyn practically jumped into his arms.

His laughter continued as he hugged her. "I take it my wife missed me."

Tamlyn bit his neck lightly. "Had you taken me with you, then you would not have missed *me*."

"Tamlyn, I explained why I did not want you to accompany me."

Putting her arms around his neck, she pulled up to his mouth. "Challon, hush and kiss me."

His fingers rubbed the three days growth of beard. "Mayhap I should bathe and shave first."

"Challon . . ." she growled a warning.

He leaned back so he could study her face, the laughter in his eyes turning serious. "I missed you, wife."

Then he kissed her. Oh did he kiss her!

Tamlyn smiled at the brush of his beard and mustache tickling her, but that didn't stop her from enjoying the taste of his lips. His hunger flared to life, pushing him to deepen the kiss, devouring her with a passion that sent her heart slamming against her ribs. Tamlyn forgot they stood in the middle of the bailey surrounded by his men. He bowed her body to his, holding her tightly.

Pagan nickered as if laughing at them and pushed Challon's shoulder. Julian broke the embrace and looked around at the midnight steed. "I think he wants his feed and is tired of waiting."

Tamlyn blushed, then looked to her cousin, as Ravenhawke helped her dismount. "Aithinne, welcome. How fare you?"

As Damian set Aithinne on her feet, she jerked her elbow from his grasp and flashed him a look that should've seen St. Giles drop on all fours and croak ribbit. Aithinne marched over to Tamlyn, embraced her, then once more flashed Damian a look of disdain.

"Well wishes on your marriage, Tamlyn. I apologize for not being there." She smiled at Challon, then lifted her brow. "So he went through the rites of the Sword and the Ring? Mayhap *this* Norman has value. Am I to stay in the same room? I tire from the ride and need to lie down."

"St. Giles is staying in that room. You may use my old room," Tamlyn answered.

Aithinne glared daggers at St. Giles. "Why does that not surprise me? He is adapt at usurping what is not his."

Tilting her nose in the air as she passed him, Aithinne strode into the lord's tower with the grace of a queen.

Her cousin was taller than Tamlyn by a hand's width, and it lent Aithinne a willowy appearance Tamlyn had always envied. Their hair was a similar shade, though Aithinne had a reddish cast, as if kissed by fire. So alike in their faces people often assumed them sisters rather than cousins. Aithinne's eyes were a deep brown with green flecks to them, though they still held that witchy, catlike appearance denoting her Ogilvie blood.

Wearing the expression of a cherub, Damian smiled. "Good day, Tamlyn. Hope you have some roast suckling ready, for I am fair starved."

"I fear not, but if you whisper to cook now, I am sure by nightfall it shall be ready. Cook has a soft spot for you," Tamlyn teased. Challon's arm came around her shoulder and she reached up to link her fingers with his.

He chuckled. "See there, Cousin. I could arrange a marriage for you. You could have roast suckling every night of the year."

Damian stared at the back of Aithinne as she entered the tower. "I am pleased *someone* looks upon me with kindness."

His eyes hungrily took in how Challon held her to his side, how she had slid her arm around her husband's waist. Tamlyn saw sadness and envy were still there, but not as strong as before. Now he seemed confused.

"If you both will excuse me, I am off to woo my lady love."

Tamlyn watched St. Giles take the tower steps two at a time. "He's going to woo Cook?"

Challon kissed the side of her head. "I wish, lady wife, you had warned me the Lady Aithinne resembled you to some extent."

"Some extent? She favors me a lot. You have to be up close to see the difference in eye color. Whilst the hair is near mine, she has that beautiful glint of red to hers."

The fiery cast made her seem more vibrant, causing Tamlyn to feel washed out in comparison. Aithinne always managed to appear the proper lady, a skill she'd never mastered. She suddenly feared Challon might look at her and now find her lacking next to her beautiful cousin.

Fearful what she'd see in his eyes, she admitted, "I always felt plain beside her."

He stopped on the top of the staircase and turned her to face him. Crooking a finger, he used it to lift her chin, forcing her to meet his gaze. "You are the most beautiful woman I have ever laid eyes upon, wife. There is not one thing I would wish to change about you. Still, I wish you had prepared me. When first I saw her, she was half in shadow. I thought you had disobeyed me and ridden ahead to Lyonglen. I was ready to turn her—you—over my knee for disobeying. Poor Damian, I am sure it totally befuddles him, has him tied in knots."

"Why should it upset Damian so?"

"Ah, that is Damian's secret. I am not sure I should tell." He kissed her slowly, then started again for the Great Hall.

"Why is Aithinne furious with him?"

"That is her *secret* to tell. I shall say this: Damian has demanded she marry him."

Tamlyn smiled at the notion, it suddenly seeming so right. "They would suit. Why is she so upset by his asking?"

"The words *demand* and *ask* have been tossed about." Challon kissed her forehead, not caring the whole fortress looked on. "Seems the Lady Aithinne dislikes an arrogant stranger telling her that she has no choice but to wed him."

Tamlyn laughed out loud.

* * *

"Oh, Tamlyn, I am sinking in a quagmire." Aithinne sniffed, then nibbled on a slice of dried apple. "It might be worry . . . but I fear I am with child."

"With child?" Tamlyn echoed, then smiled putting a hand to her stomach. "I might be as well."

"Beltane?" Aithinne asked.

Tamlyn nodded and hugged herself. "I took Challon to the orchard."

Aithinne's eyes went wide. "Beneath your tree?"

"Aye. The blossoms were so thick they blanketed the ground. On his black mantle on the white blooms it was like a dream."

"No wonder you glow with happiness." A glint of envy flickered in Aithinne's eyes.

"How far along do you think you are, Cousin?"

Her cousin bit down on the apple piece. "The apples ease queasiness. It comes in the afternoon. I always heard it was morning sickness that was the sign. Only, Oonanne says sometimes it hits a woman in the afternoon. Are you experiencing it yet?"

"Not yet, but Bessa said it could come soon. So who is the father and how long?"

"Beltane." She sighed. Going to the narrow window, she opened the wooden shutter and stared out at the fading sun.

"But you were not at the May Day ceremony—"

Aithinne laughed sardonically. "You might say I held my own ceremony."

"I do not understand." Tamlyn went to unpack her cousin's kirtles and hang them in the wardrobe.

Abruptly, Aithinne broke down crying, so Tamlyn rushed to her and held her, rocking her troubled kinswoman. "Oh,

Tamlyn, I have made a muddle of everything and I do not know how to put things right."

"Hush, sweet cousin, you shall sicken. Surely it is not as bad as you fear."

"Oh, it is likely worse."

Challon opened the door, knocking as he pushed it wide. "Tamlyn, sorry, I fear you need come tend your silly husband."

Tamlyn gasped as she saw blood dripped down his hand. "Challon, what have you done?"

"Hush, wife, it is only a small cut. I was not paying attention to what I did in the lists and Gervase sliced my wrist. It is minor, just it bleeds like a stuck pig. I need you to wrap it for me."

Tamlyn half nodded to Aithinne. "We shall talk more later. Sorry."

"Go care for your husband, Tamlyn. My troubles will still be here."

Tamlyn fed Challon a choice piece of meat, then held the cup to his lips. He rolled his eyes, but took a drink.

"Wife, it is naught but a scratch." Julian held up his arm and wiggled his fingers. "See. Bessa pronounced the wound pure. And it was my left wrist, not my right, so I am capable of feeding myself."

"Aye, Challon." Tamlyn poked another piece of roasted pork to his mouth as if he had not said a word.

He enjoyed Tamlyn fussing over him, liked how he could set her blushing when he stared at her. Devilishly, he leaned forward and ate the succulent meat from her fingers. When she went to pull back he caught her wrist and slowly he sucked her first finger into his mouth, drawing on it rhythmically. His tongue swirled around it.

She shivered. Bloody hell, he'd intended to tease his witch, but his body complained he'd be away from his wife for too long, thus was in torment as well.

"Tamlyn, I go to seek my bed. I am weary," Aithinne said, interrupting. She glared over their heads to St. Giles on the other side.

"I shall get you settled. Come." She paused. "If you will excuse me, Challon?"

He nodded, reluctantly letting go of her hand. "Do not tarry, wife. I find I am weary and need to see my bed as well."

Damian watched the two women leave, his thoughts clear upon his face. "It is amazing to see them together. You see the differences when they are side by side, but it tossed me when we entered Lyonglen."

"Tossed you? I was ready to spank the Lady Aithinne before I got close enough to see she was another woman. Once she moved in the light, I saw how she resembled Tamlyn, yet was so unlike."

"I see a few differences. Still, it is startling."

"Have you considered—" Julian started, only to be cut off.

"Do not bother saying *I told you*." Damian leaned back in his chair and rubbed his hands over his face. "My mother oft said the dreams were true. Where they became twisted was when you try to make circumstances fit the dreams rather than the dream match circumstances."

"So, now you have seen Tamlyn is not the face in your visions, what shall you do?"

"Marry the lass . . . somehow. She hates that I came to take over for my grandfather. I gather she was very close to him."

Julian sipped the wine. "Understandable, with him

raising her as his ward. I am sorry, Damian, that he died before we reached there."

Damian exhaled and nodded. "Strange. I should feel something, I suppose. I never met the man. He shunned my mother, disinherited her for marrying a Norman. After her marriage she lived in Mortain, never to set foot in her beloved Scotland again. Hard to feel something for a man who never cared enough to see you because you were half Norman. Yet, I feel an odd loss. Aithinne resents my assuming the title. Had I not, someone else would have come."

"If you marry her, Coinnlear Wood will become yours as well. Between my united holdings of Kinmarch and Glenrogha, Guillaume as Lord of Lochshane, Simon Lord of Kinloch, and you assuming command of Lyonglen and possibly Coinnlear, we are building a secure future here."

"Yea, Edward might again have to curry favor with the Dragon of Challon."

Tamlyn returned, coming to stand by his chair. "She rests. Bessa said she would look in on her later. If it is all right with you, Challon, I am going up now. I find I am wishing for bed as well."

Julian saw her eyes dance. Minx. "Very well. Have Moffet bank the fire and I shall be up shortly."

She rocked on impatient feet. "Not too long, Challon."

He took her arm and pulled her down for a kiss. The taste of cider was still on her lips, but not half as intoxicating as his Tamlyn. Nuzzling the hair at her ear, he whispered, "Bank the fire in the hearth, but not in my lady wife."

"Aye, Challon."

Damian watched her go. "She is good for you, Julian. I have not seen you this happy for years."

"Aye, Edward had no idea what a prize he was giving me. I am damn lucky, indeed."

"I raise a cup to the Dragon of Challon . . . brought low by love madness." A drunken Sir Dirk's slurred words rang through the hall. His eyes glazed from the drink and the demons that ate at his insides.

"Love madness?" The words jumped from Julian's mouth before he realized he spoke.

"Aye, it is a disease and you are infected, my lord." He gave a mock, sweeping bow. "Mayhap beyond cure. It can make a lapdog out of the strongest. Rot our brains."

"Disease?" Julian probed, wondering what maggot had gotten into Dirk's mind. A fortnight ago, he'd sent word to Dirk's brothers he wanted the man gone. Unfortunately, there'd been no reply.

Damian slammed his golden cup down hard on the table to draw Julian's attention from the knight. "Sir Dirk dips into the wine overly this night. Pendegast, close thy mouth, before you ruin our digestion with bilious nonsense."

"Any healer will attest to the truth. It is disease, say I. As with any disease, there is a cure. Does not our Church say women corrupt us, weaken us? No man should suffer such indignities to his honor and pride. Women should know their place. Obey their lord. A man never permits them to lead them around by his tarse."

Julian jumped to his feet.

Damian touched his arm and cautioned lowly. "Ignore him. His words spew forth from a green fount of jealousy."

"The healers bleed a man . . . draw out the foul poison crippling spirit and body. To sear wounds and prevent infection you slap hot iron. For a man to cure this insidious sickness that saps his soul, he must have intercourse with another woman. Then and only then shall he rid his soul, mind and body of this malady. If that does not work, he needs to discover they are all alike. Willing to lay with any man when his back is turned. A man is a fool if he thinks any one of them is special above others. A lady screams her pleasure same as the lowest swine girl. Sad when our mightiest warrior is brought low by cock fever."

Julian tossed his dagger. It landed between Dirk's first and second fingers. Casually, he strode to the table. He stared at the knight, not blinking. Reaching out, he snatched the knife and then used the tip of the blade to pare his fingernails. "You were saying?"

Dirk reached for his cup. "Nothing, my lord."

"What I thought." Julian's lashes flicked disdain.

Damian followed Julian from the hall. "You would do well to send that pup back to his brothers."

"I plan on it."

Julian closed the door to his chambers, his eyes searching for Tamlyn. Reassurance flooded him when he heard her in the solar. Unlacing the ties about his boots, he dropped them, shedding clothing as he went to her. He found his witch putting a brick of peat in the fire. On her knees, she wore only a thin chemise that left little to his imagination.

"On hands and knees and on a bear rug—lass, my heart beats fast." A smile spread across his lips. Putting a hand to his chest, he leaned against the door's edge and drank in the pleasure at watching his wife.

His wife. Soon she would quicken with his son. It was nearly enough to bring him to his knees. Two wishes he'd harbored, a dream he'd nurtured in his hardened heart.

"Challon, I am not stupid, but what does me on my knees have to do with anything?"

His laughter erupted. "I can see I am falling down in my husbandly instructions."

"Challon, I think this some game you play. You are lord of the castle, me groveling at your feet." She laughed and started to rise.

Julian swooped down and caught her under her arms. He kissed her hard and quick, tasting the cider on her sweet lips. "Oh, I would like you at my feet . . . but *not* groveling."

"I am not sure I trust that glint in your eyes." Tamlyn laughed. "With that beard it makes you appear a brigand."

"I shall shave it off in the morn. This night, I have other plans." He spun her around and pushed her to her hands and knees on the fur. "Have you ever seen a stallion cover a mare?"

"But that is . . ."

His hands smoothed over her firm derrière, relishing the firelight playing over it.

"Challon, I am not sure I want to get bit on the neck." Tamlyn glanced at him over her shoulder as he pushed the chemise over her arse and then up to her breasts.

He aided her up on her knees as he pulled the thin rail over her head and tossed it aside. Guiding Tamlyn to lean back against him, he nibbled on her neck as he palmed both breasts. Taking her earlobe into his mouth, he sucked and then bit down. Not hard, just playfully.

"Mayhap a small bite?" He laughed as he fondled the responsive breasts. Tamlyn loved him to play with them. "I lay siege to my lady."

Tamlyn made no response other than mewing kitten sounds at the back of her throat. Julian held her for a moment, allowing the emotions to play out in him. Possession. Desire. Need. Aye, need, but more than just the flesh. Tamlyn was the end to his long, lonely road. She brought him warmth, laughter and so much more. The power of what he felt for her humbled him and words were simply too feeble to explain what pulsed through his body, his soul.

Snaking his hand down, his fingers sifted through the dark curls, smiling as they touched liquid her body oozed for him. With his middle finger, he pushed into her, feeling her close greedily around it, the soft internal ripples as she moved toward her release. He kept up the tormenting motion, the slow in and out that caused her raspy approval, all the while, furiously working on the lacings of his hose.

He almost sighed as he tugged them open. "Is my lady ready to surrender or must I ram down her walls of resistance?" Tamlyn's answer was to push back against his groin. "Alas, my lady must learn to open her portcullis."

Using his chest he pushed her forward to her hands, as he slid into her liquid fire. Keeping his finger inserted and using his thumb to circle her little female button, with two strokes, she came apart. Her cry echoed against the solar's stone walls.

Julian wanted this feeling to go on, instead his body responded by following her. There was no holding back, no making it last. The release was blinding, making him dizzy. Wrapping an arm around her waist, he fell to his side, pulling Tamlyn to spoon against him.

Mayhap next time he would make this last.

Tamlyn rounded the corner to the barrack's tower, searching for Challon. She'd thought he worked with St. Giles, but she hadn't seen either of them in the lists. Glancing inside, she saw men on pallets resting, others working on their weapons or playing lots in the corner.

Sir Dirk was there with three other men. She didn't want to be anywhere near the man, so she started to back out.

"Lady Challon, you seek something?" He smiled.

That expression made oiliness roll through her stomach. Mayhap it was poor Aithinne's getting sick in the afternoon putting ideas in her head, but she'd felt queasy this past hour. Being anywhere near Dirk Pendegast only made it worse.

"I look for my lord husband."

Dirk glanced to his two friends and smiled. "I believe he went toward the stables with Lord Ravenhawke."

"Thank you," she said coolly and turned to leave.

"Want I should escort you there?" Sir Dirk moved forward.

She looked down her nose at him, a considerable feat since he was so tall. "No need. Vincent is with me."

Tamlyn stalked to the stable, hearing Vincent ten paces behind her. One of the older squires serving Challon, he would likely be knighted within the next year or so and move on to take up one of his family's holdings in Normandy. She was sure Julian's squires were bored, and maybe a little humiliated at having to play watcher for her, but Challon insisted she have one of the squires with her at all times while she went about her duties. She thought it nonsense. For the past ten years she'd run Glenrogha and never had a guard dogging her every step. Challon was unimpressed with her logic. In fact, he was quite stubborn. In this, his will ruled.

Not seeing anyone about the stables, she moved through the long rows to the door on the other side, thinking Challon might be in the paddock. Stepping out, she glanced around, though still saw no one. To her back, she heard a muffled cry, then the light coming from inside was blacked out by a man's body.

The kenning blazed forth, making her heart speed up. She was concerned for Vincent, but knew at this instant she needed to get away from here, run to the safety of Challon.

Her dread was confirmed when Sir Dirk stepped into the light. She swallowed the cold nausea rising within her, trying to stamp down on her fears, the visible reactions. Too vividly, she recalled how he fed off a woman's terror. She wouldn't gift him with what he wanted most.

Tamlyn tried to think, but this man scared her witless. She'd seen into his soul and there was such poison rotting there. She found it a contradiction. Likely, most women would find him attractive physically. All the same, what resided within the man rendered him as repulsive as a leper.

"I am sorry. I guess Lord Challon is not here after all." He moved closer. "I came to inform you."

She told herself to run, but her feet seemed rooted to the ground. Desperately, she searched for the right manner to breeze past him without touching him. Instead of thinking clearly, she just wanted to vomit. The pounding in her head saw it impossible to think.

"That was kind of you. If you will excuse me, this day I am busy and have little time to tarry. Challon will be upset if I don't finish my duties." She tried to move by him, but he caught her arm.

"That is a lie. You lead the mighty Dragon around by an invisible ring through his nose. Or mayhap, I should say by his cock."

Her heart slammed against her ribs. Her mouth was so dry it hurt to swallow. Not wasting any more time on deliberation, she pulled her knife from the belt at her waist and swung at him. He meet the arc with a counter blow that numbed her. The *sgian dubh* flew out of her grip. Not hesitating, she kicked out, catching him full in the groin, sending him to his knees. She spun to run, but he grabbed her kirtle and used it to slam her to the ground, the force causing her head to spin and her vision to darken. Desperately, she struggled not to lose consciousness.

Tamlyn attempted to get to her knees, but the mud wouldn't let her stand. The slimy muck sent her feet out from under her, hitting harder the second time. The third.

With a sly smirk, Dirk crawled forward, pinning her legs with his weight. He laughed, mocking. "Challon's lady is in the mud. But then you like to get it in the dirt, do you not. I took a hundred lashes for you, bitch. My back still heals. I plan to get my worth out of riding you hard. Mayhap the mighty dragon will see how ridiculous it is to let a woman lead him around like a gelding."

"Challon shall kill you."

Tamlyn swung out with her fist, bashing into his nose. She hoped to drive the bone back into his brain, but she hadn't been able to get a strong swing. The punch stunned him, but not enough. Grabbing her wrists, he pinned them over her head, manacling both finally with one hand. Putting his knee hard to one thigh, he forced her other leg wide.

Finally, her frozen vocal cords gave out with one loud, long scream.

Dirk slammed his fist against her jaw. Darkness swam around her, sucking at her.

Julian dismounted Lasher, unease prickling up his spine. He glanced around the bailey, yet all appeared to be a typical late afternoon.

Tamlyn.

His eyes glanced up to the tower, seeking the stained glass window. Fey whispers told him she wasn't there.

He whipped around the inner ward, eyes searching desperately for what was discordant. Suspicion bubbled as he spotted two of Dirk's men leaning casually against the barn door.

"Something is wrong." Panicked, he uttered to Damian as his cousin dismounted his gray steed.

Damian glanced at the stables, then to Julian, sharing his disquiet. As he opened his mouth to reply, a scream split the stillness of the calm afternoon.

Julian didn't hesitate. Damian followed. As Julian ran, he called to the guard, who came running on their heels.

Clearly terrified, Dirk's men bolted. Julian paid them little attention as he ran into the stable. He'd deal with them later. Halfway into the barn, he saw Vincent face down in the hay. He rushed past. Damian could check on the lad's condition.

"You rutting bastard!" Julian snarled his blind rage as he saw Dirk pinning Tamlyn in the mud. He grabbed the man by the shoulders and sent him flying, slamming him up against the barn. With a feral growl, he rammed his knee hard to Dirk's groin—hard enough to do damage. "Seize him," he ordered Damian.

Paying little heed, he knew his orders would be carried out. Julian rushed to Tamlyn and knelt beside her, wanting to touch her, to hold her, but fearing she'd reject his comfort. A knife twisted in his chest. He could hardly breathe as he stared at her disheveled condition. The bruise on her chin where Dirk had hit her with his fist. Scratches and scrapes on her arms and legs. Deep bruises already forming on her thighs. Blood under her fingernails.

Tears filled her large amber eyes as he helped her sit. Her hand trembled as she touched her fingers to her bruised lip. The shaking growing worse, she refused to meet his eyes.

Whipping off his mantle, he wrapped it around her

as he helped her up. She was so weak she could barely stand, so he lifted her into his arms.

He wanted to kill Dirk, here and now, but knew he needed to get her upstairs and to bed before she fainted.

"Take them to the pit to be held until the morrow when I shall pronounce judgment," Julian commanded before carrying Tamlyn from the ward.

Chapter 21

    The door opening roused Tamlyn from a deep sleep. She raised up on her elbow in the bed to see Julian already dressed.

    In black leathern hose, black silk shirt and black jack, Challon stood awaiting his squire. Moffet carried in the long hauberk and helped Julian into it. Once that was on and the arming points buckled, he fitted the breastplate over Julian's chest and secured that. Kneeling, the lad strapped on the greaves—protective plates on the lower legs. Finally, he pulled Julian's black surcoat over his head.

    She recalled how tender Challon had been last night, bathing away the mud from her, treating her as a mother would a babe. Then he held her and rocked her until Bessa's tansy had pulled her into the darkness of sleep. She recalled his tears hitting her cheek.

    Julian watched her as he buckled the baldric about his hips. Flicking two fingers to the door, he signaled Moffet to depart, so they were alone.

    "Where do you go, Challon?" Tamlyn scooted to the edge of the bed, still sleepy from Auld Bessa's potion. "You are girded for battle. Why? What has happened?"

"Go back to sleep, Tamlyn." He reached out and stroked the back of her head. "First, kiss me, lass."

She started to shake as she rose to her knees on the bed. It put her at eye level with him. Curving her arms around his neck, she kissed him, slowly, thoroughly, hoping to melt his armor plate. Suddenly, he yanked her hard against him, kissing her until she was breathless and wanting more. So much more.

Still, she sensed something was wrong. The kiss almost felt like he kissed her goodbye. It scared her.

Keeping one arm about his neck, she studied every line in his stunning face. She ran her thumb over his black brow, smoothed the furrow, then sifted her fingers through the thick black waves of his hair.

Her heart filled to overflowing with emotions for this man, her husband. "I think I must be the luckiest woman in all of Scotland."

One side of his mouth quirked up. "And why is that, lady wife?"

"I have the most beautiful husband. The most caring. Any woman would envy me. He is strong and brave. My people respect him. I respect him." She so wanted to say she loved him, but was unsure if he wanted to hear the words.

"Then you should respect and obey him—and go back to sleep." He gently stroked the bruise along her jaw where Dirk had hit her.

The green eyes were guarded, keeping his emotions hidden behind iron shutters. She hated when he closed himself off from her like that.

"Why do you leave, Julian?" Tamlyn twirled the curl over his left ear.

The door opened and Gervase leaned in. "My lord, it is time."

Julian turned and nodded. "I shall be there straight away."

"Straight where, Julian?" A coldness speared through her.

He gave her one of his level stares and softly kissed her again. "Go to sleep, Tamlyn. I shall be back before you awaken."

Panic surged in her. Ignoring his order, she climbed out of the bed wrapping the blanket around her. "Do not dare leave until you answer me, Julian."

He stopped and exhaled in frustration. "Would that I had been graced with a biddable wife."

"You were not so lucky, Challon. You got me. And I am shrew enough to want an answer. I mean to have an answer."

"I challenged Dirk to trial by combat." His jaw set, waiting for her explosion.

And came it did. "No! I shall not permit you—"

"You have no say in the matter, Tamlyn."

"I . . . do . . . say. You shall not risk your life because of what happened."

He half closed his eyes, shutting her out. "It is too late. I have thrown the gauntlet and Dirk picked it up."

"I do not give a fig. Kill him if you must. Hang him. Do not risk your life," she pleaded.

"Dirk comes from a wealthy and powerful family, much favored by Edward. I cannot just hang him. If I wanted legal judgment, I would have to turn him over to Edward for trial, and I doubt it would ever come to that. Edward would be bought off with enough coin to make him look the other way. If I want punishment I have to do it myself and in a fashion that leaves Edward no recourse. I do not want him coming after me, or trying to hold this against us. I face Dirk in trial by combat and God judges him. The First Knight of Christendom will understand and abide by God's law."

"Your God backs only winners," Tamlyn countered.

"Go to sleep, wife. It will be done shortly."

"Damned if I shall." She tried to block him from leaving, but the blanket tripped her.

He caught her from falling, the green garnet eyes searching her face as he memorized every line. "Tamlyn, stay here. I do not want you there."

"I do not want you there either, Challon."

He took her mouth, kissing her hard with all the passion that was between them. As Tamlyn leaned to him, he suddenly yanked the blanket from her, spinning her from him like a top. Challon deftly opened the door and closed it, locking it before she could reach it.

Tamlyn pounded on it, tears falling down her face. "Challon, do not lock me in here! Challon! Challon, answer me!"

Tamlyn heard the ravens fussing over the passes. She glanced up to see them, flitting from tree to tree, screeching and fighting. Dread eating at her heart, she picked up her kirtle and broke into a run, heading to the open field of the dead angle.

"My lady, please be careful," Moffet called as he sped his steps behind her. "You are barefoot. If you hurt yourself, Lord Challon will have my head on a pike. He shall thrash me for letting you out."

"Oh, hush up. I told you I would thrash you if you did not let me out."

People lined along the side of the field, both Challon's men and her people. A few whispered, but most remained still, watching the preparations. To the right end of the field flew the scarlet pennon with a golden eagle. She'd never seen the pennon before, so presumed it must be the Pendegast standard. Several men milled about setting up weapons, readying the white steed for the vile man. Paying little attention, she pushed through the crowd.

At the far end, she saw Challon with his squires, Gervase, Michael and Vincent. She spotted the huge wooden rack holding five lances and her blood turned cold. Shoving to break free of the people standing around, Tamlyn headed straight for Julian, determined to stop this at all costs.

Julian examined one of the lances, running his hand over it. "Gervase, change this one out."

"Aye, my lord." Gervase immediately set to doing Challon's bidding.

"Challon, I want this stopped. Now!"

He swung around to face her. His countenance composed, relaxed. How could he be so calm when her heart felt as if a thousand ravens fluttered within? She could only see him, all things about her lost. The soft breeze stirred the thick black locks on his forehead as he stared at her unblinking. So beautiful it hurt her to breathe.

"Tamlyn. I see you found a way out." His lashes made a small sweep as he swung around to stare at Moffet. "I cannot imagine how."

Damian came forward carrying the Glenrogha claymore. "I honed the edge myself, Julian."

"Damian, take Tamlyn away from here, take her to Aithinne," Julian requested.

Nodding, St. Giles stepped toward her. "He is right, Tamlyn, let me take you back to Glenrogha."

She backed up. "Why? So my idiot husband can get himself killed and I do not have to watch? You think that, then you are as big an idiot as he." He put a hand on her upper arm to lead her from the field. "Take your hand off me, Damian St. Giles, or I shall claw your eyes out."

"Tamlyn, calm yourself—" Julian began, only to have her cut him off.

"I shall be delighted to calm myself—when you come back to Glenrogha with me and forget this nonsense."

Julian exhaled and glanced skyward as if seeking patience. "I already explained why these steps are necessary. That swine dared to touch you. No one touches my lady and lives. This is the only way."

Tamlyn shivered as she saw there was no changing his mind. "Fool! Stupid, arrogant fool!" She choked on the words. "You risk all, Challon. What is honor without your life?"

His arms encircled her, pulling her to his chest, and letting her cry. "You have so little faith in me, Tamlyn? I was the king's champion, the best in all the Isles. I wish you would return to Glenrogha. If you are here you might divert me and I need no distractions."

"If you insist on getting yourself killed, then I am going to be here to go to you and kick you for it." She tried to laugh, but a sob of pain escaped her.

"If you will not return to Glenrogha, stay to the sidelines and permit me to prepare myself. I would prefer not to give you a reason to kick me." He lifted her chin and lightly brushed a kiss to her lips. "Please, go with Damian."

Tamlyn hugged him tightly, crushing him to her as if to hold him and protect him. Sucking in her emotions, she stepped back and then glanced around her. Looking at Gervase, she barked, "Give me your knife."

He blinked, startled by her command. "My lady?"

"Don't act the lackwit." She held out her hand and snapped her fingers. "Your knife. Give it."

"But, my lady . . ." He glanced to Challon, in search of guidance.

"I swear, Challon, you must deliberately seek dullards

for squires." She reached over and snatched the knife from Damian's belt. She noticed all the men except Challon backed up a step. She chuckled derisively. "Dolts."

Tamlyn ignored them and leaned down and sliced away at the hem of her woolen kirtle. When she had cut a thin band about the length of her arm, she straightened up, handed the knife back to Damian, and stepped to Julian. "If you are determined to go through with this, then you must have a lady's colors."

She tied the tartan sash of black and green around the middle of his left, upper arm, then stroked its length, wishing she could feel the warmth of his skin and not the cold of the mail.

Julian hesitated, then caressed the back of her head. He knew he could never earn Tamlyn's acceptance, but hoped she'd stand aside and let him do what he must. He had to kill Dirk of Pendegast, for he'd dared to touch Tamlyn. Women seldom understood the code of men. If he could not defend Tamlyn's honor, he'd lose the respect of his men, of himself.

"Moffet." Julian called the one-word command.

The young lad, so like Christian, took hold of Tamlyn's arm. "Come, my lady, you must follow me."

Tears filled Tamlyn's eyes as she nodded, though she continued to stare at him. "Julian, I . . ."

"Go with Moffet, my lady," Julian urged gently.

Her head dropped, then nodded. With a last look, she allowed Moffet to lead her away.

Immediately, Vincent returned to fitting the gauntlets and then vambraces, the metal guards covering his lower arms. As his squire readied his accoutrements, Julian's eyes tracked Tamlyn. She moved to the halfway point in the field, her people parting to make room for her.

She wore the simple plaid kirtle with the grace of a
queen. Nothing had the power to humble her mien.

"Damian, should I fail—" he began only to have his
cousin cut him off.

"I shall not hear such discussions." Damian patted
him on the back. "You are the best knight in Britain."

"We both know I am getting old, slower. I lack the
taste for this anymore."

"What you have lost in speed, you more than balance
with skill and intelligence. You fight with a cool head.
And lacking taste for battle—your spirit wearies at
Edward's useless slaughter. I am sure you will have a
particularly sharp appetite to dispatching this vermin.
My offer still holds. I would step into your place and
carry the challenge."

Julian patted his cousin's arm. "You have your own re-
sponsibilities now as Lord of Lyonglen. I ask only that
you protect Tamlyn. If I fail, kill Dirk. I don't want him
to live to see the sunrise."

"It won't come to that, Julian, but you have my word,"
his cousin pledged.

"Thank you. Go stay with her. She shall require
support."

Damian nodded as Julian mounted Pagan.

Aithinne joined Tamlyn as she stood trembling.

She watched the two men ride to the middle of the
field. Upon the black destrier, the Dragon of Challon
was all in black, save the stripe of dark green in the
tartan about his arm. Everything about Julian was understated. Black plates, mail and surcoat. No adornments of
any sort. A striking contrast to Dirk's brilliant scarlet and

yellows over the silver mail and plate, and seated on the snow white charger.

They spurred the steeds to midfield where Malcolm stood, garbed in the brown robe of a Culdee. The two men sat on their horses, the rising breeze ruffling their hair, staring at each other as if they were the only ones around.

Malcolm glanced to Dirk, then to Challon, his voice calling loud enough for all to hear. "Why have you come to this place and this hour?"

Sir Dirk sneered a challenge at his liege. "To do battle to prove my innocence."

Challon fixed him with hooded eyes that would have sent a sane man to trembling in fear. "I come to do battle for the honor of my lady."

Malcolm spoke. "This is trial by combat. One man lives, one man dies. God decides which. Will you fight to the death, giving no quarter and receiving none, and accept God's judgment?"

"I will." Both men swore in unison.

Malcolm nodded. "*In nomine Patris et Filii et Spiritus Santi.* So be it. Go, and let God grant judgment or vindication as He wills."

Both men turned their mounts and cantered back to the end of the field, though Tamlyn little spared Dirk notice. Her eyes remained fixed on Julian. He turned Pagan as Vincent lifted the claymore to him. Holding tip down so it formed a sign of a cross, he kissed the cross-guard and handed it back to the squire. Vincent carried the sword out several paces and drove it into the ground. At the opposite end, the squire serving Sir Dirk did the same.

Michael climbed upon the arming block to fit the full helm on Challon. For an instant, Julian's eyes met hers. Time stopped as they stared at each other, the strength of their emotions speaking what words could not. Then the helm was lowered, covering his whole head. With care, Gervace settled the long lance into his lord's grip, crosswise on the horse.

At the far side of the field, Malcolm glanced at Pendegast, who raised the tip of his lance skyward. Then the priest's eyes sought Challon, who repeated the action, signaling he was ready as well. Grasping a white cloth in his hand, her uncle held it out before him at chest level. Tamlyn sucked in a breath, as did everyone, waiting for Malcolm to let it drop.

The cloth fell from Malcolm's grip, fluttering to the ground. Before it hit, Sir Dirk set spurs to his charger. His mount cried out and leapt forward. At the opposite end of the field, Pagan jumped in response, but Challon controlled the fidgeting horse, holding, still holding the lance tip upward.

"What's he waiting for?" Tamlyn whispered in anxiety, her hand reaching out for Aithinne's, squeezing it.

Slowly the tip came down and Challon spurred Pagan. By the time the two beasts met in the middle of the field, they were going full out. Tamlyn's breath faltered as the lances slammed into both men.

The crowd groaned, and several called, "He held! Challon held!"

The knights reeled, regained their balance and immediately set the chargers to the end of the field to quickly gather another lance. Once again, Dirk was already charging down the field before Julian spurred Pagan into a gallop.

Again, the lance crashed into Challon's chest, at the same instant his slammed into Dirk. Shards of wood flew about both men, as the long lances seemed to crumble to nothing. Tamlyn grabbed her stomach in reaction, almost as if she received the blows.

Two passes. Three more to go.

Already with a fresh lance, Challon was off the mark, turning the destrier. While Dirk's horse seemed to tire, Pagan appeared to draw strength from the combat. At the last instant Dirk lifted his lance, catching Challon on the right shoulder. It flipped him backwards over the black horse and slammed him into the ground. The crowd groaned. Tamlyn cringed, shaking and barely able to breathe, her heart aching as she waited to see if Challon would rise.

Dirk dropped the broken lance, then pulled his mace and chain from the saddle. Slowly Challon staggered to his feet, only to have Dirk's chain and ball catch him across the back. There was no plate there. Only the heavy hauberk stopped the ugly weapon from mauling flesh and bone. Pivoting his horse on its hind legs, Dirk came at Challon again, the heavy spiked ball slamming repeatedly into Challon's back and helm.

Tamlyn screamed. Grabbing Damian's arm, she begged, "Stop this! For God's sake, stop this madness! He's *killing* Challon!" She started to push past Damian, but he caught and held her arm.

"Stay back, you'll get Challon killed, if not yourself."

Dirk came at Julian again. As he swung the mace, Pagan flew at the other steed. Head lowered, the midnight charger crashed into Dirk's mount. Using teeth and hooves, the screaming animals reared, fighting with the same hatred as the men. Nearly berserk, Pagan tore into the other horse's flesh, blood gushing down the animal's white neck. The dueling stallions unseated Pendegast, the magnificent destrier likely saving Challon's life.

Challon grabbed at his badly dented helm. He yanked it off and tossed it to the ground. He gasped for air and shook his head as if trying to rid it of the ringing. Forcing himself to his feet, he glanced about to get his bearing.

His eyes sighted the claymore stuck into the ground at the end of the field. Seeing that, Challon headed for the great sword. Dirk ran for his. Only Pagan charged toward him blocking his path.

Challon collapsed to his knees before the Glenrogha claymore.

"What is he doing?" Tamlyn's voice broke as she strained against Damian's grip. "Julian, get up!"

Aithinne buried her face against Damian's shoulder, unable to watch.

Challon remained in that position, looking up at the sword as if it were a cross and he sought answer to a prayer for strength. His face of such angelic beauty stared transfixed at the golden stone in the hilt. The gray clouds broke and a shaft of brilliant morning sun shone down on Julian and refracted through the amber.

Rising, Julian yanked the great sword from the ground and turned to face his opponent. The taller man wasted no time drawing his sword from his baldric and went straight into great hacking swings. The blades clanged and rang out, again and again, as Dirk kept backing Challon up with the force of his blows. Finally, Challon's blade deflected the downward arc of Dirk's. Using the momentum, Julian spun his whole body completely around, and then delivered a kick to the center of Dirk's plated chest. Pendegast appear exhausted, while amazingly, Challon gained his second wind.

Tamlyn was aware that since May Day Julian had practiced every day with the claymore under the tutelage of her cousin Skylar. Now the great sword sang in his hands. The actions were effortless, as if the blade were an extension of Challon as he fought in the Highland way. The weapon thrust, parried, then swung in fluid motion, shifting to defense, the whole sword covering the length of the back of his body. He moved so fast the taller Dirk barely had time to block the blows.

Never had she seen a man so controlled, so powerful.

Challon spun once more. The force of the feat saw his sword carry Dirk's right out of his hands, flying through the air. It landed, embedding in the earth and wobbling with the force.

Shoving her hand into her mouth, Tamlyn bit down on her knuckle to keep from screaming as Dirk picked up one of the half-broken lances and wielded it. Longer than the sword, he was able to keep out of harm's path, while swinging it as a club. Meeting each thrust, Challon used the claymore to whack off chunks of wood from the lance. Backing up until he finally neared his broadsword, Dirk tossed the now considerably shorter lance at Challon's head and lunged for the steel.

The throngs of people cheered, called warnings and moaned with each turn of events. Clearly rooting for Challon.

Dirk came up in a round swing, intending to slice Challon through the midst, but Julian jumped back, arching like a cat. Even so, the tip of Dirk's sword, ripped through the surcoat and hammered the plate underneath.

Just then, Pagan charged across the field. He'd set Dirk's stallion to running, and came back, once again, to fight at his master's side. Dirk panicked and gave an overhead blow to Challon, driving him down on one knee. Using the claymore as a shield, Challon swung the sword behind him to protect his shoulder and back. Dirk moved in and slammed his knee to Julian's chin. It sent him sprawling backward, open to a final blow before he'd be able to recover.

"No!" Tamlyn screamed and started to bury her face on her hands, but stopped.

The monstrous black destrier flew at Dirk. Rearing high, hooves slashing. He caught Pendegast hard on the head with a hoof and continued to pound at him even after the man was down.

Michael rushed to help Julian to his feet, while Gervase and Vincent took charge of Pagan. Finally able to stand on his own, Julian went to the still excited horse and patted his forehead and whispered to him.

He ordered, "Get that . . . carrion off the field." Several men moved to obey him, dragging Dirk's body away.

Tears streaming down her face, she jerked away from Damian, leaving him and Aithinne to follow. As she rushed toward Challon, people moved into the field. Several to collect the body. Most to cheer and congratulate their lord on his victory. Tamlyn was frantic to reach him, pushing them aside. Then suddenly, she was there and flying into his arms.

Sobs tore through her chest as she hugged him. Julian moaned and then loosened her hold around his waist. Tamlyn realized his back was bruised, which made her cry even more.

Challon tried to laugh, but stopped. "I think I shall forego laughing for a few days." That made the tears spring forth anew. He lifted her chin with his bent finger. "*Mo chridhe*, hush, don't make yourself sick. I told you this would not take long."

Julian sighed, then moaned at the pain. Suddenly, his eyes rolled in his head and his knees folded under him. Tamlyn and Damian caught him.

"I think I might still kick him," Tamlyn sobbed and laughed in the same breath.

"Wait until he wakes up." Damian chuckled. "He won't feel it now."

Chapter 22

"God's teeth!" Challon sucked in a breath and steeled himself to hold still. "Tamlyn, a fortnight has passed. Must you continue with these nightly tortures?"

Ignoring the protest, she pressed the poultice of sweet clover, bilberry, leopard's bane and witch hazel to his back. It was icy—why he objected. Every day she sent his squires up the mountain of Ben Shane, where snow never melted, to fetch back buckets of packed snow. She alternated between icy poultices and very hot ones, working to heal the deep bruising sustained in the combat.

"Bessa said I could stop after this night." Tamlyn leaned over and pressed a kiss to his shoulder.

"I think Auld Bessa enjoys my torments. I refused to drink any more of that foul stuff she gives me."

"You have not sickened," she pointed out.

He turned to glare over his shoulder at her. "No, but it has other . . . adverse . . . reactions upon my body."

She chuckled, suppressing her smile. "Bessa did mention that was a side effect, but that it would work to see you rest quietly until you healed. It makes one sleepy."

"Sleepy? Bloody hell, makes one positively limp—as

you are aware. You snigger at my condition each night when you say 'goodnight, Challon.' I think you let her dose me as punishment for fighting Pendegast."

Tamlyn put her hand to his back, stroking him. "Julian, promise me, never again will you fight."

He reached around, pulled off the large poultice on his spine and tossed it across the room to hit the wall. Rolling over, he took her upper arms and pulled her across his chest.

"Your back, Julian—"

"Is fine. I keep telling you. You have mothered me until I am nearly raving with madness. It is boring, Tamlyn."

"Very well, I shall tell Bessa to cease with the tansy, no more poultices."

He reached up to brush a stray strand of hair from her face. "Thank you for the small mercies, but I fare well, Tamlyn. I have fought harder and come away in worse condition, then back to my duties within a day or two. It felt soothing to have you fussing over me. No one ever cared enough to do that before. Please, stop fretting. I am well. I do not like you worrying so."

"I don't want you to fight again, Julian."

He regarded her with a crooked smile. "Why is it when you want something from me I am Julian? When you want to ignore me and do as you please, it is *aye, Challon,* or *no, Challon.* I am on to your sly ways, lass."

"I do seek to gain your indulgence. I want you to promise never to fight again. I cannot go through that another time. Watching you mauled . . ." Tamlyn's sob escaped and she flung her head to his chest, holding him tightly.

Julian stroked her long hair, letting her cry out the

horrors of watching him fight, the fears of what might have been.

"Tamlyn, I am a warrior. I have known little else my whole life. If the time comes when I have to fight to protect you or Glenrogha, I shall. You have to accept what I am, who I am."

Julian was tired and ready to seek his bed. Despite assurances to Tamlyn yestereve, his back still ached after the long day. He was older and the healing was slower. Still, he had one more chore to do before going to the tower for the night.

Night? He chuckled at this eerie pale twilight the Scots called gloaming, still unused to lacking a true night. It seemed unnatural to seek your bed when it was so bright outside. Tomorrow was Midsummer's Eve. Tamlyn warned him, as the longest day of the year, there'd be no night.

A storm approached, the wind ripping the trees around. It approached fast, would hit soon. Julian headed toward the barn, intending to make sure the horses were secure. Up ahead, he spotted Tamlyn on a course to the stables.

His lass was brave. Many women would steer away from the place that held such bad memories. With a warrior's determination, she'd stated she wasn't about to hide from anything in her own fortress.

Bansidhe was in the paddock. The mare came in season a few days ago, causing his chargers to kick up a fuss. Even so, he'd have to return her to a stall or Tamlyn would pitch a fit. Likely, why she was there now, not wishing the palfrey left out in the rain. She loved that stubborn mare. He pulled up when he caught her before Pagan's stall, feeding him an object from her hand. Nodding to Gervase, who guarded her, he signaled for the young man to leave them.

Julian strolled to where Tamlyn stood feeding Pagan a treat. "What sort of witchy magic are you working upon my charger? I suspected you slip him indulgences. He is getting fat."

She shrugged. "I bring him an apple each day and a handful of hazelnuts. Now the carrots have come in, I bring him a carrot, too."

"You will make Lasher and Dragon's Blood jealous with these lavish attention."

"They grumble, so do Bansidhe and Goblin." She smiled and rubbed the horse's forehead. "This harvest I shall see two barrels of apples stored just for your beastie. He shall have his apple even in the deepest of winter. He saved you, Challon. If you hadn't been able to rise in time, Dirk might have landed a fatal blow. Pagan did what you trained him to do—saved your life in battle."

"It is dispiriting, wife, you lack confidence in my skills. I would have won. Two more moves and my sword would have found aim. His swing to kill me already saw me roll to the side, leaving him exposed. My sword would have slid right into the seam of his mail. Even so, I was proud Pagan took matters into his keeping." He patted the horse.

There was a whinny from the paddock where Bansidhe pranced around, excited. Pagan instantly answered her call. Tamlyn's eyes shifted between the two horses, then she lifted the wooden bolt from its seat on the stall and slid it back. She swung the door wide. Pagan stuck his head out, bright-eyed and glancing about. He murmured a question in his throat, as if not believing she'd turned him loose. Understanding what she was doing,

Julian moved in unison with her to pull back the bar to the paddock and allow Pagan to dash out.

The black stallion's tail crooked high, as he snorted the air, calling to the mare. Bansidhe set to racing around the enclosed area playing hard to get. The black stallion fell in right behind the dappled mare.

Julian watched her, studying her earthy face. "I thought you didn't want me to breed her to one of my stallions?"

She shrugged, as she leaned against the door's frame. "She wants him, brute that he is."

The wind swirled around them, ruffling Tamlyn's long hair. Typically Tamlyn, she wasn't dressed as the Lady Glenrogha, but in her plaid kirtle and the worn sark. Just common clothes that most of her people wore, yet her beauty burned regal. It was real. The feral quality he'd noticed from the very first called to him.

Lightning split the darkening skies as Pagan and Bansidhe began their mating dance of lure, rebuff, lure again, working to one conclusion. Highland magic swirled through Julian's blood as he stared at Tamlyn.

The want for her never lessened, only spiraled in an ever tightening coil, overpowering all. He often found himself just watching her as she stirred about the Great Hall, wondering how his life had been so blest to have her.

He'd made a joke about Bessa's potion suppressing his natural urges, and that much was true. Only, he'd been glad of the effect. He still wasn't sure Tamlyn was ready to have him touch her in that way. Not after Dirk. She had assured him Pendegast didn't rape her. Yet some part of him feared she might be ashamed to tell him the truth.

After Auld Bessa helped him care for Tamlyn, and the potion carried his wife to the blackness of sleep, he questioned the healer, hoping she'd settle his qualms. It didn't matter to him, would make no difference in his feelings toward Tamlyn. Bessa's response would cue how he should handle his wife, especially in regard in their lovemaking. When he queried the crone, she glared at him.

Instead of replying to his question, she answered it with one of her own. "What did the lass say?"

"I have not pressed her."

"Then you should," Bessa snapped, exiting the room with another look of reproach.

He felt a knave for asking. Now, as he stood staring at his beautiful wife, he once more judged himself a callow cur for the suspicions.

"Julian, your eyes speak your thoughts. Why not say them aloud so they can be done with?" she asked sadly, leaning back against the door.

Stepping to stand next to her, he propped his lower arm on the door above her head. Though he wanted it with all his might, he didn't lean against her, just loomed over Tamlyn, absorbing the warmth of her nearness.

"What thoughts? I pondered your change of mind about Pagan breeding Bansidhe." Unable to meet her eyes, he looked out into the darkening paddock and the storm bearing down on them, turning the landscape dark.

"Julian, never lie to me, you waste breath doing so. I feel your thoughts here." She placed her palm to his heart. "Look at me."

Steeling himself, he turned to meet those witchy eyes. All his life he'd been able to control his emotions, hide them behind his will of iron. Despite, he feared looking into those all-seeing orbs. Tamlyn had the fey ability to walk in his mind.

"Pendegast did not rape me. You came in time to prevent it." She glanced to the two horses, prancing in their mating dance. "When my mother died in the solar, I no longer cared for the room. It provoked too many painful images in my heart. Then you came into my world, and suddenly, I rediscovered the joy, the beauty of the solar my father built from his love for my mother. You replaced sad memories with our happy ones. I thank you.

"So I stand here and do not recall the terror of that ugly visage, but see two very beautiful animals and the power of their quickening. I see the force of the coming storm. Both echo the passion within me, summoned by a very special man. Please believe me. That incident cannot compare to the horror of watching you fight a trial by combat. Those memories, the sounds, seeing the mace slamming into your back, you knocked from the horse by the lance—those are the recollections that haunt me. Your magic drove away the sad memories of my mother's death, my father's madness. Wield that wizardry, Julian. Give me something beautiful to warm my heart, ease my fears."

Julian leaned to her and kissed the tears from her eyes, drinking in their saltiness. What had he done in his sad sorry life to earn Tamlyn? At one point, he wanted the peace of a home, a wife . . . a son, wanted it so badly any woman would have served. That was all he asked, just a small measure of life untouched by war. Now he knew how hollow that dream had been. It was only the palest of shadows when weighed against what Tamlyn brought him.

For the first time, he no longer walked at night in his mind. He slept. He hadn't relived the nightmares of Berwick, hadn't felt himself dying inside a little each day with the grief of Christian's death, so heavy upon his soul. He no longer feared for his sanity. In time, he suspected she could heal him. The only thing that could destroy him—if something were to happen to her, to have her taken from him. He feared if that ever occurred, he would go stark raving mad. She asked him not to fight. He'd promise her the moon, but he couldn't give her that pledge. He would fight for her. Would die for her. But he would rather *live* for her.

He brushed his lips against hers, intending on deepening it. However, the minx slipped under his arm and almost skipped to the ladder, which led to the loft. Grabbing the hem of her kirtle, she pulled it up and tucked it into the leather girdle about her waist. The look she shot him was a witchy *follow me*. Then she started to climb.

Julian stood watching, enjoying how her round arse shifted with every rung. He smiled and then started after her. Out of the corner of his eye, he spotted Pagan cornering Bansidhe, then rearing to mount her.

Suddenly, life felt good.

The first thing he noticed—the hush of the loft. The piles of hay and straw muffled all sounds, giving it a unique ambience of magic. He hadn't been in a loft since he was a squire, but couldn't recall this delightful coziness.

"Have you noticed the roof isn't thatched, but lead? Hadrian said homes of nobles in the cities do this, emulating cathedrals. He wanted a stable that didn't have thatch to cut the risk of fire. He alleged chargers were too costly to risk. He used to breed the finest horses in Scotland before my mother died. After, he didn't have the heart."

"It is what I plan on doing here. Pagan, Lasher and Dragon's Blood will be the fathers of my herd."

She took his hand, pulled him toward the corner.

"The same wrights and artisans who build churches came and did the stained glass windows for the lord's chamber. They also did the barn. When the rain hits it is such a soothing sound."

She dropped down on a pile of straw, tugging his hand so he'd join her. The noise on the roof sounded like the patter of marching elves. "The rain comes."

Julian sat, listening to the calming rhythm. "You are sure it is rain and not your Unseelie Court, trooping in a dance of welcome to Midsummer's Eve?"

Tamlyn lay back like a lazy cat. "I am too lethargic to go peek. I would rather lie here all night with you and listen to the rain. Scent it on the air? It always smells so fresh."

Julian lay back on his side, propping his head up to study her in the half light. "When does heather bloom?"

"Some wee patches, mostly white heather, will bloom a bit around Midsummer's Day. Most flower in late summer into early autumn. Why?"

"I was imagining making love to you in the midst of purple flowers."

She laughed aloud, the sound musical. "Och, you shan't want to do that. Heather is not flowers, but a low growing shrubbery. The dark purple you will see growing in dry areas. In boggy lands it is pinkish."

Julian reached over and took her hand, toying with the gold Beltane ring on her finger. He desired her. Anytime he was near her that would arise. Only for this space in time, he enjoyed this solitude with Tamlyn, sharing, when all cares of the world were far away and it was just them.

He discovered he hungered for more than just their joining of flesh. Reaching out, his first finger traced her dark brow. Though she was golden, her eyelashes and brows were deep brown, as her pubic hair was. The contrast intrigued him.

"Why did you turn down all offers of marriage contracts?" he asked, suddenly curious.

She put her hand to his chest, feeling the strong, sure thud of his heart. "Because none touched my soul the way you do."

"Ah, lass." He leaned to her, brushing his lips to her soft ones, keeping the pressure light, savoring her feel, her taste.

Their passions always burned white hot, yet this time he wanted to love her slowly, exquisitely, worship her as the treasure she was. His hand cupped the side of her face, shaking. The emotions flying through him were overwhelming.

All he could do was kiss the full lips, reverence her with his.

Tamlyn tried to keep still, but she felt so happy she wanted to sing and dance. Very carefully, she reached over, tugged Challon's sark to her, and slipped it on over her naked form. The chill of dawn touched the air, though she'd slept snug against the hot body of her husband the whole night. Rolling onto her side, she stared at his beautiful face. In sleep he seemed much younger in the past few weeks. When he first came, the shadows of pain appeared etched into his countenance. The nightmares had stopped and he rested peacefully. She carefully traced her finger over the black brows, loving how they arched so expressively.

Challon was hers.

Evelynour was right. She'd fight to keep him. Fight to win his love.

She wiggled her hips and smiled. Their marriage was good for him, giving his soul peace. Putting a hand to her stomach, she wondered about her suspicion. How he would react when she told him. She'd missed her menses and her breasts felt heavier, sensitive.

Tamlyn's eyes went wide and she rushed down the ladder, barely making it to the side of the barn before her stomach heaved.

"It seems every time I turn around we are having a festival," Julian teased as Tamlyn and he trailed after his brothers, her sisters, Damian and Aithinne, all heading to the high tor where food and drink were waiting for the merrymakers of the day.

"Our people work hard. We celebrate eight times a year—four great fire festivals, Imbolg, Beltane, Lughnasadh and Samhain, then Midsummer's Eve, Yuletide and spring and autumnal equinoxes. These are all points in our cycle of harvest. A time to celebrate."

"Just so you do not want to toss me on some bonfire." Julian laughed, hanging his arm around her shoulder.

Two giggling girls ran up to Aithinne and tugged on her hands. "Come, Aithinne, we go to gather yarrow to put under our pillows so we can dream of the man we are to marry. Do you not wish to see, too?"

Aithinne blushed and tried not to look at Damian. He refused to let her duck, but shifted to stand before her. "Aye, Aithinne, are you not interested into glimpses of days to come?"

She looked to Tamlyn. "Do not toss your sweet husband on the balefire, Tamlyn. St. Giles can be spared."

Damian looked back to Tamlyn. "How can your

cousin so favor you and yet have the disposition of a shrew?"

Tilting her chin, Aithinne exaggeratedly batted her eyes at Ravenhawke, then rolled them to the sky. "Poor thing, he must have been dropped on his head as a child—repeatedly. Why else would he so favor his noble kinsman, Lord Challon, and have the disposition of a swine?"

As they neared the top of the hill, Julian noticed people working furiously on three large wheels. They were weaving straw and heather around the wheels and coating them with pitch.

"They spin the morn out of night." Tamlyn smiled at his perplexity. "The wheels of fire are meant to give our god of light more power to keep winter at bay. Cartwheels are swathed in straw and heather, then ignited and sent rolling down the hill. If it remains lit all the way down and blazes for a long time after it stops, an abundant harvest is expected. Once the fires of the wheel burn down, people will jump over the embers. Couples, holding hands, leap over it to bless their love, others to cleanse them and give them good health. The young men take heather torches, light them from that, and run around the fields and through Glenrogha purifying them."

Several young lads came running to Tamlyn. "Hurry, my lady, Skylar comes with the sacred fire. You must take it and light the wheels."

Julian watched as they pulled Tamlyn to stand before the wheels. The young Highlander who danced with Tamlyn before the balefire at Beltane, his teacher of the claymore, came rushing up the hill, heather torch held high. He ran to Tamlyn who took the torch and lit the three wheels, as the young man pushed them over the hillside. Julian watched the people cheering because all three made it down the hillside still burning, signaling their Auld Ones blessed the coming harvest.

Warrior's instincts kicked in, warning someone stared at him. He saw Tamlyn, still holding the torch to light the balefire. Swinging around he spotted an old man a few paces away. Drawn, curious why this man would gaze so fixedly at him, Julian walked over to him.

The frail old man stared at Julian with eyes much like Evelynour, almost dead and yet still they saw more than normal ones. He was dressed in the manner of an ancient druid—the long robe, sandals—and used the staff as tall as a man for a cane. "Merry met, Julian Challon, Lord of the Glen."

"I do not believe we have been introduced. Welcome to Glen Shane . . ." Julian paused, unsure how to address the stranger.

"Thomas Learmont of Ercildoune," he answered in a quavering voice of age, offering his right hand to shake.

When Julian shook it, the old man clutched it with a surprising strength and held on. "You have the makings of a king within you, my lord. The same force, same magnetism, but I sense this valley is the only kingdom you want. Pity, this land could do with a king of your mettle. Edward Longshanks would ne'er turn his eye to these northlands if you sat upon the throne, Lord Challon. Scotland's loss."

Then it hit Julian. *Thomas Learmont*. "Thomas the Rhymer, some call you?"

"Some do. Others say True Thomas. A man is called many things within his journey . . . son, father, husband. You are called Dragon, Challon or Julian. Now. Once, you walked these hills and answered to a name other. *Fitheach*, they called you." Closing his eyes, he grew silent for a breath, then words fell from his mouth,

"Time, time, tide and love that binds, the Dragon trods a path of ancient wynds."

A chill went up his spine. Hadn't Tamlyn said as much before? *I recognize you, but you don't remember me.*

"Once, at the dawn of time, you were a great warrior-king. You took a bride, a Daughter of Anne, and came unto this glen. The Auld Ones have granted you a rare gift, Lord Challon. Cherish love that has come again, keep it close, for there are those who would seek to steal it from you."

A shout distracted him. Gervase galloped his horse up the hill, calling his name.

When Julian turned back to the man to ask more, he'd vanished. His eyes searched about for the figure in the dark gray robes, but he wasn't there. Prickles went up Julian's spine. The man could walk away, but not fast enough to disappear from sight.

Gervase stopped his horse as Tamlyn, Damian and Aithinne came running. When his brothers saw them, they headed his way as well, immediately followed by Raven and Rowanne.

"My lord, a messenger," Gervase gasped. "Himself . . . King Edward."

Julian's stomach suddenly experienced a sinking sensation. The mere mention of Edward's name sent a cold dread in his heart. All eyes were on Gervase. Challon commanded, "Out with it, lad."

He held out a scroll. Julian looked at it as if it were an adder. He didn't want to touch it, resented Edward's intrusion into this idyllic glen. He snatched it, staring at the king's seal. Glancing at his brothers and cousin, he saw they weren't thrilled with the missive either. With a deep breath, he broke the seal and unrolled the parchment, his eyes scanning the words. They confirmed his worst fear.

"All prominent Scottish landowners, churchmen and burgesses are summoned to swear allegiance to Edward. They are bid to assemble on the 28th day of August this year at Berwick," Julian read aloud.

Simon snorted. "Has Edward got cork for brains? Gathering the whole of Scotland in that foul cesspit?"

"So we all sally forth to the land of the dead?" Guillaume asked. Hands on his hips, his chest rose and fell, demonstrating he was less than happy.

"Simon and you shall remain behind and protect the valley. It seems Edward specifically requests the presence of the Lord and Lady Challon, Lord Ravenhawke and Lady Coinnlear."

Chapter 23

As Julian approached the rise in the hill, he sucked in his breath. The sweet, sickening odor warned him his worse fears lay ahead.

"God's breath, what fouls the very air?" Damian snarled, clearly forcing himself to breathe shallowly through his mouth.

Worried, Julian glanced over at the women riding in pairs behind them. Aithinne had lowered her head and picked up the hem of her gown, using it to cover her nose. She appeared pale, tinged with gray. Tamlyn, riding on Goblin, yanked back on her horse's reins, trying to steady the animal as it reacted to scenting the putrid odor that polluted the air. By the stiffening of her spine, Julian knew she was as affected as Aithinne.

Julian's bark carried only as far as Damian's hearing. "We are downwind of Berwick."

"I fail to see how—"

"Remember to thank Edward for the coming experience." Julian's destrier pranced and snorted, clearly spooked by the stomach-turning scent on the wind.

Damian's pale green eyes widened. "You do not mean—"

"I do. My festering nightmare. Not many lived after three days of butchery. I had not wanted to speak of the vile atrocities to the ladies, thinking surely the foul mess would be cleared by this time. The scent tells another tale. Edward commanded the bodies should be left until Scotland was brought to heel. I fear, it is precisely what has happened."

Damian stared at Julian in horror. "Not even Edward would subject us to this. Think of the ill airs. He cannot . . . no man would—"

"Edward's mind has turned inward. They cleaned up a lot of the town, but the remainder was commanded to be left as it was. He wishes to rub the noses of Scottish nobility into the foul miasma, make certain they shall never rise against him again." Julian's mouth formed into lines of grim determination. "Be prepared, Damian. Show no tender feelings toward the Lady Aithinne before Edward. None toward Tamlyn. Let him believe we are resigned to our fate, but *not* pleased. Tell Edward whatever he wishes to hear, offer no resistance to any of his policies. Let us make haste to leave this mockery of a parliament as soon as possible. Most of all—trust no one, at all times hold close to the Lady Aithinne. Keep her safe. Then mayhap we might escape Berwick with our heads."

The road turned along the steep bank of the river, and before them appeared to be all of Scotland's nobility, making their way to Berwick. Never had Tamlyn seen such a mass of humanity converging on one spot, and there was still more than a league to travel to the town's outer walls. People mounted, traveling in curtained brancards, on foot or in carts, formed a long queue snaking along the river Tweed. The air was oppressively hot, humid, and the sun wasn't at zenith yet.

A hot wave of nausea rolled through Tamlyn. She swallowed the bad taste, her mouth beginning to water excessively, as it did when one was near vomiting. Thus far, she thought Challon hadn't noticed her morning sickness, the bouts being so light. However, this was nearly more than she could stomach.

Horses suddenly came crashing along the procession, the wild riders spooking other mounts, nearly causing several to break out of formation.

"Edward's Lordling comes," Damian smirked, "along with the rest of Bruce's sons. They come to see Bruce lands restored. Balliol took them when they refused to pay him homage as king. Annandale still expects Edward to set him in place of Balliol. He labors under gross misconceptions."

"Shan't happen," Julian stated, as he guided his mount to act as a buffer between Tamlyn and the hard-riding Bruces. "Edward never makes the same mistake twice. He knows Annandale is too weak to control Clan Comyn. Worse, the king's far-seeing, devil's breed eyes fear the Celtic blood in Carrick, despite years of molding Robert to his liking."

Tamlyn flinched as the Bruces spurred past, nearly causing her mount to shy. Julian reached over and took hold of her rein to help control the increasingly agitated Goblin.

Up ahead, there was a woman's startled scream, as the Bruces drove past the brancard under pennon of a red cross on gold—standard of Richard de Burgh. Startled jennets pulled against each other, causing the occupant to be unceremoniously dumped upon the ground. Her pale blue kirtle flew up around her hips.

"Looks as though Carrick and siblings have run afoul of de Burgh's party," Julian commented. "That must be Elizabeth, his daughter."

"What is de Burgh doing here? He does not like to leave Ireland these days," Damian wondered aloud. "Can one blame him?"

"More of Edward's machinations, to be sure," Julian muttered, his eyes returning to Tamlyn, assessing.

"Challon, what is that horrid smell?" She could barely keep her stomach quiet.

They pulled up at the crest of the hill, looking down at the mass of horses and people, converging on the once mighty town of Berwick. Never in her wildest imaginings had Tamlyn thought to see so many cattle and people in one place.

Julian's mouth flexed into a hard grimace. "So it begins."

"What?" Tamlyn's head whipped around to stare at her lord husband.

Eyes straight ahead, he replied, "The mime and mummeries."

Her mouth opened to ask what exactly he meant, but the question was cut off by St. Giles, moving his charger up next to hers, so she was between the two men.

"What say you, cousin? It seems all of Scotland comes to pay homage to their new English king. With all these people gathering on this side of Scotland, might the whole bloody isle not tip into the sea?"

Julian's face grew grim as they neared the town's outer wall. "Has Edward lost what little sense he possesses?"

"He has surrounded himself with angry nobles before. He means to—"

Julian looked past Tamlyn, across her horse to Damian. "He means to grind the nose of every personage of rank in this stubborn country in the offal that is now Berwick. God's teeth, does he not comprehend these people will only be strengthened by this outrage? He thinks this atrocity will break them, scare them into submission. By God, it shall not! He makes a martyr of the whole friggin' town."

Julian's horse pranced sideways as he addressed them. "Tamlyn, Lady Aithinne, there is no way to prepare you for what lies ahead."

"By the Holy Virgin, what sort of brainsickness is this?" Damian gasped, trying his best not to breathe. The wind shifted and the stench that rose on it was revolting! "There are no words to describe this foulness."

"It is no more than I feared." Challon's face set in hard lines as he glanced at Tamlyn with a worried expression.

As Tamlyn stared at Challon, everything began to darken and spin around her. Panic flooded her and without realizing it, she jerked back on the reins of Goblin, transferring her terror to the mare. This was the town of her dream! Only the reality was worse. Much worse. In her dream, she'd walked the wynds and vennels during the battle. This was the gruesome aftermath—four months gone, now under the hot sun of August.

"I . . . cannot . . . Challon." Unaware she was pulling on the reins, Goblin began backing up, nearly crashing into the squires riding behind them. "Please, Challon, I . . ."

As they entered the town a sound, a humming arose. Thousands and thousands of blueflies buzzed, the horrific noise matched the drone inside Tamlyn's head as faintness whirled through her mind. Murders of ravens hovered nearby, their cacophony rising, warning them against going farther.

In response to her pressure on the reins, Goblin stopped backing up and bounded on its hooves trying to rear. Suddenly, the small horse jerked sideways, almost losing footing in the muck and mire.

"Damn it, Tamlyn." Julian jerked Dragon's Blood closer so he could once more grab hold of the lead on her horse. "You panic Goblin."

"Challon . . . must . . . leave . . . I cannot . . ." In mindless terror, Tamlyn continued to jerk on the bridle, almost sending the animal into bolting. In the throng of people and animals it was madness, could result in injury or death. Yet, she had to get away from here.

Julian leaned across to grab her around the waist. He lifted her out of the saddle, pulling her sideways across his lap. Her whole body bowed, struggling against his hold and nearly toppling them both from the back of his mount. It was only the high cantle and pommel that prevented it. Dropping his reins and commanding Dragon's Blood with his knees only, he used both hands to control her.

"Damn it! Hold still," he growled, finally clamping both arms round her so tightly she had a hard time drawing breath. "Tamlyn, calm down. You shall see us both killed. Is that what you wish?"

His deep voice began to penetrate her terror, causing her unfocused stare to fix upon his face. Tamlyn's reason reasserted itself as she stared into his dark green eyes.

"Challon, please I cannot stay in this . . . this *hell* created by Edward Longshanks."

His throat worked, the muscles in the beautiful column contracting. "I understand, Tamlyn. God's wounds, I of all people understand."

Tears rose as she shook her head faintly. "You cannot. This is my . . . nightmare. I have walked these vennels of death and blood before . . . in my dreams."

His head lifted as his spine straightened. "No, lady wife, you have walked the streets of *my* nightmare. Hear the words I speak to you. Though I wish nothing more, I cannot carry you away from this becursed place. In my dealings with Edward, I tread a narrow path and must do as he wills. He commands the Dragon of Challon to Castle Berwick, along with the new Lady Challon. We dare not disobey. Believe me, if there were any other choice I would walk through the fires of hell to spare you this. By all that is holy, for the next few days you must place all trust in me, Tamlyn. Heed my council. Follow my every lead. Never allow what you feel to show. And most of all, your temper must stay hidden, lest you risk all. Look well upon the ugliness of Berwick. You do not wish this fate to befall Glenrogha. I shall do my utmost to shield you. Allow me this."

Julian held his breath, waiting for her response. The air expelled from his lungs when she nodded.

"Thank you," The words were whispered under his breath so only Tamlyn heard. He pushed her face into the curve of his neck. "Keep your face to me, Tamlyn. Take short breaths through your mouth, not your nose. Close your eyes and try to rest. I shall get through the foul murk as quickly as possible. Gervase!" he called.

"Yea, my lord." The squire spurred his steed to catch up to his liege.

"Take the reins on Goblin and lead him. Ride in front of us with Vincent and Michael. Carry the standard high. Let everyone know the Dragon of Challon comes."

Hard-bitten and dour-faced, Julian and Damian rode behind the phalanx formed by their squires, forcing their way into the fallen town. They spurred past women on foot, tearfully hiding behind their kerchiefs. Their haunted eyes pulled at Tamlyn's heart. Leaning into the curve of Challon's embrace, she tried desperately not to gag at the overwhelming pall, choking the air like a black fog.

The horses' hooves clattered over the wooden bridge, spanning the wide, dry ditch meant for defense, and then into the arched, stone entrance of Castle Berwick. Off to the side the Douglas standard hung, half dragging in the mud. Blue stars on a silver field. The flag that had flown over the castle ramparts before it was taken in spring, the proud Douglas standard was splattered with horseshite.

Tamlyn observed the halberd-bearing minions in dented jacks, as they stood positioned at the entrance asking of the people arriving, "English or Scots?"

English were pointed to the right and quickly led into the cool castle out of the noon sun. Scots were herded into a queue to the left that slowly snaked outside the bailey, through a side postern door, and into the inner ward. From there, they crossed the cobbled courtyard and were hustled toward the kitchen. They entered the castle proper through the servants' entrance. They were not permitted to break from the long line. Double ranks of armed guards, nearly shoulder to shoulder, held their halberd points like a schilltron, turning the Scots back to the line should they try to leave it.

Tamlyn looked back sadly, as Julian ushered her into the castle with Damian and Aithinne. She glanced up at her husband, feeling as if she somehow betrayed her country by entering with the English. She would've held up her chin, marched over and joined the Scots, but the nausea was increasing and she felt faint. She needed to lie down. There was no way she could take the endless waiting in that line in the sun. She glanced at her cousin, who seemed to fair no better.

More importantly, she promised Julian she'd compose her emotions and follow his lead, trust him to see them through this nightmare.

The dark stone of the castle sweated in the summer humidity. The whole area reeked of pine-pitch from the torches lining the walls. The smell was overpowering, but after the repellent haze hovering over the streets, the scent was almost welcome.

From the gatehouse to the Great Hall had seemed to take forever. By the time they entered, Tamlyn could barely stay standing. Nervously, she took Aithinne's arm, lending her support.

Julian had rushed off, but returned shortly. "I've secured a room. The four of us shall have to share the bed. I told the squires to bed down on the floor for added safety. There is just no space in this madness. Come."

In short order, the squires had carried their belongings into the room. Tamlyn guessed they were afforded an honor in having one as spacious. Though they'd have to share the bed, there was plenty of room on the floor for the squires to place their pallets. She doubted most others found such comfort.

Julian watched her with worried eyes. He walked over to where she unfolded the gown she'd wear tonight. With the back of his fingers, he traced the curve of her cheek.

"Fare you well, my lady?"

She swallowed the weariness, the fear of being in this town of death. "I manage, Challon. How long must we remain here?"

"As long as Edward wishes. I know this won't be easy, Tamlyn, but we cannot think of our personal comfort. We must think of Glen Shane. Let us get through this

ordeal, then we shall make haste to return, and merci-
fully, never shall have to put eyes on this place again."

Tamlyn nodded, but said nothing, knowing the memories of their ride into Berwick would never be banished
from her memory.

"I suggest Aithinne and you rest after you unpack.
This eve promises to be a long one."

Tamlyn was no coward, but her knees shook as they
approached the Great Hall of Castle Berwick. "*Ceum gu
foil, is fheàrr dràm toinisg na bucaid leòm*," Challon
warned. *Walk softly, a dram of sense is better than a
bucket of pride.*

As they entered, she heard Damian whispering names
to Aithinne. At the long table sat Longshanks in his royal
splendor. With him were Bishop Anthony Bek; the Earls
of Surrey and Hereford; Richard de Burgh, Earl of
Ulster; Master Hugh de Cressingham; Gartnait, Earl of
Mar; Gilbert de Clare, Earl Gloucester and son-in-law to
Edward. The few ladies were arrayed in brilliant silks
and trimmed with gold braid and heavy jewelry. Tamlyn
deemed it in bad taste.

A din of conversation filled the air, nearly drowning
out the minstrels, playing softly high in the gallery. Four
dwarves capered around doing feats of tumbling and tormenting a tamed bear. Few seemed to pay them notice
other than Edward. He occasionally pelted them with
sweetmeats, chuckling as if this were a joyous occasion.
His laughter roared and filled the vaulted hall when one
dwarf tossed the treat back to the king.

Tamlyn's eyes swung to the small makeshift table, just
behind Edward and within the king's reach. It was a
rough-cut slab of red sandstone. Upon it sat a golden
pitcher and two goblets. It seemed out of place, odd,
when Edward was trying to impress the Scots with the

English riches that he'd be compelled to use such a poorly chiseled stone as a table top.

Lines of Scots nobility pressed against the wall, wound around in a queue until it led up to small desk before the lord's table. Clerks with scrolls and books fussed about, then would suddenly call out a name. The noble came forward as one clerk checked his name off a list. He knelt before the table facing Edward, speaking his oaths of homage and fealty. When he rose, he was led to sign a sheepskin scroll to which he then affixed his seal.

Tamlyn stared at the impeccably groomed man before her—Edward Plantagenet. There was no doubt he was a king, in total control of all about him, so completely self-assured. His eyelid drooped slightly, a trait they say was inherited from his father Henry III. The eyes were what struck her the most. So vivid a blue, they were dominant, a striking feature that compelled all to quail before him. Only there was coldness to them, as if one touched ice. She'd heard he had a great mind, but flawed by a mercurial behavior, violent tempers and a deep streak of vindictiveness.

While his Eleanor was alive, she evidently exerted some control of this dark side of his nature. Tamlyn wished the woman were about now.

In his youth he'd been a handsome man. Now the once blond hair was nearly white, the cheeks ruddy from his time spent outdoors campaigning on his many wars. Dressed in red velvets trimmed in heavy gold and a wide gold collar, Edward Plantagenet was the most fearful man she'd ever met.

Sensing her hesitation, Julian placed his hand on her waist and gave it a small squeeze of assurance, then escorted her before the king. As per Julian's instructions, she made a curtsey, as did Aithinne, only to have Edward say it wasn't necessary.

"Arise. We understand the heat is stressful on ladies carrying babes in their bellies. Our beloved Eleanor fatigued easily in the early stages of breeding." Edward rose, slapping Julian on the back as if glad to see his old friend, then greeted Damian in the same fashion.

Tamlyn flinched, wondering how the king could tell she was with child. Julian showed no reaction, though she saw his eyes stared at her with a distance. She hadn't told Challon, fearing he still harbored doubts when she said Dirk didn't rape her. She almost blanched under the force of those green eyes.

Dreams of Berwick had haunted Challon since Edward's summons came. Nightly, he suffered such torment, she hadn't wanted to add to his stress by bringing up she carried his child. She hoped to wait until this was behind them until she told him of her news.

"Seems my Dragon plows a fertile field, eh?"

Challon inclined his head, feigning ennui. "Is it not what you willed? Breed these Scots females into loyal English subjects. I merely obey my king."

"Eh? My Seeding of Scotland Campaign. I see the lords of Challon wield their mighty swords for the good of England." Edward's blue eyes lit as a young woman entered. "Ah, come, join us, Lady Elizabeth, and meet the Dragon of Challon and his lady, and Lord Lyonglen and his ward, the Lady Aithinne."

The daughter of Richard de Burgh was a tall beauty, stunning. Wheat-colored hair was piled up high on her head, and vivid blue eyes flashed incisively. Their hue was emphasized by the dark blue velvet of her kirtle. The gown was trimmed with a braid in silver, accenting her high breasts. Silver fox fur trimmed her wrists and collar.

Edward laughed, leaning to Julian. "We think to make her a gift to Carrick. As one now steeped in wedded bliss, what think you? Shall they make a good match?"

Julian nodded, looking slightly uninterested. "They would make a handsome couple, sire."

"Surprised we would seek an alliance between Richard's daughter and Carrick?" Glancing around, Edward complained, "We expected to see Annandale and Carrick here before now."

Julian's eyes roved about the mass of people crammed into the hall. "They are here. You might say they nearly ran down Lady Elizabeth outside of town."

The young woman's laughter bubbled forth. "Oh dear, *that* was Robert Bruce?"

Julian nodded. "Aye, you gave him a few words on decorum, I believe."

"Oh, how precious! What a first meeting, Sire. He and his brothers, I presume, scared the jennets pulling my brancard. They dumped me on my . . . pride. I cannot wait to see his face. He told me I was impertinent. I informed him he was rude."

Julian stroked Tamlyn's hand. "First meetings are always memorable."

Behind him, Damian snorted, causing Aithinne to turn bright red.

"This sounds like two tales we would hear more of," Edward commented, arching his brow.

A sudden commotion thankfully drew the king's attention. Edward smiled. "Seems Clan Bruce has finally reached the end of the long line."

Julian was surprised Annandale and his sons had been made to wait in the long line with the rest of the Scots. They'd been with Edward when he rode into Scotland, and had given oath to him again at Wark. It seemed nothing less than a total affront to be herded into the castle with the rest of the rebel Scots.

"We see censure in your eyes, Lord Challon. Think we should exempt the Bruces from this ragmans roll?"

Julian shrugged. "Well, they did not even hold lands in Scotland at the time and rode with English forces."

"The Bruces believe we shall put Annandale on the throne. Idiocy. Traveling North to subdue Scots once is enough. We remind the Bruces there will be no such undertaking by this demonstration. Their lands are returned. I shall offer Carrick a rich bride to appease his stinging pride."

The Bruces were not only humiliated by this indignity from the king they'd served, but they received snide comments and outright slurs from the Scots that had been loyal to John Balliol. One commented his heart bled for Clan Bruce, who betrayed their true king to follow the English, only to be rewarded so shabbily.

"Come, let us a toast to the betrothal over their Stone of Destiny," Edward announced for all to hear.

Tamlyn's head snapped around to look again at that ridiculous chunk of sandstone, wondering what sort of jest was this.

Edward noticed her reaction and inquired, "Lady Challon, have you not seen your country's coronation stone?"

"No, sire, I have not,'" she replied, thinking neither had Edward Longshanks if he claimed that clumsily cut rock was what he took to be the Stone of Destiny.

This stone was not very tall. The real stone was higher, almost perfect height on which to sit. It was black stone, hard and polished like a jewel. Pictish drawings were carved all the way around its sides.

Julian asked as he lifted the cup for her to drink, "Some concern, lady wife?"

Tamlyn drank, careful of the wine, being sure just to take a few sips. With this constant struggle against dizziness, she didn't need a head full of the grape. Besides, she rarely drank wine, as it made her legs ache later. "It is not our stone. Lia Fail is a black stone, three times that size and has Pictish drawings on the sides. Is this Edward's hoax?"

"Either Edward knows this is not the stone and dares any Scot to say otherwise—or he does not know and someone played a switch with him. Yet another scenario: Edward knows they made the switch and flaunts this fake, hoping a Scot will betray the secret by blurting out he has been tricked. Little matters which one, only a fool would dare speak such to the king."

There was another commotion as Robert tried to gain the king's attention. Evidently, Carrick was incensed at having to go through this humbling and was certain Edward remained unaware of the treatment. Gilbert de Clare, son-in-law to Longshanks, but also cousin to Annandale, went to Edward and whispered something to Edward's ear. The king laughed and shooed him away.

By evening's end, Tamlyn's head buzzed. Julian finally gained Edward's leave, sighting the condition of Tamlyn and Aithinne. Tamlyn frankly didn't care what excuse he used, just so she was away from the crowd, the noise and the smells.

"Challon, how long must we endure this nightmare?" she whispered as they headed down a long corridor.

"Damian and I have an audience with Edward in the morn. I hope to gain his leave for us to return to Glenrogha after Parliament meets."

Two men stepped from the turn in the hall, blocking their way. Julian shifted in front of Tamlyn, shielding her, as Damian moved up to stand beside his cousin. Shaking, Aithinne reached for Tamlyn's hand.

"Challon, St. Giles," one man addressed them, but it wasn't in warmth.

Julian merely stared at the men. They grew uneasy under Challon's fixed glare, and shifted from foot to foot. "You have business, Pendegast?"

The tallest nodded. "We wanted to speak to you about the death of our brother."

"Your brother died in trial by combat, John. The Lord judged him guilty before all. I have spoken to Edward about this," Julian said with finality.

"But not to us."

"I owed an accounting of the circumstances to our king. He agreed the matter rested within the hands of God and He decided Dirk's fate."

A commotion rose behind them—raised voices of several men arguing. Robert Bruce and his brothers came hurrying down the hall, but pulled up when they saw the group standing in the hallway.

Robert, Edward and Nigel Bruce casually pushed past Tamlyn and Aithinne to come up behind Challon and St. Giles. Carrick turned from side to side, looking at Damian and then Julian. "Rather close to be standing in the hall, don't you think, Lord Challon? Shall my brothers and I escort you and your ladies to your room?"

John Pendegast, glared at Challon, then his eyes fixed on Tamlyn. She felt a shiver crawl over her skin. The cold blue eyes made Tamlyn feel like she looked into a grave. "My lady." He inclined his head slightly and then turned on his heels, stomping away.

Tamlyn had an odd sense of foreboding that Sir Dirk's brothers hadn't dropped the matter.

* * *

Aithinne and she shared the bed. Pallets had been placed on the floor on either side, where Damian and Challon rested. Their four squires slept just inside the door. She had a feeling Challon wanted them close because of the possible threat from the Pendegasts.

She'd heard Challon stir, knew he'd been on edge and not found his rest. He'd appeared drawn, tired . . . worried. Tamlyn glanced over and saw him staring out the arrow loop toward the night sky.

Turning to rest on her hip, she watched his still form. Clad only in a short length of white linen about his hips, his back was tensed. Carefully, Tamlyn eased off the bed, trying not to waken Aithinne, who'd finally fallen asleep.

Her steps were silent, but she sensed Challon was aware of her approach. His whole body tensed. She wasn't surprised he failed to find rest. Being here brought back all the horrible memories.

She gently placed her hand on his back. "Challon," she whispered.

His head stayed hidden in the shadows, as if he didn't want her to see his face. At last, the reply came. "You should rest. I will do my best to get Edward to let us leave on the morrow. He has paraded the Dragon of Challon before all to see that I am still his loyal lapdog. Hopefully, that shall be enough. Then we can be quit of this hellhole. Two pregnant Scots carrying English babes in their bellies make the king quite pleased with himself."

When his stance stayed shut off from her, Tamlyn ducked under his arm, braced against the wall and wrapped her arms around his waist, hugging him. "I wanted to explain—"

"Later, Tamlyn. I have little liking to discussing our troubles before others. Wait until we return to Glenrogha."

She opened her mouth to protest, but he swooped down and claimed her lips with his. He backed her against the cold stone wall, letting her feel the hardness of his body, his erection, yet keeping his full weight off her. His kiss was not gentle, not rough. Just insistent as if he used it to silence her. But soon, domination gentled and he kissed her so slowly, so exquisitely, that a mewing arose in the back of her throat.

He broke the kiss, leaning his head to hers. "Go to bed, wench, before I take you here before all."

He'd kissed her. He wanted her. But he didn't believe her. "I thought you believed me—"

"Go to bed, Tamlyn." Challon turned away to look out the window, shutting her out.

Tamlyn nodded sadly and went back to the bed, fearing she'd get little sleep this night. Fearing neither would Challon.

Chapter 24

Nine sennights after the nightmare of Berwick, Tamlyn stood watching the sparks of the Samhain balefire shoot high into the autumn night. She followed their twinkling path in the inky sky, then whispered a prayer to be carried on the faery lights. She hoped her father was safe and would return to them soon. Hoped the magic of this special night would burn away the lingering horrors of Berwick's sickness from her mind.

They'd stayed there only long enough for Edward's parliament. Longshanks received pleasure from parading Aithinne and her before all, showing the Celtic heiresses were under the power of his English knights. In the course of events, he announced Damian's betrothal to Aithinne—without any warning or consent from her—and officially conferred not just Lyonglen upon him, but made him baron of Coinnleir Wood as well. Aithinne refused to speak to St. Giles after that.

Once Edward had his jollies, Challon reminded him the foul airs of Berwick weren't good for women in the early stages of carrying babes. They, having served their purpose, were dismissed with a smile.

Tamlyn couldn't stop picturing the ugly visions of rotten corpses hanging from half burnt windows, or the piles of carcasses with ravens picking at the bones from flooding her dreams.

Worse, she still feared Challon harbored secret fears over her babe. She tried to assure him the child she carried was conceived on Beltane, warned him he'd feel the fool when she proved such by giving birth by Candlemas. He smiled, hugged her and said to ignore him, it was only the foulness of Berwick rotting his mind. Now he was away from there he knew all was right. Most of the time she believed him. But there were odd moments, when she caught him watching her, that caused her to wonder. His doubt was a knife to her heart.

Challon, resting his hand on her shoulder, gave it a small squeeze. "Sorry you are not out there dancing?"

"No, that is the last thing I wish right now." Tamlyn laughed and rested her hand on her rounded belly.

Raven had sewn several new kirtles for her in hunter green, dark blue and burgundy. They hung loosely on her body from the small pleat at her breasts, trying to give the illusion she wasn't now built like a cow. The heaviness of the child was cumbersome and often made her tired.

Nearing six months into her pregnancy, Tamlyn was more than content to watch the dancers capering around the Samhain balefire. These days, she felt awkward at best and her back ached continuously.

As if sensing her nagging pain, Challon's hand slid from her shoulder, down the curve of her spine and began rubbing. The man had magic fingers—his touch firm, yet gentle.

She leaned into him, rubbing her face against his upper arm, still relishing the scent of the man, and feeling that now familiar security of being his lady. Despite what shadows lingered in his eyes, she never doubted his commitment to her, to this glen. She'd come to love her Dragon. She only wished he felt the same toward her. He never spoke of love, though she knew he needed her. She was satisfied to wrap him up in that desire for her and the need for the world they were creating together in this peaceful valley. Someday maybe . . .

As her eyes followed the circles of dancers weaving around the great balefire, Tamlyn blinked. Her heart jumped erratically as she searched the crowd, trying to spot what had caught her attention. It was only as she focused beyond the dancers, to the people standing at the edge of the firelight on the other side, did she locate what caused her senses to flutter.

A man stood, wearing a faded plaide. His auburn hair was long, with plaits of a chief at his temples. He wore a beard, but neat. The face was so familiar. He stared at Tamlyn, the pale ice green eyes unblinking, almost willing her to look at him.

As Tamlyn locked eyes with the man, she felt the world shift under her feet.

Challon's arm wrapped around her back and held her upright and the other grasped her arm. "What is it, Tamlyn?"

She fluttered her eyelashes against the spinning flashes, then sought the man on the other side of the fire. He was gone. As if never had been. Had she imagined him? Sensing Challon's alarm, she smiled faintly. He'd been so caring, so solicitous since their return from Berwick.

"Just a twinge. The babe moved. It startled me, it was so strong."

Julian herded her toward a bench. "I told you standing

too much this night would be a strain for you. You will rest here a bit, then I shall take you back to Glenrogha. I will not hear your naysay, Tamlyn, or I shall carry you the whole way."

"Aye, Challon." She nodded absently, still searching the crowd.

"Tamlyn, when I hear 'aye, Challon,' I always feel you are ignoring me and plan on doing precisely what you want." Julian frowned his exasperation.

She suddenly spotted the man again. He was thinner than when she'd last seen him months ago. Tears sprang in her eyes. It was all she could do not to rush to him, hug him. With his index finger, he made a small circle in the air and then pointed straight down to the ground.

She counted to ten, trying to keep her emotions under control, then gave a faint nod.

Tamlyn's steps silently carried her to the old Pict broch. No longer used for living quarters, it was still good for storage. The Picts built things to last, she thought. She entered, having to bend over. The door had been designed so anyone coming in was stooped over and vulnerable, which gave people inside the advantage of first strike. She rubbed her belly and gave a small moan because the stooping set her back to hurting again.

"Mercy," she whispered to shadows, fighting a wave of dizziness. "I have three more months of this."

She allowed her eyes to adjust, then reached for the torch in the holder and struck a flint to light it. The walls were clammy, sweating, so the torch hissed as it burned off droplets of moisture. For an instant she froze, thinking she heard a noise outside, footsteps, but then they moved on. A guard making his rounds.

The stone steps were worn, uneven and damp. She moved down them one step at a time, getting both feet on one, until she moved to the next. Keeping her hand on the outer wall, she wasn't risking a fall in her condition. She followed the spiraling staircase down to the lower level. She always hated coming down here, the darkness, the silence—outside of the occasional drip of water—always closed in upon her and made her feel suffocated.

This was taking too long. Challon still slept when she slipped out, but she feared that would only last so long. He was always exhausted after they made love, but he'd soon awaken. When he found her gone, he'd come searching for her.

Reaching up to the torch holder, she tugged with all her strength and a section of the wall moved back slowly.

Bright torchlight greeted her from the other side.

There were several men there, but she had eyes for only one. He turned and smiled. "Hello, Tamlyn."

Tamlyn rushed into the arms of her father, hugging him tightly. He set her back a space and looked down at her belly, pressing to the fabric of her mantle.

She laughed through the tears. "Seems I am a wee bit different than when you last saw me." Tamlyn wiped tears from her eyes.

"A wee bit. You seem more mature in some ways. You seem happy."

"I am, now I know you are safe." A self-deprecating smile crossed her lips. "Apologies for the waterfalls. I tend to get very emotional these days."

Hadrian nodded. "It comes with carrying the bairn. Small price, eh?"

"The emotions I can handle. The back pain I can live without."

Her father put a hand on her stomach. "How far along, Tamlyn?"

"May Day." She blushed. "Carrying on a family tradition. The bairn should come on Candlemas."

"Auld Bess says all is fine?"

Tamlyn nodded. "She said I will breed a braw babe."

He nodded, mixed emotions flooding his eyes. Pride, worry, love. "Come, greet the others. We await the arrival of another. Hopefully he shall arrive soon. Tamlyn, I believe you recall Andrew de Moray and his uncle—a priest—David de Moray. Gentlemen, my youngest daughter, Tamlyn, Countess Glenrogha, now Lady Challon."

They all murmured their greetings. Tamlyn looked from her father to Andrew. "But how? We heard you both were in the Tower."

"We were, Lady Tamlyn. My father still is, along with many other nobles. For some reason, Edward had us moved to Chester. We escaped with help from Grant Drummond. From there we headed north on swift horses," Andrew replied with a devilish grin. "Like you, I am recently wed and eager to be home with my bride."

Hadrian patted Tamlyn's shoulder. "Your husband's doing. The Dragon gave plea to Edward when you were at Berwick. It caused Edward to have us moved to better conditions."

Tamlyn felt a flush of warmth. Challon had kept his promise. It only made her feel more guilty for slipping away from him.

"Tamlyn, we need to hold up here for a few days, rest. While word goes out to Andrew's people, we shall stay in the caves. There is food and water. At night, we can have a fire. Once David gets word to Petty, Avoch and Boharm, then Andrew and I will move north."

"I appreciate the shelter, Lady Tamlyn. Reginald de Chen controls my holding at Avoch. I plan to move there straight away as soon as I have enough men of Moray rallying to my standard," Andrew explained.

Torches flickered through the cave's passageway, then several men emerged. Though they were strangers, Tamlyn had a fair idea who one was. As introductions were made, she barely heard them, so transfixed by the tall man with the blue-green eyes.

"William, may I present my youngest daughter, Tamlyn, Lady Glenrogha," her father finally said.

"A true daughter of Auld Alba." He took her hand and brought it to his mouth.

Tamlyn's eyes stared unblinking at the man before her. Rumors had been filtering through the Highlands all summer and fall. The English called him an outlaw, a brigand. The Scots whispered the rebel, the patriot, William Wallace of Ellerslie. Ever since Edward crossed back over the Tweed and onto English soil, tales of his flummoxing the English soldiery had been reaching Glenrogha regularly.

Only it was not his exploits which filled her with awe. When he'd touched her hand, a jolt of lightning raced up her arm, nearly numbing her joints.

At first glance, little save the man's height would distinguish this Lowlander from others. He wore the dirty, ragged plaide with the bearing of a king, yet there was nothing pretentious about him. Though nearly a head taller than Hadrian and Challon, his power—as with them—wasn't from his physical stature. Raw force came from within. A fire burned bright in this man. It was terrifying. The vivid blue-green eyes stared at her, steeled with determination. The pain behind them nearly caused her to reel from the force.

"Glenrogha has heard of William Wallace, son of Alan Wallace. Scots speak of little else these days. I bid you *cèud mile fàilte*, a hundred thousand welcomes," Tamlyn greeted.

He smiled, yet it failed to touch his ambient eyes, as if some inner spark in his heart had died. This man had lost much, enough to cripple many others. Fires of revenge drove him. This and the lack of fear for his own life made him a formidable opponent.

"Aye, likely you have heard I am a giant, wear laurel leaves around my head and sacrifice the English in blood ritual." He laughed.

"Glenrogha is only a wee humble fief, but I offer whatever aid you and your followers may require—provided it causes no harm to the people of this glen or my lord husband." Her soft warning didn't fail to reach all ears.

"You have our deepest gratitude, Lady Tamlyn. It is vital Sir Andrew and I meet and come to a single mind. He plans on raising hell with the English in Moray. I in the south. With the backing of the Bishop of Glasgow, between the two of us we might just be able to push the English to the other side of the Tweed come spring."

Tamlyn feared this talk. She'd seen Edward Longshanks. Just pushing the English out of Scotland wouldn't last. It would only provoke Edward's wrath. She thought of the sickening images of Berwick. Did this man not understand how many would die? Men talked of freedom. It was women, who suffered for those high dreams.

Tamlyn drew a breath and closed her mind to the horrible images. "Sir Andrew and you are welcome to use the caves of Glenrogha as sanctuary anytime you need. Food is always stored here, so you may help yourself. I will see clothing and blankets are fetched for you before you leave. However, leave Glen Shane out of the troubles. I wish you well, and ken my lord father shall ride with you. But I do not want Glenrogha, Kinloch, Lochshane or Lyonglen drawn into this struggle. My lord husband provides protection for this glen and is overlord for Lyonglen. He may be Norman, but he is now lord here, he is a good man. No matter who rules Scotland I will have your word neither he nor his men shall be harried or harmed." She glared at her father, William and Andrew in determination. "Your word on this."

All nodded.

Tamlyn felt a small measure of relief at their assent. "I thank you each. Now I must return before I am missed."

As she turned to leave the storage room, William caught her arm. "May I speak frankly, my lady?"

She nodded. "Please feel free, William Wallace."

"Longshanks forced you to wed Lord Challon. You had no choice. So easily you could be made a widow." From the hard look in his eyes, she kenned he fully meant the offer.

Tamlyn trembled. "Aye, I had no choice. Howbeit, my lord father had already thought to wed me to the man, believing he would make me a fine lord and husband. In these times of the troubles, Glenrogha is well served with the Dragon of Challon as our earl. My Norman husband proves a great shield against Longshanks. The Dragon is very rich. I doubt even Edward kens how rich. Glen Shane has the lord it needs. I have the husband I want. I have bound him to this valley, our ways."

"Does he treat you well?" For once, a soft emotion touched the glowing eyes. "His repute as Longshanks' hellhound leads me to fear for your safety. Hence my offer. I would not wish you to end up like the Countess of Dunbar and March."

"Have they heard of Countess Marjorie's fate?"

He shook his head. "We can only speculate. None has seen her after Dunbar was taken in the spring. There can be little doubt she is dead."

She paused, so many conflicting emotions within her. "Once, he was Longshanks' champion, but no more. Something happened to him. Berwick, I suppose, was the final straw after the death of his younger brother Christian in Wales. He only wants to build a life here. I heard my lord husband comment to his cousin, his lands in Normandy and England were taken by Edward before he was sent here. I ken not the whole story. But he shall not rush to aid the English, nor will he fight Scots— unless they threaten this glen. Glen Shane is the only thing that matters to him. He will protect me, our people from anyone, be they English or Scot. I could never want or trust another to do that job so well."

William nodded. "Interesting. Still you have not answered my question. How does he treat you, lass?"

"I admire him. He is a just man. He treats me very well. I thank you for the offer, William Wallace. If things were different, I think you would like him and he you." She qualified her stance. "I support my lord father and respect his right to fight for what he believes. What I believe in is Glen Shane. Same as my lord husband. He will fight to shield us, so I will do naught to hamper his efforts. I would kill anyone who tried to raise a hand to Challon."

"I so hope you and your lord husband keep this valley safe, Lady Challon."

"Come, daughter, I shall see you safely to the bailey," Hadrian interrupted.

"Fare thee well, William Wallace. Go with our blessings and hopes." She watched the man move back to the small fire and warm his hands.

Her father took her and drew her into the passageway. "Thank you for the food and the shelter. We will rest here a few days, then slowly move on, heading north. Wallace will leave before dawn. You care for your Dragon, daughter?"

She nodded. "I love Challon. It has not been an easy choice, knowing he was the man who took you prisoner, destroyed Kinmarch."

"He did what Edward commanded. Had it not been him, things might have gone worse for Kinmarch's people, for me. He treated us fairly, honorably." He laughed, squeezing her to him. "My babe carries a bairn. Do you have any idea how old that makes me feel? You shall see me a grandfather."

Tamlyn reached up, stroked the handsome face, and smiled into the pale green eyes. "You are not old. Must you go with Andrew? Why can you not stay here with us? This valley can be protected against all. You would be safe here. It is a mistake to fight this English king. He is shrewd, but madness is a maggot in his brain. He will not accept defeat. You ken this. So why fight?"

Tamlyn broke down and sobbed against his chest, unable to stop the fear from seeping into her heart. Fear for her father. Fear for Challon. She loved them both and wished they'd stay within this valley. Let the rest of the world have their politics and strife. She wanted the people she loved far away from the coming war and devastation.

Hadrian held her, rocking her. "Hush, *mo chridhe*, you will make the bairn sicken." He lifted her chin and kissed her nose. "I did well in my choosing a warrior for you. Challon will protect you, Tamlyn."

She sniffed. "You might have told me."

"But you are happy with my choice?"

"Aye, I would have no other."

"Come, I shall see you to the entrance of the broch."
He linked arms with hers and helped her carefully climb
the spiraling stone steps. Pushing open the door, Hadrian
checked to see if the path to the lord's tower was clear.
"Come, you must go."

Tamlyn hugged her father, the tears coming again.
"Don't go, please—"

Suddenly, she was yanked away from Hadrian and a
sword tip was placed at her father's throat. She stared
into the hard plains of her angry husband's face. "No,
Challon!" she gasped.

"Tamlyn, step back," Julian commanded, his voice as
cold as winter. "No man touches my lady."

"Challon, stop this! He's my father!" she pleaded.

Tamlyn saw her husband blink and push past his fury
to really look at the man. Finally, recognition registered.
"Earl Shane, last we heard of you, you were a guest of
Edward in the Tower."

"Good morrow, Lord Challon. Thanks be to you,
Edward had Andrew de Moray and I moved to Chester.
While a definite improvement over the Tower, we still
had little liking for the English clime." Hadrian flashed
his white teeth in a wicked grin. He reached up and gin-
gerly removed the blade from his throat. "Let us dispense
with this. You are not going to run me through before
Tamlyn's eyes. I know it. You know it. Tamlyn does not.
Since she carries your child, let us see she does not suffer
undue stress."

Challon took hold of Tamlyn's arm and motioned with
the sword for Hadrian to precede them. "Move, Laird."

Hadrian looked to Tamlyn then to Challon. He nodded
and turned to go as instructed.

Tamlyn jerked against the hold Challon had on her

upper arm, whipped around to try and face her husband. "You are not going to take him prisoner again?"

"Tamlyn, stop fighting me. You only make this harder. Trust me to do what is right . . . for all of us." His grip wasn't painful, but insistent.

Challon marched Hadrian up the steps and pointed with the sword for the Earl to continue up the staircase. At the lord's chamber, he nodded for Hadrian to enter, then pushed Tamlyn in while he paused to speak to Moffet. Tamlyn saw the young man dash off as his lord closed the door.

"Laird, you will remain here. You will excuse Tamlyn? I have need to speak to my wife in private." Challon nodded to Hadrian. He handed Tamlyn a lit candle and pulled her out the door. He closed it firmly.

She turned and opened her mouth, but he held up his finger and fixed her with an arched eyebrow. "Challon—"

"Close your mouth, Tamlyn and keep it closed." Julian marched her back down the stairs, taking the turn for the second floor and heading to the small room that used to be hers. He opened the door, and with an upturned palm signaled she should enter. Tamlyn did so, then watched as he closed the door, then leaned against it with his shoulder, propping his sword against the wall.

"Get in bed, Tamlyn." His words were uttered softly, though Tamlyn didn't mistake the steel of the command.

"What do you plan to do with my father?" She set the candle on the table by the bed.

He exhaled, then moved to the small fireplace and set about lighting the peat in the hearth with his flint. "I have not decided. For tonight, he shall sleep in the lord's chamber. I sent Moffet for Rowanne and Raven. I assumed they would like to see him, to know he is well."

"I thank you for these kindnesses, Julian. But what will

you do? Will you send him back to Edward?" Tamlyn pressed. "I fear what your king will do."

"He's your king, too, Tamlyn."

"But he will not like that Hadrian escaped."

Challon looked up at her. "You, lady wife, would do well to worry more about pleasing me than fretting about Edward."

"You are angry with me?"

He pursed his mouth and nodded. "That would be one way to put it."

"Challon, he is my father—"

His green eyes narrowed. "And I am your husband, Tamlyn. Your first allegiance is to me now."

"Aye, Challon."

"Another aye, Challon. Is this your manner to put me off?" As the fire began to catch, he stood and pulled off his unbelted surcoat. Sitting on the chair, he unlaced his boots and dropped them. "Take your clothes off, Tamlyn."

"Challon, what are you going to do?"

"That depends. Since you are concerned about your father's fate, and how I will punish you, I should think you would be a little more anxious about appeasing me."

His words might make someone else fearful. And Tamlyn wasn't entirely confident of his mood. She knew he was angry. "Challon, what are you . . ."

He sprang at her like a big cat intent on bringing down prey. He backed her to the bed's edge. "Take your clothes off, Tamlyn. Now."

She undid her mantle. He took it from her and tossed it to the floor. With trembling fingers, she worked at the lacings at one elbow, then the other. Tamlyn paused, looking up into his stormy eyes.

"Why do you hesitate to obey, wife?"

"I cannot reach the lacing up the back."

"I have played lady's maid for you before. Turn around," he said in a low voice.

Tamlyn showed him her back. Lifting her hair, he dropped it over her right shoulder. His hand paused over it, then finally descended to smooth it. She glanced over her shoulder at him, trying to read his mood.

He slowly undid the laces up the back, then pushed the sides away and off her shoulders. The kirtle started to fall, but Tamlyn clutched it to her breasts.

"Tamlyn, are you trying to contrary me?"

She shook her head. "I am fat."

He laughed, then kissed her bare shoulder. "No, you are not fat. I loved you earlier, know how you feel. You just carry my son within your body. I have wanted a son, Tamlyn. You have no idea how much."

A shiver spread over her. "Challon, what if I carry a daughter?"

"It is doubtful. The Dragons of Challon breed sons with black hair and green eyes." He sat down and began unlacing his leathern hose. "Get into bed. You have been up too long this day. You need your rest."

Tamlyn dropped the kirtle and scooted under the covers, shivering from the chill of the bed. She was tired. Fretful of what Challon would do about her father.

Julian lifted the blanket and scooted under. Leaning over, he blew out the candle. He stretched, then rolled over on top of her, keeping his weight off her body and on his elbows.

"I thought I needed my rest," Tamlyn said, staring up into his beautiful face.

"You shall find it presently. First, you need to ease my mind, Tamlyn. I saw you embracing another man—"

"I embraced my father."

"Aye, you did. But I did not know that when I caught you. I liked not the feeling, Tamlyn. Make me forget."

She wiggled under him until her hand could close around the rigid length of hot male flesh.

"Owww . . . God's teeth, you and your icy hands." He laughed, then nipped her ear.

"I do not think my hand will be cold for long." She skimmed the velvet skin over steel down his erection and then brought it snaking back to the tip. His penis throbbed to his pulse in her grasp. "Is that helping you forget?"

She leaned up and brushed a kiss over his soft lips.

"It makes me remember how cold your hands get when you are nervous." He cradled his arms around her hips, then he shifted so he was sitting in the bed. His hands positioned her knees to either side of his legs. With a sure flex of his hips, he slid into her. "Ah, warmth again." His white teeth flashed in the shadows. With a thrust, he moved within her tight body. "Here is where you say, aye, Challon."

She used her internal muscles to squeeze hard his hot length. "Aye, Challon. Oh aye, Challon."

"Oh, aye, Tamlyn!"

Chapter 25

Julian thought festivals marked time at Glenrogha. He'd come in the spring and experienced the joys of Beltane and married Tamlyn. Since then, he'd celebrated Midsummer's Eve, Lughnasadh, Samhain and Yuletide.

Where in deep summer Scotland remained light for most of the day, the opposite proved true for the cold winter. Days were too short to finish chores, and drifting snows encouraged all to stay indoors, hovering near fireside.

He'd spent the long nights holding Tamlyn, learning to open himself to her, to speak of the loss of Christian, the brutalities of war. More importantly, how much he needed his life here with her. Each tear he shed, each soothing stroke of her hand, Tamlyn healed the pain inside him with her pagan craft. Made him live again.

Now, another festival was upon them—St. Bride's Day or Imbolg. As a Christian he called it Candlemas. To his surprise, he found in both religions the day spoke of fire and purification. The Scots took torches of heather and ran with them through the meadows and orchards at dawn to awaken them. Near dusk, Glenrogha's people returned to purify the fields and apple trees. Each carrying a fat candle, they formed a long line and paraded around them.

The corner of his mouth quirked in a smile. Tamlyn wasn't taking part in either ceremony. His wife was otherwise occupied.

Needing a breath of fresh air, Julian had climbed to the top of the lord's tower and watched the flickering lights snaking across the fields. The sight was beautiful, like faeries twinkling in the night. Oh, what he wouldn't give to have his arms around his Tamlyn and share the beauty of the pagan ceremony with her.

Next year. Next year he could stand here with Tamlyn and their son and watch.

Going back inside, Julian returned to the Great Hall. He glanced to the redheaded man standing by the fireplace— Tamlyn's father. Hadrian seemed as restless as he and not adept at hiding it.

"Any word?" Julian asked, but the reply was clear on his father-in-law's countenance.

Hadrian exhaled and shook his head no.

Before Yule, Tamlyn's father had returned late one night, wishing to see his daughters. While Hadrian was still a vital, active man, Julian thought he'd fare better at Glenrogha rather than on the move, hiding during this harsh winter. He finally talked the laird into spending the wintry season in Glen Shane. Since Tamlyn was in her final months of carrying their child, she'd been able to entreat her father to remain at least until the birth of the babe.

Hadrian exhaled frustration and looked at him. "You are calmer about this than I am."

"I am not calm."

"You hide it better. That is my little girl up there. She is going to make me a grandfather. I suppose if it were Raven or Rowanne I might have an easier time of this.

They are the elder daughters. You expect, in the natural course of events, they would be the first to have bairns. I saw them married. Mistakenly, I let them have their way, and in both cases the marriages were failures. Raven thought she needed a gentle husband, someone unlike her powerful father. The bloody milksop died because of the damp. And Rowanne—" He looked around as if he wanted to hit something. "It is the past. One I shall regret to my dying day."

Julian still wondered about the death of the Lady Lochshane's husband, a topic Tamlyn was unwilling to discuss with him. He held his tongue. Hadrian was in a flux with his emotions over Tamlyn. The man didn't need Julian giving him an outlet to vent those frustrations.

Hadrian's pale green eyes narrowed on him. "Will your brothers make them good husbands?"

"They shall. With me wed to Tamlyn, Edward is content Glen Shane is in my control. I granted leave for long betrothals. My brothers gifted the ladies until the spring to come to know them. Both of your daughters accepted the generous offer. I presume they shall marry around Beltane."

Hadrian nodded. "That was kind of you. My daughters need time. One to finish her supposed grieving, the other to trust again."

Julian finally had to sit. He'd been standing and pacing half the night. The servants were off to the Imbolg rites, save for those tending Tamlyn, so the tower was silent. He was tired, but knew there wouldn't be a breath of peace until he knew she and the babe were safe.

"I understand you likely wished for a higher born man for both women," Julian commented, rubbing his forehead where an ache was building.

It was fear. Fear for Tamlyn. He knew women often

had problems, even died in childbirth. That anxiety chewed at him. Talking to her father was a distraction.

Hadrian took the chair before the fire, opposite him. "They are honorable men, well-liked and respected. Brother to the Dragon of Challon. If they are of the same mettle—which I have no doubt—I could choose no better than I did in selecting Tamlyn's lord and husband."

Julian nodded thanks for the approval. "I have raised my brothers up to barons. None would dare cast slur on your daughters. I paid handsomely for dispensations for both marriages."

"A man is not responsible for the circumstances of his birth. It is how he shapes his fate that speaks of his worth. I know much of you, your brothers—the Dragons of Challon. My daughters can be in no better hands."

A scream cut through the tower. Both men came to their feet. They looked up to the ceiling as if they could find the answer staring at stone and wood. Julian took a step to go to Tamlyn, but Hadrian caught his upper arm and stayed him.

"Bessa will not want a man underfoot. Believe me, I have been there. She chased me out with a hot poker when the twins came." Hadrian chuckled. "Bessa and Evelynour will care for Tamlyn."

Julian looked at the man's hand, considering the advice. But then a second scream followed the first. He flung off the grip of Tamlyn's father and took the stairs to the lord's chamber two at a time.

Julian held up his son, seeing the curly black hair, nearly as thick as his own. Tears filled his eyes as he touched the tiny head, stroked the soft curls. So perfect in every way. He lifted the plaide blanket and looked at the stem poking from his belly. "Take this thing off him," he demanded of Auld Bessa.

She clucked and shook her head. "Leave that be, Lord Challon. 'Twill fall off when the time is right."

Julian's eyes looked at the tiny toes, gently stroked them. His daughter was beautiful. Daughter? He blinked, shocked to see he indeed had a daughter. Carefully scooping her up and cradling her in the curve of his arm, he stalked to the bed with his beautiful, precious daughter. "Wife, what is the meaning of this?"

Tamlyn weakly sat up, but frowned in pain. "Meaning of what, Challon?" she panted out, then grimaced again.

"This is a daughter, not a son," he stated the obvious.

Bessa chuckled. "Men," she muttered, as she folded padding and slid it under Tamlyn's legs, then rearranged the bedding.

"Aye, Challon. I am glad to see this ordeal has not affected some of your faculties," she ground out through bared teeth, her hands clutching the bedding on either side of her. "If you do not want your daughter, give her to Raven."

Raven winked at her sister and started toward him. "Here, Challon, I shall take the wee lass—"

Julian spun aside as she reached for his daughter. "I did not say the first word about not wanting . . . I am just surprised. Challons never have girl babes. They always breed sons. I never expected to have a daughter."

"You are in Scotland now, mighty Dragon," Tamlyn growled. "Wait until your daughter grows up and I tell her you did not want her, you preferred a son. She will make you so sorry!"

He again dodged Raven trying to steal his tiny daughter. "You will do no such thing, wife. She is perfect. The first she-dragon of the Challons. She is special, magical.

But then what else would she be when she was conceived under the boughs of the sacred apples, eh?"

Busy smiling at his tiny girl, it took time to register that Tamlyn's pain was getting worse, not better. He glanced to Raven, who wiped Tamlyn's brow. "What ails her? Her pains increase. Something is not right?"

"Damn you, Challon. This is your fault." Tamlyn moaned again, clearly in agony anew.

The baby began to cry as though she noticed her mother's distress. Raven flashed him a sour look and moved to take the baby. "Give me the lass, Lord Challon."

"She is fine. Just expressing her feelings." Julian used his shoulder to keep her from taking his daughter. He glanced to Tamlyn, who wailed like the Bansidhe. "Like her mother."

"Challon . . ." Tamlyn warned, eyeing him as if she wanted to sink her teeth into him.

"Tamlyn, what distresses you?" Julian felt panic rising in him again. She shouldn't be having these agonies, he thought. "What is wrong?"

Bessa barked. "Don't be a useless male. Take your daughter into the solar and rock her."

"I am not budging until you tell me what plagues Tamlyn."

"You stupid lackwit!" his sweet Tamlyn growled. "I give birth."

Julian blinked, not grasping what she said. "Aye, she is a beautiful girl babe. She will be the Challon princess—"

"Put a rag in it, Challon. Oooooo—" Tamlyn reared back, seeming to grimace with her whole body. "Not . . . I . . . gave—I . . . give . . . Oooooo . . ."

Raven glared at him. "Please step aside, Challon. You hinder things."

Bessa cackled. "Never kenned a man to be helpful when it came time for the coming of a bairn."

Lowering his brows, he frowned at the old woman. "Spare me the poker—answer me! What is the matter with my wife?"

"The lass gives birth to your bairn." Bessa shook her head as if she didn't believe his stupidity.

"She has already done that." He glanced down at the crying child, waving her fist angrily. A smile spread across his lips. He could feel it reforming his whole face. Then it nearly dropped off. "Another babe?"

"My lord husband, it dawns . . . grrrrrrrrrr." Tamlyn panted as another contraction racked her body. "I do not want to do this any more . . . I am too tired, Challon."

Evelynour suddenly materialized at his side, carefully lifting his daughter from his arms. "I shall care for the wee lass. Go sit with Tamlyn. She shall need your strength."

Julian numbly sat on the bed's edge, worrying about Tamlyn. She looked exhausted, wan. "Come wife, you are a warrior true. We have another dragon waiting to see this world." He let her take his wrists and use them to bear down on as the next contraction racked her muscles.

"Giving birth to dragons is hard work, Challon. I shall make you pay for this."

Julian smiled. "The price shall be well worth it, my lady."

His strength seemed to flow into Tamlyn, and suddenly, she had the vigor to endure her labor. From that point, matters moved fast. This dragon wanted to come into the world quickly. Tamlyn only threatened him with bodily harm twice.

Bessa slapped the babe, and another Dragon of Challon voiced its opinion. The child squalled, causing his daughter to kick up a fuss in the solar. Swaddling the child, she handed the babe to him. "Your son wishes to greet his father."

"Son . . ." For the second time this night, Julian was humbled in awe at the miracle of his second child. Then he blinked. "Tamlyn, what is the meaning of this?"

"Oh, Challon, do shut up. I am busy." Bessa massaged Tamlyn's belly to expel the afterbirth. He could see Tamlyn was in no mood for his teasing questions. "You wanted a son. I gave you a son. Now hush."

"But he has your golden hair. All Challon sons have black hair. I suppose he will have your amber eyes as well. Mayhap that faint cleft in his chin." He tried to sound properly grumpy, but the grin betrayed him. His heart moved him to tears as he fingered the straight, fair locks.

"Challon, you want a black-haired son? You have my leave to give birth to one. I am tired. Two bairns in one day are enough." She lay back, closing her eyes as Bessa pulled up the covers.

Hadrian opened the door, paused to check if Bessa was near the fireplace poker. Seeing she was across the room from it, he entered. "So, am I allowed to see my grandson?"

Julian pushed aside the swaddling to reveal his boy.

"Oh my, he has Tamlyn's hair." Hadrian smiled, a twinkle in his eye as Julian let him take his child. "The Black Dragon now has a Golden Dragon for a son. How exciting."

Julian strode into the solar and returned with his daughter. "But here is the most special gift. My wife not only gave me a son, but a daughter."

"Oh, what a little beauty." Hadrian immediately traded babies so he could hold his granddaughter. "I am partial to girls. They are a joy."

Tamlyn called, "If you two are not too busy, I would like to see my son and daughter."

Julian sat and shifted his fair son to his mother's arms. Her face softened and tears filled her eyes as she ran her finger over his toes. "Oh, Julian, he is so beautiful."

"Do not forget my granddaughter. She is the true beauty." Hadrian leaned to his daughter and brushed a kiss to her forehead. "You did well, Tamlyn."

A sennight later, Julian paced the floor, rocking his daughter. Her tiny face pruned up, then she gave a big yawn and closed her eyes and drifted to sleep. He was endlessly fascinated with this tiny person. She had his black hair. He tried to imagine a female with that riot of blue-black waves. "Oh, you will give all the lads a merry chase."

"Challon, put that baby to bed. She needs her sleep," Tamlyn called from the bed, where she sat nursing his son.

"A son and a daughter. How lucky can one man get?" Julian marveled aloud. "Is not your mother the cleverest woman in the world?"

Ignoring his wife's order to put his daughter to bed, he sat on the bed cradling the tiny bundle on his lap. "We need to name her. I thank you for allowing me to name our son after my brother Christian, but our lass needs a name, too."

"I have gone through choices. Naught seems to fit."

The little girl began waving her fist again and fussing. Julian's finger stroked the soft skin of the arm, surprised when she grasped his finger. "Look, Tamlyn, she clutches my finger. I think she wants her brother to hurry. She is hungry. She is so strong. A little warrior woman just like her mother. A pagan most likely. Glen-rogha will pass to her?"

Tamlyn nodded. "My first daughter will follow me."

"Then I shall have to build a castle at Kinmarch for our son." Julian smiled at the beautiful children, a gift. "Tamlyn, these two babes are half you and half me. A daughter like the father, a son like the mother. I think their names should reflect that. Since our son is Christian, what about naming our daughter Paganne?"

Tamlyn smiled as she removed her boy from her breast and switched babies with him. Instantly, their son set to squalling. "Tell Christian he must learn to share. His sister Paganne is famished, too."

"You like the names?"

"Aye, think they are perfect."

Julian smiled she was pleased. "Mayhap next year you shall give me a black-haired son and we can name him after your father."

"You can go shovel horse dung, my lord husband. I shall give you a black-haired son when it pleases me. I just went through this. I am not eager to rush into labor again."

Julian leaned to Tamlyn kissing her softly, slowly. "Beltane shall near soon. The apple trees will bloom and you will dance for me before the balefire."

"Oh, do cease gloating, Challon, and kiss me."

"Aye, my lady."

Chapter 26

Lightning cracked, the flash hitting so close it lit up the dark interior of Kinmarch Kirk with a blinding white light. Blinking until the flash passed, Tamlyn glanced out the stained glass window. The kenning caused a flutter of rising alarm within her.

Usually she loved storms. Loved the smells they brought, their vital, elemental force.

For some reason this storm unnerved her.

And mayhap guilt nibbled at her. She'd slipped off from Glenrogha while Challon was away at Lyonglen. If he returned to find she'd left Glen Shane and come to Kinmarch, she feared her backside would pay the price.

Even so, she had to come and for a task she couldn't reveal to Challon. It plagued her conscience. Despite promises to him to stay within Glenrogha's walls until his return, she'd kept silent about her intention to come to Kinmarch Kirk. He would've forbidden her leaving the dun. She had no aim to conceal her actions, and would face the repercussions after Challon learned of it. That he'd learn, she had no doubt. The man seemed to see all, know all. She still pondered if her husband was a warlock.

Malcolm's seven sons—Skylar, Phelan, Iain, Sean, Michael, Donnal and Jago—along with ten men from Kinmarch, were going off to fight with Hadrian and Andrew de Moray.

Her heart heavy for the deed, she'd stolen away from Challon. Tamlyn wanted them to go with the best armor and the finest mounts, and to ride as knights under the pennon of Glen Shane. She sought for them to have every advantage. The armor she filched from the barrack's tower and the fine chargers might mean the difference between them living and dying.

Malcolm finished saying mass before the kneeling men, then anointed each with holy water.

Now it was her turn to perform the adoubement—knighting these beautiful young men. When she reached Skylar, the final one, she stared into his lavender eyes, knowing he was going into harms way. Her heart twisted. Born the same day she was, they'd been childhood friends, the two of them constantly into mischief. He'd been Challon's teacher, showed him the ways of the claymore. Skills that could save her husband's life.

Her chin quivered as she lifted the sword and placed the flat of the blade on his left shoulder.

"In remembrance of oaths given and oaths received. In remembrance of your blood and obligations." She carried the Sword of Glenrogha over his head to the right shoulder, tapping it, then returning to tap the left. "Walk in honor, Sir Skylar. Rise as a knight."

"My lady."

He stood, the last of the seventeen men of Glenrogha and Kinmarch she'd knighted. Instead of giving the colée—the buffet—the slap to remind the knight he should always remember his oath, she rose up on tiptoes and gifted him with a kiss of peace to his forehead. "Return to us safely, Sir Skylar."

Lightning struck overhead, the clap of thunder terrifying. The stones of the ancient kirk rattled until Tamlyn feared they might clatter down. Outside grew strangely black. Though midday, it appeared nearly night.

"My lady!" The doors flew open and Connor Og stumbled in. "Riders, with flags flying. One scarlet . . . mayhap Longshanks' leopards. They were too far away to tell. They come this way!"

The men scrambled to gather their swords and mantles.

"*In nomine Patris et Filii et Spiritus Santi,*" Malcolm intoned as he traced a cross in the air. "Go with the blessings of our Annis, goddess of the water, Evelynour of the Orchard and Bel, our lord of fire. Come back strong and whole." Arching a brow, he shrugged at Tamlyn smiling at him. "They are my sons. I want all the protection they can get."

Everyone rushed out of the church and to the side where the horses were tied. Skylar lifted Tamlyn to Goblin. "Farewell, cousin. Be sure to thank Challon for the loan of his fine steeds and all the strong English armor. Keep safe until we meet again at Beltane."

Her kinsman departed, spurring their steeds away from the direction the riders came from. They galloped northward to join her father and Moray near Avoch.

Malcolm came before her and squeezed her hands. "Those are English forces coming this way, Tamlyn. That does not bode well for Glen Shane. Make for the passes and protection of the sacred mists."

"Come with me," she entreated.

He shook his head. "I would ride with my sons, but this body is too old. I remain here and will aid Challon in protecting Glen Shane, so our men have a safe haven to return to. You know as well as I, we can hide them for months if need. We must prepare for that possibility. Speed haste to Glenrogha and close the gates until your Challon comes. I ride to Lyonglen. Your man needs to be here with Longshanks' men approaching. We have never faced war before, lass. I don't know how strong the warding of the sacred mists is. Ride with care, you are not two months from your birthing bed."

Leaning down, Tamlyn kissed her uncle. "Travel safe." She waited until he mounted before turning Goblin toward Glenrogha. Kicking the black mare, she cantered homeward.

As her palfrey crested the knoll, she could see the pennons of the horsemen in the distance. Her stomach dropped. It wasn't the golden leopards on scarlet of Edward Longshanks, but the golden eagles of Sir John Pendagast—Dirk's brother.

While the storm's rumble upset Goblin, spooking her, the eerie darkness worked in Tamlyn's favor. They hadn't sighted her yet. At this point, they were closer to the passes and could reach them before she did, cutting off her avenue of escape.

A flash of blinding white light split across the sky, striking the tall pines nearby and ripping into one. Goblin shied. Her knees gripping the horse's barrel, it was all she could do to stay seated. A second bolt of the jagged lightning hit another tree, even closer. Sparks flying, the top half of the evergreen crashed down to the ground in front of her. Goblin reared, hooves slashing the air, tossing Tamlyn off the horse and slamming her into the ground.

Stunned, Tamlyn forced herself to her feet. The riders bearing down on her had spotted the rearing horse and now spurred in her direction. There was no chance she'd reach the passes on foot. Lifting her skirts, she dashed into the protection of the thick stand of evergreens. Her only hope lay in reaching the footpath, which snaked around Lochshane Mòhr.

Tamlyn nearly lost her sense of direction as she ran from one tree to the next, circling, ducking between the heavy limbs. At one point, she attempted to double back, hoping to steal behind them. If she could, she might be able to make a run for the passes.

A rider on a white horse suddenly loomed from a turn in the path, nearly catching her. She spun away, forced toward the loch again.

Out of breath, heart racing to the point of pain, she ducked under one ancient pine and hid in the low hanging branches. Shaking, she curled into a ball against the trunk as riders drew near. Their calls carried on the rising and falling wind.

One rider passed directly in front of where she hid. She recognized his face as one of the mercenaries that had followed Dirk around. Evidently, he'd led them to Glenrogha. "Aye, that was Challon's bitch. She cannot go far on foot, Lord Pendegast," he shouted.

Tamlyn hugged her mantle to her, pulling the hood over her head and around her face. The black wool lined with wolf fur had been Challon's Yuletide present. Rain came down, lashing the forest. It was so cold, penetrating. She was thankful for the warm protection of the fur-lined cape as the April winds were chilling, as if winter refused to let go. And for a change, she was glad her husband had a penchant for black. The color now served to cloak her in this darkness.

Her breasts throbbed. She needed to get home and feed her babes. The pressure from the milk was discomforting.

Tamlyn huddled under the pine boughs, whispering prayers to Evelynour and Annis and hoping the men would pass. Off to the east the sky turned a lighter gray, a warning the storm would soon move on. No longer would she have the shelter of the preternatural darkness. As they were far enough away, she risked leaving the sanctuary of the pines and stumbled onto the trail to Lochshane Mòhr, praying she could reach the loch before Dirk's brothers caught her.

Julian spurred Pagan hard. He'd been uneasy since Damian, Simon, Guillaume and he had lost the tracks of the riders. A small force had been camped on the other side of Kinmarch near Lyonglen. At first they assumed it was Scots rebels hiding out in the woods.

Ever since Wallace started raising hell in the south and Moray in the north, bands of young men were flocking to the woodland, searching for these rebel rousers, hoping to join up. Trouble was brewing, no doubt about it. If Edward thought he was done with Scotland, he was a fool.

Moray was drawing scores of rebels to him, many from the nobility. Young men who hated to stand by while their fathers signed the Ragman Roll. With the clear backing of the Auld Celtic Church he would be the perfect leader to unfurl banners around. Carrying ancient blood of the Picts, he was a new king in the making. One who could fashion a Scotland that might stand against the English power. Wallace pulled hordes of commoners, enough to refashion the spine of the Scottish army so broken after Dunbar. When the two met, Scotland would explode and they'd likely kick every Englishman out of the country.

"This camp is fresher." Damian shook his head and

kicked at the ashes of the fire as first drops of rain fell. "Shod horses, more than a score. I have a bad feeling about this. Just doesn't—"

Julian pressed, "Doesn't what?"

Damian shrugged, kneeling. Picking up some spilled oats on the ground, where horses had been fed, he crumbled them between his thumb and first finger. His eyes stared off in the distance, not really looking at anything. "I cannot say. Nothing here other than a score of horses and men, some oats, but—"

"Out with it, man." Julian was at the point of losing his temper.

"These are not Scots, Julian. I do not see signs here, I just . . . feel this."

Julian nodded with a harsh glare, not meant for his cousin but the situation. "Good enough. Your feelings have always been right. Which way did they go?"

"Tracks show they moved away from Lyonglen heading out of Kinmarch."

"South?"

"Southeast, but again my Scots sense tells me different than what I see with mine eyes. I get a sense they traveled off in that direction, hoping to lure us into following, but they will split and circle back."

"Glenrogha," Julian said, fear rising up his spine.

Damian nodded. "We need to get back. Ride hard."

Simon called, "A rider comes."

Whipping Pagan around, Julian drew his sword, ready to fight. So did his brothers. Oddly, he noticed Damian's sword remained sheathed.

The rider galloped up the rise, as though demons chewed on his mount's tail. He reined up abruptly, nearly causing the beast to rear as he saw he'd stumbled into horsemen. Then as the lightning flashed and he saw whom they were, he spurred forward.

"Challon! Thank God! Riders under the pennon of the golden eagle on scarlet."

"Pendegast," Julian hissed.

"They make for the passes. The mists should hold them from entering the glen."

"Thank the gods, yours and mine, that Tamlyn is within the walls of Glenrogha . . ." Julian's words died as he saw the priest's face. "Never mind explaining. Where is she?"

"She was at Kinmarch Kirk. Out of Glen Shane—"

Julian set spur to his steed. "Sir Priest, make haste to Lyonglen. Warn them to close the gates."

Tamlyn's foot hit a small rock embedded in the dirt. Slipping in the mud, her feet flew out from under her and she crashed hard to her knees and hands. A sharp pain racked her lower leg as her ankle twisted. She grimaced and bit her lip to keep from crying out as deep abrasions on the palms of her hands stung.

Even so, she forced herself to her feet and onward, up the incline. She could circle Lochshane, then use the far path to lead her back into Glen Shane through the loch pass. It was a steep trail and rocky, but it'd see her back into the valley.

Gasping for air, she turned to see where the riders were. She wasn't even halfway to the trail. Five English riders broke from the woods. Fanning out, they rode toward her. Her heart nearly exploded as she saw two more horsemen bearing down on her from the left. Shouts came. More riders appeared on the horizon to the right. The storm was still too dark to make them out. She had to act quickly or they'd box her in.

The only avenue left was the loch.

Ages ago, her Pict ancestors had built an escape bridge across the loch—the last means in or out of the glen should the passes be blocked. In the storm's half-light crossing was dangerous. She'd never used the stones except in bright daylight when you could look down into the water and clearly see the path left by the Ancients. She had to enter, landing on the first rock correctly, or she'd plunge into the icy depths of Lochshane.

Indecision held her rooted as she tried to consider the risk. Glancing around, she realized she had no option. Tamlyn rushed to the water's edge, but paused. It was too dark to spot the first stone. Well, it was trust to the ancient knowledge or face Dirk's brothers. She knew they didn't want her.

They wanted Challon.

She would not give them a weapon to use against her husband. She lifted her skirts, took a breath and walked out in the dark water.

The rain stopped just as Julian saw Tamlyn pause, glance back, then walk into the loch.

Panic filled him. He recklessly spurred Pagan down the hillside.

Five riders were off to Tamlyn's left and closing fast. Paying no heed to them, he knew his brothers and cousin would dispatch them.

"No!" Julian screamed, dismounting his horse while it was still moving. In a dead run, he followed after Tamlyn.

Instantly, he plunged straight into the water's frigid depths. With the heavy quilted aketon, and habergeon, boots and the sword with baldric, he sank like a stone. Floundering, he came up gasping for air. Blinking the water from his lashes, he tried to see. Kicking hard to stay afloat, he spun around trying to locate her. The fog rolled in, shrouding the loch.

"Tamlyn!"

He could not believe what he beheld. Treading water so icy it robbed him of breath, he watched in utter horror as Tamlyn continued across the loch. Across the loch! The hem of her mantle dragged in the water as she seemed to stride on through the surface. By the Holy Rood! She walked across the deep loch! The fog thickened, swirled around her and he could no longer see her.

It hadn't taken long for his brothers to dispatch three of the riders. The other two spurred their steeds, riding away as far as their mounts would carry them.

Julian dragged himself out of the water, teeth chattering. Damian jumped from his gray steed and helped, tugging him up the bank. Guillaume and Simon reined their stallions to a halt, leaping from the saddles and running straight for them.

Julian shoved away from Damian. "She's in the loch. Tamlyn is in the middle of that bloody lake. I saw her."

Damian finally understood Julian was fearful Tamlyn might drown. "Not in the loch. She walks upon the loch."

"What sort of madness?" Julian frowned, staring at his cousin as if he spoke a foreign tongue. Finally, the words sank into his comprehension. "Upon the loch? Are you addled? Where is my wife? Where is Tamlyn?"

Damian grabbed Julian's neck, pulling his face around so his attention focused upon him. "She walks upon the water . . . as if it were ground. See." He pointed to the middle of the loch.

Julian saw the eddying fog hovering close to the

center. For an instant, it shifted. The ghostly veil parted to reveal the figure of Tamlyn standing there, the water sucking at her feet. Slowly, she seemed to be gliding away from the shore. Her figure faded as the Highland haar closed behind her.

Blood drained from him. Pulled with a siren's call, he took several steps toward the loch's edge and waded into the water.

"No, Julian, you will drown," Damian growled, yanking him around and pushing at his chest.

"Damn it! Let me go. Tamlyn . . . my life . . . is out there. I must—"

Simon grabbed his other arm, aiding Damian to haul him back. "Julian, listen—"

"But Tamlyn . . ." A sob welled up through the fury, his mind still refusing to believe, even though he knew what he witnessed. Tamlyn walked on water!

"We saw," Simon confirmed.

Julian shook his head. "She could only move over water by black magic."

"It is an old Pictish trick," Damian assured him. "I have never seen the likes before, but heard tales of such from my mother."

Looking down at the soggy ground, Damian searched until he found the track left by Tamlyn's boots, and followed to the exact spot where she entered the loch. Carefully, he stepped into the dark waters. He stood, water lapping over his boots. Feeling his way, he stepped again. Then a third time. The fourth time he nearly ended in the loch. Arms flapping, he managed to keep his balance.

"The pattern moves, meandering." He called and kept going. Step by step, he traveled away from the shore, until he was as far as the length of five men. He stopped and looked down in amazement, a grin lighting his face.

"God's teeth, can you not see? The Picts built an escape route across the loch centuries ago. Your Tamlyn walks upon rocks. Just under the surface. They are black. Scots call it ashlar, what the true Stone of Destiny is made of. Smooth as glass, these stepping stones cannot be spotted in the water. One must be careful. They are slippery. The key is three stones to the right, then five to the left, then seven to the right. The Picts liked odd numbers. My guess is the pattern repeats. Even if someone tries to follow, if you do not see the configuration, you'd fall into the waters, which are very deep on either side. Likely, a pursuer would be too fearful to try, thinking it was Highland witchery. I would venture, dear cousin, your lady wife shall reach Glenrogha before we will, since we have to go all the way around the loch."

Remounting Pagan, Julian stared into the mist, hopeful for another glimpse of her to reassure himself she was all right.

Only ghosts in the fog stirred on the loch.

Tamlyn had to step carefully. She'd never crossed using the underwater bridge in the spring. The water was icy cold and much deeper, sucking at her legs with the power of an undertow. In high summer when it was warm and the loch was down to a summer pool, crossing the boulder bridge built by her ancestors was tricky, yet easily managed if you knew the secret. Smooth rocks were just under the crystalline water, the dark stones rendered invisible. You had to know the precise design or you plummeted into the frigid water.

The footing was dangerous since the stones were slick with moss and the spring pool was higher, close to her knees in the middle. The water was swifter, sucking at her legs, to where it was hard to pull her leg up. Each step was a struggle. The water fed from the snows of Ben Shane was glacial. Teeth clacking, Tamlyn pushed on.

As she climbed onto the bank, Tamlyn fell to her knees, so tired. Breathing hard and freezing, she knew it was vital to get to her feet and keep moving. As she sucked air, she kept telling herself that. Her body wasn't listening.

A snort of a horse and rattle of bridle fittings alerted her to someone's nearness. Her heart stopped. Then boots moved into the range of her vision. Lifting her head, her eyes traveled up the legs to the hauberk, then the scarlet surcoat with the golden eagle emblazoned across his chest.

"Lady Challon, we meet again." John Pendegast smiled.

A cry of despair came with her exhale. She staggered up, nearly losing her balance and pushed on toward the loch. Her prospects of crossing again were slender, since his men were already waiting on the opposite shore. Still, she had to try.

He was on her before she blinked. Tamlyn struggled weakly, but the iciness of the water had sapped all her strength. She went limp. He dragged her to the horses. She saw Dirk's other brother waited there. Her body was so chilled, but suddenly her blood turned icy.

"What d-do you . . . want?" She shivered so hard the question barely got out.

John Pendegast grabbed her by the waist and hauled her up, dropping her on her feet. "Want? You, Lady Challon, of course."

"Why?" She tried to tug the mantle around her as he tossed her upon his horse and then mounted behind her.

John smiled as he set spur to the steed. "Why, brotherly love, naturally. And all such noble reasons. One does not kill a Pendegast and get away with it."

"A destrier . . . ki-killed your . . . brother," she argued, desperately hanging onto the saddle, fearing to fall off and being trampled by the horse's feet.

"Everyone has seen Pagan in action. That horse is as deadly a weapon as the sword your husband wields."

Her breasts throbbed, painfully reminding her it was past time to feed the twins. "I must go to my children." She bit her lip, sorry the plea had escaped. She would never beg before these vile men, but she was so exhausted and just wanted to be home warm and safe, holding her children.

"You need milking, eh?" Ambroise Pendegast laughed. "Never fear, Lady Challon, we shall suck your tits for you. What say, John, a milk jug for us each?"

Digging down, Tamlyn summoned steel she didn't know she had. Instead of quailing before them, she stiffened her spine and summoned her warrior's mien. She was Challon's Lady, the wife of a warrior true, a man once the king's champion. "Challon will kill you and hang your guts out for the pigs."

"Mouthy bitch. We can knock that out of her or find another use for that mouth," Ambrose promised.

As they rounded the loch to the Kinmarch side, both men slowed, glancing about. The other riders were gone. Tamlyn clearly read the unease within them. Walking the horses slowly, she heard Ambrose withdraw his sword from its sheath. The men's rising fear transferred to the mounts as they suddenly grew twitchy.

The brothers glanced to each other, questions clear in their eyes. Ambrose's palfrey reverberated alarm in his throat and shied, nearly unseating its rider. It took all the knight's skill to control the sweating beast.

"What ails him?" The man sounded as upset as his animal.

Tamlyn smiled. "Blood, Sir Knight. Horses are scared of the scent of blood."

"Where are our soldiers, John?" he demanded in a querulous tone.

John surveyed the landscape, finding neither beast nor man. "They are here somewhere. Just waiting until they make sure it is us."

Ambrose pointed. "Look!"

The scarlet standard with the golden eagle lay on the grass. In this half light, it almost resembled blood spilling over the earth. Just beyond, there were figures of men on the ground, clearly dead.

"John . . ." Ambrose's voice trembled. "What happened? They are dead! All dead!"

The elder Pendegast barked, "Shut up."

"Challon. Challon happened," Tamlyn stated in a surprisingly strong voice. "If you put me down now and flee, you might escape with your lives."

"John—"

"I told you to shut up, you fool."

Tamlyn took in the thickening fog nearing the mouth of the pass. They would have to ride by it to go to Kinmarch.

Both horses shied badly as a great flock of ravens unexpectedly took to the skies. They fluttered on both sides of the passes, their cries rising to a deafening clamor. The men appeared as spooked as the beasts they rode, trying to spot what had set the birds to screaming and fighting.

"One last chance. Let me go or you seal your death," Tamlyn warned.

Warmth flooded her. Challon was near, the kenning whispered.

The mists thickened, then seemed to part, revealing the lone rider in black on the midnight charger. Arm straight, his sword was in his hand, the tip pointing to the ground. The heavy black mantle undulated behind him. Reaching up, he released the catch at his shoulder and the mantle fluttered away to the earth, leaving him free to fight.

The screams of the ravens grew louder as Challon slowly walked Pagan forward, coming right up to the Pendegasts as if they were held spellbound by the daunting image. Tamlyn thought them exceedingly stupid to let Challon so near unchallenged. Only a fool would permit her warrior husband such an advantage.

Tamlyn's breath caught and held as she stared at his beautiful visage. The hairs on the back of her neck prickled as she stared at him.

These men were taller, yet he wasn't in the least intimidated by them. His was a raw, elemental power never measured by such menial standards. The armor plates covering upper arms and thighs, the mail habergeon, mantle and surcoat were black. All black.

Not the severe Norman style of hair cutting, his locks—of the same unrelenting shade of pitch—were longer, much longer since coming to Glenrogha, curling softly about his ears and flowing past the metal gorget at the back of his neck.

Handsome—no, beautiful—Challon was born of Selkie blood. The air surrounding this dark warrior seemed to stir as scorching energy discharged from him with the sizzle and crackle of lightning. A flick of the sooty lashes bespoke his biting disdain and temporary dismissal of the two men. Few men wielded such chilling command.

His keen attention fixed on Tamlyn. The penetrating stare sent her to trembling, but not with true foreboding.

She loved this man, knew he was worth fighting for, worth dying for. More importantly, worth living for.

A great circle turned . . . and memories came alive.

He had eyes the color of the deep forest, shade of sacred green garnets said to adorn the Holy Grail. They were ringed with lashes so long a woman would cry envy, almost feminine, though none would dare to ascribe that trait to him. An inner, searing light pulsed from the hexing eyes. Heavy ebon brows brought out their mind-piercing hue. When she stared into them, the world narrowed. Nothing else existed.

There was only this knight all in black.

Challon.

His jaw was strong, square. The small full mouth, etched with sensual curves, was seductive, though touched with a trace of what might be cruelty. High cheekbones lent a balancing hint of thinness to his face, softening the arrogant planes. Glistening with a bluish cast, two jet curls fell over the hairline in a roguish air. His countenance was sinful . . . in ways no mere mortal man had right to be.

The high forehead bespoke of a willful, razor-sharp intelligence. The last man Tamlyn would want to face as an adversary. But the only man Tamlyn would want for a lover, her husband, the father of her children.

The man she loved more than life.

Images possessed her, singeing her with an ancient fire . . . of her hands on the bare flesh of his chest, how it felt to be kissed by this black knight. Smiling a secret smile, more memories flooded her. The first time she had bathed him. How he told her if she provided what he needed there would be no other women. Their dancing before the balefire at Beltane. Him taking her in the pagan marriage ceremony. How she held him and kissed away the tears as he spoke of Christian's death. This English warrior was dangerously beautiful, a killer angel with soul-stealing eyes. As upon their first meeting, he held her spellbound.

The spell broke. "My orders were not made clear, Tamlyn?" He arched a brow in censure before turning his formidable attention on the two men. "Scots. Their women are jug-headed at best. Edward does extract his punishment by leg-shackling me with this trying woman for a wife. I weary of beating her. I thank you for finding and fetching her back. I have been off hunting down rebel Scots and dispatching them. Every time I return, she is off dashing hither and yon. You both are a long way from home. If you will give her to me, we shall head back to my fortress. Not of a splendor worthy the Dragon of Challon, but I plan to rebuild Kinmarch castle, then dismantle this ancient holding. I offer you a hot meal, a soothing bath and a good night's rest after your long ride."

Challon rested the sword across his lap as if he had nothing to fear from these men. She would almost believe his words, if he hadn't made the comment about being leg-shackled to her.

Apprehension rippled through the guilt-ridden men. She saw Ambrose look to John, silently asking what to do. The elder brother seemed caught off guard by Challon's offer of food and bed. Just as she felt his grasp on her waist ease, as if he might accept the offer and live to fight another day, a score of riders came galloping up the knoll. Riders under the pennon of the golden eagle.

Ambrose smirked and sat up straighter in the saddle, buoyed by the arrival of reinforcements.

John finally spoke. "Challon, we are not here to accept your hospitality. We came for precisely this. Despite your bit of mummery, we hear you set great store by your

Celtic heiress. Whilst we should seek revenge for the loss of our dear brother, we devised a better means. Lady Challon rides with us. In five days time, come alone to Castlerock Keep. With you have the charter for the fief of Torqmond and two chests of gold."

Challon smiled. "There is a price on brotherly love after all. I hope my brothers place a higher value on my life."

"If you don't come in the allotted period . . ." John smiled, sliding his hand up to squeeze her breast. "Well, you get the idea, Dragon, we shall return what's left of her on the sixth."

Challon didn't blink, his emotions shuttered behind that will of iron. "I learned to speak the Scots tongue during this last year. Is *leam fhèin an gleann, 's gach ni ta ann*. Do you know what that means?"

"Why should we care, Challon?" Ambrose snapped, as the riders drew close. "You heard our terms."

Challon went on as if Ambrose hadn't spoken. "The words mean 'this glen is mine and all that is in it.' An old Scots adage. Do not touch what is mine. Your imbecile brother erred in daring to touch my lady wife. Dirk is dead. Just as you two shall be."

"You are an arrogant bastard, Challon. It is two to one." Ambrose watched their riders slow and fan out as they approached. "Make that a score against one."

"You forget Pagan." Julian patted the side of his steed's neck. "He already dispatched one Pendegast." The sacred mists parted as Simon, Guillaume and Damian seemed to materialize out of the fog of the passes. "Well, the odds just shifted to my favor. The four Dragons of Challon. We shall slice up a score of scum and feed the bones to the pigs without breaking a sweat. It would not matter if it were a hundred to one odds, John. You are dead. No man lays hand to my lady and lives."

He moved so fast neither man had a chance to react. His knee signals sent Pagan slamming into Ambrose's horse. The palfrey snarled deep in his throat as his teeth ripped into the neck of the roan, blood gushing from the wound. The precise instant Pagan moved, Challon brought up the hilt of the sword, slamming the rounded pommel into the jaw of John Pendegast.

Tamlyn wiggled, trying to break free, but Dirk's brother held on tightly as he fought to control his steed. Damian, Simon and Guillaume spurred past him, as Challon swung Pagan around to face Ambrose. Urging the black destrier forward, both man and animal went into action. Pagan went at Ambrose's mount again as Challon's great sword came down, clanging against the blade of the younger Pendegast.

Determined to give Challon time to handle Ambrose without John coming at him, she grabbed his sword arm, wrapping both of hers around it and hanging on, rocking in the saddle to topple them. His fist slammed into her shoulder. Her vision darkened as pain lanced through her. Even so, she held on, buying her husband time.

Challon spun Pagan on his rear hooves as Ambrose spurred his steed. At first she thought the man meant to flee, but he yanked the reins, abruptly reversing the horse's direction, then came flying at Challon.

Tamlyn kicked John's horse, causing it to rear. While they were off balance, she shoved back, forcing them rearward over the horse. Her head connected with John's chin. Already hurt from Challon's pommel slamming into it, he cried out.

She made it to her knees, but John was on his feet. He yanked her head back against his stomach as he placed a blade to her throat.

Tamlyn's eyes searched for Challon and Ambrose.

Their swords rang out as they met, but Challon caught Ambrose with the place on his sword where all the power of the blow moved into the opponent. Ambrose had hit wrong so all the vibration of the swords meeting transferred into his muscles, making it nearly impossible for him to keep his grip on the hilt. His teeth gritted as be absorbed the blunt of Challon's blow.

Challon kneed Pagan into a spinning turn and he came back at Pendegast. Ambrose tried to position himself to meet Challon. It was too late. Challon's broadsword sliced downward between his opponent's head and neck, going deep. Limp, Ambrose lifelessly slipped off his mount to the ground.

Most of Pendegast's men were down. A few galloped away. Thankfully, Simon and Guillaume were still seated and unharmed. Damian had been unhorsed, but now remounted his gray steed.

Challon dismounted Pagan and walked to where John held her on the ground, the sharp knife tip pointed to her throat—same as she once had held her *sgian dubh* to his brother. Remembering the knife in her boot, she carefully shifted to get her hand around it. Her action was slow as John held her up, spine nearly bowed. His blade permitted her no movement.

Shaking fingers brushed the top of her hidden dagger. Stretching, her trembling hand closed about the hilt.

"Unhand her, John," Challon commanded softly. "We were not friends, but I respected you as a knight of honor. Never thought you would hide behind a woman's skirts."

"Does not matter what I do, Challon. You plan to kill me. The only way I get out of here alive is with your witch."

Challon's long lashes flicked. The movement was so slight no one else could have read him. He was getting ready to move and flashed her warning. Tamlyn's hand under her mantle flexed about the *sgian dubh*.

"You are not taking her, John."

She felt the man's muscles tense as he yanked harder on her hair, stretching and exposing her throat to the long knife blade.

"Then we both die here, Dragon."

Tamlyn jabbed her small knife into his booted foot at the same instance Challon lashed out with his sword, catching the man at his throat. His body stayed upright for a moment, then fell back to the earth.

With a cry, Tamlyn fell into Challon's arms, squeezing him tight, but not as tightly as he held her. He rained kisses over her face and then took her mouth, kissing her hard, kissing her slow, cherishing her. He broke away, his labored breath panting against her hair. "Never scare me like that again . . . you have done it not once, but twice. On the loch—oh, Tamlyn, I thought you would drown. I wanted to walk into those icy waters, follow you to your watery grave. Then to see Pendegast hold you . . ."

"Poor man." She laughed through the tears.

Challon reared back and stared at her as if she'd taken leave of her senses. "Poor man?"

"Aye, when you rode up so calmly and invited him to supper and a bath I do not think he knew what to expect. You almost had me believing until you mentioned about beating me."

He flashed his teeth in a predatory smile. "That part was true. I plan to put my hand to your bottom so you will not be able to sit for a week. Then the next time you say, 'Aye, Challon,' you shall mean it."

"You may put a hand to my bottom any time you wish, my lord husband, and I might not be able to stand for a week, but it will not be because you beat me. You would

never spank the mother of your two beautiful children."
She glanced down at the milk forming stains on her sark.
"Speaking of children, can you please take me home,
Challon? I am so tired and need to feed our bairns."

"Aye, wife, I shall take you home." He helped her to
her feet as Pagan pushed his back with his nose.

Tamlyn kissed the destrier's velvety nose and stroked
his forehead. "Thank you, mighty steed, for once again
protecting our Challon."

Challon mounted in the saddle, then kicked out of the
stirrup for her, offering his hand to help her up. He settled her crosswise on his lap. Accepting his mantle from
Simon, he hung it about his shoulders and then wrapped
the heaviness around them both. He nudged Pagan with
his knees to take them home, his brothers and cousin
falling in behind them.

The terror of the moment was catching up with him.
He'd been the Dragon of Challon and had done what was
necessary to save his lady. And she loved him so. But
now she felt the faint tremors in his muscles.

"Wife, I love you, but if you ever disobey me—"

She let out with a small squeal and shifted on his lap
to face him. Wrapping her arms about his waist, she
hugged him. "Oh, Challon!"

"Stop your wiggling before you unseat us both,
Òinnseach."

"Don't distract me by calling me a fool. You said you
loved me." The smile faded as she searched the green
garnet eyes. "Do you mean it, Julian?"

He leaned forward and ever so gently kissed the
corner of her mouth. "I love you, Tamlyn. How could I
not? I think I have always loved you . . . always will."

"But you never told me."

He chuckled, then exhaled a deep sigh. "Have you told me, wife?"

"No, but—"

"Oh, Tamlyn fair, has golden hair, she won my heart from the start—"

"Challon, that is dreadful."

"Some things need no words, Tamlyn. I am a warrior, not a silly bard prancing around using words like love to where they have no value. I show you my love each time I take you into my arms, every time I look at you. Still, if you want me to recite dreadful rhymes—"

"No, rhyme, Challon, just three words."

He leaned his forehead against hers. "I love you, Tamlyn Challon."

Epilogue

High atop Dunstrathraven Tor, Julian finally found the object of his search. He paused before the breathtaking panorama, looking far out into their valley and the two beyond. Lands of Kinmarch, lands his son and daughter would one day rule. Tamlyn had heard his approach. The kenning likely alerted her to his near silent steps. But then Tamlyn needed no fey craft, since she sensed his nearness at all times. She turned her head in a fleeting glance over her shoulder, a smile tugging at the corner of her lips.

Julian knew he was a blessed man indeed. Gone were the days of inner atrophy, the black tempers, and worse, fear of losing his sanity. Gone were the vile nightmares. Even when they threatened, her warm body was there to reach for in the deepest of nights. The best healing for his tormented soul. He returned to sleep, blissfully curled around the softness of this wild Highland lass. His witch.

The pain of his brother Christian's death would always linger just out of mind, always in heart, but with Tamlyn's help he'd come to terms with it.

Loch breezes lifted, sweeping up the steep incline. Swirling about her with ghostly, playful hands, it tugged defiant whips of her honey-colored hair from the simple braid hanging down her back. Whilst the heavy mass had nary a curl, it was imbued with a will all its own. Never content to remain neatly confined, just like his lady wife. But then, Julian found he had little taste for such a paragon of virtue. No, life was sweet with this fiery, golden-haired pagan. There was naught he'd wish to change about his lady.

Julian had discovered that small measure of peace his soul had desperately cried out for, here in these mist shrouded lands of Celts, Picts and Gaels—and now English, he'd never ask for more, counting himself a favored man indeed. Some day the legend of the Black Dragon would fade into fable, told and retold by his sons and daughters to their wee bairns, and they in turn to theirs. For the present it would serve as a shield to protect all that was his, for none would dare the temerity to reive cattle or sheep from the Great Black Dragon of Glenrogha. In the dark and troubled days ahead, his Tamlyn would count it as a blessing that her lord husband was of Norman blood and, surprisingly, still had some sway with Edward of England.

Aye, his blood was Norman and might stand between Longshanks and all who lived in this sheltered glen. But his soul now forevermore belonged to these purple hills and the woman he loved more than life itself. This would never change, he knew.

He inhaled the sea-kissed wind, the familiar lavender and heather off Tamlyn's skin, the special heat that was his witch. His hands took hold of her upper arms from behind and gently drew her back against his body, encircling her with the protection of his embrace and brushing his nose alongside her face.

"At what do you stare, lady wife?"

"Kinmarch and beyond."

"Fashing your mind over the Laird of Clan Shane?"

"Oh, aye."

"Your lord father is a warrior strong, well able to take care of himself, a smart man he. Very smart. Did he not judge me worthy to be your lord husband before either of us knew the other?"

"For such a wise man, he could have told me. It would've saved me a muckle lot of troubles."

"Oh. And just what would that have changed? I cannot envision you doing one thing different or fighting me any less. Your Pict blood is strong. Proof of that strength is in you breeding me a lady daughter, first she-dragon of the Challons." He kissed her temple as he flexed his arms, squeezing her tighter. "But not the last one, eh?"

"Have you forgotten I gave you a son as well?"

"Aye, you did bear Christian, which still proves my point. The bairn has golden hair, like his mother. Another first for the Dragons of Challon. A golden dragon."

"Poor wee bairn, you cursed him with that name to bear. Christian, humpf."

"Well, I had to do something. You gave me a daughter and a son with honey-colored hair. Besides, they represent our union—a pagan and a Christian. Mayhap our next son will have my black hair and your eyes."

"I plan to breed you a whole herd of daughters, my lord husband. They shall avenge me, giving you worries enough to plague the rest of your days. I shall see they learn the ways of a warrior. They shall fight with claymore and crossbow."

The threat made Julian laugh out loud. Rocking her slightly from side to side, he swayed with her. "Your lady sisters likely plot the same fate for my poor, unsuspecting brothers. Since Edward has decreed he shall live forever, he shall be driven mad trying to find nobles for them. The daughters of the Shane vexed his efforts for nearly a decade—think what turmoil a legion of Highland she-dragons shall wreak."

Off in the distance the ravens took to wing, their screams breaking the peace of the glen.

Tamlyn's smile lessened as those Cait Sidhe eyes nervously, almost fearfully, followed their path across the far glen, seeing what his could not.

Kissing her temple once again, he was awed by the humbling emotion of love. This woman meant so much to him. Meant everything. Following her sight line, Julian tried to puzzle out what kept her staring so fixedly at that she could not really see.

"Tamlyn, *mo ghraidh*, at what do those fey eyes look upon? Why do the ravens disturb you so?"

A slight tremble shuddered through her body, as the breeze took on a strange coolness. "Challon, *mo beatha*, I scry the coming storm."

"My life—I love when you call me that." Challon leaned his head to the side of hers, studying the sky. "Only there is no storm. The sky is so clear and blue. A blue we rarely see for long in these moody Highlands."

Tamlyn's head shook slightly in denial. "The storm comes. Not this day, not the next nor the one after. Not even within a moon's passing. But soon, the Storm comes. And nothing shall stop it."

The rising chill penetrated his bones, as he comprehended Tamlyn's fear. An augury, words of the craft. She kenned what lay ahead of them.

His arms hugged this woman, his love, the mother of his children, as if his body could protect her against all the evils of the world.

"We shall face it, Tamlyn. Together we can face anything."

"Aye, Challon. We shall."

Aye, the Storm would come, and sweep the length and breadth of this pagan land.

Far off in the distance, well beyond the sight of any human, a rider made his way toward Glen Shane. The man was tired, his mount more so. But his mission was urgent. He dared not tarry.

He carried two messages of import. Young Andrew de Moray had raised his standard at Avoch Castle. And in the South, a giant of a man—a commoner—had lifted his head in defiance.

RAVENHAWKE,

Damian St. Giles and Aithinne Ogilvie's story,

available August 2007

from Zebra Books.